PHOENIX RISING

Visit Paul Henke on his website
for current titles and future novels at:
www.henke.co.uk
or email Paul at
henke@sol.co.uk

This book is dedicated to my uncle, Raymond Whalley.
With thanks to my son, OLIVER MICHAEL HENKE, who
co-authored this story.

D1362710

By Paul Henke

A MILLION TEARS
THE TEARS OF WAR AND PEACE
SILENT TEARS
TEARS UNTIL DAWN

From the Files of TIFAT
(The International Force Against Terrorism)
The Nick Hunter Adventures

DÉBÂCLE
MAYHEM
CHAOS
HAVOC

Also by Paul Henke

NEVER A WINNER

PHOENIX RISING

Paul Henke

— To Konia
Enjoy the story!

Paul Henke

GOOD READ PUBLISHING

First published in 2007 by Good Read Publishing
A Good Read Publishing paperback

10 9 8 7 6 5 4 3 2 1

A CIP catalogue record of this title is available
from the British Library

ISBN 1–902483–09–X

Typeset by Palimpsest Book Production Limited,
Grangemouth, Stirlingshire
Printed and bound in Great Britain
by Cox & Wyman, Reading, Berkshire

Good Read Publishing
Clairinch
Buchanon Street
Balfron
G63 0RL

Prologue

BLOODSHED. IT WAS all that the effete and decadent West understood. He'd give them bloodshed – more than they could stomach. His arrangements were almost complete. When he was finished he would be as famous and revered as Osama bin Laden. He made his final obeisance to *Allah* and climbed to his feet. Collecting his shoes at the door he made his way out into the busy London street, a smile on his face, satisfaction in his heart.

Ismail Salan was twenty-eight years old and born in Somalia. Of mixed blood, his father was a black African, his mother a light-skinned Iraqi, he had grown up in a strict Moslem environment. His degree in electronic engineering at Kabul university had enabled him to travel legally to the west and to study for a PhD at Oxford, England.

His work on the miniaturisation of electronic components had earned him the right of residency and a well-paid job in a research company based in Milton Keynes. He had lived quietly for two years in Barnet, North London, commuting daily, justifying the faith his employers had placed in him. During that period he had stayed away from fellow Moslems and the mosques abounding in and around the British capital. His one overriding emotion had been loneliness. In spite of the many invitations to spend time socialising with his co-workers he kept to himself. His one source of solace was his *Koran*, which he read at every opportunity. Of medium height and build, his Negroid features were softened by his Arab blood, his skin a rich honey-colour. His dark, brooding eyes had drawn many women to him but he had rejected them all. His only passion was *Allah*, and the word as given by the prophet, *Mohammed, peace be upon him.*

He had known for nearly a decade that he was one of the chosen. Which was why money had been spent on his education, donated anonymously, through a trust held in a bank in Sri Lanka. There were hundreds of recipients of this largesse scattered across the world, each primed to do their master's bidding. Who their master was they didn't know, though many speculated in the quiet hours of the early mornings. All they did know, all they needed to know, was that their cause was just.

Unlike suicide bombers – those poor unfortunates who were semi-literate cannon fodder to the greater good – Salan and the others were not expected to die for the cause. They were expected to *live*! More would be required of them until finally they too reached the end of their usefulness. Then they would be expendable. Only then would they commit their final outrage, whatever it might be.

This was Salan's second job. The first had been six months previously. Not much had been achieved then – the death of two young children and the destruction of a bank in the City of London was hardly earth shattering. Not like the attacks on America on 9/11. That had been worth dying for. Or even London on 7/7 when dozens had died and hundreds had been injured. Even so, this next operation would result in the deaths of hundreds, possibly thousands. But even this was merely another stepping stone to the really big one – when a weapon of mass destruction would be used.

His semi-detached house in the small estate on the edge of Barnet was unremarkable. What was highly remarkable were the security arrangements around the house and garden. Salan used his remote control to check the settings on the pressure pads and hidden cameras, replaying them on his video/phone. In quick time they showed only the usual – the postman, paper boy and a woman delivering some sort of leaflet. He climbed out of his car and approached the front door. Inserting his latch key he turned it and pushed the door open. The shaped charge exploded, cutting Salan in half giving him a more merciful death than he deserved.

Yorke drove sedately away. This was neither the time nor the place to be noticed. *Altogether*, he thought, *a highly satisfactory operation*. He half listened to the news on BBC Radio 4.

'*And finally. It has been confirmed that the Prime Minister's wife and two children have gone away for a bank holiday break to a secret location. A spokesman for the PM said it was to allow them privacy to enjoy themselves without the intrusion of the press. The fact that they have gone two days early has not been lost on the Opposition. Their front bench spokesman for education, Mr Tim Yale, says it's a disgrace that the children have been taken out of school early when there is a bill before Parliament threatening fines for parents who do the same thing. Downing Street has not commented other than to say it is a private matter for the Prime Minister and his family.*'

Samuel Salondi shook hands with the other man. It was agreed. One hundred million pounds worth of cocaine and heroin to be delivered in two hours time.

'Where do you have such a large quantity of drugs?'

Salondi smiled and tapped the side of his nose. A Jamaican by birth, he had started life as a mule for one of the many Yardie gangs operating in Britain. One stint of two years in Bellmarsh prison was enough to convince him that being a low-level carrier was a mug's game. Systematically he took over the small network he had worked for. His methods were simple. He killed his way to the top. The police were unperturbed and investigations into the deaths of known Yardie members were only lightly undertaken. Other, more pressing matters, took precedence with the authorities and the deaths of gang members were quickly shelved. Which suited Salondi.

He expanded his operation by rapidly taking over other gangs, rewarding those who were loyal and murdering those who were not. Within five years he controlled the largest crack cocaine and heroin operation in Western Europe. With over thirty deaths attributable to him he had no trouble keeping control of the men he commanded. Finally, he was made an offer he couldn't refuse and amalgamated his business into a far bigger one. The result was he had far more power, though not as much as the white man who accompanied him. He wielded real power.

In spite of his outward appearance, Salondi was nervous. The Head of Security of the largest criminal organisation in the world was a man to be feared and reckoned with. So far, everything had gone well. He was a man of few words and surprisingly travelled without bodyguards but then, he didn't need them. *Nobody* in their right minds would lay a finger on the hair of his head. Now that was power man! *Real power!*

'My men will deliver the goods as agreed.' Salondi walked away without a backward glance, first gesturing to the white man to go first. With a gracious nod, he did so. He was satisfied. Salondi could do the job and well.

Salondi was a big man who walked with the grace of a leopard. His black skin was ebony, his brown eyes deep set and commanding. In another time and place he could have been a charismatic African leader or tribal chief. His head was shaved bald, though the sun hat he wore hid the fact. His lightweight cotton suit fitted him to perfection, and bespoke of Saville Row tailors. Standing at the end of the wooden jetty he squinted at the setting sun, while waiting for his boat to pick him up. He ignored the two men standing near him, so used to them, he often forgot they were there. The white, impassive buildings of Cannes gave him a sense of satisfaction. To have come so far so quickly still sent a shiver of pleasure along his spine. And now, the world was at his feet. Or at least a bigger piece than he'd enjoyed so far.

Though his two black guards were big men, he topped them by an inch or two. His wide shoulders were solid muscle and although his waist was beginning to thicken he still looked like a man not to be tangled with. He watched as the thirty foot runabout crossed the intervening blue Mediterranean like an arrow and came alongside the jetty in a fading arc of wake.

Salondi stepped lightly into the stern of the boat, his body-guards following. Nothing was said as they sped towards the huge gleaming white yacht anchored half a mile offshore. The white man standing alongside him looked small and nondescript. It was a deceptive pose. He watched as they approached the yacht with disinterest while Salondi looked at it with delight.

The yacht, all 150ft of her, was the finest investment he had ever made. Hidden in her bilges was an elaborate and clever system of containers capable of holding a vast amount of illegal drugs, un-detectable unless you knew where to look. The state-of-the-art communications system was the best money could buy and kept Salondi in contact with his world-wide criminal organisation. The cleverest part of his business was the money laundering shops he'd established across Europe selling mobile phones. Even they were now becoming an embarrassment as they were turning in huge profits in their own right. One thing he was sure of – he would never be arrested for tax evasion or being unable to show how he made his money. The yacht, along with seven passports, gave him citizenship rights across Europe. Furthermore, he personally owned no property anywhere.

The boat came smoothly to a halt, Salondi stepped onto the accommodation ladder and turned to help the white man. As he did so a massive explosion blew the bottom out of the yacht's hull and the ladder disintegrated. Both bodies were shredded into tiny pieces while at the same time half-a-billion Euros worth of illegal narcotics were also destroyed.

Jack Banyon had seen the explosion through a high-powered telescope from the balcony of his hotel room. With a half smile he slipped the transmitter into his coat pocket. Time to report back.

He had been a banker for over thirty years. He had a comfortable life in the old quarter of the city, occupying a large house in its own grounds only a short ride from the business sector of Jeddah. His wife and four sons had proven a blessing, one of them even following him into banking. *Yes, he'd had a contented and happy life and the best was still to come.*

Although he was fifty-five, he still cut a dashing figure, his black hair now fashionably grey at the temples. His moustache, which he kept a deep black colour, was his one vanity. He was on his way to spend an hour of well earned rest with his mistress in the new penthouse he'd bought her, over-looking the marina. It had cost a small fortune but, by *Allah*, she was worth it.

The morning had been particularly trying. Over forty-eight million dollars had been distributed to bank accounts across the western world. Although some of the money had been charitable donations, collected in Saudi and despatched to finance the war on the *infidel*, most of it was drug money that had been laundered through his bank and was now being redistributed to cause more harm amongst the decadent Europeans. The holy *jihad* was fought on all fronts by all true believers. From kings and princes to industrialists and bankers, down the natural order of things to the suicide bombers and foot soldiers, they were all engaged in the war. And it was fought in every way imaginable. Whether it was the use of illegal drugs to rot the west from the inside, or direct attacks on their soft civilian underbelly, it was all grist to Islam's mill.

The Rolls Royce purred to a halt outside the apartment building. His chauffeur leapt out and opened the door with a flourishing salute.

'Come back in one hour,' Izzat al-Muri said.

The driver acknowledged the order and climbed back into the car, happy to escape the searing temperature outside for his air-conditioned cocoon. He would drive to the small cafe nearby and, as usual, wile away the time drinking coffee and making small talk with the owner.

The car moved sedately around a corner out of sight. The steering wheel pulled to the right and with a string of curses the chauffeur stopped the vehicle. With a sinking heart he knew he had somehow sustained a puncture. He stood looking down at the offending wheel, giving the flat rubber a kick of irritation. There was nothing for it – he'd have to get to work.

Already he could feel the sweat breaking out on his forehead and under his arms as he opened the trunk. He didn't hear the man behind him but he did feel the pinprick in his arm. As he turned his world went black.

The chauffeur's body was bundled inside the trunk and the lid closed. The man, identically dressed in a chauffeur's uniform, went around the car to the offending wheel. He located the spike sticking in the tyre and screwed a small metal bottle onto its end. Opening a valve, the tyre immediately reflated, filling with a soft rubber compound. He withdrew the spike and the hole sealed itself, a globule of black rubber forming at the hole. He looked at his handiwork with satisfaction. Many VIPs' cars now had tyres filled with the compound. The springs of a modern car guaranteed a comfortable ride while the rubber filled tyres ensured no flat tyres. Climbing into the car he drove around the block and parked outside the apartment building.

An hour and twenty minutes later Izzat al-Muri finally appeared. He looked highly pleased with himself. The driver kept his head bent, his hat over his eyes, as he opened the door. Al-Muri didn't so much as glance at him. He was used to servants being at his beck and call and rarely saw them unless things went wrong. They had been travelling for ten minutes when he did notice something was amiss and he opened the partition between himself and the driver.

'Dolt! This is not the way. Turn around immediately.'

For an answer the driver pressed his foot on the accelerator and the car speeded up.

'Stop, I say. Are you deaf?'

When there was no reply the first stirrings of fear began to grow in al-Muri's breast. He now looked at the chauffeur and said, 'Where is Ifraim? You aren't my usual driver.'

'No, sir. Ifraim is ill. I have taken over.'

The words were spoken kindly and were somehow re-assuring to al-Muri. 'But this is the wrong way, I tell you. Stop and turn the car around.'

The car slowed and al-Muri sat back with a sigh of satis-faction. He had been panicking for nothing. Still, he would teach the idiot a lesson and fire him as soon as he returned to the bank.

They were in a rundown part of the city, one that the banker never saw. High gas containers littered the landscape like carbuncles, and not far away he saw the chimney of an oil-cracking refinery. Now what? The car was stopping.

Sitting forward to remonstrate with the driver he looked down the silenced barrel of a gun. Two shots struck him in the heart, killing him instantly.

Ali Hossan climbed out of the car and walked away. His flight back to London was only three hours away and security at the airport was a nightmare.

1

STEPHEN YORKE SHOWED his ID. Although he was known, the pass was carefully scrutinised while at the same time his car was quickly but thoroughly searched. After being given the all-clear he was welcomed with a smile as the electric gates opened. His arrival was announced via a micro-wave radio carried in the lapel of one of the armed guards.

The May day was bright and warm, the early morning sun on his face making him feel good to be alive. He enjoyed England in the spring and early summer and regretted his work so often took him abroad. Though this last job had been home grown. He glanced at the briefcase on the seat beside him and hoped it contained the sort of intelligence they so badly needed. He parked the BMW Z3 at the side of the house. The building was an imposing anachronism of past glories. Built by a tobacco importer in the late eighteenth century, the huge mansion sat on the edge of the marshy flatlands overlooking Gibraltar Point on the eastern edge of Lincolnshire.

Climbing out of the car, Yorke paused a moment to admire the view and the undulating North Sea, deceptively blue-looking in the sunlight. He saw from the parked cars that Banyon and Hossan were there already. Good. There was a great deal to do.

He entered through the main door where he was greeted by another security check. The hall he was in was large, with white and black chequered tiles on the floor. The walls were oak lined and opposite the entrance was a sweeping stairway to the upper floor. There were doors leading off to the kitchen, canteen and domestic offices. Upstairs was where the real work was done. He placed the briefcase and his sidearm on a conveyor belt which fed them through an x-ray machine and explosives detector.

'Morning, sir.'

He smiled at the woman. 'Morning, Sue. Lovely day. Is everyone here?'

'Yes, you're the last. You've got time. The meeting isn't due to start for another fifteen minutes.'

In spite of the easy familiarity, his retina was photographed and compared to the details on his ID card. His case and automatic were handed back to him with a gracious nod by the male attendant. He knew he was being watched via camera and that a fully armed assault team could be in the room in a matter of moments. Security was tighter than ever, which was unsurprising considering the events taking place in the world.

Yorke moved with an easy grace – a litheness that attracted women but made men careful around him. His ID said he was 6ft 2ins tall and weighed 182lbs. In fact he'd put on a couple of pounds recently as he'd been unable to get to a gym or even go running. His photograph showed him unsmiling with curly brown hair, brown eyes and a wide mouth. When he did smile, which wasn't often, he looked ten years younger than his thirty-eight years.

He took the stairs at a fast pace and went along the corridor to his office. He deposited his pistol in his desk drawer. His ID card stated he worked for Holmes International, a think-tank involved in writing tedious and heavy papers on matters of international importance such as world-wide immigration, poverty and the globalisation of industry. These matters were dealt with but were sub-contracted to professors and undergraduates at various distinguished universities across Europe. The domestic offices co-ordinated the writing and publication of the reports, paid the necessary fees, and distributed their findings free-of-charge to anyone who wanted a copy. Governments used those reports that suited their political philosophies and aims. Mostly the reports gathered dust in the archives.

The cover worked well for the top-secret organisation known as *Phoenix*. It had been established four years earlier to fight terrorism and corruption without recourse to courts and legal wrangling that was too often tilted in the favour of the criminal. Yorke had been with them for two years.

The corridor was thickly carpeted, the walls wood lined on his left with intermittent doors and interspersed with windows on his right, giving a panoramic view of the sea. In his office he found the coffee machine had been switched on and he gratefully poured himself a mug, added a touch of milk and, briefcase in one hand, the mug in the other, went down the corridor to the conference room.

'Ah, Stephen, welcome,' said Yorke's boss, Desmond Kavanagh. Kavanagh was a retired Brigadier who had written what was considered the definitive paper on international terrorism, money laundering and drug smuggling. To it he had added a new section, people smuggling, now more lucrative and a greater problem than illegal drugs. Somehow his paper had found its way to his political masters who had hated what he'd written but agreed with his findings. When interviewed about his conclusions and how he foresaw the future, Kavanagh was gratified to discover that the government agreed with him. What surprised him was their acknowledgement that to combat the problems, any organisation would have to be kept secret. Hence the establishment of *Phoenix*. Even its name was classified top-secret and known to only a handful of people outside the group. Whenever *Phoenix* was discussed politically, only the Prime Minister, Secretary of State for Defence and the Home Secretary were participants.

'Brigadier,' Yorke nodded. 'Jack, Ali, good to see you both.'

'Morning, Stephen,' said Ali. 'I see from the newspapers your job went well.'

'Yes. It was put down to a freak accident involving a gas leak. I lifted journals and computer discs from the house,' Yorke raised the briefcase by way of emphasis, 'and put a bug in the hard drive destroying Salan's computer's memory.'

'Good,' said Kavanagh. 'Now you're here we can get started.

I've read your reports and I have to say I find it all very disquieting.'

The three men around the table exchanged wry glances. Disquieting was a strong word for the Brigadier to use. It meant he was seriously worried and highly perturbed. The four men could have been members of a company's board of directors, each wearing the civilian uniform of dark suits, white shirts and discreet ties. The only difference was three of them looked as fit as top athletes. The fourth member, Kavanagh, looked like the Chairman of the Board, except he too looked tough, a residual fitness still holding in his waistline, despite his fifty-five years. He had grey hair, a narrow face and piercing blue eyes that darkened when he was angry. Of medium height and build, he had been CO Hereford, the Special Air Service regiment, his last job before retirement.

Phoenix was outside the normal controls of the UK's security apparatus, with its oversight committees and loud-mouthed politicians unable or unwilling to keep a secret. There were only three front-line operatives – Yorke, Banyon and Hossan. Each brought complimentary skills to the organisation. Yorke had received a first class honours degree in civil engineering from Bristol University. One year working in the off-shore oil industry convinced him he had made an error in his chosen profession. However, during his time at university he also spent four years with the Territorial Army which suggested another career and he joined the Royal Marines. After general training he was accepted by the Special Boats Service where he excelled. He was a captain by the age of twenty-nine and set for higher things. That was when he married Daphne who was then twenty-seven, but had been widowed at the age of twenty-two, and the mother of Dominic, now about to be fifteen.

Daphne had understood the demands of service life as her father had been a Royal Marine Colonel and her first husband an RM lieutenant. He had been killed by an IRA bomb in Northern Ireland, a casualty from one of the last outrages committed in the Province prior to the much heralded cease-fire.

Daphne had died when a drunken driver had ploughed into her as she had been crossing the road to meet Dom from school. The man had been prosecuted on four previous occasions for drunk driving and this time had been driving without tax, a licence or insurance. It had been three-thirty on a Friday afternoon. To add insult to injury he had been given a three year suspended sentence and banned from driving for a further five years. The shame brought upon his family was shrugged off by his father, the local Member of Parliament, who claimed his son had suffered enough because of his addiction to heroin and alcohol. Rehabilitation was better than retribution, so argued the father.

Throughout the court proceedings Yorke had sat quietly, watching, waiting for justice. When it wasn't forthcoming he made his own arrangements. Establishing who supplied illegal drugs to the community of Hackney was relatively easy. Buying a quantity of pure heroin simpler still. It took three days of surveillance to discover that the culprit had not learned his lesson. He still drove his father's car and was now using crack cocaine as well as heroin. It was relatively simple to enter the crack house and inject the heroin into the young man's veins. The coroner's verdict – accidental death. Yorke was surprised that he felt no satisfaction from the death. Vengeance had done nothing to assuage his pain and unhappiness.

Help and support came in the form of his Uncle William. A boatyard owner in the west country, he had his own devils to fight, not least alcoholism. Through mutual support they had created a powerful bond. In the meantime, Yorke and Dom also grew close, each needing the other to help them through the difficult times. Yorke was given a staff job and settled for two years at the Royal Marines, Poole. Dominic went to the local school where he was forever getting into fights and scrapes of one sort or another. What eventually kept him on the straight and narrow was the threat that he couldn't join the marines with a criminal record; it was his white-hot passion to follow in the footsteps of his father and step-father. At the age of twelve, Dom went to a boarding

school at Wimborne Minster where he flourished, much to
Yorke's relief.

Yorke's next posting was to the aircraft carrier *HMS Ark
Royal*, which resulted in his seeing action in Bosnia and against
Saddam before the Iraqi war of 2003. He was then approached
by Kavanagh. He still remembered the interview.

'I've been tasked to set up a clandestine organisation to fight
the international crime cartels, terrorism and certain forms of
corruption. Interested?'

'What does it entail?' Yorke asked warily.

'Unorthodox and illegal operations in the main.'

'Illegal? I find that somewhat worrying.'

'Only somewhat?'

Yorke shrugged. 'I don't trust our courts to mete out justice.'

Kavanagh and Yorke were sitting in a pub on the outskirts
of Portsmouth, in a darkened booth. Both men had untouched
pints of beer in front of them.

'I read your file,' said Kavanagh. 'I'm sorry about your wife.'

Yorke tensed, wondering what was coming next, his eyes
wary.

'Relax. I put two and two together and came up with five.
There was no DNA to place you on the scene when that MP's
son died and you had an alibi for the time.'

'I didn't know I needed one.'

Kavanagh grinned. 'You didn't. I made my own inquiries.
Except your alibi doesn't hold water. It so happens the police
weren't interested one way or the other. As far as they were
concerned a nasty piece of work was swept away and good
riddance. You've done well in M squadron, you've a military
cross and bar to your name and are highly regarded.' M
squadron was the counterterrorist and shipboard operations
section of the SBS. S squadron was small watercraft and
minisub insertions, while C squadron was responsible for canoe
and diving operations. 'You're renowned for your patience,
attention to detail and toughness. You've never asked or ordered
a man to do something you can't or won't do yourself. The
teams under your command think very highly of you.'

Yorke moved his shoulders in a gesture of embarrassment. He hated praise even when it was well deserved.

'I'm not interested in the death of one scumbag. I am interested in you joining me. Well?'

'How long have I got to think about it?'

Kavanagh picked up his glass. 'Until I finish this pint.' Draining it in one long swallow he said, 'Ah, that's better. Well?'

Yorke couldn't help himself. He was excited and intrigued and burst out laughing. Holding out his hand he said, 'Count me in, sir.'

And that had been the start.

Operations were usually conducted alone. Unlike most military tasks where there was backup and other team members, the three men worked independently. However, they were given the very best intelligence information which to date had not let them down. Their equipment was state-of-the-art and funds seemed to be unlimited. "Wet-work" as it was euphemistically called had, to date, resulted in the deaths of thirty-three men and six women. All of whom had deserved it, of that there was no doubt in their minds. There was a war going on – one that was on the whole unseen and unacknowledged by the general public, but viscious and dirty nonetheless. At stake? As far as Kavanagh was concerned the very existence of mankind. He argued if that was fanciful look at the facts. Then come back and tell him he was wrong.

Already living patterns were being altered to deal with the threat. From the obvious precautions required at an airport before boarding a plane to the use of sky marshals in the event of a hijack. Illegal drugs were ravaging families, killing youngsters who became addicted even before they were teenagers and causing a level of crime never before seen in history. And holding it all together, the blood flowing through the veins of the whole stinking edifice, was laundered money, now running into amounts greater than most country's gross national products.

'The information you three brought back should prove invaluable. Stephen, I take it yours is in the briefcase?'

'Yes, sir.' Sliding the case across the table, he added, 'I haven't tried to look at the info, in case I corrupted anything.'

'Good. Jack?'

Banyon replied, 'Same here, sir. That's everything I could find.'

'I did look,' said Hossan. 'There are three trip-wires on each of the discs. If any help is needed . . .' he left the offer hanging in the air. With a degree in computer sciences and a PhD in AI – Artificial Intelligence – Ali Hossan was well equipped to break into computer files. Like Yorke and Banyon he had suffered from a restless personality that had found an outlet in the Armed Forces. In his case, the SAS. An apostate, as he described himself, he had proven himself time after time in tight corners throughout the Middle East. When Kavanagh approached him he had been on the verge of resigning and leaving the service to start his own business. He had been a ready and eager recruit.

Banyon had been a member of the parachute regiment. A captain with experience in the first Gulf war, Kosovo and in the war to topple Saddam, he was as tough as they come. A bachelor, enjoyed short relationships, preferably with married women. It did, he said, make breaking up easier. He had joined the paras at the age of seventeen and come up the hard way. At forty he was the eldest of the three.

'Were there any problems aboard Salondi's yacht?' Kavanagh asked.

'No, sir,' Banyon replied. 'There was a crew of only six. His bodyguard had gone ashore with him and stayed in the hotel. There were no crew around at three o'clock in the morning. I lifted the data and placed the explosives mainly around the accommodation ladder.'

'Excellent.' Pressing a button his secretary came through the door. 'Ah, Evelyn, take the cases to IT please. They know what to do.'

'Yes, sir.' She exchanged smiles with the other three men, picked up the briefcases and paused. 'Would it be in order if I left early, please? My mother . . .' She left the comment hanging. Evelyn Beckworth was a spinster in her mid-forties. An attractive woman, she had spent her life nursing an ailing and demanding mother. From time to time she had a necessity to leave work early. As she also put in extra hours when required it was rare if Kavanagh said she couldn't go.

'Yes, of course. I'll see you in the morning.'

'Thank you.' She nodded and left, hurrying once the door closed behind her. A glance at her watch told her she had plenty of time but even so, she moved quickly.

Kavanagh said, 'With the information you three have brought I think we'll have conclusive proof. The latest information we have is that a *trillion* dollars is currently washing around the world, partly financing terrorism, mainly paying for illegal drugs but also buying legitimate businesses. We know of at least eighteen insurance funds that are used entirely to launder dirty money. Their combined assets exceed ten *billion* pounds. The figures are so enormous that should the trade be stopped banks and financial systems around the world will collapse.'

'So what do we do, sir?' Yorke asked. 'Just let it happen?'

'No. We continue chipping away at them. We can do no more. You know we were created to ferret into the criminal and terrorist heartlands, to track down the Mr Bigs and put them out of action permanently. We'll keep doing so with as little noise as possible. However, I've learned some disquieting facts. It's possible, and I must stress the word, *possible*, that there's a traitor at the very heart of our government.'

'What's he doing, sir?' Banyon asked. 'There are no secrets worth giving away, never mind selling. Not even nuclear ones. Besides, who's in the market place nowadays?'

'Up to a point, what you say is true. However, there are on-going, anti-terrorist operations in particular that are classified. Not only that but many of them are highly delicate.'

'The sort that would have the politically correct screaming blue murder?' Yorke suggested.

'Precisely. If our existence was even hinted at we'd be closed down tomorrow. MI5 and MI6 are so closely scrutinised they are virtually unable to operate effectively. They've become little more than civil servants in the intelligence world. Only the SAS and ourselves operate with enough leeway to be even remotely effective.'

'So what is this traitor doing, sir?'

'A good many operations have come to sticky ends during the past twelve months. More than usual, as it happens. Our lot here have been looking for patterns, trying to find definite reasons for what's gone wrong.'

'It could be operational bad luck,' said Hossan. 'It happens all too often when you're in the field.'

'Granted. But that's why you three are here and the SAS has the selection process it does, so that when things do go wrong, you can improvise. No,' Kavanagh shook his head, 'this has been a lot worse than operational cock-ups. It's been planned sabotage. Both Five and Six have lost some good people. I'm having a file prepared of the facts. You'll get copies later on today. Let me know what you think by end of play. After that, Jack and Stephen you're both stood down for a few days. Ali, I'm afraid I've got another job for you. It's in Britain. Sheikh Omar Bakri. At long last the government have had enough. They want a nice quiet job.'

'Poison?'

'Preferably. The hospital at Finsbury Park will declare a heart attack. That's why it needs to be done next Monday. The coroner on duty there is most helpful in cases like this one. The file is in my office.'

Hossan nodded. 'I'll be delighted. It's time that excrescence was wiped away. I'm fed up with the anti-British, anti-western rubbish he spouts from his mosque. He gives Islam a bad name.'

'Our political masters see it the same way at long last.'

They discussed future operations, all three wondering how much information the IT department was gleaning from the material they'd acquired. Lunch was sent up from the canteen, soup and sandwiches all round. The talk became general while they ate. Yorke informed them that he would be sailing that week-end.

At 14.00 the IT department reported.

The Brigadier replaced the telephone. 'According to the boffins there are so many cut-outs and passwords it'll take all night to pick the information clean. They asked if you'd care to help, Ali.'

Hossan smiled delightedly. 'Gladly. I'll see you guys later.'

He nodded at the other two and left the room.

'There's nothing further we can achieve at the moment. If we get anything before you leave I'll let you know,' Kavanagh said.

Yorke headed for the basement, to hone his sidearms skills in the shooting gallery. It would kill an hour or so before he left to go home.

He took the backstairs and went down two flights. Unusually, the house had a double basement. The upper level was used by the communications and records departments, the lower to house the firing range and armoury. Pressing a four-digit coded lock, he opened the door and went in. The lights came on automatically and he crossed to the strong room where the weapons were kept. He selected a specially adapted Austrian Glock 18 and loaded the 33-round magazine with 9mm Parabellum rounds. Capable of firing on automatic at a rate of 1300 rounds per minute, it was a formidable weapon sold only to government bodies. This particular gun was non-metallic and could be broken down into eight components in a matter of a minute and reassembled in two. Even the special rounds of ammunition were non-metallic and made from a composite of materials harder than steel. The weapon was designed to pass undetected through airport security systems.

Screwing on a specially adapted silencer, Yorke, went on to the range. He fitted a stiff-paper target to the clip above his head and sent it down the gallery. The silhouette of an armed terrorist stopped at the equivalent of a hundred yards. Taking aim, he fired three spaced, single shots. The revolver kicked in his hand, the only sign that anything had happened. The silencer was superb, dampening the noise of the shots to a faint cough. He spent half an hour wasting a hundred rounds of ammunition before cleaning the gun and returning it to the safe. The weapon he had been using was identical to the one he normally carried.

There was a faint shudder in the soles of his feet and dust drifted down from the solid concrete ceiling.

What the hell?

Opening the door he was thrown back by an almighty explosion. His head hit the floor and he passed out.

2

YORKE CAME TO slowly. There was no snapping awake and full alertness. It was a gradual realisation of pain, of limbs not working properly, of nausea. Sitting up, his first thoughts were *what had happened*? *A gas leak*? It was the only thing that made sense. Alarm bells were ringing in the background. He gingerly felt his head, and discovered a large lump above his right ear. Looking at his fingers he saw there was no blood and only then realised the lights in the basement were still on. Clambering unsteadily to his feet he leant against the wall for a few seconds to allow a dizzy spell to pass. Wryly he thought about the rubbish shown in films where the hero gets blown up, knocked out, wounded and still carries on like a superman. Only it wasn't like that. He needed a few minutes to rally his strength, to get his body and brain functioning properly again. He felt bile rising in the back of his throat, swallowed it and went across to the toilets. Inside he drank a copious amount of water staring critically at himself in a mirror. He was covered with dust. Washing his hands and face, he made a cold compress using hand-towel tissue, which he held to the bump on his head.

Already he was beginning to feel better, his natural fitness and strength kicking in. He tried the door to the stairs but it was jammed solid and after a few minutes he gave it up as a bad job. Vaguely, in the back of his mind, he remembered some-thing about another entrance. Heating! That was it! The first winter after *Phoenix* arrived in the house it was found to be so cold that any other organisation would have been shut down by the Health and Safety Executive. In the interests of efficient work, rather than consideration for the workers, the old-fashioned coal-fired boiler was replaced by gas central heating. It was Calor gas delivered by tanker, the pipeline for mains gas not reaching so far into the wilds of the Lincolnshire countryside. The disused coal bin and cellar had been changed into the armoury.

Yorke opened the door and switched on the light. The room was high, long and narrow. Closed but unlocked cabinets lined the left hand side, each door marked with a list of its contents. The room was painted a dull matt grey and had the all-pervading smell of light oil, used to clean the weapons. At the far end he stopped and looked up. As he'd thought, there was the faint outline of a trapdoor, covered in thick layers of paint. Taking a step-ladder, he positioned it beneath the indentations and climbed up. Stretching his arms above his head he gave a tentative and then muscle aching push. The trapdoor was solidly bedded in place. He took a pen-knife out of his pocket, sliced through the paint around the trapdoor and tried again. Nothing.

He decided there was no time to lose and descended the ladder. In a side room was a locker marked PE, in which were various shaped charges. Helping himself to a block the size of a playing card and the thickness of half a pack, he stripped off the backing paper before pushing the PE firmly into place in the centre of the trapdoor. Flicking a switch on the side, he armed the Semtex. The face of the block consisted of an LCD display and three buttons. One increased the timing to detonation in segments of fifteen seconds, another decreased the timing and a third set the timer. Yorke set the timer for thirty seconds, pressed the start button and climbed down the steps. He took the ladder with him when he stepped through the door of the armoury. The explosion was muted by the door and he waited a few seconds to allow the dust to settle. Re-entering, he stood underneath the trapdoor and looked up in satisfaction. He could see the tunnel, angled at about forty-five degrees, a dark hole leading to freedom.

The step-ladder was about seven feet too low and he knew he'd only have one chance to get into the tunnel. He stood with his left foot on the top platform of the ladder with his right on the metal rim of the ladder's metal frame, 10 inches higher. He didn't dwell on the fact that if he missed he could seriously injure himself. Bending his legs he launched himself up, kicking over the ladder in his efforts. His head and shoulders passed into the hole while his fingers scrabbled in the rough stone as he tried to get a purchase, feeling himself sliding backwards as his legs kicked the empty room beneath him. His right hand gripped a protruding knuckle of stone and his slide backwards was arrested for a second or two. Flinging his left arm outwards, he found a crack into which he shoved his middle and index finger. With creaking muscles, he paused a few moments as the full weight of his body pulled against his precarious grip.

Heaving upwards he dragged his hips over the edge, level with his right hand, the strain easing as some of the weight came off. He let go of the knuckle of stone and felt above his head. He reached another seam, this time wide enough to take his whole hand and he pulled himself fully into the tunnel. It was the shape of the trapdoor, three feet by two feet, and he sat with his back against one side, his feet on the other while he regained his breath. After a few moments he began to inch his way up, his hands either side of him, his palms pressed flat, getting into a rhythm, moving a few inches at a time. He moved slowly but steadily, the faint light from the room below soon hidden, as the tunnel snaked to one side. After a few minutes he took the precaution of reaching above him to ensure he didn't reach the top unexpectedly and smash his head. On the fourth try he felt something.

The barrier proved to be metal. Bracing himself he pushed and felt it lift a fraction of an inch. He tried again. Still it moved only a tiny amount. He paused for a second and debated with himself whether to go back into the armoury for another explosive device but decided against it. He'd have to work his way down, drop into the armoury, climb back up, set the charge, go back down, wait for the explosion and climb back a third time. Luck had been with him so far but it wasn't something to count on.

He felt for the hinges and then reached for the opposite side. Bracing himself, he anchored his body, straining his legs and back against the tunnel, before pushing upwards against the metal cover. In the Stygnian blackness he saw red spots before his eyes, the bump on his head now throbbing in time to his heartbeat. Unexpectedly the corner he was pushing lifted an inch and then flew upwards as the grass covering the trapdoor tore open in a shower of earth and small stones.

Gripping the side of the hole Yorke pulled himself out and flopped down onto the grass lawn at the back of the house. His vision was clearing when he heard the distinct but unmistakable sound of automatic weapons being fired.

His throbbing head all but forgotten, he rolled onto his stomach and looked around him. He was at the north-east corner of the house, a few yards from the gable end. He saw the blown-in windows and shattered doors. The roof had been hit twice, possibly three times, by some sort of missile. A fire was raging at the other end of the house and above the noise of the flames and gunfire he could hear the sound of a helicopter.

Right then he would have given his worldly goods for an automatic pistol. He crawled across the lawn until he could see around the corner. Two men in black combat suits and balaclavas were hurrying out of a side door towards a helicopter sitting, like a praying mantis, on the green sward of lawn. He recognised the Soviet, Kamov Helix-C naval helicopter. It could carry an array of weapons as well as up to 16 passengers. It had been a formidable machine in its time but lack of investment and innovation had left it behind. However, thousands still flew in and around the more hostile and inhospitable regions of the world.

Dismissing the whys and wherefores Yorke knew that whoever they were he had to stop them. More balaclavered individuals appeared, carrying computer hard-disc drives and boxes.

One of the men yelled out. 'How much longer?'

The reply was indistinct but that was not what had sent Yorke into a feeling of unreality. The voice was unmistakably upper crust English! He realised that the shooting had stopped but then a few isolated shots rang out. The *coup de grace*, he thought, anger coursing through him.

He needed to get his hands on a weapon and the nearest was in his office on the first floor. The corner of the building where it was located was still standing. Suddenly he heard shrill, woman-sounding screams, until another shot abruptly cut off the noise. He couldn't wait any longer. Nearby the French-windows to the dining room had been blown open and he stepped cautiously through the entrance, broken glass crunching underfoot. The room was a wreck. Broken and over-turned tables and chairs littered the place, the floor a carpet of broken glass and cutlery. Stepping around one table he saw the body of a dead woman, the face shot away and unrecognis-able. Another body, a man's, lay by the door to the corridor. He heard a sound outside the door and he darted across the room, diving through the serving hatch and into the kitchen, landing on his right shoulder and rolling into cover.

'Who's there?' A voice called out.

Yorke crawled carefully to the door and scratched its surface.

'Come out, I won't hurt you,' called the voice in a Scottish accent. Glaswegian? West coast, anyway.

Again Yorke made the scratching noise. It would, he knew, intrigue the listener rather than alarm him. He heard footsteps crunching across the broken crockery, coming slowly and care-fully. Yorke stood against the wall, directly behind the door and made one final scratching sound.

The door opened slowly. The first thing that Yorke saw was the muzzle of a Heckler and Koch G11 automatic rifle. It's peculiar shape made it one of the most recognisable guns in the world. It was amazingly accurate, the barrel and stock of similar dimensions, making it look like a flat oblong box – 750mm long, 112mm wide and 55mm thick. In spite of its appearance it was comfortable to use and shot well. It had been designed for use by the German army but politics had inter-fered and the gun had only been issued to German Special Forces.

The intruder followed the weapon, stepping slowly but softly forward. 'Come out, come out wherever you are,' said a soft, lilting voice, reminding Yorke of a cat playing with a mouse.

The man closed the door quietly behind him and stood with his back to it. The balaclava hiding his face, restricted his vision and hindered his hearing. Some movement on the part of Yorke must have been sensed by the man for he began to turn his head as Yorke brought the straight edged sides of his palms smashing down onto both sides of the man's neck. Normally such a double blow would have been totally incapacitating but the slight movement caused Yorke to miss the exact spot he'd aimed for and instead of the man dropping at his feet he stood like a wounded bull, shaking his head, rallying his strength. Already the gun was coming up to point at Yorke's midriff, the assassin's finger curling around the trigger.

In one fluid movement, Yorke hit the rifle to one side, stepped in the opposite direction and thrust three fingers into the man's throat, crushing his larynx, closing the airway. The man gurgled, his eyes popping, as he stared into Yorke's. This time he collapsed, a harsh grating rattle came out of his silently screaming mouth, his heels drummed a brief tattoo and then fell still. Yorke didn't need to check for a pulse to know his assailant was dead.

Grabbing the G11, he checked the safety on the left side above the trigger. It was forward one notch, on single shot. He pushed it forward a second notch to "3". Now it would fire a three-round burst of 4.7, 33mm caseless cartridge. It meant for a surer kill than a single shot. Quickly he felt in the dead man's pockets and found a spare magazine. Grabbing the balaclava he pulled it off the man's head and stopped in shock. Sergeant MacLean? It couldn't be. But there was no mistaking the man from the Gorbals. They'd worked together often enough in the old days. *MacLean? It was impossible! He was the last man Yorke would have expected to go bad.*

The standard ear radio and mouthpiece lay on the floor and Yorke grabbed it. Placing the earpiece in his right ear he clearly heard the words . . . 'report in. It's time we got the hell out of here.'

Yorke was already out of the kitchen and hurrying across the dining room. He didn't know what was going on and he didn't care. He would kill as many of the bastards as he could before they got him.

3

YORKE PAUSED AT the shattered window and looked out. Men were hurrying towards the helicopter. All had on balaclavas, carried guns and wore dark combat fatigues. The way they moved, the way they held themselves told Yorke they were trained operatives. Ex or serving special forces?

Through the ear-piece he heard a voice ask, 'Mac, we're leaving.'

As the men climbed into the waiting helo Yorke aimed the G11 at the third man from the end, fired, changed aim, fired and . . . there was no other target. The third man was already diving under the belly of the helicopter and going in through the other door. The two men Yorke had downed had been hit with head shots and wouldn't be going anywhere. The helicopter took off like an express elevator even as Yorke opened fire. This time he was aiming at the side window, trying to hit the pilot. The helicopter was very quickly out of range and Yorke stopped shooting. Even as he watched, the helo's aspect changed and he realised it was turning to face him. He didn't wait. He took off like an Olympic sprinter, across the room, shouldering open the far door, along the corridor, heading for the back exit. Just as he flung it open an almighty explosion sent him staggering as two air-to-ground missiles struck the front of the building where he'd been standing only moments earlier.

He kept running as the entire building began to collapse. A second and third explosion followed. A large amount of explosives had been set within the house. Slate, bricks and other pieces of the building rained down. A blow to his left shoulder caused him to stumble but he kept his feet and ran harder still. He could hear the masonry falling behind him but above that he also distinguished the clatter of the helicopter's rotor blades.

Changing direction, Yorke weaved his way across the lawn, heading for a copse of trees two hundred yards away. The chattering of a machine-gun was followed by the eruption of the grass in front and to his right.

Flinging himself towards the ground he twisted in mid-air and landed with a bone-jarring thud on his back. He sighted the G11 whilst flicking the safety to fully-automatic and opened fire. He had the satisfaction of seeing his bullets strike the helicopter as it wheeled away and clawed for height. Immediately he was up and running once more. This time in a straight line, the copse less than fifty yards away.

The only sounds he could hear were his laboured breathing and the crackle of fire from the demolished house. Glancing over his shoulder he saw the helicopter was a distant speck heading towards the coast. Yorke kept going. He wanted cover before he stopped and took stock.

There were eighteen or twenty beech trees. Tall and leafy, the undergrowth was kept clear, giving very few places to hide. It was a precaution in case of a sniper attack or someone setting up a listening post. Movement caught his eye. Two policemen appeared, wearing blue uniforms and carrying handguns. They were thirty yards away and watched as Yorke ran towards them. One of them spoke into a microphone but Yorke was too far away to hear what was said.

'Don't shoot! I'm from the house.'

He still had ten yards to go when he saw the slight change of stance of both men. That and the fact the guns they were carrying *weren't* matt-black Glocks warned him. Diving to the right he was shooting at them before they had time to take aim. One man died from a head shot while the second stumbled backwards, saved by his Kevlar body armour. Yorke forward-rolled back to his feet and fired two single shots again into the policeman's body. The force of the blows knocked the man off his feet, winding him and cracking ribs. Yorke reached the man and kicked him in the side of the head. The policeman went limp. Reaching down, Yorke took the gun out of the man's hand. A glance told him it was a silver SIG P225.

Grabbing his would-be assassin by the shoulders, he dragged the semi-conscious body into the trees. He propped the man against a tree trunk and quickly searched him. There was no ID, only handcuffs, spare magazines and a radio. Slapping the man's face, Yorke got no response. He placed the muzzle of the SIG into the palm of the man's hand and fired. The man screamed with pain and came wide awake.

'You bastard!'

'I knew you were faking it,' said Yorke. 'Who are you?'

'You'll never know, Yorke. But we know who you are.'

Although shocked to the core to hear his name, Yorke kept his features straight. 'I asked you a question. Who are you?'

'You'll never know. But my people know you. They know you're alive. You're a dead man walking.'

By way of response Yorke placed the muzzle of the gun against the man's left knee cap. The man smiled, ground his teeth and died. His head lolled forward, his mouth dropped open and drool oozed from his lips. Yorke recognised death from cyanide but checked for a pulse anyway. There was none.

In the distance he could hear the sound of sirens. The last thing he needed was to be arrested and questioned; which was why he couldn't take any of the guns with him. It would take the authorities days to unravel what had happened. And the fact was five men were dead at his hand. *Phoenix* had always been a deniable organisation, operating outside the law. Would his political masters come to his aid? Admit that *Phoenix* even existed? Christ, the political fall-out would be devastating. Human-rights organisations would have a field day. There would be demands to uncover the operations he'd been involved in. He could see the Court of Human Rights in Strasbourg arraigning British ministers to account for their actions. War crime indictments? Possibly. After all, *Phoenix* had assassinated generals and politicians in Bosnia. Men who had deserved to die, without doubt, but they'd been denied a fair trial. Even if he did somehow manage to get off, he was finished. *Phoenix* was finished. The organisation was as moribund as its namesake. Except for one vital ingredient. He was still alive and free.

And after all a phoenix was a mythical Egyptian bird of great beauty which lived for 500 or 600 years in the Arabian Desert. It consumed itself by fire, rising again from its ashes, young and beautiful, to live through another cycle. If he could get away undetected there was a possibility that this particular *Phoenix* could rise again long enough to extract vengeance for what had happened.

He looked back at the house. The entire complex had been razed to the ground. Not a wall, not even a chimney-breast, was left standing. White hot rage swept through him.

He moved swiftly through the trees. At the edge of the copse he stopped. To his right was a nature reserve, to his left, a golf course about a mile away. In front was open land leading down to the beach. Stooping, he dug a shallow hole using the barrel of the G11. Carefully he wiped the gun clean of any possible fingerprints and pushed it into the soft earth. He replaced the dirt on top and threw a handful of twigs and grass over the bare ground. It was the best he could do under the circumstances.

Keeping the trees between him and the house he hurried away, the sloping land quickly taking him below the skyline. He scrambled down the cliff to the beach, slipping and sliding, maintaining a precarious footing. He dropped the final five metres onto the balls of his feet, his knees flexing, the sand cushioning his landing. There was nobody in the immediate vicinity but he heard a dog barking and he looked south along the water's edge. A gambolling dog was a few hundred metres away, its owner trudging along behind. Yorke turned north towards Skegness and walked with a long, loping stride that ate up the distance. There weren't any men wearing dark suits on the beach and he slid his jacket off and rolled up his shirt sleeves. He removed his tie and put it in his pocket.

The going was soft and his shoes filled with sand. Stopping, he took them and his socks off while he pondered his options. The man who'd killed himself had said that they knew who he was – that he was a dead man walking. What did that mean? Was it pure melodrama? Or was he actually at risk? And from whom?

Seacroft, the southern end of Skegness was ahead. People were strolling along the beach, enjoying the afternoon sun. A few pointed behind him and Yorke looked over his shoulder to see a wisp of smoke rising in the air. It must have been from the house. He was surprised more people weren't rubbernecking, alerted by the sound of the explosions.

He was passing one elderly couple when the man called out to him. 'I say! Did you see what happened?'

'Where?' He decided to play it dumb whilst at the same time taking out a tissue and blowing his nose.

'At Gibraltar Point. We heard loud bangs. Sounded like a gas explosion or something.'

Speaking nasally, he replied, 'Sorry, I was on the beach. Heard the bangs but saw nothing. Sorry.' He hurried away, his head averted. The last thing he wanted was to be remembered.

Stopping at a set of concrete steps he wiped the sand off his feet as best he could and replaced his socks and shoes. He hurried up to the pavement and headed for the railway station. On the way he passed a hole-in-the-wall and stopped to insert his Visa card. He tapped in his PIN and requested £100. The screen apologised, announced it was keeping his card and closed down.

What the hell? *It was impossible*! His card was paid automatically every month. There was no reason to keep it. He reached into his wallet and extracted a second card, was about to insert it then thought better of it. Something was seriously wrong. Somebody, somehow, had instructed his bank to take his card. It also meant that if his card was being monitored then his whereabouts would be known. *What was happening*? *This was crazy*! *Nuts*! The thoughts swirled around his head. He walked on, alert, keeping pace with the crowd as they ambled past the shops, window shopping, killing time until it was a reasonable hour to go into a local pub. People were on a short break vacation, enjoying the bank holiday.

Feeling in the lining of his coat he touched the square of plastic he kept there. He forced the threads apart and pulled out a credit card. One thing he'd learnt in his time with *Phoenix*, a second identity was always useful. The next ATM machine accepted the PIN number and he requested a current balance. £98,434.46. It was about what he'd expected. He extracted two lots of £500 and put the notes in his pocket. He had a complete new legend on the *Lucky Duck*, including a passport. Thinking about the yacht reminded him he was due to meet Dom that evening for a week-end sailing trip. Damn! There was no chance of that. He'd have to disappoint him. Reaching into his pocket he took out his mobile phoned and paused. Reluctantly he put it away. He'd use a phone box; mobile phone calls were all too traceable.

He stopped at a coffee shop outside the station and, sitting at a table two in from the window, he scanned the area. Anyone looking in would have difficulty seeing him in the darker shadow of the shop. Outside looked quiet and peaceful. But he knew from his own experience that appearances could be deceptive. What was out of the ordinary? Who didn't fit the usual pattern of pedestrians around a railway station? An ice-cream van, half hidden in an alley, was doing very little trade. In the time Yorke sat at the window he saw only one customer. The man serving looked to be what he purported.

The *Big Issue* seller fitted the profile – in his twenties, dressed casually, polite, smiling into the faces of those who refused to buy, scowling at their backs. Two men in suits stood by the main entrance, looking around, alert.

On the corner were two young women, chatting. Passengers went through the entrance, some ambling, others in a hurry. A small queue was building up at the taxi rank. His eyes went back to the two men in suits. One of them nudged the other and pointed. A man hurried up to them, handshakes were exchanged and the three men went away. False alarm.

But there was something; he knew it! Or was he being

stupid? Seeing enemies where none existed. He was now regretting his decision not to have brought one of the SIG's carried by the two gunmen. What the hell was niggling him? It was . . . the ice-cream vendor. First of all the van was in the wrong place. Secondly the man served the occasional customer but the rest of the time he was looking around, quartering the area with his eyes. Usually someone doing something so tedious and mundane sat with a paperback or a newspaper, waiting patiently for the next punter. Yorke fixed his attention on the man. He was in his thirties, wore a tee-shirt, looked fit. If the area was this well covered he was in dire need of a weapon. Glancing over his shoulder Yorke checked out the back entrance.

He waited patiently until a customer appeared and asked for a coffee, whereupon the waitress turned her back to the room. As she did he stepped over to the door and went through. He was in a short corridor, at the end of which a glass-paned door led outside. Through the door he found himself in a small yard, a gate leading to an alley. Moments later he was in the high street. He sought a gents outfitters, where he bought a light-coloured sports jacket, jeans and a floppy sun hat. Next he went to a newsagent and purchased a copy of the *Daily Mail*. Rolling it up tightly, he carried his old clothes in a carrier bag in his left hand and the newspaper in his right. With the hat pulled low over his eyes he shambled back towards the railway station. He thought himself into character. A holidaymaker, one or two drinks over the odds, spending money; wanting an ice-cream.

Nobody else was at the van. A glance around showed no one was even looking at it. Yorke walked up to the hatch, kept his head bowed and mumbled, 'Ice-cream, please. Medium cone.' He slurred his words.

Holding out his hand he offered a ten pound note to the man who in return proffered the ice-cream. At that moment Yorke looked up into the eyes of the other man. The man couldn't help himself. The shock of recognising Yorke caused him to freeze momentarily, while his eyes widened in disbelief. It was all Yorke needed. Dropping the carrier bag, Yorke grabbed the man's belt and pulled him towards the counter with a jerk. The man had dropped the cone and was reaching underneath the counter when Yorke rammed the end of the newspaper into the other's throat. Two inches of rolled newsprint was like a solid piece of wood. With his throat crushed and larynx smashed the man collapsed in a gasping heap. Yorke let him drop, picked up his carrier bag and quickly went around to the driver's door.

The man was gasping, losing his fight for breath, his face ashen and caked in sweat. From under the counter Yorke extracted the automatic lying there. A glance showed it to be another SIG P225. Tucking it out of sight under his coat, he buttoned up the jacket, closed the hatch, lifted the van's keys and climbed out. Locking the door behind him he walked away without a backward glance.

The next train was at 16.01. Change Grantham and London, arrive Poole 22.29. He paid cash for a standard single to London. He had made the journey often enough and knew the routine. He walked onto the platform with only a few minutes to spare. Skegness was the end of the line and the train was waiting to depart.

Unhurriedly, he made his way to a carriage and climbed aboard, loitering in the doorway, watching the platform. With grim satisfaction he saw two men hurrying to catch the train. It wasn't the fact that they looked tough but the faint creases each had in the left side of their coats. If you knew what to look for, you could usually tell if a man was carrying a gun.

4

HE LOOKED AT the goal posts, fixed their position in his mind, stepped back two paces, then three to his right, concentrated on the ball and made his move. His right boot connected with a satisfying thud and the rugby ball sailed high into the air and between the two uprights. A loud cheer went up, the whistle blew and they'd won! His final kick of the match had won it for the school. Dom raised a mud stained hand above his head and let out a resounding yell of sheer, unadulterated happiness.

Dom was clapped off the field, smiles on the faces of the pupils from Wimborne Minster School for Boys, scowls on the faces of the supporters from Harrow. It was the first time in living memory Wimborne Minster had beaten the Harrow team and it had been in no small measure thanks to Dom. He couldn't wait to tell his father. Although Stephen wasn't his real father, he was better than a lot of the fathers who visited the school.

Dom would be fifteen tomorrow and he had a long weekend pass to visit Stephen. The original plan had been for Stephen to come to the school in the morning and collect him but he had persuaded him that he could take the bus to Poole that evening and meet on the boat. A few days of sailing the Solent aboard their 38ft, single-masted, sloop, *The Lucky Duck*, was exactly the sort of present he relished. He argued it was good training for when he joined the Royal Marines, like his real father and Stephen.

The boys sung lustily as they showered – favourite rugby songs coarsened by childish lyrics and resulting in great hilarity. Afterwards, his hair still wet, Dom threw a few things in his grip and reported to his house-master that he was leaving. He

collected £20 from his account run by the school and walked
out the front door and down the steps, eager to get away. He
was tall for his age, just touching 5ft 10ins, his shoulders
widening, the child becoming a man. As yet he had no need
to shave, his light-brown hair suggesting it would be some
years before the boring necessity arose. His eyes were blue,
his nose thin, his forehead high and when he smiled his wide-
mouth formed dimples in each cheek. He was good-looking,
but still too young to appreciate the fact. His youth and living
in an all-boys school meant he had little experience of girls,
and when he did meet them he was often tongue-tied and
awkward. The boys exchanged stories and banter about what
it was like to kiss and feel a girl *there*, but somehow, Dom
thought, none of them really knew.

A half-mile walk took him to the bus station in the centre
of town. The next bus was at 16.30 and he had plenty of time.
He bought himself an ice-cream and sat in the sun, enjoying
the cold strawberry taste. Only another half-term to go before
the dreaded exams, he thought. Still, they shouldn't be too
difficult. He'd done well in his mocks just before Christmas.
Then two more years, A levels to pass and off to university.
Three years and then a commission. His holidays would be
spent with the RM at Poole. In his head he had his life mapped
out; he only wished his mother was there to be a part of it.
And his father, he thought, feeling disloyal to his memory,
though the truth was he could remember nothing about him.
Only half-thought, hazy stories, told by his mother, fading
with time.

His bus drew in and he climbed aboard. Paying the fare to
the driver, he settled in the back seat, his bag by his side.
Another dozen people climbed onboard, mainly women with
shopping bags. Dom let his thoughts drift to the weekend ahead
and he smiled. *It would be great fun.*

He passed the twenty minute journey replaying the rugby
match in his mind. What had he done wrong? What could he
do to improve some of the moves he'd made? It was a habit
Stephen had taught him. After an operation a de-brief was vital.

Mistakes were to be admitted and corrected. The future must learn from the past.

The bus stopped regularly, disgorging and taking on passengers. Finally they came to his stop and he alighted with alacrity. A pang of hunger reminded him that the last thing he'd eaten had been his lunch – the ice-cream didn't count – and he entered a fast food joint for a burger and fries. Slinging his bag over his shoulder, he ate while he walked, the marina only a few hundred yards away. It was a lovely afternoon, the sun still high enough in the sky to cast a warmth over the land. He hoped they would take the yacht out and anchor somewhere for the night; that was great fun, setting the drag coefficients, listening to the creak of the cable in the hawse pipe; talking to Stephen about the marines. Naturally he had an idea of what Stephen did although little was said. Dom knew it was terribly hush-hush, and that national security was involved. One day, he hoped, he'd be a part of it. Wouldn't that be something?

He debated whether or not to buy a few groceries, milk and bread and stuff, at the shop in the marina, but thought better of it. Stephen would probably do that at a local supermarket. His feet clumped over the wooden slats of the short pontoon and he stopped at the gate. Tapping in the security code he pushed the gate open with a loud creak.

He paused at the rubbish bin and threw his empty cartons away, hoisted his bag in his left hand and walked along the main pontoon, paralleling the road about 8ft away. At the end he turned right, nodding and saying hullo to some of the people who had already arrived for a weekend of sailing and partying. The yachting fraternity were a sociable lot.

The *Duck* was berthed on the left, off a secondary pontoon. Hoisting himself aboard he was disappointed but not surprised to find that Stephen had not yet arrived. The large, open cockpit could sit half a dozen people comfortably. The wheel was in the middle; forward of it was the double door and sliding hatchway to the companionway that led to a small navigation cabin on the port side while aft and under his feet was the main cabin. Forward were two more double bunk cabins, one

either side of a centre aisle. In total there were berths for six.
Right forward was the sail locker and workshop where the
diving gear was stowed.

Taking a Yale key out of his pocket he unlocked and opened
the right-hand door. He slid back the bolt holding the left-hand
door and pushed it open, simultaneously sliding the hatch
forward. It moved with a slight squeak, reminding Dom he had
promised Stephen he would grease it. In fact there were a dozen
small jobs he could get on with while he waited. He stepped
lightly down the companionway. His first task was to check
the bilges for water and gas.

He was unaware anyone else was aboard until he heard the
words, 'It's only the kid.'

A hand covered his mouth while an arm fastened itself
around his chest and pinioned his arms to his side. Fear and
desperation lent him strength and Dom struggled furiously.

'Help me hold the little bastard,' said the man behind him.

Still wriggling, Dom lifted his right leg and swung it back
with all the force he could muster. He felt the satisfying jarring
up his leg when his heel smashed into his captor's shin. The
man yelled, letting loose a mouthful of profanity. Dom felt the
man's grip slackening and renewed his attempt to get loose. A
sharp prick in the side of his neck galvanised him a little more
but he felt himself growing weak. His vision was blurring and
he wondered if he was being strangled. With legs like rubber,
he couldn't stand and his knees began buckling under him. His
vision tunnelled, began to blacken and he collapsed.

He stood in his office, a phone to his ear, impatient to end the
call. 'Yes, yes. I understand. I'll take care of it. Now I must
go, I have a board meeting.'

He didn't say goodbye, merely replaced the receiver. He
adjusted the cuffs of his immaculately cut, grey suit, to show
half an inch of white cotton shirt. He ran his fingers either side
of his head, pushing his hair off his ears. I need a haircut, he
thought. He looked at his reflection in the ornate mirror across
the room. At 53 he was still trim and fit, working out regularly

in a gym in the Old Kent Road. Not one of those health and fitness spas for over-weight and over-pampered men and women with too much time and money on their hands, but a proper gym, where sparring and real weight-lifting still took place. Where the air was rank with old sweat and Old Spice, where, to put it succinctly, *men* were *men*. Where women weren't allowed. Not that he didn't like women. He'd been married three times, divorced twice and still kept two mistresses.

He examined his image critically. As usual by that time of the day he had a six o'clock shadow. Running a hand over his jowl he thought about having a shave but then dismissed it. Deep blue eyes looked back steadily at him. As always he thought his mouth too thin and his nose a little too big. He'd pondered having a nose-job a couple of years back but in the end didn't bother. His vanity was legendary amongst those who knew him well, not that there were many in that category – mainly his ex-wives and mistresses. He rarely drank and ate healthily. His hair was black, the grey covered up by the latest hair dye. He liked to think of himself as having only two weaknesses, women and horses. He had a string of race horses which he was inordinately proud of. His driving force was a combination of money and power – with one came the other. In his quest to acquire both he was insatiable.

The corner room reflected the man. It was large, the rosewood furniture was highly polished and ornate. The view from his Canary Wharf office was breathtaking. On one side was the Limehouse Reach stretch of the Thames and on the other was the main section of the West India Docks and The International Hotel. The cars below looked like toys, the people like dolls. It was a scene he never tired of, a reminder of how far he had travelled. Not only in distance, but also in achievement.

He had been born János Kadras in Budapest. His family had been refugees after the Soviet army had quashed the Hungarian uprising in 1956. By November that year they had gone from a five-bedroom villa over-looking the Danube in the south of the city to a two-bedroom apartment in Venice next to a stinking and filthy canal. A move that had turned the 5 year old's world upside-down.

His father opened a tobacconist shop. It thrived and a second and third quickly followed. The family moved to a bigger and better apartment. János had a sister two years older and a brother two years younger. His father began abusing his sister on her eleventh birthday. János didn't hear about it for nearly two years although he had been disturbed by the changes he saw in his sister during that time. János' own abuse began at the age of eleven. His sister was 14 when she committed suicide. János dreamed about escaping. Suicide or running away, it was all the same to him. However, he understood the fate that awaited his younger brother when he too reached 11 years of age and he curbed his plans for his brother's sake.

The day before his brother's birthday his father came into János's room. Now his sister was dead the boys had a room each. His father was drunk. He *boasted* what he would do to János' brother the next day. János was filled with hatred and had decided that whatever happened he had to protect his brother. When his father got on the bed János whipped out a kitchen knife and held it in front of him.

'Do not touch me, father, ever again. Or I'll kill you.'

His father was a nondescript man, of medium height, prone to violent outbursts of temper. Seeing the knife he looked at it incredulously and burst out laughing! It was the final humiliation. János plunged the knife into his father's neck, severing the carotid artery, missing the spinal cord, the knife sticking through like the bolt of Boris Karloff's Frankenstein. His father had reared up, choking, his hands to his throat, the blood pumping out, like water from a tap.

János leant forward and said, 'I *hate* you.' He was staring into his father's eyes when Kadras Snr died.

The bed was covered with blood; it dripped off the side and onto the floor, creating a widening pool. János sat and watched it, mesmerised. So simple, he thought. That was all it took to end nearly two years of fear and abuse. He shivered. If only he'd done it sooner! His sister would be alive. The thought made him cry and he sat for a while with his knees up to his chin, trembling, tears coursing down his cheeks.

He knew he couldn't remain. On shaking legs he got his school bag and stuffed some clothes into it. He knew his mother would be in bed, pretending to be asleep, continuing to live the lie that there was nothing wrong. He hated her as well! Hated her for her indifference, her unwillingness to face up to what her husband had been doing to them all these years. Even with the death of his sister she had not been prepared to act. I'll kill her too, he thought, but then remembered his brother. He couldn't take him away, yet the youngster couldn't stay there alone. He sighed, his sobs passing, the shakes stopping. He decided he would let her live.

Downstairs he knew where his father kept his money. The key to the locked drawer was in its usual hiding place in the pantry. Opening the drawer he took every lira he could find.

He put on his coat and let himself out silently through the front door. Without a backward glance he set off. He had thought about running away so often that he knew exactly what he had to do. His heart soared. He was free!

He came back to the present with a start. Too often of late, he was remembering the past. That was then. Now he was John Kennedy. He looked out across London. Storm clouds were gathering in the east, and he fancied he could smell the coming thunderstorm, a ridiculous notion as the air conditioning neutered all smells. A last satisfied look at himself and he crossed the room, throwing open the door. A dozen men and one woman sat around the table. He was ten minutes late but didn't apologise. He hadn't done so in thirty years.

'Let us begin. What's the latest on *Phoenix*?'

'It was completely demolished,' began the man sitting on Kennedy's right. His name was Leo Agnew, an American who had been with Kennedy for twenty years. A fact Agnew often reminded others about.

'I know that, Leo.' Kennedy kept the exasperation out of his voice. Agnew was a loyal right-hand man. Ideal for the job as he had no personal ambition, no imagination and was utterly ruthless, as he'd proven on many occasions. 'What about the man who escaped?'

'We know it was Yorke. He's on a train for London. He killed one of our men in Skegness. In the centre of the town. Some of our men know who he is. Special Services is a small world.'

'Thank you, Leo. So what are you doing about him?'

'We've two men on the same train. It left Grantham a few minutes ago. It ends at Kings Cross. They know what to do.'

'They'd better. I don't want any slip-ups. Ingrid?' Kennedy looked at the woman. Ingrid Kahn was in her early thirties, with blonde hair so light as to be almost white, blue eyes, pretty in a washed-out, insipid way. Behind her gentle gaze lay a mind like a steel trap with a talent for computer hacking. It had cost Kennedy two million dollars in bribes to keep her out of a German prison but she'd repaid him fifty times over during the last four years.

The men in Kennedy's organisation called her the ice maiden, a sobriquet she relished and took great pleasure in living up to. 'I've got enough to go on. He's got a yacht in Poole and a stepson in a school down that way. The boy is in our care onboard the boat. Two of our men are waiting in case Yorke makes it.'

Agnew glowered at the woman opposite him. If Ingrid was in any way perturbed or intimidated by the look she didn't show it. The bitch hadn't told him any of that. Trying, as always, to make him look incompetent in front of the boss.

'Good. Let's hope we are finished with *Phoenix* once and for all. I want this man Yorke out of the way so we can draw a line under the organisation and get on with other things. I hope I make myself understood.' Kennedy smiled benignly around the table, like the Chairman of the Board who had just settled a particularly difficult business deal.

A glass of water lay on the table in front of him and he took a sip before proceeding. 'Let us get back to why we are gathered here. I know you have already met but I would like to welcome Sheikh Mohammed al-Gari and his colleague Mr Mustapha Hamza. Gentlemen, it is indeed a great pleasure to have you with us.'

They nodded and smiled. They were dressed like successful merchant bankers, dark suits, dark ties, white shirts. Both wore heavy, gold, Rolex watches, Hamza was clean shaven, the Sheikh had a bushy moustache.

Kennedy continued. 'As we all know, London is, without doubt the terrorist capital of the world.'

This brought a few chuckles and broad smiles from everyone. Nobody disagreed.

'It has enabled us,' Kennedy waved an all-encompassing hand around the table, 'to take advantage of the fact. We have uniquely brought together three fundamental, shall we say, industries? Banking, narcotics and terrorism. What a perfect match! What a superb amalgamation of businesses with which to create not only massive wealth,' he paused and looked around the table, staring into the eyes of each person there, enjoying his moment, 'but power! Vast power which will enable us to influence governments, control governments, *own* governments.' Some of his audience had heard it all before but still they felt the thrill of his vision, the sheer magnetism of the man sending their hearts and minds soaring at the prospect of what lay ahead. They never tired of hearing the words.

'Thanks to Mr al-Gari we are now able to launder unlimited amounts of money through his network of banks across the world.'

There was a faint smattering of applause and al-Gari nodded his moustached head in acceptance of the praise, the smile on his lips failing to reach his eyes.

'According to the stock-exchange the first trillion dollar industry will be telecommunications. Probably reaching that figure within two years.' A wide smile lit up Kennedy's face, 'Of course we know that the first trillion dollar industry will be reached this year and it isn't in telecomms but a combination of drugs, people smuggling and money laundering. Of which we now control as much as ten percent thanks to Mr. Lopez and Mr. Kepler.'

Lopez smiled, full teeth and crinkling eyes a reflection of his Colombian heritage. He wore the same smile when he killed, or maimed, depending on the merits of the situation. His paunch was hidden beneath an ill-fitting suit that looked as though it had been bought in a charity shop. He needed a shave and if Kennedy hadn't strictly enforced a no-smoking ban his nicotine stained fingers would have been busy. His speciality was cocaine; growing, refining and smuggling.

Kepler was a Georgian from T'bilisi. His sallow, pock-marked complexion and white, round face was evidence of an early life of bad food and poor medical attention. He headed a coalition of Georgian Mafia gangs simply because he had proved more ruthless than his counterparts. His country, situated between the Caspian and Black Seas was ideally positioned to take advantage of the heroin growing countryside in the countries making up the Caucasus region to the north, Turkey, Armenia and Azerbaijan to the south. From there, through the porous borders, the narcotic flowed from Iran, Afghanistan, India and Pakistan. The trade was huge, the money involved was greater than the GNP of virtually every country in the world except America, Japan and possibly Germany. Immensely wealthy, he lived and behaved like the peasant he was. He had no conception of what to do with his money, only that he wanted more. Even political power was of no interest. However, Kennedy had persuaded him of the benefit of controlling Georgia and as a result he was financing a new political party that was sure to win the next election. The organisation would have a country in its complete control. Recognised by the United Nations, the World Bank, the World Trade Organisation and every other world-wide institution, their access to the highest echelons of government anywhere in the world would automatically follow. Especially with the money Georgia would have to invest in *legitimate* businesses across the world.

'As you all know,' Kennedy continued, 'our fast-food franchises are making healthy profits in every quarter of Europe.

We will be expanding into the USA shortly. Mr. McGill, I believe you have something to say about that?'

McGill cleared his throat. He was in his early thirties, Harvard trained in business studies, but went on to take degrees in accountancy and the law. He was there representing his mentors, the heads of the American crime cartels, founded by the Italian Mafia in the twentieth century. They had realised some years earlier that crime had come of age and needed to be controlled and directed. Otherwise, as in the bad old days, turf wars could result in *real* wars and that was bad for trade. With that knowledge came the search for the right man to co-ordinate and effectively be the Chairman of the Board. They had settled on Kennedy after he had explained his intentions to the Americans a year earlier.

It had been, as the American contingent said, a no-brainer of a meeting and Kennedy had been voted in unanimously. His clear, far-reaching ideas were just what the Americans had been looking for. They wouldn't be buying only fast-food businesses, which were used to retail illegal drugs, but heavy industry such as electricity generating companies – gas, nuclear and oil companies, construction companies, airlines, telephone companies – the list was endless. And it was all there for the taking.

'As you know,' McGill spoke in a Bostonian accent, 'we have now agreed the purchase of a five thousand outlet burger chain.'

Kennedy stopped listening. There had been a fly in the ointment. It was known as *Phoenix. Had* been known, Kennedy corrected himself. Kavanagh and his people had come too close. The deaths of Salan, Salondi and al-Muri had been a wake up call. Thank goodness for his contacts in the British government.

McGill stopped speaking and the board looked expectantly at the Chairman. 'The next item,' Kennedy announced, 'is people smuggling. We estimate it will be worth as much as fifteen percent of our business in the next year to eighteen months. I have the figures here.'

5

YORKE GOT OFF the train at Grantham. The station was busy with commuters and he wandered around, keeping a lookout for the two men he was certain were following him. His movements were random; from newspaper vendor to the station bar to the exit and back to the newspaper stand where he purchased an Evening Standard, a can of coke and a disposable lighter. As he paid he made a brief phone call to the school. They confirmed Dom had already left.

After disembarking from the train, the men had split up, making it more difficult for him to keep an unobtrusive eye on them but at the same time giving him an idea. Timing was everything. When his train arrived passengers would be alighting, mingling with those waiting to get on. It would be busy but the likelihood was the toilets on the platform would be empty. If they weren't he'd have to think of something else. As far as he was concerned, collateral damage was unacceptable. He doubted such niceties applied to his adversaries.

The train was approaching when he walked along the platform and into the Gentleman's toilets. The urinals were on his right, the closets on his left. A solitary man was standing at a urinal, he finished, zipped up and walked away. A quick glance showed all the doors were open and the closets unoccupied. Knowing he had only a few seconds, Yorke closed the door to the second closet, gratified to see it swung shut and stayed there. He stepped into the first closet and stood with his back to the side, hidden from the main door.

He heard footsteps and one of the men came into view, heading for the second closet. Yorke only needed a nano-second to bring the butt of the revolver he had liberated from the ice-cream vendor smashing against the side of the man's head. The man fell, pole-axed. Yorke hit him a second time, dragged him into the first closet and propped him on the toilet. A quick search revealed a wallet and another SIG, both of which he dropped into his carrier bag. Closing the door, he reached under and propped the man's feet against it. He'd be unconscious for a while and with luck nobody would open the door.

He paused at the entrance and looked at the train. The doors were beginning to close when he darted out and dived into the carriage. He smiled an apology at the woman he'd bumped into and moved further into the train. There were no empty seats and a number of passengers were standing. The smile froze on his face when he saw the second man standing with his back to the next door watching him. All pretence was over. He must have seen Yorke coming out of the toilets and not seen his friend. There could only be one explanation.

Yorke turned around and went along the train towards the rear coaches. He had to jostle past a few people who glared at him but said nothing. Tempers were held in check by weariness. If some idiot wanted to push his way along the length of the train in the hope of finding a vacant seat then so be it. Only he wouldn't find one. Didn't the stupid sod not know that? Hardened commuters inwardly gloated, superior in their knowledge of the hardships and vagaries of travelling on Britain's trains.

Yorke reached the end of the last carriage and stopped. The reason he had made the move was simple. If the gunman began shooting there was nobody behind him to get hit. In turn, he would have to be damned careful where his bullets went. The train would be making no stops and was due to arrive at King's Cross at 19.12. If it came to a shoot-out and he survived, a police armed response unit would be all over them. Most likely the train would be stopped somewhere in the wilds, helicopters would fly in the ARU and they would wait him out. He would get years in prison even if it was proven that he had shot in self defence. Merely having the gun on his person would get him five years; such were the gun laws in Britain. His only way of escaping a term of imprisonment would be to get shot to death. All this had been explained to them when they had joined *Phoenix*, and it had been accepted. In the backs of their minds had been the belief that the Brigadier would come to their rescue; *Jesus, what a bloody mess*!

Yorke kept a watchful eye on the far end of the carriage. The other man didn't appear and after a while he was beginning to wonder whether the man intended waiting until King's Cross to make his move. More likely, he would have phoned for backup. The man's job would be to finger Yorke, not shoot him – yet.

The train was slowing down for the run in to London when the gunman appeared. He stopped at the far end of the carriage and looked directly at Yorke. He smiled. Yorke kept a straight face and ignored him. What did the man intend doing? Wait until the train had stopped? What then? Either Yorke would have to leave the train and walk along the platform past the man and possibly into a trap with more gunmen waiting for him, or the man would try his luck himself. With the train stopped, in the panic and pandemonium of gunfire, the killer could hope to escape after shooting Yorke.

The train slowed further and Yorke saw they were seconds from coming to a stop. The carriages juddered to a halt and the doors opened. People were standing, patiently queuing. The front doors were jammed with bodies while those at the rear were slightly less congested. Yorke waited until passengers began to step out. Then he charged, barging through the door, knocking people flying, some to the ground, others stumbling out of the way. Yells of anger mingled with screams of fear. He hit the platform and sprinted along it, darting in and out of the throng that was teeming towards the exit. More yells and screams from behind indicated that the gunman had done the same thing.

Yorke had his ticket in his hand as he approached the barrier, shoving past the other passengers, he ignored their protests. He vaulted the turnstile to be faced by two burly ticket collectors, grim looks on their faces.

'Here's my ticket,' said Yorke, 'in a hurry. Death in the family.'

The two men looked nonplussed as Yorke took to his heels. A glance at the ticket showed it was valid and they exchanged shrugs. The man hadn't broken any law. More commotion attracted their attention as a second man pushed his way through. What the hell had gotten in to people?

'Here, you, where's your ticket?' The older man stood in front of the gunman.

The gunman reached inside his hip pocket and felt for the ticket. It wasn't there! Another pocket. Empty! Where had he put it?

'Come on, let's be having you. Where's your ticket?'

The gunman saw Yorke's retreating back. He was getting away! Without hesitating the man drew his automatic, shot the ticket collector through the chest and ran after Yorke. Behind he left a platform in total chaos.

The concourse was teeming with people at that time of the evening. Yorke ducked his head and threaded his way through the crowd and out onto Euston Road. He ran past St Pancras Station, the New British Library, the Elizabeth Garret Anderson Hospital and Hospital for Women, and cut right into Eversholt Street. As far as he could tell no one was following as he hurried into Euston Station and down into the underground.

His heart was hammering and he was sweating but he was gratified to know that his breathing was steady after the mile long dash. He bought a ticket for Waterloo and continued down into the bowels of London's underground to the Northern Line.

At the far end of the platform there were relatively few passengers. He was wearing the sun hat and clothes he had bought in Skegness, and carried the plastic bag. He changed his jacket and removed the hat. One of the automatics he tucked in his waistband out of sight, the other he dropped in the plastic bag after first removing the ammunition, which he pocketed.

His train came in and he climbed aboard. As far as he could tell nobody was taking any notice of him. At Waterloo he alighted and took the escalator above ground. There he bought a ticket for Poole. He then left the station to wander the streets. While he did so he began to dismantle the gun in the plastic bag, wiping it clear of fingerprints. He used his Swiss army knife to undo the two screws holding the plates of the butt in position, took the slide and barrel apart and dumped the lot in different rubbish bins.

In a back street he found a half empty rubbish skip. Using the lighter, he set fire to some waste paper and dumped the sun hat and plastic bag inside. Other items in the skip caught fire as he threw the lighter in on top and left. A skip fire was such a common occurrence the fire brigade probably wouldn't bother coming out.

In a doorway he found a beggar, sitting on a strip of carpet, a mangy dog at his feet. He gave the man the jacket and a five pound note. A disinterested nod his only thanks.

Back at the station he washed his hands and face and combed his hair. He'd missed the first train and had another hour to wait. He wandered the concourse. It took less than five minutes to identify at least three men who were out of place. Two were carrying guns, the third he wasn't so sure about. Surely for them to be at Waterloo was a co-incidence? If it was, then all the major stations were covered. What sort of organisation had that big a force to be able to deploy so many men? It was incredible! It was . . . bullshit. The thought hit him with the force of a hammer blow. They, whoever they were, were after him. They knew who he was and everything about him. So it was safe to assume that they knew about the *Lucky Duck*. Dom! Christ! Were there men at Poole waiting for him? And if so, had they already hurt Dom in some way? Killed him maybe? His mouth was suddenly dry, fear gnawing at his belly.

He needed to find out. He knew that directed anger was an asset. It heightened the senses and channelled the power of action. Dom was in danger and the men currently walking around the station possibly knew something about it.

By that time the crowds on the concourse had thinned out. Yorke pondered his options. There were too many commuters for any direct action to be taken. Furthermore, the station was well covered with CCTV cameras. Anyone even suspected of having a gun could expect the police to be there within minutes. There was only one thing for it. His train was waiting to depart in eight minutes. He kept out of the line-of-sight of the three watchers, moving slowly, blending in with the other commuters. Time stood still . . . then there was only five minutes to go . . . three . . . two . . . time to move.

Yorke walked boldly past one of the watchers. The man glanced at him but continued to scan the other faces. Out of the corner of his eye Yorke saw the man suddenly jerk his head back round to look directly at him. Turning towards the trains, Yorke saw the second watcher look his way and figured the first one had radioed the others. Good. Yorke climbed onto the train with a minute to spare. Two of the watchers followed. The third was left running down the platform as the train pulled away.

Yorke sat as though he didn't have a care in the world. Passengers got on and off at various stations, each time fewer people were left behind. He sat in the end carriage, his back to the rear in an aisle seat. One of the watchers appeared, glanced in his direction, and sat down half-way along. After the first stop, the second man came in and sat at the opposite end of the carriage.

They were, Yorke decided, making the right moves. So they knew what they were doing. That had a distinct advantage. Amateurs did the unexpected because they did the *wrong* thing. With professionals it was easier to predict their actions.

A drinks trolley appeared and Yorke got a coffee and a sandwich. The train had departed on time, at 20.50 and was due in at 23.19. Having taken the train many times, he wasn't surprised to find it was running twenty minutes late; in railway timetable parlance, it meant the train was virtually on time. It was fully dark when he recognised the outskirts of Poole. By this time there were fewer than ten passengers in the carriage. They drew in to the station, the guard announced the train was terminating and that all passengers should collect their luggage and alight.

Yorke saw the middle-aged woman struggling to drag her

suitcase out of the stowage between the seats and stepped forward to help.

'Here, let me. I'll carry it for you.' He smiled disarmingly.

The woman looked at him a little flustered but must have decided he wasn't a pervert planning to rape her or a stealer of women's cases and smiled in return. 'Thank you. That's most kind.'

'It's my pleasure. I'll carry the case to the taxi rank.'

'Thank you very much.'

The woman didn't seem to think there was any call for small talk and they fell in step alongside each other. The other two men worked a pincer movement, one in front, one behind. It was precisely predictable. *Time*, he thought, *to go walkabout*.

Dom had no idea how long he was unconscious. When he came to it was dark, he couldn't move and he felt the urge to vomit. He lay still for a few seconds, gathering his strength. Blinking, he saw it wasn't as dark as he'd first thought. He was lying on a coil of rope in the fo'csle of the *Duck*. Groaning softly he tried to sit up but couldn't. He lay still, puzzling what was wrong, his mind fuzzy. His shoulders ached, his back hurt where something dug into him and his arms were pinioned behind his back. That was it! He felt a surge of relief at understanding his problem. He was tied up. The pain in his back was a knot in the rope.

Memory came flooding back. A man had grabbed him. He'd been stung on the neck and then blacked out. A hypodermic, he thought. What was going on? He lay still, gathering his wits and trying to guess where they were. Not at sea, that was for sure. Was the yacht still in the marina or had she been moved? Was it a yacht-jacking? No, the man's words came back to him. *It's only the kid*. So were the men waiting for Stephen? If so, what did they intend doing? Had Stephen arrived already? Horror struck him as the next thought logically followed the last. Was Stephen dead? Had the men killed him?

He listened intently. There was the gentle sloshing of water lapping against the hull and faintly, somewhere, a motor was running. Friday night usually meant the boat owners arriving, having a party and sleeping it off until the morning. Only then would the serious business of sailing begin, the men handling the boats, the women below frying bacon and making coffee. It was part of the ritual. Comforting, pleasant, *safe*. Tears welled up and he angrily blinked them away. He had to stay focused. He had to remember the advice given to him by Stephen and think!

If the men were still on the boat he needed to be extra careful. If they heard him the next time it may not be a drug to knock him out but something more permanent. His legs weren't tied and awkwardly he got to his knees. A dizzy spell washed over him and he stopped for a minute or two. The feeling of nausea he'd experienced was receding to be replaced by one of thirst. His lips were dry and his tongue felt swollen, too big for his mouth. He could feel a few inches of rope hanging down behind him and he took a frayed end in one hand, rolling it between his fingers. He instantly recognised the man-made fibre, corelene, and guessed it was the line used to connect a diver to a marker buoy.

He tried moving his wrists and found he could twist them a few degrees either way. Bending down he stretched his arms as far as they would go. Awkwardly, he tried to pull his right foot through the loop of his arms but after a few seconds realised it was hopeless. The heel of his trainers caught in the rope and nearly sent him flying. He sat down on the deck, his heart pounding, fearful he'd made enough noise to warn the men he was conscious. After a few moments of silence, while his heart rate slowed back to something approaching normal, he removed his shoes. Still sitting, he forced the heel of his right foot into the bight of rope and, ignoring the pain of the corelene digging into his wrists, inched his foot through. With a sigh of relief his foot slid free and he was able to relax for a moment. His other foot quickly followed.

Better, he thought. In the gloom he looked intently at the knot holding his hands together. A reef knot with two half-hitches either end. He grabbed the end half-hitch with his teeth and worried it, shaking his had. He felt the bight loosen. The bight had become a small loop and he managed to get his tongue through it and pull it open. He attacked the second half-hitch and pulled it free. He did the same with the other end of the rope. All that was now holding him was the reef knot. Gripping the end of the corelene in his mouth he pulled it against the lay of the knot and it immediately slackened a fraction. He did the same with the other end, then gripped the small bight he'd created and pulled it loose. Moments later the rope slipped free. *Idiots, if they'd used sisal or some other natural fibre he would never have been able to untie the knots.*

Dom tried the door to the fo'csle, silently turning the handle. He pushed against it and to his chagrin found it locked. Letting the handle spring back he turned his attention to the forward hatch. It was locked from the inside by a hasp with a shackle through the staple. It was designed to keep intruders out, not prisoners in. A quick examination showed Dom that nothing had been tampered with and he undid the pin of the shackle. Quietly he slipped the shackle free and pulled the fastening off the staple. Cracking the hatch a fraction of an inch he was about to push it fully open and make a dash for it when he had second thoughts. What if one of the men was waiting in the peak? Was it likely?

God, he didn't know! Oh, God! Oh, God!

Dom found he was shuddering, like palsy, his teeth chattered and he felt immobilised by fear. *What* was it Stephen said about fear? Harness it. Use it. It helped you to focus. It kept you alive! It was all right to be scared, just don't let fear rule your thoughts and actions. Gradually his breathing came under control and the white mist he'd felt enveloping his brain dissipated. He began to think with clarity once more. No one would be in the peak. There was nowhere to hide. If they were waiting for Stephen they would be hidden inside the hull. People were outside. Other yachtsmen and women. There had to be. He listened intently but heard only the sound of the rigging strumming against the mast. Time? He looked at his watch. Ten minutes past midnight! He'd been unconscious for nearly seven hours. Stephen should have been here long ago. Was that why it was so quiet? Had he arrived and had something happened to him? He mentally shied away from the thought that Stephen might be dead. It was too horrible to contemplate.

He decided he couldn't stay there any longer and he pushed the hatch gently upwards, slipping his fingers between the lip and the deck. What else had Stephen told him? Senses. Use your senses. In the dark, sight was a poor third to hearing and smell. His ears told him nothing. He sniffed the air. He concentrated, distinguishing the smells – the tang of the sea, the mixture of oil and diesel from the boats, and a faint cooking smell. No body odours. No sour breath or smoking cigarettes.

Easing the hatch up further he got his arm through. Should he fling it back and scramble out and make a dash for it? Or should he stay with his programme of stealth? The indecision made him shiver. The thought of being captured again filled him with dread. Quietly does it. He'd sneak away. Go to the police. Tell them what had happened. Bring them back with him. What if they didn't believe his story? He'd *make* them believe, he told himself fiercely.

Easing the hatch up further, he pushed it gently all the way back until it lay across the deck. Dom climbed stealthily through the hatchway and quietly replaced the cover. He stayed where he was, looking intently around the yacht, trying to see if any shadow was where it shouldn't be. The fact was there was nowhere to hide. The ambient light around the marina lit the deck, reflected off the water, and cast wide and deep shadows.

There was no one around. He stayed still. Movement was eye-catching. It drew attention. Eyes gleamed, white faces shone but movement drew attention in the first place. He had to embrace the dark like a friend.

The fore-peak was three feet above the finger of pontoon. If he climbed down the hull would rock. If we went to the centre, he'd be six, possibly nine inches lower. The hull would be steadier, weight of the mast and engine making it so.

He slithered along the deck, slowly, avoiding bumping or scraping anything, aware how the sound would reverberate through the hull. He reached the cockpit and stepped lightly down.

He was at the rail when a hand shot out and grabbed his shoulder. 'Got you, you little bastard.'

The meeting continued for hours. Dusk fell, lights were switched on, London lit up, it's grime and squalor hidden by the shadows cast between neon lighting.

Much later, as they came to the last item on the agenda, Kennedy was irritated by a gentle knock on the door. 'Come in!'

The door opened and his secretary put her head through, nervously. 'Sorry, to disturb you, Mr. Kennedy, but you said I was to tell you if anything came in about Yorke.' Doris had been with him for ten years, was probably the highest paid secretary in Christendom and utterly trustworthy. 'The message is, Yorke has been found. Two of our best men have him and are herding him to the yacht.' She withdrew.

'Excellent news, excellent.' Kennedy rubbed his hands together. 'I think we can safely assume *Phoenix* will not be rising again to bother us.'

6

DOM'S FEAR HELPED. It gave him strength. As the hand grabbed his shoulder, Dom yelped, ducked and flung himself over the side of the yacht and onto the pontoon. He landed on all fours and took off like the wind. Behind he heard the crash of a heavy body landing on the wooden boards and running after him. It never occurred to him to duck and weave in case the man shot at him. Ahead he saw a marked police car draw up and could have cried with relief.

'Hey! Hey, wait for me!' Dom yelled at the top of his voice.

The footsteps chasing behind petered to a halt and Dom felt a surge of exhilaration in his breast as he reached the gate. He grabbed the round knob, his fingers slipping on the smooth metal surface. The handle turned and he flung the gate wide, running across the short pontoon to the pavement.

The police car held two uniformed constables who sat looking impassively at him. Dom reached the car and hit the window with his hand.

'Hey, take it easy. What do you think you're doing?' asked the driver, opening the window.

'Please. You've got to help. Two men,' he panted, at a loss for words.

'Calm down, take a deep breath and start again.'

Dom gulped air.

'Get in the car. Talk from there,' said the driver. The driver stretched his arm over the back and opened the door, giving Dom no option other than to get in.

Dom entered and closed the door.

'Now start again,' the driver said kindly. The other policeman looked steadily at Dom, not saying a word.

'I'm on my father's yacht. When I got there this afternoon there were some men there. They injected me with something and I was knocked out for hours and hours. I think they're waiting for my father to come to the boat.'

The two policemen exchanged cynical glances. 'Come off it, son, pull the other one.'

'No, it's true, honest.'

'Why would anyone want to hurt your father? He rich or something?'

'No. He's . . . I can't tell you. Please believe me when I say he's important in the security services.'

'That puts a different complexion on it. Why didn't you say so?' The car's engine had been idling and now the car pulled away from the kerb. 'I think we'd better get some help.'

'Where are we going?'

'To the police station. We'd better report in.'

After a few minutes Dom said, 'I thought you said we're going to the station?'

'We are.'

'But that's at the Civic Centre. And that's back there.'

The two men exchanged looks. The driver said, 'We know. We're going to the other one. That's where the senior duty officer is tonight. And we need special help if security is involved.'

'Oh!' Dom had been sitting forward and now sat back in his seat. 'The one at Ashley Road.'

'That's the one.'

Dom was reassured for a few seconds. His brain was insisting something was wrong but he couldn't figure out what. Then it struck him. There was no radio. He'd seen plenty of cop shows. The radio would be a background noise as instructions were given and acknowledged to constables on the beat and in their cars. Furthermore, wouldn't it have made more sense to radio in for help? Or at least tell control they were on their way in? Dom looked closer at the man in the front passenger seat. He wasn't wearing a hat and his hair looked too long. There was something else. What was it? Yes! He'd been in a police car once before when his school had had an open day and the police had been there extolling the advantages of a career in the force. The car's back doors could not be opened from the inside. A policeman had to open the door from outside, yet the door *had* been opened from inside.

The man chasing him had given up too soon. Where had he gone? If the police had stayed where they were the men on the boat would have been trapped. Unless they swam for it. No! The events of the last few minutes only made sense if these policemen had something to do with the men on the *Lucky Duck*.

His heart was hammering with the knowledge. He had to get away. But where and how?

The car turned onto Springfield Road and passed neat rows of houses and bungalows on either side of the street. Dom frowned. He was being stupid. This was the way to Ashley Road so he was worrying for nothing. A sigh of relief escaped him. The car turned right and came to the T junction that was Ashley Road. They turned left and sped away, accelerating quickly.

Dom looked behind him. The police station's lights were fading in the distance.

'Hey, the station is back the other way.'

'We know. We just a got a message to go to Ringwood.'

'Why?' Dom called out. 'And how did you get the message?'

'On the radio.'

'I don't see a radio.'

'Of course not. It's hidden beneath the dashboard. Now shut up and let me concentrate on my driving.'

The man was so self-evidently lying that Dom didn't pursue it. If he made too much of a fuss, showed he was on to them, they could take the initiative and hurt him or restrict his movements in some way.

'That's okay. But we must hurry and get to Ringwood,' Dom spoke ingratiatingly.

The looks that passed between the two men weren't lost on Dom. Traffic lights ahead were on red and the car slowed down. Another car was stopped at the lights and the police car drew up behind it. Dom didn't wait. Reaching for the door handle, he flicked it open, shoved the door and fell out into the gutter. He scrambled to his feet as one of the men yelled at him to stop. He ran for all he was worth, back the way he had come. Behind, he heard the squeal of tyres as the car turned and came racing after him. Looking back he saw they were less than a hundred yards away and gaining fast. He couldn't outrun them and so his plan to get to the police station was dashed. They could easily run him over instead of trying to capture him. He swerved into the drive of a detached house. He caused an outside light to come on that startled him but he almost immediately plunged into darkness again as he darted around a garden shed. He heard the car screech to a halt and a door slam. The car took off immediately.

Footsteps ran along the concrete driveway. A voice called out, 'Oi! What do you think you're doing?' There was no reply and the voice came again. 'Officer? Are you a police officer or should I dial 999?'

'Police, sir. We're chasing a suspect. Nothing for you to worry about. Go back to bed.'

Dom had stopped at the end of the garden and crouched beside a wall. He was perhaps fifty yards from the rear of the house and in shadow. The householder had appeared at a back bedroom window and challenged the fake cop but now he withdrew, closing the window. The man came slowly forward holding something in his right hand. Against the backdrop of the safety light, which suddenly switched itself off, Dom saw it was a handgun with a long barrel.

The wall was six feet high and made of brick. He reached up, grabbed the top and scrambled up, making too much noise in the process. He was lying across the wall when something impacted the brick near his face and sent a smattering of small pieces exploding in all directions. A sob caught in the back of his throat as he realised how close he had come to being shot.

Fear masked his pain as a sliver sliced his left cheek, his blood mixing with his sweat. He dropped to the other side, fell awkwardly, landed on his feet and stumbled to his knees.

Looking around him he found himself in another garden with a house fifty yards away. He heard footsteps running towards the wall which galvanised him into moving. His instinct was to run across the lawn but he stopped himself. A half moon had risen that was just visible over the roofs of the houses; a sea of light separated him from deep shadow on the other side. If he tried to cross, the bogus policeman would spot him easily. Dom could hear the man scrambling up the wall and knew he had only seconds to get away. Bent double he sprinted alongside the wall, the shadow of a bush beckoning him on. Glancing behind, he saw the gunman had dropped to the ground and was standing still. Dom dived to the ground and slid behind the bush. He knew that if he raised his head to look the movement and whiteness of his face could draw attention to himself. It took will-power to keep his head buried in his arms. After a few moments, during which he tried to control his gasping breath, he could resist no longer. Carefully he looked around the edge of the leaves.

His heart missed a beat as he saw the man walking along the side of the wall – away from him. Dom didn't wait. Staying bent over, he hurried in the opposite direction until he reached another wall.

'Hey!'

The loud yell sent Dom over the wall in utter panic. If the man did fire again Dom didn't feel any bullets anywhere near him. A dog barked nearby, startling the boy. Another dog further along replied. The call was taken up by others until half a dozen or more had joined in the chorus, from a deep-throated German Shepherd to the yelp of a poodle. A few householders put on their lights, the barking turned to howls and silence returned.

Dom was tempted to knock on the door of one of the houses and ask for help. But he realised that if the fake policeman turned up he'd be handed over to him. Or worse. Such an action would give the gunman time to catch up and he could merely shoot both Dom and the householder.

He was breathing hard as he came to a wooden fence and tried to scale it. When he reached up to grab the top he had to stretch his arms. His fingers curled around the wood beading lining the top and he began to haul himself over. There was a loud crack and the section he was on broke, throwing Dom to the ground. Hearing a noise, Dom quickly got to his feet. He looked behind him but couldn't see the gunman. It didn't mean he wasn't there and for a terrifying moment he had a vision of the man aiming his gun and shooting him. Backing up, Dom bent his shoulder and ran at the rotten fence, hitting it as though tackling an opponent on the rugby field. The wood broke apart and he fell headlong into an allotment. Something stung his leg, provoking him into action and he got to his feet, running hard again, leaping over serried ranks of some plant or other. By now a cloud had scudded across the sky and turned off the moonlight like a switch. It gave Dom a small sense of security while at the same time making his path more treacherous. He stepped onto a loose stone and went sprawling, lying prone on the earth, his breath coming in sobs. He knew he had to move but the instinct to just lie there and let it be over was strong. Maybe they wouldn't kill him. Maybe . . . Maybe what? Shaking his head, Dom climbed to his feet just as the moon shone once again.

He could now see where he was going and with that realisation came the knowledge that the gunman could probably see him as well. Dom bent low and weaved left and right. Something buzzed past his head and he fell headlong once more.

Climbing unsteadily to his feet, he stole a glance back. The bogus policeman was lumbering after him, thankfully still at the other end of the allotment. Dom passed numerous sheds, each offering a false sense of security should he hide in one. Another glance behind and he saw with a surge in his heart that he was getting further away. The gunman was floundering, running awkwardly.

A hedge loomed in front of him, black looking in the moonlight. A glance to his right and he saw a five-barred gate. He took it at the run, placing one hand on the top cross-bar, his other on the middle and vaulting over. He landed on packed earth and found himself in a lane. By now he had no idea where he was and in which direction to go except there was a glow of street lights to his left and darkness to the right. He elected for the darkness.

His legs were aching and he felt as though he'd played two rugby matches, back-to-back. He dredged up the last reserves of his strength and sprinted. His one thought was to put distance between himself and the gunman. The lane wound away from the houses and was surrounded on both sides by neat hedgerows. It was wide enough for one car with passing places every hundred yards or so. On his left was a nettle filled ditch, on his right, solid ground. He looked behind; nobody there. Ahead there was nothing except . . . except the loom of a car's headlights.

Was it coming his way? Yes! Bugger! Who was it? Was it the police car? The thoughts tumbled through his brain, causing indecision. The lights were stronger, closer. Who would be out at this time of the night, on this back road? He was still running – towards danger, or away from it? *Think*! *Do something*!

He looked at the ditch. The nettles were thick and high. The lights were just round the next corner and would have him fixed any second. A gate! He vaulted over, landed on his feet, dropped to the ground and hid his face. The car came past, driving more slowly than normal and Dom sneaked a peep, lifting his face from his arms. He caught a glimpse of what appeared to be a police car.

He lay still for a little while longer, getting his breath and strength back. Where could he go? Where was safe? Back to school? But what about Stephen? What had happened to him? Was he safe? Was he dead? The thoughts swirled round and round leaving him in a quandary of indecision. One thought surfaced above all others. He couldn't stay where he was. He had to move, but where?

*   *   *

Yorke wanted to know how good the two men were so he
turned right suddenly, away from the marina. The man behind
stayed where he was, about a hundred yards back. Around
another corner and the follower was no longer there. Instead
the lead man appeared, fifty yards ahead. It was perfect strategy.
The men were good – very good and obviously well trained.
In an urban situation, knowing the general direction the mark
was taking, you moved in and out of sight, until it was time
to close up and take out the target, if that was the objective.

Or you let yourself be seen and then your task was to herd
the mark to a particular place where you then took action. It
was all SOP stuff – Standard Operating Procedures. Yorke
grinned ruthlessly. But it also made his job easier. He only had
a single objective – to get to the yacht and ensure Dom was
safe.

There was nobody about. Each of the three men moved
uncannily like ghosts, their rubber soled shoes making no noise.
They *had* to know that he'd escaped and evaded a series of
obstacles that had been set up to stop him – with extreme prej-
udice, as the CIA euphemistically called it. So they knew he
knew and they knew he knew. Good. They had to be so very
sure of themselves that they must have special services training.
But from which country? MacLean had been British. The voice
on the radio during the attack on *Phoenix* had been English.
Were these two Brits as well?

The front man was now eighty yards away and turning
towards the main road leading to the marina. Yorke turned down
an unlit side street, another lit street loomed fifty yards away.
The second man would appear in about ten seconds. Yorke
expected them to be in touch by radio, probably ear phones
and wrist mikes.

Yorke knew he had to neutralise his shadow before the man
could transmit a warning to the other. On his left and right
were the back gardens of rows of houses. All had solid wooden
fences. He opened the first gate and stepped in, pushing it to,
leaving a tiny gap.

It wasn't the man's footfall that warned Yorke but the rustle of cloth. The man appeared, walking steadily, unafraid, even contemptuous of Yorke. He was half a pace past the gate when Yorke swung the gate open and stepped out. The movement and noise warned the man far too late. Yorke brought both hands together in slashing cuts, using his hands like blades, either side of the man's neck. The man collapsed. Yorke checked for a pulse and was relieved to find it beating strongly. The last thing he wanted were dead bodies turning up all over Poole. Squeezing the side of the man's neck, Yorke induced a deeper level of unconsciousness. As he did so, Yorke studied the man's face. He was a stranger.

Wearing a pair of thin latex gloves, Yorke searched his victim's pockets, extracted a wallet and a bunch of car keys. He found a silenced automatic in a shoulder holster, a earpiece in the man's left ear and a microphone strapped to the gunman's left wrist. Yorke removed all the items.

A voice spoke through the ear piece. It was in a language he wasn't sure of but *thought* it might be Serbian or Russian. Yorke replied making a hissing noise, pushing the transmit button on and off.

He was rewarded with a short burst of what he guessed was profanity followed by silence. *Time to stop buggering about and get to Dom.*

Yorke moved quickly back the way he'd come. The other man would be expecting him in the next street, not coming from behind. He ran lightly along the pavement, stopped at the corner and looked carefully out. The second gunman was less than thirty yards away, on the other side of the road, standing in the shadows, waiting patiently, looking towards the lane. There was nobody else in sight and nothing moving; no cars, no cats, and no insomniacs out walking their dogs. Yorke was halfway across the street when some instinct warned the man. He was turning when Yorke shot him twice, both chest shots. Both in the heart. So much for not leaving bodies littering the streets, he thought.

Another search yielded a similar haul to the first killer. This time Yorke left the gun and radio where they were but took the wallet. He'd examine its contents later. Dragging the body further into the shadows he left it there and hurried away.

Soon he was opposite the gate to the marina. Stopping in some shadow, he took out his cell-phone. He dialled a special number and looked at the screen. The connection was quickly made and the screen lit up, showing the yacht from a camera situated on the top of the mast. It was state-of-the-art, tiny, unobtrusive and with a lens that had one hundred and twenty faces covering the world like a golf ball. By selecting the right button, Yorke could look down, up, sideways. He could look close-up or out as far as three hundred metres with good resolution. After that the picture began to get a little fuzzy. The camera started recording as soon as somebody approached within a metre of the boat. It stopped if the person continued past. It recorded everything if the person came aboard.

Two men arrived at 15.40. They opened the door without any difficulty and climbed inside the hull. Yorke fast-forwarded the picture. The camera had a transmit range of less than a mile. He had developed some of the technology with a friend during their university days. They had patented the software, put together the hardware and sold a few to security companies. His friend, Martin Shearer, had gone on to build a highly profitable business while he'd taken a 20% shareholding and joined the Royal Marines. Each year a dividend appeared along with an invitation to go to a shareholders meeting or vote by proxy. He took every opportunity to attend. The dividends grew along with the company. Now there was talk of a stock-market flotation. Should it happen, somewhere in the back of his mind was the realisation that he would be rich. It wasn't something he thought much about. He saw Martin occasionally, their friendship picking up each time from where it left off. Martin had been there for him when Daphne had been killed.

Yorke saw Dom arrive and vanish inside. Then nothing. He fast-forwarded again, terror gnawing at him. If they'd killed Dom, he vowed, they would have the worst death he could devise.

The picture was now only of the deck. He saw the forward

hatch move. Then Dom appeared! Christ, one of the men was in the cockpit. Oh, dear God, no! He watched as Dom was grabbed and how Dom escaped and raced along the pontoon. Changing the lens coverage, he watched as Dom raced towards the gate, the gunman perhaps twenty yards behind. He wondered why the man didn't just shoot and then saw that he wasn't carrying a gun. He saw the man stop. The picture was beginning to blur and he made slight adjustments. The police car came onto the screen. The rear door opened. Yorke played it again. He didn't need to check the picture of the gunman walking back towards the *Lucky Duck* with a smile on his face. Yorke had understood the significance of the rear door being opened from inside. He watched the car drive along the street and out of sight. He saw the lack of aerials and lights which confirmed the car was a fake.

Dom, where the hell have they taken you?

7

BECAUSE HE NEEDED so little sleep he often became irritated with those who wanted more. The news that Yorke was being dealt with had put him in a good mood. Excellent. He didn't like loose ends. It was the middle of the night and Kennedy sat with a glass of diet coke, iced with a twist of lemon, in his hand. The house was a mansion in Belgravia. It was opulently yet tastefully decorated. It had cost a fortune to buy and a bigger one to renovate. The interior designer who'd been given the job had been neither gay or precious. Instead, he'd been down-to-earth, pragmatic, drove a bargain with the suppliers and pushed his men like a Tartar, finishing ahead of time and on budget. Kennedy smiled with gratified memory. It had taken very little to show the designer what could happen should the reverse be true. However, as a result the man now had many other jobs across Europe, looking after the network of contacts affiliated to Kennedy's organisation. Of course, the designer wasn't happy about the 29% stake that Kennedy insisted on having in his company, but what the hell. The designer now earned three times more money than previously. So everybody was happy.

The computer screen glowed. Kennedy rose to his feet and crossed the width of his study. It was on the second floor, wooden shelves lined the walls, holding hundreds of books from reference to the classics and modern thrillers. He had read many of them, his taste wide and eclectic. The furniture was counterfeit Hepplewhite, so good that many experts had been fooled by the room's contents. A smile played his lips. Good. The report from Moscombank. He sat at the desk and his fingers played over the keyboard.

One hundred million dollars worth of false invoices had been sent to Russia by his shell company, Bowlux. Ostensibly it was for electronic goods received, such as computers and play stations. In reality nothing was despatched except the invoices. The money was paid into a Bowlux account in Jersey and from there it was sent as legitimate transactions to accounts in London and the USA. In eight months over twelve thousand transactions had taken place totalling in excess of $5 billion. With the fees generated by such a huge sum it was in everyone's interest to allow the trade. Officials in the regulatory authorities couldn't compete. And those that tried were either bribed or had unfortunate mishaps, often resulting in death.

Another message appeared. *Excellent*. It was what he'd been waiting for. The Sudanese and Arab slave trade was now his. Teenage boys and girls in the Southern Sudan region of Bahr el Jebel, on the borders of Uganda and the Republic of Congo, were captured and taken north to the Arabic region of Sudan. There they were sold into slavery, often ending up in Saudi Arabia, United Arab Emirates, Oman and other Arab countries where slavery was rife. Some were house slaves, doing chores and looking after younger children, while many were sex slaves. Once they reached their middle teens the latter were often sold or killed. The profit on each slave delivered to the end purchaser was in excess of 1000%.

The latest batch had just been sold. Almost a thousand slaves had been collected and taken in separate caravans northwards. Only eight percent had perished en-route. He knew what that meant in spite of warning the caravan masters. The children had been sodomised or sexually abused by the slave-drivers. Once that happened they lost their value and were killed. It was a waste but one he had factored in as an inevitable expense. At two thousand pounds sterling each for a virgin boy or girl it was a very good trade.

Another report came in. This one made him grit his teeth in anger. A heroin consignment had been stopped in the South China Sea as it was being shipped from Shantou to Taiwan.

The tramp steamer carrying the drug had been intercepted by an American customs cutter on loan to the Taiwanese. There had been no resistance and ten million dollars worth of heroin had been confiscated and the crew imprisoned. Had the Americans known about the heroin or had it been a coincidence? After all, dozens, even hundreds, of ships were stopped and searched in the Taiwan Strait every day. Usually to no effect. Kennedy shook his head. He didn't believe in coincidence. The Americans had known. Therefore there had been a leak. Ergo, he needed it plugged. He put it on his "to-do" list for Mr Frobisher, his general factotum, to pass the details to Colonel Roberts.

The next message was from Italy. The steamer carrying 350 illegal immigrants had arrived safely off-shore Loreto on the east coast. Due to bad weather the ship had been forced to stay an extra three days ploughing a furrow in the Adriatic before being able to land its cargo. Even then it hadn't gone smoothly. A dingy had capsized and eight people had drowned, six men and two women. What the hell, it didn't matter. They had each paid $3,000 up-front for the journey. Total $1,050,000. Operating costs, $150,000. Profit, Kennedy grinned – better than drug smuggling. Plus most of them would be going into black labour jobs controlled by him. The women, unknown to them, would be forced into prostitution. He nodded with deep satisfaction, *a highly lucrative business to be in*, he thought with typical understatement.

Other reports came in from all over the world. With one exception it was good news. The exception was a consignment of explosives and arms for Columbia in exchange for nearly a ton of cocaine. The shipment had been intercepted by a Colombian warship. The dilapidated steamer carrying the cargo and the weapons had been confiscated. A phone call and one million dollars would release both. But that still represented a total profit in excess of $25,000,000. Not a bad night's work. Total gross profit on all activities $285,000,000, currently running at slightly over 30% of turnover.

Now that *Phoenix* was out of the picture he could move

forward even faster. The satisfied look on his face was wasted on his reflection in the mirror across the room. Who would have thought that the British government would have been so hard-nosed and duplicitous as to establish such an organisation? Kennedy chortled. He had the PM in a tight grip and he would squeeze – as hard as necessary. He had to admire the British. In spite of what had happened at Skegness there was no hint of it in the media. A blackout had come down so hard and fast it was awesome. The gas leak story had taken hold, injuries had been reported but no deaths. Already the story was fish and chip paper.

Sitting down he closed his eyes and started his transidential meditation mantra. In seconds his mind was set free and the memories came bubbling back.

He had walked to the railway station in Venice. It had taken him most of the night as he started at shadows, hid from cars and worried about the police finding him. He knew his mother would not even try to enter his bedroom before daybreak so he had time. It began to rain and he stopped in a doorway to shelter. The doorway was deep and displays of mens' suits on dummies stared out at him. The hand on his shoulder made him shriek and he spun around to see who had grabbed him. A tramp, bleary eyed, foul-breathed, stood before him.

'This is my place. Move!'

János needed no further encouragement. He took to his heels and fled, indifferent to the wind and rain that was sweeping the city. It was fully ten minutes before he had his emotions under control and he stopped running. He was in a part of the city he didn't recognise and he was fearful. It was now after midnight and he was cold, wet and tired but he knew he couldn't stop. To his relief he saw a street sign indicating the way to the post office. He wasn't as lost as he'd thought. Once there he'd be able to find the railway station. He crossed the Canal Grande using the Ponte di Rialto, his shoulders hunched against the wet, shivering, on the verge of tears, sustained by his anger and hate for his father. Being out so late for the first time made him realise how alive the city was in spite of the hour. And not just gondolas still plying their trade, and late night revellers going home, but the underbelly of the city was there in the shadows. The hookers, the down-and-outs, the street robbers and muggers. His imagination was running riot and if he heard footsteps near him he broke in to a sprint until he was alone once more.

In that way he arrived at the railway station a few minutes before 04.00. The huge concourse appeared empty until he walked around it. Then he found the people sleeping rough, some with empty wine bottles alongside them. One had a dog at his side, the mutt pricking up its ears and lifting its head as he passed.

He found a quiet corner and sat down, exhausted. When he awoke it was to the raucous yells of the railway employees rousting the sleeping people and kicking them out of the station. Some were rougher than others.

Now that he was here, he didn't know where he was going to. The realisation came as a shock. He couldn't walk up to the ticket counter and ask for a ticket to anywhere. He looked at the huge destination board as it flicked to life, announcing the destination of trains, the times and platforms. The first train was 05.45 to Roma. That would do!

He bought the ticket without any problem. He purchased a cold drink and a sandwich at a kiosk and was on the train long before departure time. It left punctually and he breathed a sigh of relief. He was free!

Yorke had no way of helping Dom. He couldn't trace the car and had no backup. He only had the men on the *Lucky Duck*.

The best time to attack a target or effect a clandestine penetration is in the small hours of the morning when bio-rhythms are at a low ebb and concentration is poor due to tiredness.

Using his cell-phone Yorke switched the camera to infrared and heat-seeking. From the masthead it easily looked down onto the cold deck and into the hull. If the engine had been running the images would have been blurred but, as it was, the heat signatures of two bodies showed clearly. Both were in the main saloon. One was lying down on the starboard side, the other was upright, unmoving. Were they both asleep?

The figure lying down moved slightly, an arm extended and stilled. It was the normal restlessness of a sleeping person. The other image was still, sitting with legs crossed and stretched out. It moved. The head went back and the legs uncrossed. Then it stopped. Asleep or merely dozing? Certainly not fully awake. Yorke sat watching the images for nearly half an hour. 03.30. Time to make a move.

Opening the gate he walked softly along the pontoons. All the time he watched the images, ensuring neither stood up or came on deck. Alongside the yacht he stopped and removed his shoes and socks. In spite of the rubber soles on his shoes they would still make a noise, and socked feet were slippery on wooden decks made damp by the dew.

He knew that if he stepped onto the deck the hull would rock. The only way to prevent that happening was to climb up the stern, along the centre line. He removed his jacket and lowered himself into the water next to the stern. Attached to the *Lucky Duck's* transom was a short aluminium ladder. It had been placed there to help swimmers and divers climb in and out of the water. Grabbing the rungs he slowly climbed up, keeping his feet placed exactly in the centre of the ladder. He didn't hurry, gratified to feel the hull remaining steady beneath him. On the deck he checked his phone. The bodies hadn't moved location only their posture.

There were two ways into the boat. Dom had escaped through the forward hatch and so presumably had been locked in. It was where he would have placed a prisoner, albeit, he would have somehow locked the hatch from the outside. That left the door into the saloon. There were six steps leading inside, about 10 inches apart. He could walk down without having to turn his shoulders sideways with a quarter inch either side to spare. From the images on the phone he knew the person sitting was in the chair, port side, next to the ladder. He would have to lean forward and put his head around a bulkhead to see him.

The other man was on the sofa, starboard side, lying with his feet to the steps. He only had to open his eyes to see Yorke. He had to assume they were both armed and both ready and able to shoot him.

Ideally, he wanted a distraction. Very, very carefully he worked his way forward keeping one eye on the images, the other where he was putting his feet. Since Dom had undone the catch on the hatch nobody had bothered to lock it again. Opening the hatch, Yorke lay on his belly and reached down. He found a coiled up rope and lifted it on deck. Stretching further he found a cross of lead, used as a diver marker, and lifted that out. The 10lbs weight had a ring in the middle to which he attached the end of the rope. He dangled it over the lip of the hatch, paid out the rope and lowered it to the deck below. Reaching inside again he found a diver's football-sized poly-styrene blob with two feet of broomstick through the centre. Pulling out the stick, he made his way back to the cockpit door. He placed the stick in the small of his back beneath his belt. A glance at the screen showed the figures still motionless.

In the cockpit Yorke slowly inserted the key into the Yale lock. He knew it was well oiled and moved silently, though he wasn't so sure about the hatch. The door opened the merest fraction. If he opened it any further, a draft of air could be enough to warn the men. It would all have to be done in one move. He placed the SIG on the deck ready. His phone, with the screen facing him, he propped on the combing above the door. He held the key turned in his right hand. In his left he had the rope. He put tension in the rope and raised the weight a fraction off the deck. He let it drop. The noise was insuffi-cient to disturb the recumbent figures. Yorke did it again; a bit higher this time. The seated figure moved a little more than he'd been doing but not much. Yorke repeated the procedure. This time the figure sat upright and leaned forward. A fourth knock and Yorke saw the figure get up and cross to the prone man, waking him. The figure got to his feet and both men moved slowly for'ard, past the companionway. From their posture Yorke figured they were holding guns.

Never give a mug or an enemy a chance.

Raising the weight about a foot off the deck he let it down with a loud thump. Grabbing the automatic, he slammed open the door and hatch, breaking the wood around the bolt. He went in feet first, to land on the deck, the gun pointed at the two men who were turning to meet him. In the narrow corridor the man furthest forward was hampered by the other gunman. A double tap took the nearest man out with a combined head and torso shot. Yorke's next shot shattered the second man's gun hand while the fourth bullet blew his left knee apart. He went down heavily, landing on his companion's body. The trauma that had hit the man's body was so massive that the nerves where the wounds had occurred were momentarily over-whelmed and no messages of pain were getting through to his central nervous system. As pain began to overwhelm the man and before he could react, Yorke stepped across the deck, grabbed the gunman, forced his mouth open and rammed the broomstick lengthways across his mouth, breaking teeth, stop-ping his jaw from closing.

Yorke used the butt of the automatic to knock the man out. The blow was savage and hard. A search with his index finger in the man's mouth showed that one of his back molars was slightly proud. In the ready-use toolbox he took out a pair of pliers, felt for the tooth and with a savage jerk extracted it. He applied the pliers to the middle of the tooth and carefully cracked it open. A glass capsule fell into his cupped hand. He wondered what sort of people would take cyanide rather than be taken prisoner or arrested.

In minutes he had the man trussed up like a turkey, his mouth held shut with silver-backed masking tape. Yorke quickly went through the engine start checks, opening cocks and fuel lines. On deck he removed the fore-spring, aft-spring and two breast ropes, leaving only the head and stern ropes. The engine was warming through nicely and he let go the stern rope. Forward, he hauled the bow in and removed the head-rope. Back in the cockpit he pushed the gear lever into reverse, heard the solid clunk of it engaging and steered the yacht out stern first from her berth. As the bow cleared the finger-pontoon, he pushed the gear lever into neutral, paused two marching paces, and pushed it ahead. The screw bit, he swung the wheel hard to port and the bow came round. He kept the *Lucky Duck* to starboard of the waterway as she nosed her way downstream, sliding past Brownsea Island to starboard and the sandbar to port.

He didn't look back and failed to see Dom yelling and waving as the yacht passed the marina outer-marker buoy, the noise of the engine drowning out the boy's voice.

8

THE STORY DIDN'T make sense. Catherine Colbert sat with a
pencil tapping her teeth and a mug of coffee going cold at her
elbow. After five years covering national politics she knew
when kidology was being used. Something was wrong, she
could sense it. Alex Beaton, the Prime Minister, was looking
overwrought. Strained even. Was that the right word? She shook
her head. No, it was more than that. She'd only caught a glimpse
of him and frankly he looked dreadful. But what could be so
awful? There were no scandals on the horizon as far as she
knew, and she usually did. She'd scooped many of her fellow
journalists to good stories – to their chagrin and her complete
satisfaction. She still remembered the snide comments about
her getting the reporter's position with the London Times above
more senior correspondents. Most of them were on the lines
of her sleeping her way to the job. It simply wasn't true but
the rumours forced her to try harder than anyone to get the
story and the angle and then write good copy. Now, at age 31,
she had taken the big step and gone freelance. It terrified and
excited her at the same time. She had a pleasant flat in
Woolwich, bought seven years earlier with a legacy left by her
mother. The mortgage was a mere £30,000 while the property
was worth at least £350,000 – probably more if she bothered
to check it out. Two bedrooms, one en-suite, a kitchen/diner,
lounge and study-cum-office were sufficient for her needs. She
sat at a table cluttered with two phones, a fax, a desktop and
laptop computer, a colour ink-jet printer and an in-tray stacked
high. Her latest story on Iraq had just been filed and had been
bought by both a London and American newspaper.

Whenever she had a story in her head, as now, she couldn't sleep and she'd been up since 04.00 after a restless night.

Sitting looking north out of her window, her eyes were fixed on the Thames. It moved like undulating sludge in the orange glow of the street lights lining each side of the river. She wasn't really seeing the view, she was replaying the last twenty-four hours in her head. Her interview with Beaton had been cancelled after she had arrived at No 10. That in itself was out of character. Beaton was always courteous, oozing an old world charm that was almost a parody – but it worked, even on the most cynical of hacks. Therefore, it followed he would never have let her arrive at Downing Street before cancelling. Worse, he hadn't personally apologised but sent Stuart McIver, his patronising and oily press secretary, to relay the news that the PM was ill. However, Beaton had been in the room behind the secretary where she had caught a glimpse of him, pacing the room.

Something big, of mega-proportions, was going down and she needed to find out what it was. Then, only that morning, had come the announcement that due to a bout of flu the PM was cancelling his engagements and going home for a complete rest. Something, so it was claimed, not possible if he stayed in Downing Street.

Another thing niggled at her. She *knew* Beaton had a very good and close relationship with his wife and doted on his kids. It was unheard of in four years of office for them to take separate holidays. But Mrs Beaton had gone away for a few days – her destination a closely guarded secret. Was that the problem? Marital strife? Not flu at all. It could be. But if so it had blown up out of nowhere. She picked up the receiver to call a colleague but changed her mind and replaced it. First of all, he wouldn't appreciate a call at such an ungodly hour and secondly, if she was right, then as an exclusive it would be worth a fortune to her to file it. The currency of the story would diminish significantly if others got to hear about it. Pensively she crossed the room to a filing cabinet, pulled a drawer and extracted a buff file. As she thought. The PM had been ill on two previous occasions, once with flu, two years ago and last year with a chest infection which had triggered the asthma that plagued him. On neither occasion did he go to Aldingbourne, near Chichester, to rest and recover.

Both times he had stayed at Downing Street, soldiering on, still with his finger on the pulse of state as the Daily Mail so quaintly put it. So it didn't add up. She was leaning on the filing cabinet flicking through her notes when something else struck her as very strange. Who got the flu at this time of year? Colds, possibly. But flu? Surely it was a winter complaint. Besides, Beaton would have had the flu jab last October/November. Was it something else? Was he seriously ill and were the politicos trying to find a way of informing the public? Damn! She replaced the file and pushed the drawer closed with a loud thump. None of it made sense.

She opened a sideboard cupboard and rummaged around looking for a forgotten packet of cigarettes. Just one, she told herself. Cold turkey for three weeks was a record and now she needed just one to help her think. Pulling papers and shoving things about she rummaged anxiously. Nothing. But then, the last time she'd quit, she'd succumbed to the need for just one cigarette. And she'd been hooked again. She'd vowed that next time she wouldn't allow temptation to get in her way and so had emptied the flat of all packets of fags. She swallowed cold coffee, pulled a face and went to make fresh.

Her new coffee maker was too much hassle and she put on the kettle for a cup of supermarket instant. In the hallway she caught a glimpse of herself in the mirror and thought, *God, I'm a mess*.

She was 5ft 9ins tall, had short, black hair and hazel eyes. She showed dimples when she smiled, her nose she considered too big and her mouth too wide. She was of mixed parentage, a West Indian father and a white mother from Birmingham.

Her mother had seen herself as something of a radical – equal rights for all, marching and protesting in the early seventies instead of knuckling down and getting a decent degree. By the time she went down from Durham University she had a third in political history and a bun-in-the-oven, as her mother so quaintly described it. The result of a stoned party of which she remembered nothing. She hadn't been as much of a radical as she'd liked to believe – she'd insisted on Catherine's father marrying her. He dropped out of Durham three months before his finals and out of the marriage one year and five months after Catherine's birth. With a small inheritance from an uncle, her mother had finally got her act together and opened a small delicatessen in south London that had somehow thrived. The two of them had lived happily above the shop until Catherine went to Oxford University. Even after Catherine had left home they had remained close, although Catherine had never agreed with her mother's cannabis habit. In Catherine's third year her mother had been diagnosed as schizophrenic and was sectioned under the Mental Health Act of 1989.

After 6 months hospitalisation her mother had returned home. During that time the shop had been well run by a local woman who proved a natural in the specialised market of the delicatessen. Furthermore, as far as the accounts showed, the woman also appeared to be that rarest of rare people, completely honest. The shop had thrived and the two women shared the work amicably. Which was why, two years later, while Catherine was working for the BBC, it came as a complete shock when her mother drowned herself in the river Thames. The letter she had left behind had talked of demons stalking her. The authorities shook their heads sadly and suggested the schizophrenia was more deep-rooted than they'd been led to believe. Not uncommon with certain cannabis users. Catherine sold the shop to the manager, bought the flat and a Series 3 BMW and invested a further £100,000 in an insurance bond. She used the remainder of the money to hire a private detective to track down her father.

By the time she flew out to Jamaica to see him she had spent nearly £10,000. Her father was a wasted, crack-cocaine addict with AIDS. She gave him £1,500 and fled from the scene. She didn't attend his funeral two months later.

Catherine wrote a moving tribute about her mother and a scathing one about the Mental Health Act. It brought her notice and a job with the Daily Mirror. Two years later she went to the Times.

She looked at herself critically in the mirror. Her skin was coffee coloured and smooth. She had a slim waste, a bust she thought was too big and a backside to match. She had never considered herself pretty but as she had never lacked for boyfriends she guessed she was okay in the looks department. Most of her relationships didn't last because she was focused on her work and career, loving every minute of being in the forefront of the cut and thrust of modern politics. Seeing things happening and then writing about them gave her a buzz. She also enjoyed giving her own spin, her slant, her perspective on what was happening. Occasionally, she even managed to influence what people thought, a fact that brought a smile to her lips.

Then the shambles that was her personal life intruded. Her last boyfriend she'd sent packing when she'd learnt he'd made a pass at a girlfriend of hers. How dare the insensitive slob put the blame on her, claiming it was because she didn't pay him enough attention. That she thought too much of her career! How dare he! Even now, after eleven weeks, her blood boiled at the indignation of it all.

Dismissing thoughts of the creep and accepting the absence of a cigarette she contented herself with a coffee and chocolate biscuit instead.

Her mind came back to the business in hand. There was another thing she didn't like the look of. She sat at the table, her computer in front of her. The business about the house at Gibraltar Point. There was something odd about that whole affair. When she'd tried to discover more she'd been told there was nothing to find. A tragic accident. A huge gas leak. Only that didn't square with what she knew. First of all it just didn't happen nowadays. It was unheard of. A fire in a small residence leading to a gas leak and an explosion she could buy, but not one in a premises like the one that housed the so-called think-tank. Had she read too many political thrillers, she wondered? Was she seeing a conspiracy where none existed? For a while now there had been rumours about a top-secret organisation that committed assassinations at theirs' and the government's whim. She pulled her files. She'd been collecting and collating data for nearly three years. She checked certain dates and events, whilst letting her thoughts dwell on the problem of the Prime Minister.

As she thought, an announcement in Parliament about the unproved criminal or terrorist activities of certain individuals had resulted in their deaths a month or two later. It was as if the victims were being declared *persona non grata* before being removed. It was true each one appeared to have an exceptionally unsavoury past, but surely even such creatures deserved a trial before justice was meted out. Besides which, Britain didn't have the death penalty. In fact, wouldn't even extradite known criminals or terrorists to countries that did have one without the assurance that it would be waived. As that was tantamount to interference in a country's legal system that assurance was rarely forthcoming with the result that there were few, if any, people extradited. Which was another reason London was known as the terrorist capital of the world. Well, she didn't believe in the death penalty. An-eye-for-an-eye was not a philosophy she would or could live by. Most terrorists were someone else's freedom fighters. History was full of such people.

What should she do first? Check on the Prime Minister or visit Gibraltar Point? Or make a few phone calls to verify a few facts? With a sigh she decided on the latter.

Dom ran full tilt, calling at the top of his voice but it was no use, the yacht was too far away. He stopped, his hands on his knees, panting, tears of frustration in his eyes. Since escaping the bogus policemen he had jogged for what seemed like hours to get back to the yacht, to see if Stephen had returned. To see the yacht sailing away with Stephen at the helm was a blow. He got his breath back and wondered what on earth he should do. He could go back to the school, but was that safe? What if the men came for him? One possibility was to get to the school and hide. He could camp out in the cricket or rugby pavilions. The most important thing was to make sure he wasn't caught again. With the thought came fear as he looked around him, expecting to be spotted at any second.

He was near the front. He ducked under the railing, over the wall and scrambled down to the tiny strip of beach. Out of sight he felt calmer and could think clearly. Dom sat on a rock, his head in his hands. Waves of tiredness swept over him. Suddenly he groaned. *What an idiot*! Stephen had a mobile phone. He got up and started walking over the sand, the darkness making it difficult for him to see where he was putting his feet, causing him to worry about stepping on a rock and spraining an ankle or twisting a knee.

He'd gone a couple of hundred yards when he climbed back up to the road. The phone box he knew to be in the vicinity was only a few paces away. Feeding fifty pence into the slot, he dialled Yorke's number.

It rang . . . and rang . . . and . . . 'Dad? It's Dom!'

'Dom! Thank God! Where are you?'

'In Poole by the marina. I saw you going. I ran after you but you couldn't have heard me. I was taken by some policemen. Only they weren't, if you see what I mean.' He was becoming incoherent in his desire for his father to come back for him.

'Take it easy, old son. Now listen, walk down the harbour road and go onto the Canford Cliffs. Then head for Bournemouth. You know where the path is? Down to the beach?'

'I know. By the green hut. We went there last year.'

'That's the one. Get down there and I'll come in with the inflatable. Dom, it's five miles, can you manage it?'

'Sure, dad, no problem.' There was a smile in his voice matching the one in his heart. Now Stephen was there, everything would be all right.

'Okay, synchronise watches. I've got zero four zero eight.'

'Roger that, dad.'

'Okay, two and a half hours from now. I'll be there. You got that?'

'Sure. Two and a half hours. I'll be on the beach.'

'Good lad. Now move it before those policemen come back.'

Dom made his farewells and hung up. His tiredness sloughed off him like a discarded skin. He was built for stamina, not speed. He settled down into a loping run that he'd learnt on the hare-and-hounds cross-country jaunts the school organised. He never caught the hare, and was never first, but he hadn't been out of the top three in the last eight races. His trainers made hardly a sound as he ran along the pavement, the cold early morning breeze off the sea keeping him cool. Everything would be all right now. His father would see to that.

Now he knew how Atlas would have felt having the pillars of heaven removed from his shoulders. The relief of knowing that Dom was safe at least for the time being was immense. He was a tough lad who could be relied on to do what was needed. What was necessary at this juncture was to get information and the methods he would have to use were not appropriate for a fifteen year old boy to witness.

There was a gentle swell from the southwest and a breeze that once he was clear of the land backed to the northwest. Yorke engaged the autopilot, checked the horizon for contacts and, satisfied it was clear, went below. He put on the kettle and spooned coffee and sugar into a mug. Normally he drank his coffee without sugar but he knew he needed the energy and lift it would give him. While the kettle boiled he checked on his two visitors. The dead body had brains and blood oozing onto the deck. Yorke went forward, stepping over the bodies, into the forward cabin. He found an old sail and cut it to the size he wanted.

Carrying it back into the saloon, he wrapped the dead body in the canvas and secured it. Next, he manhandled the body to the forward hatch. He checked on the other man. His pulse was steady, though blood was seeping slowly from the shattered knee. Roughly he placed a bandage around the wound.

He went back on deck, the mug of coffee in his hand. Sipping, he checked the yacht's position and the sea for other ships or boats. In the distance he could see the white steaming lights and red port lights of two passing freighters. He checked their relative bearings but it was clear they would pass well ahead. The yacht was now four miles offshore, moving at a steady six knots. It wasn't far enough, but he had to get back for Dom. Besides which, dawn was already lightening the sky to the east.

He went forward and dropped through the hatch. Lifting the body, he shoved it through and onto the deck. He wrapped a length of chain he normally used to secure to a buoy around the dead man. Without a moments hesitation he shoved him over the side. The body vanished with barely a splash.

The next task he wasn't looking forward to. He dragged the injured man through the hatch and onto the foredeck. The inert body had his hands tied behind his back. Yorke threaded a diver's belt with old-fashioned lead weights and placed it around the man's waist. Next he filled the deck-swab bucket with sea water and threw its contents over the inert man's face. Nothing. He did it a second and a third time. The man groaned and slowly began to regain consciousness. Yorke ignored him while he dropped the forward guard-rails on the port side.

Then he rigged a lifting tackle to the end of the main boom. He used a twin-sheaved block for the standing or boom end and a single sheaved block for the moving end, giving a four-fold lifting ratio. With the tackle roved-to-disadvantage he could easily move the body of a man. He then hauled up the boom until it was at an angle of forty-five degrees and secured it in place. He tied the moving block to the rope around the inert figure who had been lying watching Yorke's preparations. As he did the body began to struggle, the masking tape muffling the man's protests and curses.

Yorke hauled on the rope lifting the man off the deck, his head and legs trailing down, his back was agony as his spine threatened to break. Yorke easily held the wriggling weight with one arm as he swung the boom outboard. He let the rope slide through his fingers and watched clinically as the body sank beneath the water. This was the man who had chased Dom along the pontoon. Who had already possibly hurt his boy and who could die one way or another. Easily or hard. It was up to him.

He counted thirty and pulled the body back to the surface. Yorke kept it there for a minute, staring down into the man's eyes as they stared back. If the man in the water was fearful, he didn't show it. Without a hint, Yorke opened his hand and let the rope run through, the man sinking suddenly from view. He waited forty seconds before bringing the body back to the surface. It thrashed and wriggled on the end of the rope like a beached shark, but to no avail. After the fourth time, Yorke pulled the body up far enough to reach down and rip the masking tape off the man's mouth.

'Who are you? What's your name?'

No answer.

Yorke let him drop again. Fifty seconds later he pulled the man back up. The repeated immersions were beginning to have their effect. Death by drowning is a hell of a way to die, half-drowning, followed by the luxury of breathing, sapped the will to resist in the strongest minded person. Yorke knew. He'd been through the routine during escape and evasion exercises and shown what it was like. At the end, you got what information you needed, the prisoner appeared unharmed and you could claim he'd been treated in accordance with the Geneva Convention. Nobody believed it but it didn't matter.

'Who are you?'

'Roger Wiglow.'

'Who do you work for?'

No answer.

He went under again. This time, Yorke left him there for a minute and ten seconds. When he pulled the body back up the man was gasping, spitting and sneezing water.

'I can keep doing this for as long as it takes. You were on

my boat. You were waiting for me. You threatened my son. Why?'

'Orders.'

'*Befehl ist Befehl* doesn't wash with me. Who do you work for?'

The man groaned. 'Get me aboard and I'll tell you. My mouth hurts like hell, you bastard.'

'I took out your cyanide pill,' Yorke said callously. 'Now, who sent you? Who do you work for?'

For the first time fear showed in the man's eyes. 'My pill? You took my pill?' His jaw began to work frantically back and forth.

'There's no easy way out. Tell me what I want to know. Or we'll keep doing this.'

'Your a dead man walking, Yorke.' The man spat at him, 'Only you don't know it. You and the kid.'

'So I've already been told.'

This time Yorke thought he'd gone too far. One minute and twenty seconds later he hauled the unconscious body onto the deck. Placing it on his side, he kicked him hard in the solar plexus. The man gasped and water vomited from his throat. He was still groaning when Yorke put him back over the side. He kept the body on the surface until full knowledge returned to the eyes and he and Yorke stared with undiminished hatred at each other. Five dunkings later, each over a minute, finally had the man cracked.

He was gasping and heaving for breath. 'I was hired through an advertisement. Ex-special services only need apply,' he paused.

'And? Come on you bastard. I want more than that. Who did the hiring?'

'All right! All right! Let me think! The man who interviewed me was Jack Bacon.'

'Bacon? Ex-SAS? Captain?'

'That's right. You know him?'

Yorke didn't answer. He knew *of* him. Bacon had been considered for *Phoenix* at one time. Only his assessments hadn't been quite right. There had been something wrong but Yorke couldn't remember what. He shook his head. 'Who else is involved?'

'I only know a few. We operate in small cells. Need to know and all that crap.'

That made sense.

'Who did Bacon report to?'

'I can't tell. I . . .'

He was cut off as Yorke let the rope slip between his fingers. This time he let the rope continue travelling. At about thirty feet he hauled the dead weight back to the surface. He had been under the water less than forty seconds but the panic had well and truly set in when he hit the surface.

'Roberts. Colonel Roberts.'

'Mack Roberts?' Yorke couldn't keep the shock out of his voice.

'Yes. Mack the Knife. He's the new boss.'

'But why?' There was incredulity in Yorke's voice. Roberts was a highly decorated war veteran who had cut his teeth in Bosnia and fought in both Iraqi conflicts.

'For me it's easy. Money. Ten thousand a month, tax free. Half a mill if killed on duty, paid to next-of-kin.'

'My God! Who's doing it?'

'I don't know. I swear I don't know.' Panic and fear vied for the uppermost emotion as Yorke looked into the man's eyes.

'I'm getting soft,' said Yorke. Reaching into his pocket he pulled the man clear of the water until he was at deck level. He popped the cyanide capsule into the open mouth and said, 'Crunch on that, you scum.' He slammed the mouth shut, the capsule broke, the man arched his back and died.

Using his free hand to click open the spring shackle Yorke let the body drop free. Wearily, he thrust the engine into ahead, set the autopilot and now, running with the wind broad on his port beam hoisted the main and jib. He adjusted both until he was happy and then cut the engine. The yacht raced along on a broad reach, her speed wavering between seven and eight knots. Now he needed to get to Dom.

9

DOM RAN A mile, walked half a mile. Ran a mile, walked half a mile. He was aware that the darkness was giving way to grey. Twice he had noticed car headlights ahead of him and had dived into cover. Both times had been false alarms but they had set his heart racing and the adrenaline going. Canford Cliffs was on his right, the water of Poole Bay an unseen, undulating mass of black beyond. Far out he could see the occasional steaming lights of vessels heading up and down Channel.

To his left was the golf course and then a row of detached and semi-detached houses. Although he was jogging, he was slowing down. Weariness left him going through the motions rather than eating up the distance. A car came up behind him, catching him in its headlights. He was unaware until it was too late to hide. It passed by, the single occupant not so much as looking in his direction. He licked lips made suddenly dry with fear. He knew he had to stay alert. The false policemen could come his way at any time. He stared out to sea, willing himself to spot the combined green and red masthead lantern of the *Lucky Duck*. Nothing. His heart sank but he knew he was being ridiculous. Stephen would be there. He just knew it!

The thought galvanised him and he picked up his pace. Finally he stopped, his hands on his knees, his head hanging down, gasping for breath. He'd made it. He crossed the narrow strip of green grass and stood near the cliff edge, scanning the sea. He saw a faint green light that changed to red. There it was again. It was the masthead lantern, heading straight in. Then it went out.

The light was strengthening and turning opaque as the sky

streaked grey and orange. He walked further along, looking for the steps cut into the cliff, leading down to the beach. Finding them, he paused at the top and looked to sea once more. Yes! It was the *Lucky Duck*. He'd recognise her anywhere.

Squealing tyres jerked his attention back to the road. The police car! They were back! Dom took to his heels and started down the steep and uneven concrete steps towards the beach.

'Come here, you little swine,' one of the men yelled.

The cliff face was on his left, a metal bar, waste high, on his right. His breath came in ragged gasps, fear lent his feet speed. His rugby training coupled with his youth gave him an agility lacking in the two men chasing him. There was an angry buzz past his ear and a bullet fired from a silenced gun smacked into the concrete three steps in front of him. *Oh No, no, no, don't let me die. Not now! Dad is there for me!*

The cliff face curved inwards and he was out of sight. He was holding onto the rail, his hand sliding down the metal, the steps getting darker to see as he went downwards. He didn't hear the outboard starting up, nor see it racing towards the shore.

Another chip of rock blasted off the cliff next to his head, shards of stone hitting his face. Dom knew he couldn't continue down in a straight line and he did the only thing left to him. He swung underneath the railings and launched himself at the beach. If he landed on rocks he'd be seriously hurt or worse. He prayed he would land on sand.

Yorke had been watching the cliffs with night-vision binoculars and saw Dom and the two policemen. He knew one of them was shooting at Dom as he turned the *Lucky Duck* into the wind and brought her to a graceful halt. He had been sailing without lights for the last half mile, a ghost on the water. He didn't bother lowering the main sail. Instead he sliced through the main and jib halyards and let the sails float to the deck. In the bows he grabbed the anchor and threw it over the side. The inflatable was being towed astern, he pulled it alongside and leapt into it.

Tugging sharply on the starter cord, the engine immediately

burst into life. The new silencer box encasing the motor meant there was barely a gurgle as the exhaust bubbled to the surface. He engaged the gear, opened the throttle and headed for the beach. The water was flat calm, the breeze barely ruffling the surface. The inflatable was speeding towards the shore with Yorke standing athwartships, the steering column of the motor between his legs. He withdrew the SIG from his belt and pulled back the slide, cocking the weapon. There was no safety as such, only a de-cocking lever in the left of the butt with a thumb-piece just behind the trigger. The breaking dawn lit the cliff tops while lower down was still in darkness.

He could see the two men in police uniform taking the steps two at a time while Dom was a faint blur a hundred feet away from them.

He saw Dom jump or fall from the steps about fifteen feet above the sand. Yorke was icy cold. He was almost at the beach, fifty yards from the cliff, tearing in at twenty knots. He throttled back but left the gears engaged. The inflatable's speed was bleeding rapidly away when he raised the Glock and aimed.

Still the two men hadn't noticed him. It wasn't surprising as the surface of the water was black and they were concentrating on running down the steps to avoid a fall and potential injury.

The shore was five yards away when he opened fire. The magazine held eight rounds. He fired four in rapid succession at the first man and the remainder at the second. It was the equivalent of a turkey shoot. Both men collapsed against the cliff.

'Dad! Dad!'

'Here, old son. Take it easy.'

Dom was at the water's edge and wading out to the inflatable. Heaving himself aboard he felt Yorke's strong arms around his shoulders, giving him a hug.

'You okay?'

'Yes. Fine.' There was a catch in Dom's voice. 'Now I'm with you.'

'Good lad. We need to get out of here. The cliffs may have deadened the sound of my shots but we can't be certain. Now listen up, I don't want to leave the bodies lying there. So I'm going to bring them here and we'll dump them at sea. All right?'

'S . . . Sure, dad. Fine.'

'Now hang in there, Dom. And remember, they tried damned hard to kill you. It was you or them. Okay?'

Dom nodded, his shoulders lifting, his back straightening. 'I'm fine.'

The inflatable beached and Yorke leaped ashore. He ran across the beach and up the steps. A quick check showed the first man was dead. All four bullets had struck him in the torso. He darted up the steps, two at a time. The other man lay against the steps, gasping, blood seeping from his mouth.

'Who are you?' Yorke asked.

'You'll never know. You're a dead man Yorke. I'll be seeing you in hell.'

'After you,' said Yorke, placing his hands on either side of the man's neck and squeezing. He shoved both bodies over the side of the steps and hurried down to the beach.

Slinging a body over his shoulder, he picked up the man's automatic, tucked it under his belt and trudged across the sand. He dropped the body in the water alongside the inflatable. 'We'll drag them out. I don't want any blood in the boat. Tie the painter to his belt.'

While Dom did as he was told, Yorke went back for the other body. He carried it into the water and tied the bodies together. Climbing into the inflatable, he turned it towards the *Lucky Duck*, a dim outline twenty yards away.

'When we get aboard, flash up the engine, haul anchor and get us away from here.'

'Right, dad.'

The inflatable nudged gently alongside the yacht. Dom leapt aboard and tied the bow painter to the stern cleat. He started the diesel and spun the wheel, turning the bow towards the open sea. Leaping forward he grabbed the anchor rope and hauled it up, placing it neatly in its stowage. Back in the cockpit, he engaged the gears and the boat headed away from the shore.

While Dom carried out his instructions, Yorke systematically went through the pockets of the bogus policemen. The false IDs told him nothing. There was nothing else on them. He made sure the bodies were well secured and hauled the inflatable round to the stern of the yacht. He climbed into the cockpit and smiled at Dom.

'It's great to see you, old son.'

'And you, dad. I,' his voice caught and he cleared his throat, 'I wasn't sure I'd see you again.'

'I'll always be there for you. Now, tell me what happened while I splice the halyards and we get sailing again. Dom told the story of his adventures from the time he'd left school fourteen hours earlier. While he did, Yorke repaired the ropes he'd cut, hoisted the main and jib, set a course to the southeast and cut the engine. The silence blanketed them as the sun came over the horizon. It was a perfect day for sailing. Yorke went below and prepared two mugs of coffee.

'We've got beans and hardtack but that's all. Fancy any?'

'No, thanks,' Dom smiled. 'Dad, what's going on?'

'I don't know,' Yorke said, shrugging his shoulders. 'But I mean to find out.'

'Why are these men trying to kill us?'

'I'm sorry, Dom. Let me get my thoughts together.'

Dom looked over his shoulder at the two partially submerged bodies tied to the side of the inflatable. 'I've never seen a dead man before,' he said softly.

'It's not a pretty sight. If you get in to the marines you'll see a few more. We'll get rid of them soon but we need a bit more water.'

'Who are they?'

'According to their IDs, nobody. Their wallets held only money. Nothing to say who they were.' Yorke had cut up the wallets and ditched them overboard. What the hell could he tell the boy? It was a question that had niggled at him all the way down in the train. 'I suppose you deserve to know the truth. I work for a top-secret government department . . .'

'I know that,' Dom said, scorn in his voice. 'I've known for simply ages.'

Yorke smiled and ruffled the boy's hair. 'Well, yesterday, the place where I work was attacked and wiped out. A lot of people were killed and the building destroyed. Furthermore, when it was attacked some important men were there.'

'I bet you're one of them,' said Dom loyally.

'Well, possibly.' Yorke knew it wasn't a time for false modesty. 'What I mean is, the boss and three agents were there. Now, that's pretty unusual. It happens maybe a dozen times a year. So how did they know? And who are they?' Yorke was settled on the starboard side, leaning against the angle of the yacht as she cut through the water, pensively voicing his thoughts. 'I need to know who, why and how. I'll be back in a moment.'

He went forward and below, returning moments later with two weighted diving belts. 'This'll do, Dom. I'll get rid of our cargo.'

He hauled the inflatable alongside and jumped in. Awkwardly he put a belt on one of the corpses and cut it free. It dropped from sight beneath the water in eighty fathoms. The second followed. Climbing back on to the *Lucky Duck* he said, 'I need to swab below decks. You set the auto-pilot and find some white hull paint. Paint out the name on the bow and stern. You know the drawer with the stencils in?'

Dom nodded. 'Sure. What are we doing?'

'Hiding. The hull paint will be dry in thirty minutes. We'll paint a new name. What shall we call her?'

'The *Outlaws*?' Dom smiled.

Yorke laughed. 'Close. How about the *Outlaw*?'

Dom suddenly went serious. 'Are we? Criminals I mean?'

Yorke shook his head. 'I wouldn't have said so. All we've done so far is defend ourselves. But you have to understand, the law may see it differently. You aren't in any trouble. But I could be.' He dropped his mobile phone in the water. 'They could be tracking it. I'll get another.'

'What about the organisation you work for?'

'It's called deniable ops. The government says, hey, it's not us. We didn't authorise any of this action.'

'So why do it?'

'Good question. I really believe we've made a difference. And I suspect because of what's happened that others found our operations too dangerous. Too threatening. Though how in God's name they found out about us is beyond me.' Yorke felt his eyelids drooping and shook himself awake, standing up. 'Stay alert while I clean up. Okay?'

'Sure, dad. You can rely on me.'

'That I never doubted it for a moment.'

Below deck, Yorke cleaned the blood away as best he could. A rug had a splattering of blood on it and he disposed of it overboard. When he'd finished, there was nothing to be seen with the naked eye but he knew it wouldn't fool a forensic team for more than a minute or two.

Back up top he found Dom standing at the wheel, his head nodding, his eyes drooping. 'I'll take over, Dom. You go below and rest. We'll head for Cowes and hide amongst the yachts there.'

'I painted out the *Lucky Duck*. The stencils and paint are there.' He nodded at a ready-use locker on the port side.

'Thanks. I'll paint in the name.'

Yorke altered course and set the sails for a broad reach, with the wind coming over the port stern quarter. He checked the radar settings and auto-pilot before awkwardly leaning over the stern and carefully stencilling in the new name, *The Outlaw*. He did the same up for'ard, port and starboard, before retiring to the cockpit. The sun was well above the horizon on a clear day. The wind was steady, the sea was calm, and the ships and boats dotting the Channel were all passing clear. He settled on the seat and closed his eyes, drifting off to sleep.

The insistent buzz of the radar warning system brought him wide awake. He looked ahead and to starboard, the sector of the sea from which any craft would have the right of way and he would have to alter course. Nothing. As was his habit, he had a pair of binoculars around his neck and he put them to his eyes and scanned forward and then aft. Coming up fast astern was a large Fairline cruiser. The elegant *Phantom 40*

was a beautiful craft, capable of speeds up to 31knots. It was
approaching on a steady bearing and if the helmsman didn't
look out he would be on top of the yacht in about three minutes.

There were two men on the upper bridge, one with a pair
of binoculars trained on him, the other standing by the helm.
As a sailing boat he had right of way and so he waved at the
two men to keep clear. They took no notice as they closed to
two hundred yards, a cable, and kept coming.

By his side, Yorke had two fully loaded automatics which
he'd empty into the other boat if it came too close. He held
the binoculars to his face with his left hand, obscuring his
features, while with his right he waved the boat away. They
kept closing. He looked at the hull, trying to read her name.
Sally-Anne. Meant nothing. He'd never heard of it but that
wasn't surprising. She could have been berthed in Poole and
he'd still never have known her.

The boat was within about twenty yards when her bow paid
off to port and she began to overtake the yacht, picking up
speed. Staying in character, Yorke waved a fist at them, to be
rewarded with a V-sign. As the wake went past the yacht rocked
before settling down again.

Yorke had no doubt the men on the boat were the enemy
and were looking for the *Lucky Duck*. He hoped they were
fooled by the name change. Of course, should anyone come
aboard they wouldn't be fooled for a second as the yacht's
name was in the log, engraved on the radio consul with emergency frequencies and written on other nautical publications
and chart folios.

The boat was turning to port, headed for another yacht about
three miles away. He sat watching it for a few minutes before
making a decision. It was time to break out the heavy arma-
ment. Below decks down aft he pulled up the deck boards
around the engine. He reached down through the bilge water
until he found a small handle. Pulling and twisting it, he lifted
a sealed box free and out of the bilge. It was three feet long,
a foot wide and six inches deep.

Hidden in locations along the hull was a total of six similar watertight containers. In them was everything from Semtex charges to various types of weapons. In one were Dutch passports and ID cards for him and Dom along with £20,000.

The box he'd taken out contained an Italian Beretta AR 70/90 automatic rifle. This model was long-barrelled with a folding butt, the 30 round magazine having been modified to take 150, 5.56 X 45mm SS109 (Nato) bullets. A specially adapted silencer was in the case and Yorke screwed it on the end of the barrel. It made the weapon more cumbersome and awkward to aim but was ideal when the rifle's tripod was fitted. Yorke had used a similar one on numerous occasions and knew how deadly effective it was. He took out the magazine, pressed the spring and then loaded it. The manual selector was a combined safety catch, "S" for safe, "1" for single shots, "3" for three shot bursts and "30" for full automatic. All the weapons and explosives he had secreted around the yacht had been taken during one operation or another and were untraceable.

The men in the boat would cover the sea quickly. It wouldn't take them long to figure out the only yacht fitting the description of what they were looking for was the newly named *Outlaw*. Which would mean they'd be back. If they were, he'd be ready for them. He replaced the container and lifted out a second. From it he withdrew two grenades, and dropped them into the pockets of the light-weight body warmer he was wearing.

Satisfied, he went back on deck to scan the area. There was no sign of the boat but there were other vessels passing within a couple of miles of the yacht.

Slipping below, he checked on Dom. He was fast asleep in his cabin next to the forward workshop. In the saloon, Yorke helped himself to a spoonful of energy drink. He dissolved it in cold water, added sugar and drank it in one swallow. He knew it would keep him awake and alert for the next four hours.

Opening a tin of beans and helping himself to hardtack emergency ration biscuits he went back on deck. When he glanced at his watch it came as a shock to find it was only

07.53. He adjusted the mainsheet, hauling in the boom a few degrees. He turned the autopilot five degrees to port and adjusted the jib sheet. He thought about hauling up the spin- naker but decided against it as more of his view would be obscured.

He sat in the cockpit, spooning cold beans onto a biscuit, eating it thoughtfully, his eyes never still. He needed answers and knew of only three places to go. One was the Prime Minister, two was the Secretary of State for Defence and three was the Home Secretary. Officially, they were the *only* people who knew of the existence of *Phoenix*. And unofficially? That was a bigger question. Who could know? A lot of people, said a voice in his head. From senior civil servants to members of the armed forces – albeit, senior personnel. Secrecy could only work so far. Desmond Kavanagh had always known that. He'd maintained that after a few years of effectiveness, the politically correct would learn of the organisation and insist it be closed down. It was inevitable. How? Yorke had asked. Easily, had come the reply. From a disgruntled ex-Home Sec or Def Sec out for revenge.

Finishing his makeshift meal he put the remains below and boiled the kettle for another mug of coffee. He was standing in the bow, the mug in hand, when he saw the boat in the distance turning towards the yacht.

Bending down he threw open the for'ard hatch. 'Dom! Dom,' he yelled.

'What?' came the groggy reply. Then more strongly. 'Dad! What is it?'

'Come here, quickly.'

Dom stumbled out of his bunk, bleary eyed. 'What's up?'

'Sorry, son. We've got company. Bad company. Here. Take the SIG.' He handed down the revolver. 'You've fired guns often enough. There's no safety. I'll probably take them out. If I fail or make a cock-up, it'll be down to you. Stay down there and listen up. Okay?'

Dom managed a tentative smile. 'Sure, dad.'

'Listen, Dom, these are really bad men. Remember what I've always told you . . .'

'I know, dad. Get your retaliation in first and don't give then an inch.'

'That's right. Stand-by. They'll be here in about a minute and a half.'

Unhurriedly Yorke went back to the cockpit and levered a round into the chamber of the rifle. He left it lying next to his hand, on the deck, out of sight.

He wondered what the men would do. Run the yacht down or shoot him? The latter, he decided, as there was a danger of damaging the fibreglass hull of the other vessel.

Whenever he was going into conflict or a dangerous situation he felt an unnatural calm come over him. His senses became hypernatural and he saw things with a clarity and perception way beyond what was normal. He was aware that he had surprise on his side and felt reasonably confident about the outcome. But not sanguine. Never sanguine. Sanguineness led too quickly to death. His only fear was for Dom.

10

HE WAS RAPED twice. On consecutive nights. Both times by
Italians. After the second time he vowed it would never happen
again. He bought himself a sheath knife and strapped it to his
right leg, underneath his sock. After the second time, János
Kadras took buses to Milan. It took three days. During the
nights he slept rough, hiding under hedges, away from other
people. By the time he got to Milan he had made up his mind.
He'd walk to England if necessary.

He spent two days in the city. On the evening of the second
he was walking past a bar when a well-dressed man came stumbling out. He was obviously drunk and staggered along the
pavement with János following. A plan began to take shape in
his mind. Not much of a plan it was true, but one he thought
could work. It was nearly midnight and the small square they
were now traversing was deserted. Snatching the knife from
under his trouser leg, János ran after the man. He was upon
him before the man realised something was amiss. János didn't
hesitate. Plunging the knife into the man's left side, as luck
would have it, it sliced through the man's heart and he dropped
dead. Quickly he rifled the man's pockets and removed a wallet
and loose change.

Shoving them into his own pockets, he took to his heels,
exhilaration and fear surging through him in an odd mixture
that left him feeling ecstatic. His haul had been the lira equivalent of £21. Not bad work, he decided.

By the middle of July he was in Turin. He had robbed three
other men, killing one and seriously wounding two. Each time
he had attacked and stabbed a man he had felt nothing but

great joy. When he examined his feelings he found he had not a shred of remorse or pity for his victims. He didn't know it but he was a sociopath, without any regard whatsoever for his fellow human beings. People were there to be used, it was as simple as that.

Three local buses later found him in the village of Bardonecchia, next to the French border. It was there he discovered the requirement for a passport. The main road led to a French village called Névache, while a mountain track went over the Alps to Modane alongside the railway line.

He made discreet enquiries and learnt that the only way was through the Frejus Tunnel, by train, but he'd need a passport. Which he didn't have. Instead, he bought a knapsack, filled it with food and went hiking along the trail as far as the tunnel. He stayed hidden in the trees for 24 hours. At the end of that time he knew when the trains were due and in which direction they were travelling. What he didn't know was how long the tunnel was. He hadn't thought to enquire.

The longest gap between trains had been from 01.30 to 04.45. He decided to walk through the tunnel the following night. The train was fifteen minutes late when he finally began trekking alongside the track and into the tunnel. It was single-track, with metre wide paths either side. The torch he'd had the forethought to buy stood him in good stead as he walked briskly.

The tunnel was solid rock. Every 100m or so was a recess, the cigarette butts lying on the ground testimony to the fact that maintenance crews stood there when trains passed. A draft caused him to look up and he saw an open chimney about 10cms in diameter and realised it was to help dissipate the smoke from the engines. He kept walking, the Stygian darkness oppressive, broken only by the beam of his torch. The tunnel seemed to go on forever but finally he could see the faint outline of the end of the tunnel just as the forlorn horn of an Alpine train sounded and a dazzling beam of light lit the walls of the tunnel. János turned and ran back the way he'd come, searching desperately for the nearest recess. The thunder of the train was booming around him, bouncing off the walls, magnified to numbing proportions when he stumbled and fell, gasping for air, as the train passed by in a blur of yellow lit windows. The tunnel filled with smoke, leaving him coughing, his eyes watering, his sleeve over his mouth and nose as he gasped for air. He stayed where he was, regaining his breath and eyesight for a few minutes, before he struggled to his feet and stumbled the rest of the way to the fresh air.

He'd gone perhaps half a kilometre when a voice called out in French. A man suddenly appeared out of nowhere. He was dressed in workman's clothes and spoke with a thick French patois. He grabbed János' arm and shook him roughly.

János spoke idiomatic French with an Italian accent. 'Let me go, monsieur, I beg you.'

'What are you doing here?' The man stunk of rotten wine and cigarette smoke. His unshaven chin of grey bristle and thick moustache leered at the frightened boy and panic rose in János' throat.

'Nothing. Let me alone.'

'You're coming with me. To the police station.' He had a powerful grip on János' arm.

'Let me be! You're hurting me!'

The reply was unintelligible. János stumbled on the track and would have fallen if the man hadn't been holding him so tightly. Already fear had given way to blind hatred and János went quietly. When they reached a beaten up old truck he climbed meekly into the vehicle and sat quietly while the man climbed in as well. Before starting the engine, the man lit a foul smelling cigarette, blew out a long stream of blue smoke and switched on the ignition. The diesel motor turned over slowly, picked up speed and burst into life with an explosion of black exhaust. The gears engaged with a loud grinding noise and they set off with a jerk. The worn springs made the truck lean to the left and each bump on the track was a jarring blow in the rump.

'How far?' János yelled above the noise of the labouring engine.

Without taking his eyes off the track the man replied, 'Ten kilometres. Now shut up.'

The track wound down the side of the mountain. Ahead, János could see a Tarmac road and knew it was time to act. Stretching down he grabbed the hilt of his knife and slid it out of the sheath and placed it under his right thigh. He waited a moment before pointing out the driver's side window. 'What's that?'

The driver wouldn't have been human if he hadn't turned his head to the left to look. Seeing nothing he was turning to look forward again when the knife flashed under his chin and dug deeply into his throat. He jerked back, shock and horror on his face as his hand grasped for the handle and he tried to pull the knife free. His fingers clasped convulsively around the shaft and he pulled it out of his neck. Blood spurted over his hands as he turned to the boy, ready to strike him with the blade. He'd let go of the wheel and the truck swerved to the right, hitting a tree, throwing the weakened and dying man against the windscreen. His head hit the glass and he passed out, the blood gushing out in decaying spurts in time with his heart beat. János had sat watching, mesmerised, too enthralled by his actions to move as the man had turned to thrust the knife at him. Shaking himself, he came to his wits. He clambered down from the cab, went round to the other side and pulled open the door. Reaching in, he clutched the man's shoulder and heaved him out and onto the ground. Struggling and straining he dragged the body into the undergrowth. There he checked the corpse's pockets, relieving it of twenty-eight francs and thirty-five centimes.

It had been his intention to steal the lorry, but the blood covering the steering wheel made him think twice. The engine had stalled and in the gathering silence he heard the sound of rushing water. He found the stream moments later and threw himself onto the ground. His mouth was as dry as a desert. He drank copiously but still felt thirsty. With a sigh he got to his feet and went back to the truck. Quickly finding his knife on the floor he retraced his steps to the corpse. He cut some cloth from the front of the man's coat and soaked it in the stream. He began the task of washing the blood from the steering wheel and windows.

When he was satisfied he started the engine and rammed the gear lever into reverse. The truck leap-frogged backwards in a series of jerks. János had learnt to drive a tractor when helping out on a local farm and then, after the farmer had an accident and broke an arm, he used to drive the truck around the fields collecting the crops. With a loud grating of the gears he finally managed to get the truck moving forward along the track towards the road. Reaching the road he turned left, knowing it was westwards, into France.

The steering was slack, the brakes spongy and the gear shift hard to change. However, the truck was getting him further from the border and nearer his destination. One problem loomed ahead. He'd need a passport to get into Britain. There was no convenient tunnel.

Kennedy sat eating his breakfast, the memories intruding, reminding him of how far he'd come. Not in distance – Italy to Britain was nothing. But in stature and status.

His private phone rang and he answered it, first switching on the scrambler. Anyone calling that particular number would also be on scrambler.

'Sir? It's Frobisher.'

'Ah, Mr Frobisher, I trust you are calling me with good news.'

There was a slight pause and Frobisher cleared his throat. 'I'm afraid not, sir. Yorke seems to have escaped to sea on his yacht.'

'Mr Frobisher,' the voice was silky smooth, 'I don't pay you to make mistakes. I want this resolved immediately.'

'Yes, sir. I thought I'd better keep you informed. We're working on it. We've got three fast boats out looking for him. He won't get far.'

'I trust that is the case. Let me know when this matter is resolved. Not before.'

Though the harmony of his mood was shattered, he replaced the receiver gently, holding his temper in check. He ignored the three-minute boiled eggs and instead sipped at his specially blended coffee. The high caffeine content was to his liking and was one of the few stimulants he permitted himself.

He dismissed the problem of Yorke from his mind. After all, there was very little one insignificant man could do against him and his organisation. It wasn't as though he had the whole of *Phoenix* working against him. And the other services he held in great contempt. The police were useless except when dealing with petty crimes and those who broke the law when driving, while MI5 and MI6 were virtually ineffective. The parliamentary oversight committees saw to that.

He cleared his head of the problem and logged on to his computer. Seconds later he was into the main computer at the European Union Bank of Antigua, owned by a Bahamian shell company called Swiss Investment Association which in turn was a wholly owned subsidiary of Moscombank. Of course, there was no such bank in Antigua, it existed only in cyberspace, courtesy of the internet. The computer running the bank's accounts was actually in his castle in the Highlands of Scotland. Yesterday it had reserves of $89,000,000 and change, today it was dollars short of $100,000,000. Excellent. He checked where the money had come in from. Much of it was drug money, but half was for a lucrative arms deal with Osama bin Laden's cohorts. The man himself might be ill, but he would be leaving the world one hell of a legacy. All that was needed now was to buy the bank in Jersey. He would have to work on the final arrangements himself.

Yorke watched the Fairline with her sleek lines turning. She was now less than twenty-five yards away and coming round to parallel the yacht's course, drawing ever closer.

'You Yorke?' A voice yelled across the water.

The two men on the open bridge stood looking down at him from a height of about 20ft.

Yorke didn't bother answering he merely stared at them.

'Did you hear me?' The man at the helm was getting angry and he said something to the man next to him.

The other man raised a pistol in his hand and fired off a shot that hit the water just astern of the yacht's transom.

Yorke swept up the rifle and fired a long burst, the burping of the silenced weapon in sharp contrast to the yells of the dying men and the shattering of glass and the shredding of pieces of boat. The deck of the Fairline was flush with the hull. Sudden movement caught Yorke's eye as a head appeared in the for'ard hatch. Yorke moved his aim smoothly and blew the head off the man who had appeared with a machine-gun in his hand.

The boats were now less than ten yards apart. There was no further sign of anyone aboard. Yorke sat watching, allowing the vessels to draw close enough to allow him to throw a grappling iron and pull the hulls together. He swapped weapons for a grenade in one hand and a SIG in the other.

'Dom, stay there and keep watch.'

'Right, dad.'

Yorke was grateful that Dom spoke in a steady and strong voice. Yorke leapt aboard and went up to the bridge. The two men were dead, their pooling blood in sharp contrast to the white plastic surface. Ignoring the sight, he went below. The cabins and saloon were beautifully furnished to the point of luxury. Under the for'ard hatch the man he'd shot lay still and a glance told Yorke he too was dead. Searching everywhere he found little of use apart from a signal log, a list of frequencies, and telephone numbers with initials alongside. He also took the boat's log and registration documents.

Awkwardly he shoved the two bodies into the saloon and closed the door. Opening the hatch to the engine room he lay on his stomach and reached down to the deck plates covering the bilges. Lifting a plate, he pulled the pin on the grenade and dropped it into the bilge, letting the deck plate fall back into place.

He was back aboard the newly named *Outlaw* when the grenade went off six seconds later. The metal deck plates meant that most of the force of the explosion was down and a section of hull was blown out. The boat quickly began to settle while Yorke removed the grapnel and turned the yacht away, catching the wind. The boat was out of sight beneath the sea by the time they'd sailed one and a half cables – 300 yards.

How many more boats were out looking for them or was that the only one?

'Dom? Come here, there's a good lad. Take the wheel. Head towards the Isle of Wight. I'll hide the guns.' Yorke opened a ready-use locker under the stern seat. 'See this knot?' he pointed at the round discoloration of wood. 'It's hinged.' He put his index finger through and lifted out a panel of wood. The small recess was big enough to hold the SIG. 'There's another in the locker on the other side. In the chart-house, on the port side of the door, is another knot. Push it and a catch is released opening a long locker. The rifle will fit in there.'

'I didn't know about all this,' Dom sounded peeved.

'I know. It was better you didn't. Now you need to know. There are other things I have to tell you but they can wait. The best hiding places are in the bilges. But these will do in case we need quick access. I'm going to work the radio. You all right? You're looking a bit white around the gills.'

Dom nodded. 'I guess so. It's not like in films is it?'

'No, I suppose not. Listen, old son. I know I'm repeating myself but these men are out to kill us. The worst of it is, we don't know who they are and we don't know why.'

'Can't we just go to the police? Let them deal with it?'

'How? Think about it. First of all if we go in and tell them we've killed a bunch of men who we *thought* were trying to kill us, we'd be the ones to land in jail. Secondly, whoever is doing this is well financed and that usually means powerful. I know some of the men involved. Trust me when I say we wouldn't stand a chance.'

'I'm scared, dad.'

'It's all right to be scared provided you don't let fear rule you. *You* must rule it. And use it. Let it help keep you safe by making you cautious. I'm hungry. What about you? Beans and hardtack?'

He was rewarded with a lopsided smile and a nod. 'And a coffee.'

'Good. I'll get it. Keep a sharp lookout, son. And call me immediately if you're at all suspicious of anything.'

While the kettle boiled and the beans warmed, Yorke sat at the navigation desk and fiddled with the radio. If it was examined closely, anyone knowing and understanding marine radios would have been very surprised. This particular set was state-of-the-art. He could contact anyone, anywhere in the world, either using the radio set or the built in sat-nav telephone. He could also programme it to listen in on different frequencies and simultaneously record twenty at a time.

There were twelve phone numbers. The initials alongside meant nothing except for the top one. M the K. Mack the Knife. Was that Colonel Mack Roberts, ex-SAS, ex-Army? A hero of the first Gulf War and Kosovo. If half the stories about his time in Northern Ireland were true then the man was a living legend. So what had gone wrong? What had happened to him to make him do this? Or did he think *Phoenix* was the enemy? Was that it? Some incredible cock-up? It was a possibility. But somehow, Yorke couldn't see it. If they'd been after him alone, then maybe, but to go after Dom as well, made it highly unlikely. Ruthless though it could be, the British government weren't *that* bad. Not yet, anyway.

It took a few minutes but he set the frequencies to be listened to and set the recorder. Next he took the sat-phone and began calling the telephone numbers. The recipient would get number withheld on their receiver. The first one he tried was unobtainable and he wondered if he was going to strike out with all of them. However, the second was answered.

'Yeah?'

'Hullo? Is that you Dick?'

'Who is this?'

'Who's that?' countered Yorke.

'Listen mate, you called me. So identify yourself.'

'What are you doing with my friend's phone?'

'This is *mine*. Now get off and go to hell.'

'Temper, temper.' Yorke's voice was patronising. 'That is 07710782916, isn't it?'

'Yes, and it's my number.'

'So who is that? It's not Dick.'

'Never mind who I am. Get lost!'

The phone went dead and Yorke grinned. He redialled. 'Is that you, Dick?'

'I told you . . .'

'Hang on. I checked the number. If you aren't Dick who are you? I must know you as you're in my address book.'

'My name is Josh Oldboy.'

'Lt Oldboy? Ex-SBS?'

'Yes. Now who . . .'

But Yorke didn't bother with him any longer. He cut the connection. He'd known Joshua Oldboy on and off for two years. A good man. Tough. Dedicated. If he spent any more time on the phone there was the danger Oldboy would recognise his voice.

He tried the same ruse with the other numbers. He hit pay dirt four more times. One other name meant something. Ian Williamson's file he'd read with a view to recruiting him into *Phoenix*. The reason the approach hadn't been made was because the man had dropped out of sight. Even with their extensive connections and abilities, *Phoenix* hadn't been able to find him. When had it been? Three months ago? The waters were getting murkier by the minute.

One thing he knew, if he was to solve the problem, he needed to move fast.

Back on deck, Yorke adjusted the sails and the yacht's heading. 'Dom, I'm getting some shut-eye. Call me if you see anything unusual.

'Right, dad,' Dom nodded, managing a smile.

'You okay?'

'I think so. Only, I've been thinking. We can't keep running and hiding. They, whoever they are, will find us.'

'Well done!' Yorke smiled at him. 'You're right. So we need to get to them first. But we can hide, Dom. For as long as we want. I've false identity for us both down below. Passports, birth certificates, the lot. We could vanish, you know.'

Dom frowned. 'If we did that I'd have to leave my friends. Leave the school. We won the rugby match, by the way.'

Yorke was immediately stricken by remorse for not having asked about the game but then he remembered another fact. 'Christ, son, I forgot. A very happy birthday.' He held out his hand and Dom ceremoniously shook it.

'I'd forgotten as well. Thanks, dad.'

'Right, I want to hear all about the game, kick for kick, pass for pass. Come on, give.' He settled in the stern and watched as Dom replayed the game, understating his part in the team's success. Skilful questioning by Yorke got the full story of how Dom had won the game for the school. When the boy had finished, Yorke knew he had to find an answer to the problems they faced. It would break Dom's heart to have to leave all that he was used to and knew. And the death of his mother was enough heartache in one young life.

Telling the story about the game lifted Dom's spirits and he was once more like his old self. 'I'm okay, dad. You can get some sleep, if you like.'

'Thanks. But first I'll check the radio.'

In the charthouse he examined the recording equipment. Of the frequencies he'd logged in, three had been in use. He pressed the play button and listened to each in turn.

One frequency was being used ship-to-ship. Two boats, one south and the other west, had been trying to contact a third.

'*Oakleaf*, this is *Charybdis*, over.'

'This is *Oakleaf*, nothing heard from *Baywatch*. Any word on that yacht he was going to take another look at?'

'Negative. It could be radio problems.'

'I tried his mobile. No answer.'

'I'll call you back. There's a contact I need to check out.'

The second frequency had been ship-to-shore. 'Mack? *Oakleaf*. We lost contact with *Baywatch*.'

'What do you mean, you lost contact?'

'Just that. No radio, no phone.'

'When did it happen?'

'An hour ago.'

'Where was he?'

'East. Looking for Yorke.'

'Where are you now?'

'West. *Charybdis* is south.'

'Right, I'll have boats out of Falmouth trawl eastwards and south. He can't have passed Falmouth so he must be in the Channel somewhere. You and Fitzroy head east at full speed. Look for *Baywatch* and Yorke's yacht. Once he gets amongst the marinas at Cowes it'll be like looking for a needle in a haystack.'

Alongside one of the telephone numbers were the initials CF. Charles Fitzroy. Another name, another enigma. He'd been a high-flyer until Northern Ireland. Something had happened over there but for the life of him Yorke couldn't recall what it was. He'd sleep on it.

The third call was on an ultra-high frequency, shore-to-shore. It took highly sophisticated and specialised equipment to operate in the range but it meant that speech was virtually guaranteed secure.

'Mr Frobisher? Roberts.'

'Ah, Colonel. I hope you have good news for me.'

'I'm afraid not. Yorke is still on the loose. And I appear to have lost one of the boats. It could be a radio fault, but I doubt it.'

'So do I, Colonel. Yorke is becoming an irritant rather than a nuisance. There is very little he can do. If you haven't stopped him by 6pm, abandon the quest. We have other, more pressing matters to deal with.'

'Understood. I'm sorry to have let you down.'

Contriteness was not an emotion Yorke would ever have associated with Mack the Knife Roberts. He was famous for his toughness which went hand-in-hand with his personal bravery. Which begged the question, *who* was Frobisher?

'One failure is permissible. Don't let it become a habit.'

'*Charybdis* this is *Oakleaf*. Report position, over.'

The latitude and longitude were given. *Oakleaf* gave theirs. Instructions for a course and speed were passed to *Charybdis* while *Oakleaf* gave her intentions. Yorke wrote them down.

The final recording was Roberts back to the *Oakleaf*. 'I won't tolerate failure. You have until 17.00 hours.' The colonel had reduced Frobisher's time by one hour.

The recordings stopped. Pensively, Yorke plotted their position and the position of the other two vessels. They would be in the vicinity of the *Outlaw* in precisely fifty-five minutes. Time to muddy the waters.

'*Oakleaf, Baywatch*, over.'

'*Baywatch,* this is *Oakleaf*, come in, over.'

Yorke said nothing. The call was repeated three times. Then he replied. 'Under attack . . . South of St Catherine's . . . five miles.'

'*Baywatch*, did you say you are under attack, five miles south of St Catherine's Point, over?'

'Affirmative. Out.'

The callsign was repeatedly broadcast but Yorke ignored it. After a couple of minutes he heard *Oakleaf* and *Charybdis* agree to change course and investigate. Good. By the time they arrived and found nothing there, the *Outlaw* would be berthed in the marina near Yarmouth on the Isle of Wight. He lay down on the sofa in the saloon, closed his eyes and promptly fell asleep. It was a knack most military men had.

He slept for an hour. Waking refreshed he went up top to find Dom dozing, his feet splayed out in front of him, his head lolling back. Yorke looked at his adopted son with affection. *He's a great kid. Nothing must be allowed to happen to him.*

Shaking Dom's shoulder he said, 'Come on, old son, time to hit the sack. Why don't you go below?'

'Okay, dad. Sorry, I must have dozed off.'

'The radar and video alarms would have warned us of any approaching vessel. That's what they're for.'

Dom went below while Yorke checked the wind, made slight

adjustments to the sails, and then checked their position. According to the chart and the speed of 8kts they were making good over the ground, as opposed to their speed through the water, they would be at the marina in about an hour and a half. The rocky points of the Needles were now only 3 miles away, and an awesome sight in the clear air.

As the time was now approaching 10.00, he turned on the radio to listen to the news. He tuned in to the announcer when he mentioned the Prime Minister. Brian Perkins said, in his authoritative voice, 'And finally, Mr Beaton, the Prime Minister, is resting at his private house in Aldingbourne near Chichester, recuperating from what had been reported as a bout of flu but is now described as a heavy head cold. His few engagements have been cancelled until further notice. BBC Radio 4, news.'

It looked as though his next move had been made for him.

11

THE MARINA WAS fine to starboard when he heard the radio messages between the two boats searching for them. Unsurprisingly they had seen nothing, although they had approached at least a dozen yachts in the vicinity. With the bank holiday, the Solent and Channel were inundated with hundreds, even thousands of yachts. Searching for one would prove to be a daunting task. Yorke heard them decide to search the marinas on the south side of the island. Good. It would take them all day.

Aldingbourne was 45 miles away by sea and 5 miles inland, north of Bognor Regis. If the wind held steady they'd be there by the middle of the afternoon. Plenty of time to make the necessary arrangements. He tacked the yacht to port and headed for the gap between Hurst and Sconce Point. Now the water was covered with yachts, jibing, going-about and tacking, many claiming right-of-way and, on the whole, disregarding or misinterpreting the Rule-of-the-Road as it applied to the sea. It kept Yorke busy, as he steered a course through the narrows and up to Cowes. Under any other circumstances he would have been enjoying himself.

Just after 11.00 Dom appeared. 'I'm hungry,' he greeted Yorke.

'Me too. What say we stop off at Cowes, and one of us can go ashore for some vittles.'

'I'll go!'

'I thought you might volunteer. Okay, we'll make a list of what we might need. Starting with the basics like bread and milk.'

A short while later the yacht turned into the wind and Dom dropped the anchor while Yorke lowered the sails. The inflatable's engine was flashed up and Dom headed ashore. The lad didn't have far to go, just a few hundred yards. He tied up at the marina and hurried ashore to the supermarket. While he was away, Yorke checked out the specialised equipment the yacht illegally carried, shifting some of it to the ready-use locker in the charthouse.

When Dom returned, the youngster took the helm while Yorke raised and secured the anchor. The wind was a gentle breeze that had gone round to the north and the yacht sat at a comfortable angle to it, heading 090. When he was satisfied with the trim of the sails, Yorke went below and began washing and slicing vegetables for a mixed salad. He liberally coated two steaks with black pepper and garlic salt and put them on to grill, before cutting slices of fresh bread. When the steaks were cooked he put them onto plates and carried them topside.

They ate the meal in companionable silence, broken only by the hiss of water round the hull and the wind in the rigging.

'What are we going to do, dad?'

'Good question, Dom. I need to talk to a very important person. That's where we're going now.'

'Who?'

'The Prime Minister.'

'What?' Dom looked at him wide-eyed. 'The PM? You know him?'

'Not exactly. But he knows who I am, that's for sure.'

'How can he?' Dom was excited by the thought of Yorke being known by the Prime Minister.

'Because of the nature of the work I do. He won't know me personally, but he'll know where I've come from.'

'Ah,' Dom looked crestfallen, 'I thought you meant he'd know your name.'

'Cheer up, old son,' Yorke smiled, 'he'd never know that as it's secret.'

'Your *name* is secret?'

'I mean in the context of what I do for the government. Did do, I suppose I should say.'

'How will you get to see him? He's in London.'

'No, he's not. He's at his house in Aldingbourne, not far from Bognor. I'll go there.'

'Will he see you? I mean, surely you can't just walk up to his front door and knock and ask to go in?'

Yorke's smile this time had a frigid veneer to it. 'That's more or less what I will be doing. You'd better come ten degrees to port. We'll edge past Ryde and stay on this side of the Solent. I'm going to check on the radio.'

There were a number of transmissions, nearly all between the two boats looking for them south of St Catherine's Point. The enemy had established a search pattern and were setting about the task in an orderly fashion. The power boats had approached eight yachts and the searchers were beginning to lose patience. That was evidenced by the report given to Mack Roberts. Yorke grinned when he heard the boats being ordered to move further south and out into the Channel.

Spitbank Fort was abeam, a reminder of the wars with France during Napoleonic times, which meant the newly named *Outlaw* was making good time. They tacked a few times to avoid other yachts under sail and held a steady course when boats-under-power came their way. A Royal Naval destroyer was in-bound and though the rule "power gives way to sail" was the norm, Yorke told Dom to tack to starboard and give the grey behemoth a wide berth. The sailors aboard were busy preparing for the ship to enter harbour, running out ropes and fenders, a bee-hive of activity. Over the tannoy, the ship's company was ordered to fall-in and face to starboard; the men left what they were doing to make a single line forward and aft, ready for entering Portsmouth. Yorke waved to the quarter-deck officer, who waved back. *HMS London* had been away for seven months in the Gulf and this would be the ship's company's first time back with their families in all that period. It was, Yorke, decided, a thankless profession. All work, no play and lousy pay. He grinned. Salary-wise, *Phoenix* wasn't much better. But there'd been many opportunities to enhance his income on various operations around the world and he'd taken them. After all, why leave money in the hands of drug dealers, gun-runners, terrorists and sundry other criminals? Various investments had paid off handsomely, and he supposed he was wealthy by normal standards, but the fact was, money meant little to him. It was a means to an end. A commodity to be used. Frequently he had paid bribes and rewards out of his own pocket, not bothering to tell Desmond Kavanagh back at Gibraltar Point. Having access to cash had saved his life on at least two occasions.

And he had the investment in the camera business. There was also a job there if he wanted it. He grinned mirthlessly. His friendship with Martin probably relied on the fact that he wasn't involved with the business. But also there was the more pertinent fact that he didn't want it. He sighed. Even so, as soon as he'd solved the problem of whatever was going on, he'd retire. Provided, of course, he lived.

They tuned in to the weather forecast which predicted showers later in the day for the sea areas of Dover, Wight and Portland. The day wore on in peaceful passage as they rounded Selsey Bill and turned for the home leg to Bognor. Tea-time saw them dropping anchor half-a-cable south of the famous seaside resort.

'Dom, I've been thinking about what to do with you. It'll be better if you don't stay here while I'm away. So we'll moor up. We'll go ashore and find a hotel.'

'Leave the *Duck* unattended? In an open sea? You've always said that's a bad idea.'

'I know, but your safety is far more important.'

'Dad, I've got an idea!' Dom slipped below and appeared a few moments later with a copy of Admiralty Sailing Directions for the south coast.

'What do you want the Pilot for?'

'We never come this way, do we? We always go across the Channel or west. Sometimes to Wight. But I'm sure a pal of mine at school goes up the River Arun for quite a distance.

Here it is. You go in at Littlehampton. Look, there's loads of places we can berth. We can get past Arundel if we want. There's plenty of water.'

'Can I see?' Yorke asked, holding his hand out.

A few moments later he smiled at Dom. 'We'd better weigh anchor and get going. We'll be off the open sea, and practically impossible to find up there. If we need to we can take the mast down and go even further. We can leave the *Duck* safely while we find a hotel. Let's get going.'

Dom raised the anchor while Yorke hoisted the Mylar/Kevlar mainsail. Since time immemorial sailmakers had been experimenting with different materials to manufacture the ideal sail. The new materials of the late twentieth century had resulted in quantum leaps in technology applied to an ancient art form – sailing. Only the spinnaker tended to be made from nylon and nothing was made from canvas any more. The yacht picked up the wind, Yorke spun the wheel and they headed east. Dom adjusted the mainsail before raising the spinnaker, the *Duck* immediately responding with a lift of her bow and an increase in speed.

'We've only an hour to go,' called Dom, 'perhaps less.'

'Okay. I've been reading the Pilot. We keep to starboard as we enter. Work out the tide, please, height, flooding or ebbing. You know what we need.'

Dom was delighted to be trusted with such an important task and set to with a will. Five minutes later he reported, 'Plenty of water under the keel. We'll be on a flood tide which is ideal. I reckon we'll have two knots of current against us for the first mile or two and that'll increase the further upstream we go.'

'Okay. In that case we'll stop around Arundel. See if there's a hotel there we can check into. How about a cup of tea?'

'Aye, aye, skipper,' Dom smiled.

The yacht settled down on a broad reach that would take them half a mile off-shore of the harbour entrance. Yorke checked the time of sunset, 21.11. Plenty of time to do what he needed. Clouds were building up from the west and they both got their foul weather gear ready to wear. As a squall hit and it started raining they both clambered into their yellow waterproof trousers and jackets. The shower passed quickly and the sun reappeared, dropping down towards the horizon and what promised to be a glorious sunset.

Other small yachts and pleasure craft were approaching and leaving Littlehampton. As the *Duck* turned north and spilled most of the wind from her sails, Yorke engaged the engine and motored, leaving Dom to lower and store the mainsail and spinnaker.

They went slow and easy, following the other traffic. Regular visitors and berth holders peeled off, port and starboard, while the *Duck* continued upstream, past the mooring buoys and pontoons. From both sides came the noise of cars and other vehicles as they passed the picturesque houses that made up the town. The yacht went under the A259, with plenty of headroom above the mast. By then the banks had given way to countryside with isolated buildings and the occasional pub. They were underneath the bridge when a train went over, the wheels a loud echo of noise in the tranquil early evening.

Arundel Castle was ahead when they came to a small inlet in the river. There were two empty mooring buoys. Yorke manoeuvred the yacht up to the furthest one, stemming the river, allowing Dom to use a boathook to grab the orange float. Minutes later, they were secured with the motor switched off. Blessed peace descended, interrupted only by the sound of birds as they foraged for their evening meal, sending warning signals, or singing for pure enjoyment.

'What now, dad?'

'We go ashore and find a hotel. Your stuff all packed?'

'Sure. I never unpacked when I got here last night.'

'Okay. You stay here while I get changed and pack myself a grip.'

Yorke went below. He selected his wardrobe very carefully, a wry smile on his face. Practically everything he wore was a weapon of some kind, or a constituent of one. By the time he was finished he was a walking arsenal, from the heels of his shoes to the collar of his jacket. His credit card, driving licence and other means of ID all proclaimed him to be Stephen Yarrow from Huddersfield. His business card showed he was a director of a computer company. If asked he would also claim ownership. Like all good legends there was a backup system in place which only he knew about. Should anyone phone the number it would be answered by the company name, and if required a message could be taken. So sorry, Mr Yarrow is out of the office at present, but is expected back soon.

The river bank was about three yards away. Yorke tied the inflatable's painter to a longer piece of rope and threaded it around a forward cleat. A second rope was tied to the stern of the boat. They climbed into the inflatable and a hefty shove sent them to the bank. Dom scrambled ashore, followed by Yorke. The head rope was pulled tight and the boat floated back to the yacht. Both the head and stern ropes were then tied to a convenient bush near the bank. Neither could be seen with a cursory glance though it wouldn't take anyone looking more than a few seconds to find them.

A pathway led alongside the river and a short while later they were in the picturesque village of Arundel, dominated by its castle. A hotel offered two rooms at a price that made Yorke wince but he took them anyway. He paid with his American Express credit card in the name of S. Yarrow. Dom booked in as his son.

The rooms were en-suite, small, and chintzy. Yorke arranged for a taxi to pick him up at the front of the hotel at 22.00. Destination? Barnham, for a late night party with friends. He assured the receptionist that he'd take the front door key as well as his room key.

Dinner was excellent. The service punctilious but not obtrusive. They both ate paté, followed by game pie and Dom had home-made ice cream to finish. They drank water, Yorke declining the wine list, much to the chagrin of the waiter.

A few minutes before he was due to leave, Yorke tapped on Dom's door. He entered and closed it behind him.

'Listen, old son, I won't be back until very late. Possibly

breakfast time. Just don't worry. If I'm not back by ten, take a taxi to school. Here's two hundred quid. It's more than enough. And here's your birthday present.'

He waited while Dom unwrapped the parcel to find a mobile phone. With a beaming smile he said, 'Thanks, dad! It's just what I wanted.'

'Good. Only I'll be borrowing it tonight. You use the sat-phone. Why not go and programme in your new number? And then set your phone to vibrator and no ringing tone. But Dom, only call me in an emergency, okay?'

Dom smiled tremulously. 'Sure, dad.'

'Okay. Now, there are a few other things. Let me show you something.' Taking the phone from Dom he pressed a button. 'See that? That's our latitude and longitude. I say our but in fact it's mine. I have small signalling devices in my shoes and in my clothes. It works on your new phone and the sat-phone.' He showed Dom how to operate the device. 'Martin developed it.'

Dom nodded. He knew and liked Martin.

'I'll send a check signal from this phone at least every eight hours. Here, let me show you.'

Dom's phone gave a bleep and OK appeared on the display. 'Cool!' was his response.

'Next. This credit card is in the name of D. Yarrow. It's yours in case you need it. Your PIN is easy to remember, it's the month of your birthday, mum's and mine. Okay?'

Dom nodded. Mention of his dead mother no longer brought him the anguish it once did. When he'd told Yorke that, and that he felt he was being a traitor to her memory, Yorke sat him down and explained how pain lessened with time. Love didn't diminish, only the pain. It was normal. Much relieved, from that day on Dom could refer to his mother without guilt or torment.

'One last thing. Here's a passport in the same name as proof of identity.'

'Wow! Just like in the films.'

'Except this is real, Dom and don't forget it.'

'I won't, dad. Not after last night and today.'

'Good. All right, I'll see you in the morning. Night, son.'

'Night, dad. And be careful.'

Yorke was closing the door behind him when Dom called out.

'Dad. I just wanted to say I love you.'

'It goes for me too, Dom, in spades. See you later.' Yorke closed the door and sauntered downstairs. As he arrived outside his taxi drew up. Twenty minutes later it deposited him outside the corner shop in the village of Barnham.

By now it was fully dark, the sky was cloudy and the showers that had been promised earlier were in the air. Yorke carried a small bag, slung over his shoulder, the contents of which, should the police search it, would have resulted in his immediate arrest. He set off at a leisurely stroll, following the signpost for Eastergate. He had plenty of time. He wanted to break in to the house around 03.00, when even regular night-shift personnel were at a low ebb. And nothing was as mind-numbingly boring as mounting a guard on a British politician. Few, if any, were worth killing. Not even the Prime Minister. Maybe a crank would want to try something, but rarely a professional, unless they were members of the IRA and they'd been quiet for at least three years because of the concessions made by the government. And cranks and madmen rarely, if ever, got close to a target.

That didn't mean Yorke would or did underestimate the police who made up the protection unit. They were highly trained and exceptionally skilled, only they were also seriously limited in their ability to act in any given situation. They couldn't shoot first and ask questions afterwards. After all, a tramp could wander onto the grounds of the PM's house and trespassing didn't result in the death penalty – not in the UK. So the police were very, very careful when it came to using firearms or any form of force. Yorke wasn't so inhibited, only he had no intention or desire to seriously hurt or kill a member of the constabulary who was only doing his or her job. After all was said and done, *they were on the same side*.

The road was deserted, with only the occasional car passing. Fairly soon he found himself in Eastergate and passing the pub, the Labour in Vain. Another mile and he was in Aldingbourne, near the church. He followed the road to Tangmere, the old air station that had been an integral part of the war effort against the Germans in 1939-45. Now it consisted of open spaces and an expensive housing development. On the far side of the field sat the PM's house with the quaint name of Anna-Drew, a combination of the PM's children's names, if he remembered correctly. It was ideally situated as he often travelled by helicopter, avoiding the rush hour traffic, the hellish congestion and the nightmarish roadworks that plagued Britain. Naturally, travelling that way was justified because of safety issues. Its convenience was secondary.

At midnight, Yorke positioned himself across the open field opposite the house. From his bag he removed a thin, grey coverall, that was far more effective at night than the camouflaged "can't-see-me-suits" of the armed forces. He quickly pulled it on over his slacks and blazer. Taking out a pair of binoculars, he settled himself down on the ground. These were no ordinary glasses as they had a built in infra-red, heat-seeking capacity that was invaluable. He took his time. Anna-Drew was five-bedroomed, detached, modern. It sat in about an acre of landscaped garden, lawns front and sides, bordered by flower beds. Behind the house he knew there was a two-car garage and a swimming pool with more lawn. There was also an outhouse that had been converted into a comfortable room for the police. Inside were monitors hooked up to cameras, pressure and vibration detectors. Surrounding the grounds was a nine-foot, chain-link fence and Yorke could see it was no ordinary one. A series of boxes gave away the fact that the fence was interwoven with a clever array of pressure sensors. He looked at the fence with a feeling of despondency. How far under the ground did it go? This was all new and had been installed since his one and only visit. It was a double deterrent; vibration detectors with a taut wire system made cutting the chain-fence impossible.

On the other side of the fence the lawn was as flat and smooth as a billiard table. He looked more closely and saw the very slightest bump running the width of the grass. Unless he was very mistaken, a subterranean pressure cable. If it was the type he thought, then the cable's flux would give it a detection range of about six feet. Once past those two obstacles he'd have the house to contend with, but that problem he'd face after he got there.

Silently, he moved further around the perimeter of the housing development. From one angle he could see the converted shed, a light showing. One major factor about VIP protection in the UK. It was meant as a deterrent. Not to capture or kill a wrong-doer. And so it was in-your-face, obvious. That had its plus side. It meant there were few, if any, unseen obstacles. Even the pressure cable wasn't that well hidden.

The houses he was passing were well spaced out, their gardens inevitably adjoined. And as this was rural England woebetide the owner who didn't look after his plot of real estate. Trees grew in abundance. Some were mighty oaks, others were beech and elm. They were protected by law and couldn't be felled unless in an emergency. Dutch elm disease would do it. Or damage by lightning causing a weakness in the tree. Otherwise they were as protected as an endangered species – unless a new road was being built or other politically useful development undertaken. The removal of a tree because it *might* interfere with the security arrangements of a British Prime Minister did not fall into that category. Indeed, an oak tree has taken hundreds of years to grow, a politician is here today, gone tomorrow. No competition as to which was the more valuable.

He was lying beneath a small bush and slowly extracted himself. Keeping low he went back the way he'd come, until he reached a copse of trees. Amongst the trees he searched for a straight sapling, about two inches in diameter and about eight feet long. He found one to his satisfaction and, taking the razor sharp throwing knife from his left sleeve, he cut the sapling down. Clearing the branches, he placed it on the ground and swung off it. It barely bent.

In the middle of the PM's lawn was a tall, ancient beech, it's spreading branches casting a wide shade in the summer. In the neighbouring garden was an old and sturdy oak tree, towering above the houses. It was precisely as he'd remembered it. He threw the stave like a javelin, watching with satisfaction as it sailed through the air to land at the bole of the oak.

He slid over the garden fence like a wraith. Across his shoulder he carried a thin, lightweight length of nylon with a flexible steel core. On his belt was an odd looking gun with a barrel the diameter of a shotgun's and as long as a pistol's. The firearm he carried strapped to his right thigh fired darts that could put an oxen to sleep for four hours, provided the target was hit in the right spot, such as the side of the neck. He wore the latest night-vision-goggles which fitted like sunglasses. The world was bright with a slight greenish tinge and thanks to microchip technology, in the event of moonlight or artificial light, the goggles automatically compensated for the change.

The lowest branch of the tree was some six feet above the ground and Yorke climbed onto it. Staying close to the trunk he scaled the tree until he was at least fifty feet above the ground. From there he had a panoramic view across the country and down to the sea. It wasn't a view he stopped to admire. Taking the gun from his hip, he fitted a short handled grappling hook with its four prongs folded along the haft, into the barrel. It was spring operated and had a range of 100 metres in a straight line, 150 metres when fired at an angle. The distance to the tree in the PM's garden was 80 to 90 metres. The underside of the barrel was an open slot, from which dangled the thin rope, it's breaking strain in excess of 500lbs. It was secured to a hole in the base of the haft. When fired, the grappling hook remained folded and aerodynamic, the prongs springing open only when the hook reached the end of its trajectory and the wire-rope brought it up short.

The secret of success when firing the gun was to ensure the smooth running of the rope. Carefully, he coiled down the rope in a fork in the tree, ensuring there were no snags or snarls. Satisfied, he aimed the gun across the lawns and into the beech tree. He had a choice. He could fire and secure the end of the hook level to where he was and work his way along the rope, hence giving him a way back, or he could shoot lower, and slide down, and have to egress the property by another route. He decided on the former. The wire in the centre of the rope did two things. First, it gave the thin nylon significantly more strength, but secondly, by loosening the hook and pressing a button at the end of the rope it retracted the prongs and enabled the hook and line to be recovered, leaving no trace. His preferred *modus operandi*.

The gun fired with barely a sound, the suppressers built into the weapon doing their job. The line snaked out across the gap and the hook fell between the bole and a sturdy branch. Yorke pulled the line taut, gratified to see the prongs snag in position. Hauling the line as tight as possible he secured the end to the oak's trunk. He knew that no matter how hard he pulled and tied the line it would have an almighty dip in the middle.

Now wearing a pair of thin leather gloves, reinforced with Kevlar to protect his hands, he slung his bag over his shoulder, grabbed the rope and launched himself onto the line.

He swung his feet over the rope, tucked one foot on top of the other, and set off, hand-over-hand, feet first. The rope sagged as he went along but he kept up a steady rhythm, ignoring the leg breaking drop beneath him. In the middle he had to work harder as he was now pulling himself up to the grapnel. Suddenly, somewhere in the vicinity, a dog barked and then began howling. Another dog took up the cry which galvanised Yorke to move faster. The last thing he needed right then was for some householder to come and see what was causing the dogs to make such an infernal row and spot him against the night sky.

His feet touched the tree and a few moments later he was standing still against the trunk of the beech. He stayed where he was for a few minutes, listening intently, gratified to find he was barely out of breath in spite of the strenuous journey along the rope. A harsh voice called out, a dog yelped and blessed silence returned.

All static security systems have a major flaw. They can be set off by wildlife, the weather, or children fooling around the perimeter. In order to reduce the number of false alarms they are set carefully to configure with the intrusion of an adult person. Hence weight and more importantly, weight distribution, are taken into account. It also meant that if you acted outside the set parameters, the sensors automatically ignored the warning. The only sure way to protect a position, any position, even in Great Britain, was by using armed patrols. But that had it's own drawbacks. First, it was very expensive on a 24/7 basis. And secondly, the patrols could set off the alarms. To prevent that, the alarms had to be switched off, which in turn devalued their use. It was a conundrum that security personnel faced continuously but one which worked in favour of the attacker. Yorke knew that in this case the police ran a static operation, relying on the equipment, staying warm and comfortable in their outhouse.

Yorke climbed down the tree. From a pocket he removed a voltmeter and looked at the dimly lit LCD display. He slowly went back towards the underground pressure sensors that encircled the boundary. Although the cable was some way off, the electromagnetic flux of the cabled sensors created a detection field six to eight feet wide. The needle on the voltmeter flickered and then moved steadily upwards. He knew the cable was designed to leak the electric flux that was detected by a second cable and hence create a detection field that was also two feet high, making a rectangular box. A thirty pound animal wouldn't set off the alarm but a ninety pound young adult would. Wind and snow, leaves and rain would all interrupt the flux but the computer system would filter out the effect and not react. There was no way to tamper or fool the system, the only way was to go over it. He lay the stave with one end at the edge of the field. It was his emergency route out. The system, as well as the fence, could identify where a break in occurred. If he set an alarm off in the house and made a run for it he hoped it would take the police a few vital seconds to deploy around the perimeter – by which time he'd be away.

Stealthily, he approached the house, and went around to a side entrance. This had been the door he'd used in the past. Set in the wall was a discreet touch screen. If he pressed the correct numbers the alarm would be deactivated. From his bag, Yorke removed a small atomiser of fine powdered charcoal and sprayed the pad. The oils left by the fingers would show as a pattern and Yorke hoped he'd be able decide on the sequence of numbers. Blowing gently on the display, four figures showed they were in use, 3, 4, 5, 9. What wasn't shown was the order. He knew he could afford three attempts before giving up. After all, anyone could press the wrong numbers by error. The problem was the combination of four numbers was so large that it would be sheer luck if he got them. What was the PM's date of birth? His birthday was recently. A few weeks ago. May 4th 1956. That was it. Hence the 4 and 5 possibly. It didn't help much. He pressed the buttons in order. 3, 4, 5, 9 and enter. The red light stayed obstinately red. He then pressed 4, 5, 9, 3 and enter. Nothing. Damn it! One last try. 9, 3, 4, 5 and enter. It didn't work. Then he hadn't had much hope it would. But luck often played a large part at times like these. Now it was time to make his own luck.

Taking a penlight, Yorke examined the edge of the door. He found two screws in the bottom corner. That had to be where the contact switch was placed. The alarm circuit was complete because a magnet in the bottom of the door kept the contacts of a ferrous-metal switch together. Open the door, break the switch and off would go the alarm. Taking a powerful magnet from his bag, he used a fast acting glue to secure it to the door, holding the switch closed.

The mortise lock used a Chubb key and probably engaged at least three bolts, one in the centre and another top and bottom. The door would be solid steel with a wood grain cover and if he couldn't tease the lock open he'd never get in.

From the knapsack he extracted an electronic key sensor. He placed it carefully into the lock and pressed a button. Tiny rods of tempered steel moved in all directions, expanding to fill the lock's recesses. A twist of the wrist and the lock was open. He withdrew the rods and removed the electronic key. All being well, when the door opened, there'd be no alarm. One thing he knew, if it did go off it would be with a raucous noise, designed to frighten any intruder into an early coronary. Easing open the door he was greeted with complete quiet.

12

HE CLOSED THE door behind him. The corridor he was in led
to the kitchen at the back of the house. Off that was a dining-
room and to his left and right were two public rooms.
Immediately by him was a cloakroom and toilet. The loudest
noise in the house was the ticking of a grandfather clock on
his left side. He stood still, letting his senses tune in to the
house, the seconds ticking slowly by. He knew that with the
house occupied, any photo-electric cameras and sensors would
be switched off.

Yorke moved like a ghost from room to room, in case there
was a sleeping sentry somewhere on the premises. Downstairs
was empty. In the kitchen he found a three-quarters empty bottle
of Famous Grouse whisky, a dirty glass and a postcard alongside the bottle. Turning over the card he saw it was from the
Prime Minister's wife. *Having a wonderful time. Wish you were
here. Kids missing you and send their love. Hope cold gets
better soon.* The front of the card was a picture of Crieff Hydro
Hotel. He'd never heard of it. He slipped the card into his pocket.

Yorke flitted upstairs, the dart gun cocked and ready. At the
top was another corridor with two doors along one side, three
doors on the other and one facing from the far end. The first
door on the right opened onto a bathroom. The one on the left
was an empty bedroom. The second right was another empty
bedroom, as was the second left, except it had en-suite facilities. The third right was another empty bedroom which left the
one ahead. He presumed it was the master bedroom, which
made sense as it would be the largest with the best view.

Yorke stopped outside the door and listened. Above the

sound of his own shallow breathing he could hear the movements of a restless sleeper. Cautiously, he gripped the door
handle and very slowly eased it down. Gently he pushed at the
door, moving it millimetre by millimetre. The PM was bound
to have a panic button, either on him or nearby. He'd press
first and ask questions afterwards.

The door swung on oiled hinges. When it was far enough
ajar to slip through, Yorke put his head in. A single lump filled
the right side of a double bed. There was a door opposite he
assumed led to a bathroom. The body moved and a gentle snore
disturbed the tranquillity of the room.

Yorke moved slowly, testing each floorboard before putting
his weight down. Standing beside the bed he looked down at
the clean cut features of the Prime Minister, his face more
youthful looking in repose. His left arm was on top of the quilt
and Yorke recognised the watch as an alarm transmitter
requiring only a push on the switch next to the furled knob.
Waking a sleeping man was a risky business. He was liable to
fight and kick before being made to relax and listen. And in
this case the PM's instinct would be to sound the alarm. Where
in the room would the static alarm button be? Yorke grinned
and picked up the clock/radio. Next to the on/off button was
an unmarked button. What was more natural than to reach for
the clock in the middle of the night? He placed temptation on
the floor away from the bed.

The watch was secured by a leather strap. Infinitely carefully Yorke began undoing the strap. The PM twitched. Yorke
froze. The body began to snore softly and Yorke continued his
task. It was an incredibly delicate thing to do and one Yorke
wouldn't have attempted except for the almost empty bottle of
scotch and the pervading sour smell of whisky breath. A fuddled
brain was also unpredictable. The watch fell free and he placed
it out of reach.

One factor *did* work in his favour. And that was the Prime
Minister would have been used to have his sleep disturbed,
especially in times of crisis. He was counting on it now.

'Prime Minister, sir, wake up. Prime Minister.'

The PM grunted, turned over.

'Prime Minister.'

The PM's eyes snapped open.

'Prime Minister, please wake up.' Yorke's voice was smooth, unthreatening.

The Prime Minister sat up, his features reflecting his bewilderment. 'What? . . . What?'

'Please pay attention Mr Beaton. We need to talk.'

The PM was quickly coming round, his faculties returning to normal. His hand reached for his left wrist.

'Don't bother, Prime Minister, I've removed your alarm. Where are your servants?'

'I have a house-keeper who lives in the village. This is the one place where we can come and be a normal family and I keep it that way. Now, who are you?' If he was frightened, Beaton wasn't showing it.

'My name doesn't matter. I'm here to talk about *Phoenix*.'

Beaton gasped. '*Phoenix*? What do you know about it?'

'Only that they've been wiped out. And I want to know who betrayed us and why.'

'Us? You're one of them?'

'Was. They're no more. As you know only too well.'

'I can't help you.' The Prime Minister had been leaning on his elbow, now he sank back onto the pillows. 'Get out before I call my security people.'

'I admire your courage PM but not your intelligence. You'll not manage to do more than open your mouth before I stop you. That'll be both unpleasant and undignified. For you, that is. Only three people knew about the organisation; what it really did. You, the Secretary of State for Defence and the Home Secretary. It was always agreed that it would be kept that way. The whole place was tagged with a security code higher than atomic top secret. So don't bullshit me. I won't insult your intelligence if you don't insult mine. I want to know what's going on. I *need* to know.'

'Why the urgency? What's so important that you broke in here to talk to me?'

'They, whoever they are, are trying to kill me and my son. I mean to stop them.'

'You can't,' said Beaton, 'they're too powerful.'

'What do you mean? How can they be more powerful than the Prime Minister of a sovereign country? It's impossible.'

'It's not. Look, I'm at a disadvantage. Would you mind turning the side light on so I can see who I'm talking to?'

'I'd rather not. It may be some sort of signal. Or it may cause your protection unit to check to see if you're all right. Just lay still and talk to me.'

Beaton folded his arms in an act of defiance and said, 'No chance. Get out while you still can. Or I'll call for the police. And they're armed.'

'I'm aware of that fact. Sir, I need your help. I say again, my son's life is in danger as well as my own. They've been trying to kill us since yesterday afternoon. I've just about kept a half-pace ahead of them but if we're to stay alive I must get to the men behind my attackers.'

'You can't,' said Beaton with an air of defeated despondency about him.

'What do you mean, I can't? Why not? What do you know you're not telling me?'

'Nothing!' The PM's voice was harsh. It sounded like anger but Yorke could see there was a good deal of fear in him as well.

'Something's happened. What is it? What's made you so scared?'

'Nothing, I tell you. Now get out!'

'I'm not going. I have to know what it is you won't tell me. I'll do anything to save my son.'

'I'll do the same for my family . . .' the PM suddenly stopped talking, his face now horror stricken.

'I thought so. All that nonsense about your family being on holiday is a sham. Where are they?'

'They are on holiday. Believe me. I swear to God they are.'

For some reason Yorke knew he was telling the truth but not the whole truth. Then he understood. It was a flash of inspiration and he said, 'Of course they are. Somewhere pleasant. In communication with you. *They* believe they're on a break while you know better. Brilliant. What is it? They die if you don't do certain things?'

Beaton squirmed, the truth hitting a raw nerve. 'Drop it! I know who you are now. I just realised. You've a stepson. His mother's dead. Yorke! That's it! Stephen Yorke!'

'Who told you my name? It wasn't Kavanagh.'

'No, it wasn't. I was given your name recently.'

'By whom?'

'Never mind who told me, it's not relevant.'

'You have to tell me!'

'I cannot! Don't you understand? I cannot!'

'My God, over thirty people died to save your wife and children and you won't give me a name?'

'I had no choice, I tell you. Besides, I didn't expect them to kill anybody. Who's ever heard of an attack carried out like that apart from in a war? It was the last thing I envisaged.'

Yorke couldn't blame the Prime Minister for that. He'd never have expected such a response either. It was unheard of.

'What would you have done? The worst I'd been expecting was exposure and political ruin. A price I'd happily pay to save my family.'

'What would I have done? I don't know, to be honest.'

'I've often wondered how far I'd go to save my wife and children. Now I know. There are no limits. I'll sacrifice anything and everybody to save my family. It's as simple as that.'

'Why don't you just get them home?'

'There are people watching them . . .' he tailed off despondently.

'What about your family's protection detail?'

'Two extremely capable and dedicated policewomen. You know the families of politicians, even of Prime Ministers, have never needed protection as such. It's always been more a token than anything. Hell, to keep the paparazzi away rather than fight off a threat. This isn't America.'

'Times have changed. Taking out *Phoenix* was a massive display of their power. A quasi-military operation.'

'Exactly. And we have no way of combating them. We cannot use troops to attack people in this country no matter what their crimes. We can only use the police and occasionally an armed rapid response unit. We arrest felons. We don't kill them. That was the whole purpose of *Phoenix*. To take the war to the bastards. Your problem was you were getting too close to the top. It made a lot of very powerful men angry.'

'It also made them very scared,' Yorke said reflectively. 'Hence the reason they reacted like they did. But I don't get it. Desmond Kavanagh never hinted at anything to me. Or the others, I'm sure of that.'

'He was beginning to pull it all together. He'd said as much to me. When I asked for names he told me he could only speculate so far. That he'd tell me as soon as he had proof. He used language that, quite frankly, scared the hell out of me.' Beaton frowned and looked at the dark outline of Yorke. 'Desmond was frightened by what he'd learnt. I'd stake my life on that.'

'Him? Frightened? I don't believe it.'

'That's your choice. He's dead. He had the right to be frightened.'

'Yes, how stupid of me. What happened to coerce you into giving away *Phoenix*?'

'Annabel, my three year old daughter went missing for thirty minutes. I had a call on my private line at Number Ten. It made the situation crystal clear. That half an hour was the longest of my life. I didn't require a second lesson. That would have involved Andrew, my seven year old. He has asthma. When he's frightened or nervous it brings on an attack. It was too much to risk.'

'So you gave them *Phoenix*, just like that?' There was no hiding the contempt and anger in Yorke's voice.

'No, not just like that. It was curious but the way I was approached and questioned made me think they already knew about Gibraltar Point. I was merely confirming what they knew.'

'Who did the questioning?'

'I can't tell you.'

'Can't or won't?'

'It amounts to the same thing. However, I am aware of the fact that as I gave into them with their first demand what's to prevent them making more? That is unacceptable and so is the danger to my family. I cannot and will not place the government under the control of such men.'

'But how will you prevent it? You've just said, if you've given in once you'll do it again.'

'As soon as my family return from . . .' he paused and then continued, 'from where they are, I shall resign with immediate effect. I'll be of no further use to them then.'

'But what's to stop them doing it to somebody else? To whoever takes your place?'

The PM sighed heavily. 'I cannot speak for what my successor may or may not do.'

'Sir, that's the coward's way out.'

'Don't you think I'm not aware of that? But I see no other way.'

'Fight them! Use every means at your disposal.'

'The only means I had has been destroyed. This was precisely what *Phoenix* was set up to do. We've known for a long time that if we're to win the war on terror and crime we'd have to do it without recourse to the law. I don't need to tell you what would happen if the press found out about you. Even now, we'd be pilloried. The people behind this whole mess would orchestrate every civil liberty group and bleeding heart in Europe. Can you imagine what it would be like?'

'Of course. We discussed it often enough at Gibraltar Point. In fact why didn't they just do that? Expose *Phoenix* instead of destroying it?'

'I've asked myself the same question. Because that's what I'd expected. Exposure. Closing down. Political flak. The conclusion I came to was that there was a message.'

'A message? To whom? You?'

'No, I don't think so. I think to others of their ilk. Terrorist groups. Organised crime. God alone knows. It was a message of power and utter ruthlessness. A convincing good way to deliver it, don't you think?'

'Yes.' Yorke couldn't keep the resignation out of his voice.

'So you see, there's nothing you or I can do about it. I suggest you keep a very low profile and let it all blow over. My family will be back in three days and I'll resign. I suspect the Home Secretary will take over. Whatever happens after that will no longer be my responsibility.'

'What if they won't let you resign?'

'What do you mean? How can they stop me?'

'By the same threats they've used already. It's what I would do, in their place.'

The PM gasped, the thought never having entered his head. 'I'll do it suddenly. Before anyone knows.'

'Does anybody know? Have you mentioned it to a member of your staff? Or a colleague? Someone you trust implicitly?'

'Of course not. Only Brian Calthorpe, the Chancellor. He'll have my endorsement in the party. I don't want Gordon Whitley to get the job.'

'The Home Secretary? Why not?'

'I don't trust him. No reason in particular. Anyway, I've an agreement with the Chancellor.'

'That's like offering the man a poisoned chalice.'

'He's a bachelor with no close relatives still living. He'll be a hard man to blackmail.'

'They'll find a way, believe me.'

'It will no longer be my problem. It'll be his.'

'It will be everybody's!' Yorke said harshly. 'You'll have sold out the country like a third world banana republic. And once it happens it'll be virtually impossible to reclaim it. What's going to happen in the future? Will we have a secret government within our elected parliament who'll be pulling the strings?'

'Damn it, man, don't you think I haven't had the same thoughts? I'm not a fool.'

'I know you're not. So we need to find an alternative. We have to stop them.'

'How?'

'There's only one way. We have to cut off the head of the monster.'

'It's impossible. We don't know whose head to cut,' the PM spoke wearily.

'We find out. I've got a name I can use. I'll go after him. I'll make him talk. Get to the source.' Yorke spoke in staccato sentences, anger boiling in him. Britain was on the road to Armageddon all due to the cowardice of the man on the bed. But where would he find Colonel "Mack" Roberts?

'I wish you luck. Only I won't be able to help you.'

'Be able to, or willing to?'

'It amounts to the same thing in the end. Look, Yorke,' no mister this time, 'I came into politics to make life better for ordinary people. But *not* at the risk to my family. It's contrite, I know, but I am truly one of those rare individuals in politics who is a happily married, family man. I can live without politics, but not without my family.'

It was an honest admission to which Yorke had no reply. One luxury he enjoyed which was priceless – he and Dom existed in a world shrouded, on the whole, in anonymity. It was an advantage denied the Prime Minister and his family. Yorke felt less inclined to be so judgmental.

'I repeat, I don't think you'll be allowed to resign.'

'They won't know until it's too late.'

'They probably know already.'

'I told you, only the Chancellor knows of my intentions and I have honestly said it's to spend more time with my family, clichéd though it sounds.'

'Then the secret is out.'

'How do you mean?'

'Think about it. Are you telling me that Calthorpe isn't briefing journalists right now? He's a politician, for God's sake. Off the record, secret, prepare the exclusive – you can write the agenda better than I can.'

Beaton looked like he'd just been hit below the belt. Wearily he nodded. 'I suppose I was so caught up in the idea of getting out and what had happened to *Phoenix* I didn't think it through properly.'

'You should work with the knowledge that they've found out and expect an unpleasant phone call.'

'What are you going to do?'

'Go after whoever it is. The country must not be sold down the river. There's no telling where it'll all end. I'd better be going.' Yorke looked at his watch. It was 03.38. 'I'd appreciate it if you kept my visit a secret. Can I get hold of you, if I need to?'

'E-mail is your best bet. I'll give you my family address. Nobody else has it.'

Yorke made a mental note of the address and said goodbye. He headed straight for the front door. He had just stepped outside when alarm bells rang out with a cacophony of noise. It seemed to Yorke that the Prime Minister had had a change of heart.

13

HE RAN. IT was the only thing to do. The bells were ringing in the house and the police would be appearing any second. Floodlights were coming on even as Yorke grabbed the stave, took two paces, jabbed the end of the stave into the lawn and swung himself over the pressure sensors. The general alarm wouldn't pinpoint his position. If he set off the flux or the alarm on the fence the police would know precisely where he was.

He ran with a long, loping stride, the pole gripped at one end by both hands. Half a metre from the fence he slammed the end of the stave into the ground and swung himself upwards with all his strength. If he missed now he wouldn't get a second chance.

Even as he flew upwards he heard yells behind and expected the sound of gunshots at any second. His body was horizontal to the top of the fence when he swung his legs across the wire, thrusting his whole body over the top. He let go the stave and went flying over backwards, facing the house, landing on the balls of his feet and flipping over backwards in a handspring to take away the momentum he'd built up. He landed on bent knees and dived for cover. His glimpse of events in the garden showed the police converging on the front door of the house.

He kept low and moved fast. Why the hell had Beaton done that? Why agree to something one minute and change his mind the next? That kind of vacillation didn't bode well in a country's leader. The noise stopped and blessed peace descended, if the barking dogs and lights coming on in the other houses could be called peace.

What would the police do in this situation? Their sole task was to ensure the safety of the PM. Once that was accomplished, then and only then would they try and track down the perpetrator. However, they could and probably would have phoned in the intrusion and even now squad cars were very likely converging on the area. Even as the thought took root he saw blue flashing lights in the distance.

Yorke stuck to the hedgerows. He also moved at speed, knowing distance was his best protection. He wasn't concerned. He'd pit his abilities against the police any time, most of whom lived such sedentary lives they'd have difficulties in a hundred yard dash never mind a long yomp across country. More blue lights were flashing over to his right and ahead of him and he realised that they were building a cordon around the area.

A scan of the horizon showed eight sets of lights. The police were too stretched to have more that two men per car, but even if they had four, thirty-two men was totally inadequate. Yorke knew that. He'd been on enough escape and evasion exercises in his time. He saw a flashlight shining about two fields away, pointing away from him. In a copse of trees he stopped for a few moments to take stock of what was going on. Already he was at the periphery of the blue lights, the nearest about a third to half a mile away to his left. The hedge he was standing next to was high and dense. A tree with low, spreading branches stretched above him. Reaching up, he swung arm over arm until his feet hit the hedge. He walked over the hedgerow, his arms taking the weight. Dropping into the lane he saw he was at the outskirts of Aldingbourne, near Eastergate. The road was called Hook Lane. He was now outside the cordon but in danger of being seen by a prowling police car. Headlights appeared at the crossroads in front of him and he dived over the nearest hedge. He was in the small front garden of No 2. He stayed hidden as the lights swept passed him and went up the road, vanishing into the darkness. He leapt the fence and jogged to the crossroads, passing a convenience store on the left. Turning right he saw the gates of a level crossing, just before a pub called the Prince of Wales. More headlights appeared before him and he plunged along the railway track in the direction of Barnham.

By now the sky was taking on the hue of an oyster shell, pearly gray in the new day. As he ran alongside the track Yorke became aware that he was able to see the railway sleepers and where he was placing his feet. In ten minutes he was at Barnham, where he paused at the road. There was no sign of life in either direction and he decided to stick with the track. He knew he was well away from the police and only bad luck could spoil his chances of escape. He kept up the mile eating pace until he arrived at North End. Again, the track crossed a narrow lane and here he stopped to rest for five minutes. The problem of why the Prime Minister had betrayed him had been playing around in his mind to no avail and finally he dismissed the thought. Instead he wondered what the PM meant about being questioned with regards to *Phoenix*. He had said whoever was questioning him knew about the organisation. But if that was so, who else could have betrayed them? Jesus. *Jesus, what a bloody, sodding mess*. Speculation was distracting him from the main objective and that was to return to the hotel without being seen. He stuck with the railway line. Alongside it ran a beaten path, used by workmen when repairs to the line were needed or when routine maintenance and surveys were called for.

There was a rumble in the air and Yorke looked up at the sky. The few scattered clouds were just visible against the lightening sky as the stars faded. The noise and vibration became louder and he realised it was the sound of an approaching train. He plunged into the undergrowth and lay with his face hidden as the train swept by. Glancing up he saw it was a goods carrier and he rejoined the path as the train swayed away in the direction of London. Minutes later he found himself on a bridge and knew he was at the River Arun. If he continued following the track he'd end up about a mile to the west of Arundel itself and so he climbed down the embankment to the river. There he followed a pathway upstream. As the sun came over the horizon its rays hit the majestic walls of Arundel Castle.

Yorke reached his room without being seen. He stripped off, took a shower and flung himself onto his bed. He fell asleep instantly to be woken by a loud knocking on his door.

'Yes?'

'It's me, dad.'

'Hang on a second.' Yorke climbed out of bed and slipped on a robe, courtesy of the hotel. 'Come in, son.'

'Hi, I wondered about breakfast.'

'What time is it?'

'Breakfast ends at ten and it's a quarter to.'

'Give me five minutes and I'll meet you downstairs. Once this is all over we'll do something special. How about a diving trip to somewhere hot?'

'That'll be great.'

'While I'm away have a browse of the internet and see what you can find. Not the Red Sea, mind. Mauritius or Scotland.'

'Dad! Scotland!' He spoke with disgust but departed with a happy smile.

Yorke shaved, showered, dressed and made a phone call but couldn't get hold of the person he wanted. He arrived at the dining room with two minutes to spare. The breakfast buffet was still hot and Yorke helped himself to a plateful of scrambled eggs, bacon and local sausages. The coffee was hot and very good. Dom had the healthy appetite of a growing youth. Corn Flakes was followed by waffles with syrup, fried eggs and bacon.

'That's some combination,' said Yorke with a grin.

'It's what we had in America last year, remember?'

'Sure, I remember. Well, it's your stomach. So enjoy it.'

'What are we doing next?'

'I want you to stay with the *Duck*. I have to go north for possibly two days. I need to know you're safe.' Seeing the crestfallen look on Dom's face Yorke added, 'It's for the best, Dom. If we're to get our lives back there's things I need to do.'

'Like what?'

Yorke ignored the question. 'I'm not happy about leaving you but I don't have any choice. You'll be all right on the boat.'

'Where are you going?'

'To Scotland. But I also need to go to a place near Skegness. There's some stuff I need from there.'

'Why don't we go by boat?'

'It'll take too long. Besides, this is a good haven. I need to know you'll be safe. But keep a low profile. Fix up the TV aerial and watch television and get some DVDs.' Yorke could see the unhappiness in the boy's eyes and almost yielded to Dom's wish to go with him.

'But I can be useful,' argued Dom. 'I can be cover. Two of us travelling together. A father and son, what can be more natural? And I can cover for you if I need to.' Dom lowered his voice. 'You know I'm a good shot with a rifle and a pistol.'

'I know, but shooting up targets is one thing, shooting a man is another. It's not on, old son, really it isn't.' Yorke managed an encouraging smile. 'Listen, I was thinking about the diving trip. Why don't we go away for the whole summer? Cruise the Med in the *Duck*. What do you say? Not only some diving, but wind-surfing and para-sailing.'

Dom shrugged disconsolately. 'Whatever. Yeah. That'll be great.'

'Okay.' Yorke paused, unsure whether or not to involve the youngster any more but he had no choice. 'Listen, I need you to know what's going on. You're my backup if things go wrong. Every operation has headquarters' staff to guard our backs.'

'What about Uncle Phil?'

'I tried phoning him but he's away. I'll try him again later. He's the one I want you to get the information to. He'll know what has to be done.' Yorke paused with a fork of bacon and eggs halfway to his mouth. 'Dom, I can't tell what's going to happen. So we need to cover as many bases as we can. To do that I need backup and I'm afraid you're it. There isn't anybody else. I *need* you on the yacht. You're my ace-in-the-hole.' Yorke could see that his words were having the desired effect and that Dom was looking happier about his role in matters.

'Okay. You can count on me.'

Yorke's smile was one of genuine pleasure. 'I never doubted

it for a second. One more thing.' He paused. He knew there was nobody else. *That* was his dilemma. 'I can also send an emergency signal. It's not to your phone but to the communications system on the *Duck*. If you get the signal, contact Martin or Uncle Phil and tell them where I am. Get one of them to send the police in p.d.q. Okay?'

'Yes, dad.' Dom's voice was small, strained. He cleared his throat. 'I know what to do.'

'Good lad. Right, we'd better pay the bill and get going. Have you packed?'

'No. It'll take about a minute and a half.'

'Same here. We'll meet in the lobby in ten.'

Yorke was standing at the check-out desk when the muted television caught his eye. A picture of the PM's house in Aldinbourne appeared. He wondered what the story was about.

He used his credit card in the name of Stephen Yarrow and he and Dom left the hotel. They stopped off in the village and bought bread and milk before returning to the yacht. Dom knew all about the cameras aboard and waited while Yorke checked the security around the *Duck*. Nobody had been near. They worked the ropes and pulled the dinghy across the intervening narrow stretch of water. The dinghy bounced against the hull and Dom, the painter in his hand, leapt aboard the yacht.

Yorke checked the communications system. He and Dom listened as the men searching for them in the Channel finally admitted defeat and gave up. That had been yesterday evening. There was one final transmission. The boats were ordered to return to Mevagissey.

'Why there?' Yorke asked rhetorically, to which Dom shrugged. 'There are a few jobs you can do about the boat, but I don't need to tell you what.'

'Okay, dad. I'll be fine. Don't worry.'

Yorke put his hands on Dom's shoulders and looked him in the eyes. 'And don't you worry about me. I know what I'm doing. Trust me.'

'Sure, dad. Only . . . take care.'

Yorke gave Dom a hug. 'I will. Now, I'll pack a few things

and get going.' The last thing he did before leaving the yacht was to hand Dom a phone number and e-mail address. 'This is Uncle Phil's number at Hereford. As Adjutant somebody will know how to get hold of him in an emergency.'

'I'll get on with my chores. I'll get the hatchway greased and do that splicing.'

'Good lad. That's the idea.' Standing on the river bank he waved goodbye to Dom, an overnight grip in his hand. He was carrying two guns, the one concealed in the bag was a specially modified Smith & Wesson, with a built in silencer. It held 11 rounds of 9mm Parabellum and had a safety catch on both sides for ambidextrous use. The other, a short-barrelled Walther PPK, was strapped to the calf of his right leg. The jury-rig to hold the gun in place was uncomfortable but he knew he'd get used to it. It was an old gun that had been altered and refurbished, holding 7 rounds of 9mm Shorts.

He struck out across country for a mile before he reached the hamlet of Crossbush. He had timed his departure so that minutes later he was on a train northbound, after picking up a handful of newspapers. As he'd expected they were full of the death and carnage at Gibraltar Point. One or two papers went along with the gas explosion story while others were already threading a huge conspiracy theory around the event. The problem was, as Yorke knew only too well, the conspiracy theorists were much closer to the mark though their conclusions weren't. He alighted at Crawley and took a taxi to the light aircraft field at Gatwick Airport.

Knocking on the door of Captain J. Phillips, Instructor and Planes for Hire, he went into an immaculate office occupied by a middle aged, fit-looking man wearing a pilot's short-sleeved shirt with four stripes on his epaulettes. A young woman sat in front of a computer terminal, typing.

'May I help you?' she smiled pleasantly at Yorke. In her late twenties, she had a wide smile and blonde hair out of a bottle.

'Yes. I'd like to hire a plane.'

'John?'

'I heard, Sue, thanks. Mr?'

'Yarrow. Stephen Yarrow.'

'What can I do for you, Mr Yarrow?'

'I'd like to hire a plane. What do you have?'

'Cessna Skyhawk.'

'Excellent. I've got over two hundred hours on the Skyhawk.'

'Can I see your log book and licence? Coffee?'

'Please. White, no sugar.'

'Coming right up,' said Sue. She busied herself with the coffee machine in the corner. It hadn't been used so far that morning and the fresh smell of ground coffee soon permeated the air.

'Here's my log book and licence,' said Yorke handing over his Pooley's Pilot's Flying Log Book and his pilot's licence.

Phillips flicked through the book, satisfying himself as to Yorke's experience. 'I see you did quite a bit of flying in Florida.'

'I went there to get my licence originally and since then I've taken every opportunity to keep my hours up.'

'I see that. You've flown in some odd places. Gibraltar, Greece, even Egypt.'

'Just the nature of my job. If I've time to spare I like to take a look at a country from the air. It's amazing the difference in aspect you get when you fly around the pyramids.' He didn't mention the numerous flights he'd made which weren't logged. Especially those around the Middle East and parts of the old Republic of Russia.

'Thirty hours on twins as well?'

'Longer range and heavier loads. I'd toyed with the idea of becoming an airline pilot once upon a time.'

'What happened? Thanks, Sue,' Phillips broke off to acknowledge the coffees being handed out.

'Not enough money.'

Phillips smiled. 'Eighty grand a year not enough?'

'Not if you're in the City. And besides, I hear airline pilots have a rotten matrimonial record.'

This time Phillips laughed. 'You're right there. As I know only too well. I'll have to check you out. That okay?'

'Of course. Whenever you're ready.'

'A few questions first.' Phillips lifted a clipboard off a pegged board behind his head and started working his way down a check-off list. Name, address, date-of-birth, medical details, total flying hours and then more pertinent questions regarding flying. All basic stuff to anyone with a Private Pilot's Licence.

'When did you get your PPL?'

'1997. Fort Lauderdale.' Brief questions on procedures followed.

'Okay, that's fine. Let's go and make a circuit. That suit you?'

'Yep. No problem.'

Yorke followed the pilot out of the office and round a corner to a hangar. The doors were wide open and various aircraft were scattered around the building, some with open cowlings as mechanics worked on the engines. Next to the left-hand door stood a new-looking Cessna Skyhawk, its registration emblazoned in red down the side of the white fuselage, GBZPT. It was a sleek and beautiful looking craft, a single-engined, four-seater with a high wing. With the fuselage slung underneath the wings it made for almost 360 degrees of vision.

Phillips handed over a check-off list for the externals and he and Yorke went around the plane. It took a few minutes to check the surfaces, the aileron, elevator and rudder movements, the three tyres, even the cleanliness of the windscreen. Satisfied, Yorke handed back the ticked-off list. They climbed into the cockpit, Yorke on the left, Phillips on the right. This time the pre-start check-list took a lot longer. Happy with that, Yorke went through the starting procedure from engine prime to start-up. The engine noise was barely above that of a formula one racing car.

Phillips sat beside him and said nothing, leaving Yorke to handle everything as though the older pilot wasn't there.

When he was ready Yorke radioed the control tower. 'This is Golf Bravo Zulu Papa Tango, request flight clearance, over.'

'This is control, please taxi . . .' detailed instructions followed and Yorke followed them precisely. At the end of the runway the tiny aircraft was third in line for take-off. When given the order Yorke increased the revs and the plane picked up speed. A third of the way along the runway the plane lifted gracefully into the air. Yorke performed a box turn, each leg 5 miles long, before turning in for finals and his approach. He rapidly went through the landing check-list prior to the Skyhawk kissing the runway and settling on her tricycle under-carriage.

'Very good, Mr Yarrow. Let's taxi back to the office and complete the paperwork and she's all yours. We had full tanks when we started. That's about forty gallons imperial usable. How long do you want her?'

'Thanks. Three days I should think, at the most.'

In the office an imprint of a credit card was taken after establishing the fact that there was sufficient value to cover the hire and insurance costs. A short while later Yorke was back in the air and heading north at a height of 10,000ft, and a speed of 122 knots through the air, 127 knots over the ground thanks to a slight tail wind.

An hour later he was passing over the shoreline of the Wash. King's Lynn was clear to starboard, the ribbon of the Great Ouse sparkling in the sunlight. Ahead he could easily make out Gibraltar Point. Even at that distance he could see the utter devastation caused to the building. Cars were in abundance and uniformed police swarmed the area. It was as he'd expected. Forensic teams would be taking the place apart. The problem was they were all looking in the wrong place.

14

BY THE TIME he was twenty years old János Kadras had killed eleven people, ten men and a woman. The latter had been a prostitute who had tried to steal his wad of cash after an hour of her company. She had thought him asleep. It was the last mistake she ever made. He had pushed a stiletto between the second and third vertebrae, cutting her spinal cord in half. Death was not immediate. All electrochemical functions to her muscles ceased although there was very little pain, merely a warm sensation in her neck. She couldn't breath or move and he'd had to turn her body to face him. János looked deeply into her eyes as realisation of her impending death dawned on her, fear struck just as the spark of life faded. It was, for him, a highly gratifying moment.

He bought a run-down apartment in a crummy area of Paris for less than it was worth. After painting it, he sold it for twice as much as he'd paid. He repeated the process, keeping some apartments to house prostitutes who dealt in heroin and sometimes a little cocaine, still a relatively unused drug by the ordinary consumer. Ruthlessly he built a portfolio of slum properties. From the combined incomes of the drugs, prostitution and rents he began buying up city centre sites and building multi-storey car parks. Using inflated valuations of the slum properties he borrowed heavily from the banks and built more car parks in other French cities. His cash flow was excellent thanks to the illegal part of his business. When the law got too close it frightened him sufficiently to sell off the slum buildings and connected trades and go legitimate. By his mid-twenties he was worth a conservative ten million pounds. He never bothered with French valuations. He was still set on going to England. At age 25 he arrived in style and set up offices in the City of London. His first act was to change his name legally to John Kennedy.

He stayed clear of all illegal activities. Then in September 1976 sterling collapsed and the Chancellor of the Exchequer, Denis Healey, was forced to borrow from the International Monetary Fund. The London Stock market fell heavily and property values went through the floor. From being rich, Kennedy was bankrupt with all the major lenders screaming for their cash.

That was when he remembered the advantages of his illegal operations in France. He quickly set up deals with his old colleagues and began moving in large quantities of heroin into Britain. The stumbling block he hit was unexpected. Established gangs didn't like him muscling in on their turf. Also he couldn't make the deals quickly enough and was forced to buy time from the banks by the simple expedient of explaining that if they called in his loans they would lose a great deal of money. They responded by agreeing and imposing stiff penalties. The banks gave him six months to pay in full.

His British connections and the people who worked for him were utterly respectable. As far as he was concerned, contemptibly so. He had a fortune in heroin stashed in England and no means of distribution. He called on his old friends from France to lend a hand. They were delighted at the opportunity. At this time there was very little gun culture in the UK. Kennedy introduced one. Ruthlessly he and his men exploited the use of black gangs in south London many of whom were from French Africa and spoke English as a second language. They inhabited a twilight world of slum living made bearable by using drugs. They preyed on their own people turning a life of misery into hell on earth. But they made money. A lot of it. Kennedy began repaying the banks. It was the beginning of his second empire, this time founded on crime. He concentrated his efforts on building cash businesses that enabled him to launder drug money, establishing over 200 coffee outlets that thrived beyond expectation. Next he built a chain of pubs, buying up large old properties such as banks and railway stations to convert into suitably welcoming hostelries. No music, no slot machines, good food and excellent beer at affordable prices. Ideal for washing drug money through. Even without the illegal income his businesses thrived. And whenever he was tempted to legitimise his operations he remembered the bad times and decided to stay with the drug dealing.

The cross-connection to terrorism was almost by accident. A happy accident to be sure.

There was a dip in the ground. If he flew in low from the sea he would be out of sight of the destroyed house. He kept at wave-top height, lifted the plane over the cliff with only feet to spare and came down on flat, even land. Yorke taxied to a low, corrugated iron hut. He was about a mile from the house as he sat in the cockpit, the engine running, the prop no longer turning, examining the countryside around him. Nothing stirred. Finally, as satisfied as he could be, he pulled the cut-out and switched off the engine. Climbing down from the plane he left the door unlocked. There was no such thing as a fast getaway with an aeroplane, but even a few seconds could make all the difference.

He made his way through a small wood of stunted trees, prevented from blossoming to their full glory by the poor marshland soil. He went slowly and carefully. At the edge of the trees he halted by the bole of a tree and used a high-powered telescope to examine the area. The badly damaged building was brought into sharp relief. He could even see the striped police tape warning people not to cross the boundary as well as signs stating that the building was dangerous and in danger of collapsing.

Taking his time, he watched as uniformed police and plain-clothes men and women walked purposefully around the scene. Ambulances were drawn up and bodies were still being carried out. It took will-power to prevent the surge of anger and hatred from over-whelming his senses. Off to one side, sitting forlorn and neglected was a low concrete building a hundred yards from the house. Yorke studied the ground around the building but saw nobody taking any interest. Hanging an ID card around his neck he stepped out of the trees and boldly crossed the intervening lawn. If he was seen no one took any notice of him. His ID identified him as a superintendent of police, special branch. It was a position and organisation nobody would argue with or question. This was the third time he'd used it. If anyone questioned his identity and ran a check on him the computer would list him as Superintendent Stephen Yarrow, giving him a clean bill of health. The ID was real, the legend was fake.

The low building was about twelve feet long by six wide. The walls were eight feet high, made of brick coated with roughcast, the roof flat felt. A green painted door was locked, a single side window was coated with dust and cobwebs. The oddity was the punch-pad lock. He pressed a series of numbers and was rewarded by the sound of a whirring and scraping as locks opened. A glance around showed nobody was in sight and he stepped inside.

The room was bare, the floor solid concrete apart from a trapdoor set in the middle. Closing the door behind him, Yorke stepped to the trapdoor, hooked a finger into a ring along one edge and raised it wide open. He walked down concrete steps, closing the lid behind him. It was pitch black. From his bum-bag he took a pair of electronically controlled night-vision goggles and switched them on. An updated version of the old NVGs, these were chip-controlled and reacted in the event of a bright light suddenly shining in the wearer's face. Light blindness was now a thing of the past. They were also far easier and more comfortable to wear. He was at the end of a corridor that led straight to the house.

Although bare lights were embedded in the roof above his head, Yorke didn't switch them on. Instead he walked silently towards the far end, his feet making little sound on the stone slabs of the tunnel. A rat was walking towards him and suddenly stopped in alarm, his whiskers and nose twitching as it tested the air. It couldn't have liked what it sensed for it turned tail and ran, vanishing in a crack in the wall. The cats in residence had kept the rats at bay but they had already returned like the vermin they were. As he approached the end more cracks appeared until the walls and ceiling were honeycombed with them. Only the floor appeared intact.

A ten digit electronic lock was on the right-hand side. Yorke entered the required four numbers and the door opened a crack towards him. There was no handle. Hooking a finger around the door he opened it a few degrees. He continued opening the door until it was wide enough for him to step through.

Yorke was in the west end of the upper basement. Here the main computers were stored, linked to the offices upstairs by protected cables. Yorke thought of the irony of the precautions that *Phoenix* had taken to protect its true purpose and to look after its personnel and the information it collected. All wiped out in one devastating attack. Something not even Desmond Kavanagh had predicted in spite of his almost paranoid tendencies.

The dark room appeared as bright as day. Yorke could see that everything was covered in a fine coating of dust and from the look of the scuff marks on the floor and surfaces the police had already been inside. One thing Yorke was sure about. The encryption processes used by the organisation would take a great deal of cracking – weeks rather than days. However, one fact was indisputable, the computers *would* be broken into and their secrets read. The question was, who would be doing the reading?

It took only seconds to establish the fact that the backup electric power was operating. Sitting at a computer terminal he switched the machine on. A series of passwords got him into the guts of the computer. After a few questions it was obvious that somebody had already tried accessing the data. To date, whoever it was, hadn't been successful. He began downloading the files he wanted. New suppression techniques enabled him to transfer a vast amount of information quickly, even so he had to be selective as the amount of information contained in the system was vast. He particularly wanted one personnel file; Evelyn Beckworth's. Had Evelyn left before the attack? Where was she now? Had she been to the police? And if so, what had she told them?

He ran through a number of files to no avail. He knew Kavanagh's propensity was to use code words based on WWII, so what was appropriate? With a smile of inspiration he typed in "Overlord". Yorke spent nearly forty minutes finding and downloading the information he wanted on to a 1gb USB high speed, pen drive. Finally, he was as satisfied as he'd ever be. His final act was to send a deletion instruction into the computer. Unlike other systems, after answering a series of questions, he was able to erase all memory from the computer, including the re-cycle bin and the hard-drive. It was, he thought, too much like closing the stable door after the horse has done a bunk, but there was nothing more he could do.

Powering off the computer, he taped the pen drive to his back, alongside his spine. A quick search and pat down often missed that part of the body, whereas if he carried it in a bag or a pocket it would inevitably be found.

Retracing his steps along the corridor, Yorke paused in the doorway of the outbuilding, removing the NVGs and placing them in the bag while he searched the landscape. It appeared clear but he stayed where he was, ever vigilant, ever careful. There was no movement but his ears detected different sounds. In the background he could hear distant voices, a car engine starting, an occasional yell. Nearer to hand the breeze rustled the leaves in the trees and hedgerows. All seemed peaceful and, in view of what had occurred, normal. But he was troubled. Something wasn't right. Frowning, his eyes quartered the land-scape. Nothing. So what was bugging him? Birds! There was no sight or sound of birds in the offing. The thought sent a chill through him as he searched more closely. Birds had the sense to stop chirruping and singing when there was a poten-tial predator in the offing. They were exercising that sense right then.

A few seconds later he spotted something behind the bole of a tree. It was the hint of a moving shadow where no shadow should be. He stayed completely still and looked a few degrees away from the tree. He knew that peripheral vision saw more clearly than direct sight. Could detect more. There it was again. The shadow had taken substance and was more clearly defined but as what he had no idea. Was there somebody kneeling? It could be a shoulder. Or a knee. Yes. There was the shoulder. Now a head looking around the tree. Yorke frowned. Who the hell was it? Police? The attackers back again?

The dark shape turned colour. Blue. A paler face. Black hair. Soft features. A woman. Yorke decided his best option was boldness and he stepped out of the doorway and closed the door behind him. He walked away, leaving the copse of trees on his left, skirting around the figure, heading back the way he'd come. He kept moving his head, looking around him. His legend was very good but he preferred not to put it to the test.

He moved further left, closer to the trees. A stillness had descended over the countryside, not even the slightest of breezes disturbing the peace. The noises in the background were fading when he heard footsteps on his left. He kept walking purposefully away, his nonchalance an act as the adrenaline began pumping, heightening his senses. Footsteps and the rustling of undergrowth was coming from two different directions. Turning his head to the left he saw a flash of blue and heard something about thirty degrees right of the woman. Dark shadows hardened and two men appeared. They were dressed in police uniforms, one a sergeant the other a constable. Both men were armed. They saw him and called on him to halt. He did, watching the men closely, aware that something was seriously wrong.

At that moment the woman in the blue dress appeared and approached. Yorke couldn't help noticing how attractive she was. Not exactly pretty, but striking. The two policemen looked at her, their attention flicking between Yorke and her.

Yorke's attention was on the policemen. Their uniforms were correct but they were bogus. Armed police didn't carry their automatic pistols, they were holstered until needed.

Furthermore, whatever guns they were carrying they weren't Glocks, the weapon of choice carried by the British police. Finally, *no* policeman used a silenced gun. He would have liked a private chat with the two men, but with the woman in attendance there was little he could do about it.

Belligerently the constable said, 'You! What are you doing here?'

The question was addressed to Yorke who changed his demeanour and marched briskly towards the bogus policemen. Feigning anger he said, 'Don't speak to me like that.' He was now only a few yards from the men who were regarding him with suspicion tinged with condescension. Yorke recognised the type. Tough men with guns in their hands. They thought themselves in control of the situation. However, the guns weren't actually pointing at him.

Before either man could speak, Yorke said, 'My name is Superintendent Yarrow.' This was the time to defuse the situation, not make it worse. Hence he didn't ask to see their identity cards. He doubted they carried one, trusting to their uniforms to give them all the cover they needed. Instead he flashed his own ID at them. Except they'd made a few mistakes when it came to their guns. Yorke could see they were carrying Smith and Wesson Third Generation Pistols, the same gun he had – far too sophisticated and expensive for the police in any country, never mind the UK.

Before the two men could respond the woman approached and said, 'My name is Catherine Colbert. I'm a journalist.'

Yorke turned to her immediately and said, 'You have no right to be here. I must ask you to leave before I have you arrested.'

'I represent the press,' Catherine bristled with suppressed anger, 'and have the right to ask questions.'

Yorke summoned up a smile which wasn't reciprocated. 'You do indeed and I have the right not to reply.'

His eyes were on the woman who was standing only a few yards away, but his attention was on the two men to whom he'd sidled closer when he'd turned to face Catherine. There was palpable tension in the air and Yorke knew they were only moments away from possible violence.

'I insist on going across to the house and conducting interviews.' She turned to the two gunmen. 'Why don't I start with you? Can you tell me what happened?' Taking a small recorder out of her shoulder bag she added, 'If the damage was caused by a gas explosion why are armed police patrolling the area? Can you tell me that?'

The two men exchanged uneasy glances. Yorke could guess what was going through their minds. If they refused to speak and she went to the house and mentioned an armed patrol all hell could break loose and they would be on the receiving end. By the same token, if they assumed he was for real, he'd be asking awkward questions pretty soon as well. The only thing that had probably saved him so far was the appearance of the reporter. The four of them were standing far enough from the house to be hidden from view and certainly the sound of a silenced gun shot wouldn't be heard at that distance. It was as though a telepathic thought passed between the three men, with Catherine oblivious to the danger she was in.

The bogus policemen were beginning to raise their guns when Yorke made his move. He had had already noted that the sergeant's safety catch was up for safe, while the constable's was horizontal and the pistol ready to fire. Yorke stepped into the man, turning his back to him. Grabbing the gunman's arm by the wrist he clamped his other hand around the barrel of the gun, aimed and jerked all in one smooth motion. The gun fired with barely a cough shooting the sergeant through the chest, throwing him onto his back, his arms and legs outspread. The other man didn't respond quickly enough. Middle-aged looking police superintendents didn't react as Yorke had done and the gunman was shocked into indecision for the second Yorke needed. He slammed his elbow into the man's midriff, knocking the wind out of him while at the same time pointing the gun at the ground. He didn't want a stray bullet hitting the reporter. Yorke slammed the flat of his hand across the gunman's neck and the man collapsed unconscious.

Catherine stood still in utter and complete shock. The violence was all over in a matter of seconds and her startled wits were just returning to her. She opened her mouth to scream when Yorke crossed the few yards to her and clamped a hand over her mouth.

'Shut up, for God's sake,' he hissed in her ear. 'There may be more of them around.' He removed his hand from her mouth.

'He's d . . . d . . . dead,' Catherine stammered, staring at the body, blood beginning to seep out of its back and onto the green grass. 'You killed a policeman.'

'He wasn't a policeman. Neither of them are. They were about to shoot us. We have to get away. Come on.'

Yorke turned to go but Catherine stood where she was, her head moving back and forth between the two inert bodies, her hand to her mouth.

'Come on! We must move!'

'No! No! I don't know who you are. I saw you kill this man and knock out the other. I'm going to the house.' She turned to flee.

Yorke leapt after her and grabbed her arm before she could go more than a couple of paces. 'Listen to me! They aren't policemen. Trust me. They may be wearing uniforms but they also have silenced guns of a type not used by the British police.' Reaching into his pocket he withdrew a warrant card. 'Look, for Christ's sake. I'm a superintendent. I haven't a clue what's going on only that we were in danger. These men were going to shoot us.'

'How do you know?'

'I do. That's all you need to know. We have to get out of here.'

'I'm going to the house. I'll tell them what's happened. And about you. I read your name. Stephen Yarrow. I'll let them sort it out.' She was getting her equilibrium back. She'd been twice in the Gaza and once in Iraq and had seen more than her fair share of dead and mutilated bodies. After the initial shock her reporter's instinct was already at work. She had a story. A cracker. A senior police officer shoots down one policeman and incapacitates a second. It would be front page news. It was a pity she couldn't get a picture of Yarrow. Still, she had more than enough. Excitement coursed through her.

Yorke needed time to get away and was about to render her unconscious long enough to make good his escape when there came a yell. Looking over his shoulder he saw four men in paramilitary outfits stepping out of the trees, each carrying a weapon. One of them pointed towards him and Catherine and the men raised their guns and aimed in their direction. Yorke's reactions were instinctive. He flung himself onto the reporter knocking her to the ground as she began to protest.

'Shut up, you fool they're shooting at us.'

'Don't talk rubbish . . .' There had been no sound of shots. However, a lump of dirt exploded in Catherine's face and she screamed.

'They're using silenced weapons,' Yorke said with a calm he wasn't feeling. Reaching down to his right calf he took out the unsilenced Walther and fired four rounds at the men who were now about two hundred metres away. If they hadn't been grouped so close together he doubted he would have hit anyone at that range but by luck a shot struck one man in the abdomen. That and the sound of the firing sent the others diving for cover. Even as they hit the ground Yorke was up, dragging Catherine with him, sprinting away from the gunmen and away from the house. Already the sound of the shooting had brought men from the destroyed building to investigate the noise. Yorke looked back over his shoulder and fired the last three rounds in the magazine at the men still prone on the ground. He hoped it would encourage them to keep their heads down and at the same time attract more attention from the house.

Catherine screamed and stumbled, clutching the top of her left arm. Blood seeped through her fingers. 'I've been hit!' Hysteria clutched at her throat.

'Faster, for God's sake,' Yorke yelled. A sound like an angry bee buzzed past his ear and he hunched his shoulders. He expected at any moment to be shot down and the feeling made a spot between his shoulders itch.

Catherine stumbled again and he grabbed her arm and held her up. Her breath was coming in ragged gasps and her legs threatened to give way. Whistles sounded behind and a loud-speaker rent the air ordering them to halt. Yorke glanced back and to his relief he saw that policemen from the house were converging on the men dressed as soldiers. They were up and retreating towards the trees, carrying their fallen comrade with them. A dip in the ground and they were out of sight.

'Keep going,' Yorke urged Catherine.

Catherine tripped and would have fallen if Yorke hadn't grabbed her uninjured arm. Sobs escaped her lips as she stumbled again. Yorke debated with himself whether to leave her or not but he had no idea who was behind them. Was it the legitimate police or the enemy, whoever they were? He caught a glimpse of his plane in the distance and made Catherine move a little faster. As he did so he heard the unmistakable sound of a helicopter and looking to his left saw one rise in the sky and swoop over the cliff and out to sea. He'd seen the same type only the day before when it had ferried the men who had attacked the house.

'Not far now,' he encouraged the reporter.

They reached the Cessna and he unlocked the passenger door. Helping her into the cockpit he ran around the front and climbed into the pilot's seat. Hurriedly he worked his way through the start-up checks, ran up the engine and let it warm while he completed the post start-up list. In under a minute he was taxiing the plane and lining up for take-off. He opened the throttle and in less than a hundred metres he had the plane in the air and banking to starboard and out to sea. At 1,000ft he levelled off and headed directly east for about five miles. Then he began quartering the sea, looking for a ship.

Catherine had regained her breath and was sitting in fearful dejection alongside him. Her arm ached, and there was a rip in her jacket where the bullet had gone through. Carefully she removed the jacket and looked at the red stain on her white blouse.

Yorke glanced at the wound. 'Another inch and you'd have

been in trouble. Gunshot wounds aren't like you see in the
movies. The muscle and tendon damage can be serious. Here,'
he reached under the seat and extracted a First Aid kit. 'take
this. There are probaly antiseptic wipes and plasters inside.'

'Thanks.' Her voice was husky with stress. She shuddered.
She'd never been shot at before and the experience had terrified her. Taking the box she found the wipes and tentatively
cleaned away the blood that had seeped from the wound. 'It
stings like hell.'

'I'm sure it does.'

'Who are you?'

'You saw my name on the warrant card. Stephen Yarrow.
More to the point, who are you?'

'My name is Catherine Colbert. I'm a freelance journalist.
What on earth's happening? Why have you kidnapped me?'

Yorke looked at her in utter astonishment. 'Kidnapped you?
What the hell are you talking about? I was saving your life,
lady. You want to go back? I can land and throw you out if
that's what you really want.'

She stared into his brown eyes that glared fiercely at her.
Catherine shook her head. 'I . . . I guess not.' Her reporter's
instinct began to take hold and she asked, 'So tell me, what's
going on?'

'I don't know. How's your arm?'

'It stings.'

'You were lucky. We were lucky. That was too close for
comfort.'

With another sigh, Catherine covered the wound with a
plaster. As she did, she asked, 'You said you're a policeman.
Are you?'

'Sort of.'

'For God's sake, either you are or you aren't. Which is it?'

He decided to prevaricate. 'I'm a cop undercover. I use my
ID when I need to, which isn't often.'

'Aren't you a bit senior for such work?' she asked slyly.

Yorke knew he was on dangerous ground but before he could
answer he saw what he was looking for. In the distance was a

merchant ship of about 20,000 tonnes and sitting on it's stern deck was a Kamov Helic-C. An unusual helicopter to find on the stern of a civilian ship.

Yorke headed towards the sun, turned the Cessna, until the sun was directly behind him and dived towards the ship. At half a mile and 500ft above sea level he clearly made out the name – the S.S. Invergowrie. He turned the plane sharply away and headed towards the sun again, preventing any lookouts from getting a good look at the plane and possibly seeing the registration along the fuselage.

'What are you doing?'

'The helo on the back of that ship took the men who shot at us. I wanted to find out her name. I may be able to trace the owner. Perhaps then I can begin to find some answers about what the hell's happening.'

'What do you think is going on?'

Yorke shook his head. 'I've no idea.' Anger coursed through him and he clenched the control column until the white of his knuckles showed. 'I only know some extraordinary men and women have been killed. I intend to find out who's responsible which I guess will lead me to why.'

'What will you do then?'

Yorke glanced at her. She was staring out of the cockpit window but, sensing his look, she turned her head towards him. Considering what she'd been through, she appeared calm enough.

'That all depends on what I find.'

The bleak words coupled with his stare sent a shiver down Catherine's spine. He was not, she thought, the kind of man to cross.

For the next few minutes Yorke busied himself with the plane. Air traffic control had to be contacted and details of their flight path passed for approval and monitoring. Height and speed were agreed. He set the automatic pilot and relaxed.

'Where are we going?'

'Scotland,' came the terse reply. Now that she was safe Yorke wanted rid of her. There was no way he could afford to have her tag along. Already she knew too much and had seen more than was good for her.

'Scotland's a big place.'

He sighed. He had no intention of telling her his destination was Crieff Hydro. 'We'll land at a small airfield near Cumbernauld. It's on the outskirts of Glasgow. From there you can get a taxi to the station and into Glasgow.'

'And where will you be going?'

'Elsewhere,' was the abrupt answer.

Catherine was about to protest but saw the look on his face and wisely decided to say nothing. The flight north was uneventful apart from the few alterations of course required by ATC and the necessity to go around a large anvil-shaped, dark cloud.

The plane landed with the slightest bump on the oddly undulating runway. Yorke had been there before and taxied over to the hard-standing. He was greeted by a member of the ground staff and taken to the office. There he paid the landing fee, arranged refuelling and phoned for a taxi.

While they were waiting, Catherine excused herself and went into the Ladies. Using her mobile she telephoned a local car rental service and arranged to have them meet her at the railway station. A short while later, in hostile silence, Yorke and Catherine left the airport in the back of a taxi. After the station the taxi was to take Yorke to AAA car hire.

When the taxi drew up Yorke said to her, 'Have a good journey and goodbye.'

'Thank you,' Catherine replied stiffly.

Even as the taxi drew away Catherine was signing the necessary papers to take hire of a nondescript Nissan. A few minutes later, armed with directions, she set off after the taxi. She arrived at the Triple A garage in time to see Yorke climb into a Ford Mondeo and drive off. She kept well back and began to follow.

Yorke turned north on the A80 and then towards Stirling on the motorway. Using the hands-free on his mobile he telephoned directory enquiries and then rang Crieff Hydro.

Catherine had no fieldcraft and no training, but had enough sense to stay back, closing up only if a turning was sign-posted ahead. The road was reasonably busy and she kept three or four cars between them. Yorke drove within the speed limit, not wishing to draw attention to himself. The gleaming silver car was easy to follow and Catherine allowed herself the luxury of wondering where he was going.

At the services Yorke turned off for Stirling and then followed the road to Springkerse Retail Park. Once there he left the car and went into an electrical retailers. He returned to the car thirty minutes later, carrying a computer case and box. Placing them in the boot, he casually looked around the car park as he climbed into the driver's seat and made his way back to the motorway.

Just after Dunblane, on the A9, Yorke indicated he was turning off and Catherine followed, nervously aware there were no other cars between them. She slowed right down, giving Yorke a chance to pull away. Around a bend and Yorke floored the accelerator, the car speeding away rapidly. Through Braco and past the old Roman fort and there was nothing behind him. He cut off the main road at Garrick and headed for Muthill. At the edge of the village, where the road rejoined the A822 he came to a halt and waited. He didn't have long. The Nissan he'd noticed back on the motorway swept past and he caught a glimpse of the driver. A wry grin parted his lips.

15

YORKE WAITED HALF an hour before continuing his journey. As he entered the small town of Crieff he followed the signs to the Hydro. The roads twisted and turned until he came to the entrance to the hotel complex and drove through the gates. The imposing main building was on his right as he stopped at the car park and alighted. He paused for a moment to savour the view and look up the hill at the self-catering cottages. He wondered which one was occupied by the Prime Minister's family. The question he needed answered was whether or not the PM was acting under coercion or voluntarily.

At reception he gave an imprint of a different credit card and checked in. With his grip and two computer bags he went up the stairs to a second floor room overlooking the car park and the lodges. The first thing he did was to call Dom.

'Hi, son!'

'Dad! Where are you?'

'In Scotland. A small town called Crieff. I'm staying at a hotel. Want to check out the lat and long?'

'Sure, dad. I'll do it right now. Fifty six degrees, twenty-two minutes north, three degrees fifty-one minutes west.'

Yorke could hear the uplift in Dom's voice. He knew it was unfair on the fifteen year old to wait on the boat but Yorke saw no alternative. Sending him back to school was not an option. It was possible Dom would be ignored, no longer part of the equation as far as his attackers were concerned but he didn't dare take the chance.

'I can refine that down to hundredths.'

'I know you can, Dom. Don't bother right now. Switch it

off otherwise the reading wanders and eventually goes haywire. For some reason the fix only lasts a few minutes. We think it's to do with the satellite but aren't sure. Martin's working on it.'

'Okay, dad.'

'Is everything quiet?'

'Sure. I've stayed aboard. It's just . . .' his voice rallied. 'It's just, I guess, I'm feeling lonely.'

'That's perfectly natural. But it won't be for too long. Nobody been around, bothering you?'

'Not a soul. Is it all right if I go into the village this evening and buy some fish and chips?'

Yorke hesitated. 'Of course it is. If anybody asks what you're doing tell them you're on a holiday with me and I'm in the pub. Try not to get into conversation too much as it's easy to trip yourself up and say the wrong thing or contradict yourself. Don't make anyone suspicious, okay?'

'Sure, dad. You can count on me.'

'I know I can. Look, I have to go. It's now 16.28. I'll try and call again before midnight. Okay?'

'Okay, dad. I ran up an aerial and now have wireless connection here. What about you?'

'Let me check.' Yorke powered up his PDA. 'Got it. Web meeting?'

'Great, dad! I'll be on from 23.15. What's the meeting name and password?

'Use Crieff and outlaw.'

'Right. See you then.'

Reluctantly, Yorke made his farewells and broke the connection. There was another option open to him that was extremely attractive. Make a run for it. He had money. He and Dom could vanish. Go and live a pleasant life in some other country. He'd always fancied Switzerland or Italy. Sighing, he shook his head. He couldn't do it. Something was rotten at the heart of the British government and he appeared to be the only person in a position to do anything about it. Whether or not he'd succeed was another question. However, he knew he could never live with himself if he cut and ran. The British people may not have been aware of it but it was all out war. At stake was one of the greatest and oldest democracies in the world. Yorke sat down and closed his eyes for a moment.

After a few moments he'd made up his mind. Taking the pen drive he plugged it into his PDA. One of the programmes he'd downloaded gave him access to every government data base in the land. He accessed the vehicle licensing centre in Swansea and tapped in a car registration number. He learnt the name of the hire company that owned it and telephoned them.

'I'm sorry to trouble you,' he began, 'but I'm a friend of Ms Catherine Colbert. She hired a car from you earlier today?'

'Possibly, sir,' was the cagey reply.'

'Look, all I want you to do, should she contact you or when she returns is give her a message. Can you do that?'

'Certainly, sir.

'Tell her Stephen Yarrow called and give her my mobile number.' He related the number, thanked the person and broke the connection. *She doesn't know it, but Ms Colbert is about to have the scoop of her life.*

Changing the file, Yorke checked the latest additions to the system. He was relieved to see that the information brought back by Jack Banyon, Ali Hossan and himself had been loaded. There hadn't been time to read or interpret the information. He browsed through different files, taking notes, writing down names and places. None of it meant much. He didn't have the overall picture of Desmond Kavanagh and Yorke knew he had a lot to learn. The task was daunting. He switched back to the programme giving him access to government data bases and put in the name of the ship he'd spotted in the North Sea. The S.S. Invergowrie was registered to a Panamanian company. He continued searching. The company was in turn owned by a bank registered in Montserrat which was owned by . . . So it went on. Forty-five minutes later he traced ownership to a Swiss company whose total shares were owned by a trust. The Goodchild and Everest Trust was rich – over a billion dollars in assets – with no named individuals. A dead-end.

He changed files again. This time hopping to the personnel

file of Kavanagh's secretary, Evelyn Beckworth. There wasn't much. She was a spinster, aged 48, lived with an ailing mother, had spent her working life as a civil servant before joining *Phoenix*, listed her hobbies as travelling and reading and hadn't had so much as a parking ticket or speeding fine. She'd lived an exemplary life to date. *Was she*, Yorke wondered, *still alive?* He made a note of her address and telephone number.

His mobile rang and he glanced at the screen. He didn't recognise the number. 'Hullo?'

Catherine's voice greeted him suspiciously. 'Is that Stephen Yarrow?'

'Catherine! You got my message.'

'Evidently. I called the car hire firm to arrange returning the car out of hours and they gave me your number.'

'Where are you?'

'Why?'

'Look, we can spend all night playing twenty questions. You followed me. I lost you. I now wish to rectify that. I have a story that will blow your mind. Do you want it?'

Her journalistic instinct immediately got the better of her and she replied, 'Yes.' Just like that; no questions, no hesitation.

'Good. So please tell me, where are you?'

'At the Stirling Services. I stopped for a coffee.'

'Good. I'm at Crieff Hydro. It'll take you about an hour to get here. It's a busy place. Don't bother registering but come into reception and up to my room.' He gave here the number.

'And where am I sleeping?'

Yorke grinned. 'You aren't shy, are you?'

'No dammit. But I don't leap into bed with just anybody, not even for a Pulitzer Prize winning story.'

'I hear you. Rest assured, I don't wish to sleep with you. I've a bedroom and sitting room. That do you?'

'All right. Expect me in an hour.' Catherine broke the connection.

There was a kettle in the room and Yorke pensively made himself a cup of instant coffee. The sitting room he was in was comfortably furnished with a sofa, two armchairs, occasional tables, a desk, a bookcase with paperbacks and tourist books for the area, and a TV with DVD player. A sign said there was a library of videos and DVDs downstairs. The sofa did not look particularly inviting but on the other hand he hadn't been expecting much sleep that night.

He continued working on the PDA, taking notes, making connections. When it came, the knock on the door surprised him.

Yorke opened the door to Catherine, standing nervously with a small knapsack in one hand and a new suitcase in the other.

'I don't remember seeing this before,' he greeted her, taking the case, ushering her in.

'I stopped in the town and bought a few necessities. Nice room.'

'The bedroom's through there. Would you like a coffee or something?'

'Tea, please.'

'Coming right up.'

Now she was there Yorke was having second thoughts. But the fact was he couldn't see any alternative. Catherine spent a few minutes in the other room before returning. With her she had a small tape-recorder, stenographer's pad and a fistful of pencils.

'What are those for?' Yorke nodded at her hands as he offered her the cup.

'I can take diction. For the story,' she added lamely.

Yorke shook his head. 'It's not that easy.'

'It never is,' she replied dryly. 'So what is it?'

'Look, now I'm about to tell you it sounds ludicrous and melodramatic. First, you have to understand I don't know everything. A lot is supposition. However, I have ideas to confirm my suspicions which is one of the reasons I'm here.'

'In this beautiful place?' She looked at Yorke in utter astonishment.

'Yes. I'll explain shortly. But I also need your help.'

'My help? How?' Catherine was bristling with suspicion of

her own. She ran a worried hand through her hair and thought
longingly of a cigarette.

'This is going to take some time. Have you eaten?'

'What? No. But now you come to mention it I am hungry.'

'We'll get food delivered. There's a menu on the desk.' They
settled for sandwiches and bottled water. While they were
waiting Yorke began his story.

'The organisation I worked for, the one that was attacked
and destroyed was set up to fight organised crime. Occasionally,
our operations spilled over into anti-terrorist work but not often.
It wasn't our remit. The problem is that crime and terrorism
work hand in glove.'

'So what did you do? What form did these operations take?'

'Primarily we accumulated information. Much of it was
passed to the relevant authorities all over the world. Usually,
the people we dealt with had no idea where we got our information from and we never told them.'

Catherine had a flash of inspiration. 'I take it this information was gotten illegally?'

Yorke was sitting opposite her and watched as she crossed
one shapely leg over another.

'Let's just say that the evidence we acquired could never
be used in a court of law. It's why the government was keen
to keep certain individuals in Bellmarsh Prison. We know
they're terrorists but wouldn't be able to prove it. The dog's
dinner they have isn't working as the last bomb showed.' Two
individuals who had been held under the anti-terrorism act of
2003 had been allowed out of prison with others of their ilk.
The curfews and home-detentions hadn't worked. The two men
had died in a suicide bombing attack which had killed 106
innocent people and maimed hundreds more. Yorke continued.
'Even so, there were voices in Britain that said it was a price
worth paying for ensuring civil liberties. Naturally, the price
had been paid by others.'

'And you don't think so?'

He shrugged, ignoring the question. 'Sometimes we were
able to supply information that enabled the police to get a

warrant and make arrests. Sometimes, the information we had was overwhelming but unusable.'

'So what did you do then?'

Yorke thought for a moment and then replied, 'Let's just say they didn't get away with it.'

It took a few moments for the implication of what he was saying to sink in and she said, 'You *killed* them?' Her voice rose as indignation and revulsion swept through her. 'Is that what you're saying? What about due process? Innocent until proven guilty?'

'I'm not saying that. You're assuming it. Let's leave it at that. The organisation I worked for no longer exists. It was wiped out in an armed attack that was quasi-military. I know we have a traitor at the heart of the British Establishment, although I don't think he's a volunteer.'

'Who is it?'

'I'm not ready to tell you yet. But I will, I promise. I need to check a few things out first.'

Catherine shook her head. 'I'm not sure about all this.'

'What in hell do you mean?' Yorke asked more aggressively than he'd intended.

'I think we should go straight to the police.'

'Christ!' He leapt out of his chair and began pacing the room. 'Have you heard a word I've been saying? We wouldn't live twenty-four hours. Look,' he was almost pleading now, 'you met some of those men today. Christ, you've a bullet wound to prove it. They shot first with *no* intention of asking questions after. Get real, Catherine.' Seeing the obstinate look settling on her face he said, 'Okay, I'll make a deal with you.'

'What kind of deal?'

'You check out the files I lifted from Gibraltar Point. I've made a start. You can use anything you find. But bear in mind, we're looking for names. We need to find who the top people are.'

'What will we do then?' She couldn't keep the sarcasm out of her voice. 'Kill them?'

Yorke sighed. 'Not this time. We'll hand the information

over to the appropriate authorities.' He held up his hand as she began to nod vigorously. 'Only not until I tell you. Deal?'

'Deal!' She held out her hand and Yorke shook it.

Neither of them intended keeping to their side of the agreement.

A waiter arrived with a tray of sandwiches and the water. While they ate Yorke continued telling Catherine about the now defunct *Phoenix* organisation and the events during and after the attack. From her sceptical look he wondered how much of his story she believed. Not a lot, it appeared from her expression.

In exasperation, he said, 'It's the truth, damn it. Why don't you believe me?'

Catherine looked uncomfortable for a second. 'I don't know,' she paused. 'It's just so unbelievable.'

Yorke acknowledged her sentiment. 'What chance is there of convincing the authorities if you think I'm lying in spite of you being shot at?'

Instinctively Catherine put her hand to the slight graze on her arm and nodded. 'Already it seems like something I read about, or seen in a movie. Does that make sense?'

Nodding, Yorke said, 'Of course. The total abject fear of getting shot and running for your life has to be dealt with. The mind plays tricks. You don't forget the incident, that's not possible, but you do forget the emotion that went with it. It's how we cope.' Yorke looked at his watch. 'Let's get working on the computer. I need to go out in an hour.'

'Where are you going?'

'I'm looking for somebody. Don't worry, I won't be far. The person is here at the Hydro.'

'I wasn't worried, merely curious. What are you hoping to learn from the computer?'

'I downloaded a pile of files. Whenever we have an operation . . . I should say, had an operation . . . it was given a code name. Kavanagh loved to use code words from the Second World War. Operation Gold, for instance, was named after one of the beaches for the D-Day landings. I knew he was working on something very big indeed and when I went into the system the obvious name was Operation Overlord. That's what we have on the pen drive.'

Catherine said, 'I could use a proper drink.'

'Wine?'

'Please. Red.'

Ringing room service, Yorke placed the order before replacing the receiver and then said to Catherine, 'I've merely browsed through the information. If it's half right it's dynamite. If, as I believe, it's one hundred percent accurate, then governments will fall.'

'That's one hell of a big claim.' Catherine was sitting with her shoes off and feet tucked under her. A second button on her blouse had come undone and the sight was distracting Yorke.

'That's as maybe, but it's true. You'll understand when you read what's on there.' To distract his thoughts and eyes, he stood up and walked over to the sideboard to make a cup of coffee. Glancing in a mirror, he saw Catherine smiling knowingly. With the smile came the realisation that she knew her button was undone and that she was deliberately tormenting him. *Jesus H. Christ! This was no time for playing games!* Or perhaps flirting in that way just came naturally to her. Her method of getting more information from whoever she was grilling. He smiled at the thought and wondered how far she would go.

'What's so funny?'

'Funny? Nothing. I just had a ludicrous thought.' Before he could say more there came a knock on the door and a waiter appeared with an opened bottle of Australian Shiraz and two glasses. Yorke gave a two pound coin as a tip and took the tray. He poured a glass for Catherine.

'You aren't having one?'

'Later perhaps. I'll need my wits about me when I go out. Let's get started.'

For an hour they skimmed through the contents of the files. Even Catherine's cynicism was held in check by what they were reading. Her glass of wine had stood untouched from the moment the first file had been opened. Now, as the time approached 22.30, they paused and she absently reached for the glass and drained half its contents.

'Is this all true?' She spoke in a whisper.

'It looks like it. It explains why they went to such lengths to kill me. Just in case I knew what Kavanagh knew.'

Catherine looked at Yorke through narrowed eyes. 'Two things spring to mind. First of all, how did they know *Phoenix* knew?'

'I've already asked myself that question and I have one possible answer.'

'Which is?'

'I'll tell you when I'm more sure. What's the other point?'

'There's obviously a traitor in a senior position in the government. Though God alone knows who.'

'I think I know.

16

JOHN KENNEDY WAS in a good mood. He could afford to be. In spite of losing Yorke, he still held all the cards, including now having three European governments in the palm of his hand. With the British, Italian and French governments ready to do his bidding there was nothing he couldn't achieve.

There was a knock on the door. 'Mr Frobisher, what can I do for you?'

Frobisher was in his late forties; a tall, spare man with gray eyes and hair to match. The avuncular look he wore was misleading. Frobisher could and did order the deaths and serious injury of others without a second thought.

'I've taken care of that little unpleasantness in Sweden, sir.' His voice was soft, even gentle. He had never been known to raise it in anger and he *never* swore or used profanity.

'Good, spare me the details. I take it nothing like that will occur again?'

'I have passed the message out, sir.'

Three men and a woman had been skimming 2 – 3% off the profits of drug deals in Stockholm for over two years. It had taken a particularly punctilious accountant, a woman, to spot the discrepancies. She had been offered a share in the takings which she'd sensibly declined. The total amount stolen was over 50 million kroner, or 4 million pounds. The culprits' deaths had been very slow and unpleasant. By way of a concession, their families had died quickly, in front of them. A painful lesson, but one that was nonetheless important. Provided others learnt from it. Kennedy sighed. That was the problem, of course, mankind rarely did learn, in spite of the severity of the teacher.

'What are you doing about Yorke?'

'I've scaled down the search, sir. I think he has been suit-ably neutralised for now, but we are still looking. We have all the usual points covered. If he contacts the police we'll hear about it quickly enough. We think he and the boy will make a run for it.'

'All right,' Kennedy nodded. 'There's nothing further you can do about him. For us it's business as usual. Is Crieff secure?'

'Yes, sir. Mrs Beaton appears happy enough, though natu-rally she misses her husband.'

'Naturally.' Kennedy's tone was not lost on Frobisher. Neither man gave a damn whether the Prime Minister's wife was missing her husband or not. A compliant Mrs Susan Beaton was more easily handled than one under duress. But at the end of the day it was all the same to him. 'What about this nonsense that he's going to resign?'

'All taken care of, sir. He'll be staying on the job for a while until we finally decide on the replacement. As you know, we have two preferences for the position.' Anyone listening to them speaking would think they were discussing a lowly manage-ment job in one of Kennedy's companies, instead of Prime Minister of the UK.

'Good. I'm relying on you. Is everything ready for Cornwall?'

'Not yet. Colonel Roberts is there now, overseeing the arrangements.'

'The good colonel has proven himself an able replacement for von Diesen. He was an excellent choice. Thank you for bringing him to my attention.'

'My pleasure, sir.'

Kennedy nodded with satisfaction. Roberts, like Frobisher, was completely reliable. If there were more men like them and, he thought, more women like Ingrid Kahn in his organisation, he'd rule Europe inside three years. Instead, it would take at least five.

'That's all for this evening. Oh, where is Mrs Kennedy?'

'Asleep, sir.'

'Drunk, as usual?'

'Yes, sir.'

'Then telephone Mrs Carter. Send Maxwell to collect her.'

'Certainly, sir.'

He was looking forward to a satisfying but busy night.

At a few minutes after 23.15 Yorke typed into his PDA – www.myvideowebmeeting.com/join. The screen came up "loading". He clicked twice on "Agree" and once on "Guest". He entered the meeting name, Crieff and the password, outlaw. Onto his screen came a grinning Dom.

'Hi, dad!'

'Hi, Dom! You okay?'

'Sure, dad. I was watching *Die Hard* on the video.'

'You practically know the dialogue.'

'True, but it's such a classic.'

Yorke chuckled in spite of himself. 'Hardly that. One day I'll have to introduce you to the real classics like *Casablanca* and *Gone with the Wind*.'

'No, thanks. Who's that with you?'

Yorke moved his head and aimed the built-in camera at Catherine. 'This is Catherine. She's a journalist. I'm briefing her.'

'Is that wise, dad?' There was panic in Dom's voice.

'I don't know. But if you come up with a better idea, let me know. Say hullo.'

'Hullo, Catherine.'

'Hullo, Dom. This is incredible. I've not seen this before. How does it work?' The question was aimed at Yorke but Dom answered.

'It's supplied by an American company called My Video Talk. Neat ain't it? We can also send video e-mails. It's voice and video over the internet.' Dom realised he was sounding enthusiastic and said, 'You can ask dad.'

'I will, thanks, Dom.'

Dom scowled at her suspiciously.

'Don't worry, Dom, we can trust her.'

Dom nodded reluctantly. 'If you say so. I just hope you're right, that's all.' There was no conviction in his voice.

They checked the positioning transmission on the mobile phone before saying goodbye and logging off the internet.

'I hadn't realised you were married.'

Yorke sighed. 'I'm not. And truth to tell he's my adopted son. His mother was killed some years ago by a drunk driver.'

'I am sorry.'

'As Nelson said to Hardy, as he lay dying, *kismet*.'

'I thought he said, kiss me.'

'No. He used the Turkish word for fate.'

Catherine shook her head in mock wonder. 'One lives and learns. Speaking of which, if half of what we've found in these files is true then we're in deep, deep trouble.'

'I can't imagine deeper. And believe me, it's twice as bad as is shown there. Desmond Kavanagh was a cautious soul. He would never have written those files without first double and treble checking. Whenever we had a sanction . . .'

'Sanction?'

'Yes!' Yorke snapped, irritably. Then seeing the look on Catherine's face he was immediately contrite. 'Whenever we were given the order to assassinate somebody you could be sure that person deserved to die.'

'How can you be so sure?'

Yorke shrugged. 'We checked and rechecked the evidence until we were absolutely certain. We never made a mistake.'

'Not once?'

'Not once. Trust me on that.' Yorke looked at his watch and then went across to the window and peeped through the curtain. 'Good, it's as dark as it's going to get. I have to go out.'

'Where are you going?

'To find somebody I know is staying here. Keep working on the files. Make as many notes as you like.'

'Stephen.' It was the first time Catherine had used his name and for some inexplicable reason he liked the sound of it. 'You will take care, won't you?'

'Sure. I always do. Excuse me a moment.' He went into the

bedroom and changed. When he came out he was wearing dark grey slacks, matching high-necked sweater and a grey blazer.

Catherine looked at him with curiosity.

'Contrary to popular belief, on a night like this black clothes are more easily seen than this garb. I don't know how long I'm going to be.'

'I'm going nowhere.'

That was all the goodbyes they said. Yorke left the room, went quickly down the stairs and out through the main entrance. In the boot of his car he found what he wanted and walked up the hill towards the trees and lodges. Once he was around the first bend he stepped off the path and into a small copse, near the tennis courts. He stopped to listen, smell and *feel* the night. He still remembered his instructor at Poole telling him to do exactly that. To embrace the night like a lover, having made it a friend in the first place. Don't rush in. It was true – only fools did.

The night was fine but overcast. There were odd noises in the background. A car door slamming, music playing, a voice calling. All usual, all exactly what one would expect at a place like Crieff Hydro. So what was unusual? Anything? He took his time and finally decided nothing was.

All the lodges had names as well as numbers. The nearest was called McEwen. The one next to it, McDonald. From an inside pocket he took what looked like a conventional fountain pen, albeit a little fatter than usual. Into his left ear he put an earpiece, aimed the bottom of the pen at the nearest window and clicked the switch at the base. From inside the lodge he clearly heard two people talking. The pen was a directional listening device. By twisting the two halves he could widen the scope or narrow it to pinpoint an individual on a telephone, cutting out much of the surrounding noise. It had been developed by a sound man working in Hollywood and the patent had been bought by Martin to incorporate in the camera. The pen Yorke was using was a beta version.

The conversation he overheard was mundane and not the person he wanted. Without moving he aimed at McDonald. A television programme was on. He waited a few minutes and then heard a slurred male voice asking, 'Do you want a drink?'

'No. And I don't think you do either. You've had enough.' The female voice was sharp, peevish.

Yorke didn't bother waiting to hear if there was any reply. Slowly he made his way up the hill, pointing and listening at every building he passed. Glen Devon became Ben More as he moved higher. There had been four lodges where he'd been unable to identify the occupants, two being empty while in the other two he had heard only monosyllabic grunts along with the television.

He had reached McJames, the last lodge before the top road. It was empty. Across the road, next to the golf club house were adjoining lodges, Corrie and Brae. After those there were only the Culcrieff Cottages to check – unless they were staying in the main hotel, but somehow he doubted that. Security would have been a nightmare as well as too many gawking people pointing and nudging each other.

Brae was empty, although a light was showing downstairs. By turning up the volume control to maximum it was possible to hear breathing under the right conditions. All Yorke heard was utter silence. Corrie was pay dirt as soon as he aimed the listening device at it.

'Ma'am, I'm sure it'll be all right to go ice-skating in Perth.'

'No fuss. Just us.'

'Of course. We'll have to inform the local constabulary.'

'I appreciate that. Thank you, Monica. Goodnight.'

'Goodnight, Mrs Beaton.'

Yorke crossed the road like a ghost and made his way behind the lodge. He found himself on the edge of the golf course. Again he spent time absorbing the night, sniffing the air, listening. It was quieter up here than lower down. Even so, he clearly heard a car engine start up. A door opened and shut close by. Aiming the pen at the lodge containing the Prime Minister's wife he listened intently. He heard the sound of someone preparing for bed, including the noise of gargling.

Pointing at the adjoining lodge he heard a female voice ask, 'Is Mrs Beaton okay?'

The policewoman Yorke now knew as Monica answered. 'Fine. She tell you she wants to take the kids ice-skating in the morning?'

'She mentioned it. But said she hadn't made up her mind. It's definite, is it?'

'Looks like it.' The accents were London East End.

'I'll tell the CC in the morning. He won't take it kindly being called at this time of night.'

'I'll leave it to you. I'm going out for my walk.'

'You and your walks. Every night you've been out.'

'It clears my mind. Helps me sleep. This sedentary life sitting around all day, baby-sitting two kids and a Prime Minister's wife is getting me down.'

'So why'd you volunteer?'

'I didn't. I was sent.'

'But I thought . . .' the voice tailed off.

'What? What did you think?'

'Nothing.'

'Good. I'll take my fags with me.' Monica slammed the front door a bit harder this time. Her footsteps quickly faded.

Yorke debated with himself whether to follow or stay where he was. The policewoman who had just left sounded an unpleasant individual and he wondered where she fitted into the scheme of things. He had the pen still pointed at the lodge and what he heard gave him pause for thought.

'Mack? It's me. She's going to Perth ice-rink.'

Yorke listened intently. Mack? Colonel Roberts, known as Mack the Knife? Was the bodyguard one of them? If she was it would explain the ease at which the PM's daughter had first gone missing. What about the other policewoman, Monica? But then why wait to make the call, if it was to Roberts, if Monica was a part of it? Yorke shook his head and concentrated on what he was hearing.

There was a few seconds of silence. 'Good. If Beaton's learnt his lesson then there's no need for me to lift the kid again. We may not get away with it so easily the next time.'

Yorke now had some of the answers he'd been searching

for. The PM had told the truth. He had been coerced. He tuned in again.

'Wilson said she was sent. Can't we get rid of her and get one of the others?'

Even with the pen turned up full Yorke couldn't hear the reply. He surmised that whoever she was talking to had other people who worked in the protection squad on their payroll. But definitely not Monica Wilson. The next thing he heard was the woman saying she had to go. Then the door opened and Monica Wilson was back.

He listened until they went to bed. It had been a clever move, to place one of their own people with the Prime Minister's wife and children. Open surveillance. Far superior to covert and all the inherent risks of being seen. Particularly by such highly trained officers as those who worked on protection for VIPs and foreign dignitaries. Another disquieting thought was how far did the organisation's forces stretch?

Yorke walked pensively back to the hotel. Letting himself into the suite he said to Catherine, 'I think I'll have that drink now.' He poured himself a glass of red wine.

'I can't,' Catherine greeted him, her voice hollow, her eyes stricken, 'believe what I'm finding.'

'What are you finding?'

'Names, lots and lots of names. Not just people, but organisations and businesses. It's like an evil octopus with tentacles everywhere.' She shook her head in wonder tinged with fear.

'Better show me what you've got.' Yorke pulled out a chair and sat alongside Catherine, looking at the computer screen. He was suddenly aware of her, her perfume, her body. She still hadn't done up the second button of her blouse and he glanced at her cleavage.

She saw where he looked and hid a smile. She pointed at the screen. 'Look at this file. It's all about a bank named The Royal Bank of Sark.'

'Never heard of it.' Yorke sipped his wine. He rarely drank and right now he needed to keep his wits about him.

'It started life as a licensed deposit taker back in the seventies, even though it called itself a bank. It grew on the back of drug money until 1983. It then had assets in excess of $200 million and applied to become a proper bank. It was turned down and the whole kit and caboodle moved to the Cayman Islands. There, they had no trouble in being a bank. Even the name was kept. They advertised as private banking for the discerning individual. Audited accounts were produced by one of the largest accountancy practices in the world and sent to some of the wealthiest people around the globe. The promise was total secrecy and instant access via a credit card with no limit. Look,' she pointed at the computer, 'ten million pounds can be taken out from any bank in the world by just presenting the card, proof of ID and a password.'

'What the hell use is ten mill in cash? That's nonsense.'

'Of course it's nonsense. But what a great gimmick. Can't you just hear the wives of the rich and famous? And how much will your platinum and diamond studded credit card pay? Only a million? Mine pays ten!'

Yorke grinned. 'I can just imagine the conversations.'

Catherine smiled back. 'Money poured in, but it still wasn't enough. The bank started dealing in drug money. Or maybe it never stopped, I can't tell. Follow this.' She moved the cursor along, highlighting what she was saying. 'A company in Liechtenstein bids for a plot of land in London Docklands. The bid is backed by a multi-national company registered in Hong Kong which in turn is financed by a back-to-back deal in Saudi Arabia and the Caymans. All nice and legal. Only the actual money belongs to this man.'

Yorke sat up with a jerk when he saw the name.

'It's not possible.'

'It appears to be true.'

'Osama bin Laden? My God!

'Ah, but it doesn't end there. Look! Another two companies lead to one name, John Kennedy.'

'Who's John Kennedy?'

'You've never heard of him?' Catherine looked surprised as

Yorke shook his head. 'A big man in the City. Into everything. Gives heavily to political parties. Well, two anyway. The Conservatives and Labour.'

Yorke snapped his fingers. 'I know who you mean. Sorry, I wasn't thinking.'

'What's really, really interesting is that his name keeps turning up.'

'What do you mean? Keeps turning up?'

'Kennedy's name is like a black plague all over the place.'

'Let me try something,' said Yorke thoughtfully. He changed files on the computer and used his mobile to access the Lloyds Register of Shipping. 'Remember the ship we took a look at? Let's see who owns it. Here we are, registered in Vadüz, Liechtenstein, through an IBC. What on earth is an IBC?'

'An International Business Corporation,' said Catherine. 'A shell company.'

'Do you understand all this stuff?'

'Some. I've written a number of articles on finance. At the legitimate end of the market place. I don't know much about the criminal side. Although, it's true to say, there's a sort of inter-mingling, a cross-over, between what's legitimate and what's illegal.' She paused, took a gulp of wine and continued. 'It's like the information on the computer. Unless you're looking for it, at face value it's all legal. Corporations owning other corpora-tions owning real assets. The only people affected are the govern-ments of the countries who are losing massive amounts in tax revenues. I do remember one incredible statistic. 40,000 people live in the Caymans and there's a bank for every 76 residents. What's more, the total wealth owned by the banks is in excess of $900 billion. That's over $22.5 million per resident.'

'Where do they stow all that cash?'

'They don't. The Caymans have no vaults. They hold no cash. The money is in London, New York, Frankfurt, Hong Kong and so on. The wealth is just green dots on a computer screen.'

Yorke shook his head. 'I suppose that all makes sense at one level. What else have you found out?'

'Tons and I've only just scratched the surface. There's enough to write a book here – not just a few articles.'

'Do both.'

'Are you serious?'

'Of course I am. If you live long enough, that is.' The smile he gave her did nothing to dampen the flare of alarm that had erupted in her stomach.

'Are you serious?' She repeated herself.

'About what? The book or you living?'

Catherine shrugged, unsure how to reply.

Yorke stopped smiling. 'I'm serious about both. I'm alive because I . . .' he paused, took a sip of wine and said, 'because I might not know about the stuff on the computer but I'm bloody good at what I do. And that's not a boast. It's a fact. When I phoned you . . .'

'Yes, why did you phone me?'

'It struck me that the only way to get out of this mess is to expose it. The corruption is deep, wide and cancerous. And spreading. Where will it end?' The question was rhetorical and Catherine didn't bother replying. 'I realised that as soon as I read just a few of these files. But I also know it from first hand experience. I've told you what happened. Let me ask you something. What has there been in the news?'

'What are you talking about?'

'Think! The report of the house blowing up and the people who died has already faded from the papers and from the TV news and radio. It's unheard of. And what about the other events? I heard a gunshot when I was leaving Waterloo station yet there's nothing about it on the news. There may be an increase in gun crime in this country but not so much that the discharge of a gun isn't reported. And was anyone hurt?'

'Yes. A ticket collector.'

'How do you know?'

'It was briefly mentioned on 5 Live late at night. But,' pausing, Catherine frowned, 'it is unusual. I remember thinking poor man. Shot by someone who didn't have a ticket. What on earth is our society coming to? That was the sort of fatuous thought that went through my head. But that was the last I heard of it. And believe me, I'm a news junky.'

'Did he live?'

'Does it matter?'

'It does to him,' Yorke said dryly.

'What I meant was the reporting would be the same whether he'd lived or died. Just being shot would be enough to cause a feeding frenzy of reporting and comment. But in answer to your question, I think he was alive when he was taken to the hospital. It did say that he was shot in the chest.'

'With a wound like that he's got no chance,' Yorke said matter of factly. 'That being the case it would be in every newspaper and on every broadcast. But there's been nothing. A few events of the past couple of days also should have been made public. Somebody, with a hell of a lot of power is wielding a very big stick.'

'Oh, God!' Catherine had seen only the story. The glory. Suddenly reality flooded in. 'You've put my life at risk,' she gasped.

Yorke nodded. 'I'm sorry. But it's not too late. No one knows you're here. No one knows *I'm* here, so you'll be okay. Just bow out. Your car is downstairs. Leave now. Say nothing. Write nothing. Do nothing. Get out while you can.'

Catherine stood up, drained her glass and sat back down with a heavy thump. 'Make like the three monkeys? It's too late. I'm hooked. And anyway, I can't do that. Not now. Not with what I've learnt. But even if I do write an exposé who will we get to publish it?'

'We start with the internet and take it from there.'

'I suppose,' she said pensively. She sighed. 'That won't get me the Pulitzer.'

'No, but it might save your life.' Yorke placed his hand on her forearm. He could feel her warmth and his tongue suddenly felt too big for his mouth. Clearing his throat he removed his hand and said, 'Catherine, you have to understand how dangerous this is. If we get it wrong . . . If *I* get it wrong, it won't be a messy court case where we argue our corner. It'll be a bullet in the head and a cold, lonely grave. If we're lucky.'

'Lucky?' In spite of herself, her voice was hoarse. Was it the man or the situation, she thought? 'What do you mean, lucky?'

'It's clichéd, but there are a hell of a lot of things worse than a quick death.' Looking into her deep brown eyes he fought a desire to kiss her. With an effort he stood up and walked across the room to freshen his glass, though it was still more than half full.

Having broken contact, the moment passed and he sat beside her once again. 'Let's try and follow the trail of the ship. The name of the IBC is Earth-Fuller. It doesn't take us anywhere.'

'Here, let me.' Catherine pushed him away from the keyboard and began typing. 'I had to do this before when I was writing about tax avoidance. This is Liechtenstein's Registrar of Companies.' Her fingers flew across the keys. A few moments later she had what she was looking for. 'Issued shares, one hundred. There are two named shareholders with one share each, the other ninety-eight are held by a trust registered in Switzerland. When all else fails, follow the money. Look this is going to take a while. Why not leave me to it? If I find anything interesting I'll give you a shout.' She didn't add that his closeness was disconcerting her.

Yorke looked at his empty wine glass in surprise, nodded and went over to the sofa. 'I'll take a nap. Wake me if you do find anything.'

Catherine turned on a lamp by the computer and switched off the overhead lights. 'That better?'

'Thanks.' Taking off his shoes, he settled down and was soon asleep. The military habit of storing up sleep standing him in good stead at times like this.

He awoke to a stiff back, a keyboard tapping away and a grey light in the room. Fully alert, he stayed still and then sat up.

'You're awake,' Catherine greeted him, glancing in his direction.

'Have you been at it all this time?'

'Yes. Once I get started I never know when to stop. All night I've been thinking, I'll just do a bit more and a bit more. The next thing, the dawn is here.' Catherine yawned. 'However, I know my limitations. I'm going for a few hours sleep. Is that all right with you?'

'Of course. What time is it?'

'Just after half past five. I've filled two notebooks with information. There's no order to it but what I've discovered is unbelievable.' Catherine looked at Yorke with sad eyes. 'Only I do believe it. I'll leave you to go through what I've found.'

Yorke nodded. 'Just let me brush my teeth and freshen up and the bedroom's all yours.' When he returned he found Catherine on the sofa fast asleep. He took the duvet off the bed and placed it over her. She hardly stirred as he looked down at her. She wasn't beautiful in the conventional sense but she had a certain, *je ne sais quoi*, and Yorke found her very attractive. It had been a long time since he'd been with anyone. Somehow he'd never had the time, or the inclination – not since Daphne had died.

He walked softly across the room and put on the kettle. He didn't notice Catherine open her eyes for a moment and watch him, a smile on her lips before she went back to sleep.

17

DOM WOKE SLOWLY. The boat creaked and he heard the slight strumming of a halyard vibrating along the mast. Apart from those sounds it was utterly quiet and Dom lay at peace with the world. Then the memories of the day before came back with a vengeance and he snapped awake, his peaceful thoughts shattering like broken glass. He looked at his watch. Nearly 08.00. He'd stay where he was for a bit longer. Then he'd get breakfast and start on some of his chores.

The thought of school intruded. After this bank holiday weekend there would be no more rugby. He was going back to cricket. He was second bat for the second eleven. With luck, next year, he'd be in the first eleven. He knew it would look good when he applied for the Royal Marines, something he intended doing in a few weeks time. In his head he had his future mapped out. After "A" levels he'd go to university. Exeter, probably, to read military history and politics. After that, he'd go straight into the RM. Of course, he'd spend his holidays with the Marines. He couldn't wait. Why, oh why, did it take so long to grow up? The lament of youth echoed in his mind.

He fell into an uneasy doze, snapping awake when his mobile phone played "What shall we do with the drunken sailor?".

'Hullo?' Dom answered tentatively, not recognising the number.

'Hullo, Dom. You okay?'

'Sure, dad. I'm just getting up. I didn't know the number.'

'I forgot to charge my battery so I borrowed a phone. What're you up to?'

'I've a few things I need to do. I'm also going to tidy up the paint job we did on the *Duck's* name. Where are you?'

'Still in Scotland. I'm not sure how long I'm going to be. Want to check the positioning signal?'

'Sure. Doing it now. Same co-ordinates as last night.'

'That's it. Good lad. Right, I'll phone you to-night or once I start moving. Take care, Dom.'

'I will. Bye, dad.' Dom broke the connection, unzipped his sleeping bag and climbed out of his bunk. He shivered in the cold morning air before putting on his old rugby shirt and a pair of shorts. A superficial brushing of his teeth and he was ready to begin his day.

In the galley he poured a glass of orange juice and a bowl of corn flakes with sugar and milk. Barefooted he went up on deck and sat in the cockpit. There wasn't a cloud in the sky and it promised to be a warm day. His simple meal finished, he opened the forward hatch and all the port holes to allow fresh air to move through the hull. He ran up the engine and started the three bilge pumps. The merest trickle spewed out and he switched the pumps off.

From the forward locker he took a can of marine grease and smeared a thin layer on the runners of the hatch over the companionway. He pushed the hatch back and forth but the squeak was still there. More grease and nothing changed. Dom gave up in disgust. As his right hand was already covered in the muck, he applied the grease to all the sheaves, careful not to put on too much, or to drop any onto the wooden deck. Finally, he greased the bottle screws, used to slacken or add tension to the rigging.

The sun was high in the sky and he saw it was after 10.00. Time for stand-easy. Cleaning his hands, he put the grease away and made himself a cup of tea – NATO standard – milk and two sugars. A couple of chocolate digestive biscuits took away his pang of hunger.

Next, Dom tied the inflatable under the stern, took a can of white paint and covered over the new name, *The Outlaw*. When his father had painted the name some of the black had run. He did the same on either side of the bow. Lunch was a cheese sandwich and a packet of crisps, followed by an apple, his concession to eating healthily. The white paint was now dry. Taking thin metal stencils he began to carefully paint the new name back on. This time there were no rivulets of black staining the white hull.

When he was finished, Dom took a paperback from the bookshelf in the saloon and settled in the cockpit. He hadn't read two pages when he fell asleep, waking to the sound of voices in the distance. He ducked down inside the cockpit and then wormed his way down the stairs into the yacht. Two people appeared on the pathway a few yards away. A man and a woman. They stopped to look at the yacht. The man read out the name, *The Outlaw*.

'Do you know it?'

'No. I thought this was Eva's mooring.'

'It is. Whoever owns the boat has no right to be there. Oi! You on the boat!'

Dom decided not to reply. He was going nowhere and didn't intend getting into an argument with two adults. It was one he couldn't win and the last thing he needed was for the police to take an interest in him. Better to lie low than draw attention to himself.

After a few minutes he heard the man say, 'There's nobody there. Let's go. We can tell Eva when we see her.'

Dom didn't hear what the woman said. He sighed with relief as they vanished out of sight. What should he do? Indecision paralysed him. If he stayed and someone came back would they arrest him? He shook his head irritably. That was stupid thinking. Of course they wouldn't. But somebody might come aboard and see the yacht's name in the logs and realise she was the *Lucky Duck* and not the *Outlaw*. What would happen then? Suppose it was reported and the enemy found out? The questions whirled around his head. He needed to decide. Go or stay? Or phone dad and ask him? With relief at the thought he picked up his mobile and speed dialled the number his father had last called him on.

* * *

'Dom? You okay?'

'Yes, dad. It's just some people came by and I heard them talking about this being somebody's mooring. I don't know what to do. Should I move or what?'

'Stay there for today and move tomorrow. I doubt anything will happen on a Saturday evening. The owners are probably away for the weekend so you'll be safe enough. Tomorrow go south towards the sea. Let me know if you find a berth. If you don't, cruise the river all day and go back to where you are. If it's still vacant you can moor up tomorrow night. I expect to be back before then. You got that? Just keep a low profile.'

'Will do.'

'Good lad. I'll speak to you tonight.' Yorke broke the connection.

'Is he all right?'

'Appears to be.' Yorke told Catherine what had happened.

'Sounds a sensible boy.'

'He is. I couldn't be prouder of him if he was my own son. Back to work.'

'It was a good idea getting the flipchart from the hotel. We can follow the convoluted paths of the criminals more easily.'

Yorke smiled. 'Credit where credit is due, I like the new wallpaper.' He nodded at one blank wall which had held a number of prints by Scottish artists. These had been taken down and in their place the wall had been covered with sheets off the flipchart. The sheets of paper were three high and ten wide. Each one followed a company or a name. Different colours made identification easier.

'I forgot. I have a boat's registration documents here.' He crossed to his bag and extracted the papers. 'Can we trace the owners?'

'We can try. Let's take a look.'

Ten minutes later Catherine announced, 'Registered to an off-shore company in the Caymans. It's a dead-end, I'm afraid.'

'Okay. Not to worry. It was a long shot anyway.' Wandering across to look at the sheets plastered to the wall he pointed to three areas. 'I was involved with operations connected to that, that and that.'

'In what way?'

Yorke shrugged and smiled diffidently. 'Getting information. All obtained illegally. No warrants. That sort of thing. The problem, as far as our judicial system is concerned, is that we have to do things in a certain manner.'

'But . . .'

'I know,' he held up his hand. 'But me no buts. We understood at *Phoenix* the ramifications of what we were about. But look on it this way. Suppose for a moment we are at war, with organised crime which is hand-in-glove with active terrorism. How do we fight it? We have no answers. We could not have fought World War II with one hand tied behind out backs. Christ,' as he warmed to his theme, Yorke became more agitated and began pacing the room, 'if it was *only* one arm we might stand a chance. It isn't. It's two arms a leg and a foot. What we're facing is horrendous and we're only scratching the surface of it.'

Catherine nodded. 'I agree. But I am yet to be convinced that what your organisation did was right. What about civil liberties? The rule of law? Innocent until proven guilty?'

Yorke shook his head. 'Please don't let me sound patronising . . .'

'Which means you're about to.

He stopped his pacing and nodded. 'Probably. But you still don't understand what we're battling. These people don't resort to the law. They kill, maim, frighten, threaten. You name it and they do it. Bribery and coercion are employed as a natural way of doing business.'

'All I've found are damning connections between some terrorist activity and layers of businesses that make enormous amounts of money and pay no tax. The links to terrorism are tenuous to say the least but appear to exist. There are at least a dozen companies that make money but don't appear to have any product . . .'

'Drugs.'

'Probably.'

'Or people trafficking.'

'Possibly. But I need to delve a lot further before I'm convinced.'

'Of what?'

'Where this is all leading.'

'It's leading directly into the heart of the establishment.'

'How can you be so certain?'

'Trust me. I am.' He hadn't told her about the Prime Minister's wife and his discovery of the evening before and Catherine hadn't asked. It was information he was going to keep to himself until it was needed. 'Would you like a coffee? Or something more quaint like afternoon tea? They are serving it in the conservatory.'

'Oh, the conservatory?' Catherine emphasised the word in a voice that brought a smile to Yorke's lips. 'What about all this?' She waved a hand at the wall.

'We'll take it all down. I'll hide the sheets under the carpet. We can't be too careful.'

'I'd better get changed.'

'Tight jeans and a tee-shirt without a bra may be a bit scandalous for the ladies of Crieff Hydro.'

Catherine had the good grace to blush but said nothing. A few minutes later, dressed in a summer frock and short blue matching jacket she followed Yorke down the stairs.

The room was busy, large, light and airy. Afternoon tea for Catherine was Earl Grey with a special infusion of bergamot, the orange oil that gave the tea its unique flavour. For Yorke it was black China tea, served without milk or sugar. Scones and other cakes were served on platters.

'This,' said Catherine, licking cream off her top lip, 'is frightfully refined.'

'Frightfully.' Yorke mimicked her and then looked over her shoulder at a slight commotion at the door.

Catherine looked back and said, 'Good Lord, is that who I think it is?'

'Mrs Beaton, kids and bodyguards. Yes.'

Catherine looked at him sharply. 'You're not surprised. Are they to do with whatever you got up to last night?'

'Clumsily put, but yes.'

'What did you do?'

Yorke sipped his tea, playing for time. 'I'll have to take the fifth on that. Put it this way, what I learnt didn't surprise me.'

Catherine paused with a scone lavishly decked in strawberry jam and cream halfway to her mouth. Slowly she placed the cake on a side plate. 'The heart of the establishment? Is that what you're meaning? The PM? I don't believe it.'

'It's not what you think. When I know more I'll tell you. Okay?'

'I suppose that'll have to do for now. I don't suppose I can go over and ask for an interview?'

'I thought there was a protocol to speaking to family members.'

Catherine sighed. 'There is, really. It's not on. Hell, it's not the spouse's fault if their husbands or wives enter politics.' She glanced across the room again. 'I see everybody is having the good manners to ignore them.'

'It's the British way,' smiled Yorke.

'What will we do about dinner tonight?'

'The restaurant looks pretty enticing. Or we can have room service.'

'I fancy the restaurant.'

'Good. So do I. We have a date.'

'A date?' Catherine raised a quizzical eyebrow, a smile playing on her lips.

Yorke suddenly found his mouth had gone dry.

They left the table and returned upstairs. Together they continued examining the files. There was eye contact and occasional hand touching, each time adding to the tension building between them. After a few hours, they sat back in their chairs and Catherine let out a sigh.

'The further we're progressing the more I don't like it. You see we've finally tracked the ship?'

'Yes. Back to John Kennedy. The cut-outs and blind alleys have been astonishing.'

'The files are riddled with them.'

'Look, I don't know about you but I've had enough. I'm for a shower, a drink and dinner.'

'Sounds good to me. I bags the shower first!' With that Catherine bounded to her feet and went into the bedroom.

Yorke listened to the tantalising sound of the shower being turned on. He wondered how she would react if he volunteered to scrub her back.

When Catherine came in from the bedroom she was wearing only a towel. 'The shower's free.'

'Thanks. I won't be long.'

She looked into his eyes and smiled. He thought there was a definite invitation there, but he wasn't sure. He never was when it came to women. As he left the room he wondered if that had been a promise he'd seen. Or just his fevered imagination?

When they went down to dinner it seemed natural to walk side-by-side, with Catherine's hand resting on his arm as they entered the restaurant.

They were directed to a table for two in a corner where Yorke could observe the room without being obvious.

After perusing the menu for a few minutes he asked, 'What do you fancy?'

'I'll have the smoked mackerel to start and the venison to follow.'

'I'll have the scallops and the venison.'

The waiter appeared. Yorke ordered and added, 'A bottle of Sancerre and a bottle of still water.' When they were alone he said, 'Eat, drink and be merry, for tomorrow . . . Ah, yes, tomorrow. There's always tomorrow.' But he spoilt it by adding, 'Maybe.'

'I hope you're right, without the maybe. What are we going to do?'

'In all honesty, I don't know. I'm at a loss. Exposure seems to be our best bet. But I don't know how effective it will be.'

Yorke shrugged. 'Alternatively, I threaten exposure, and as long as Dom and I are left alone I'll leave them alone.'

'Can you do that? Knowing what you know?'

Before Yorke could answer the waiter returned with an ice bucket and a bottle of the white wine. He poured a taster but Yorke just waved at him to pour two glasses. When the waiter left Yorke raised his, 'Cheers. Here's to a bloody war and a sickly season.'

'What?' Catherine clinked glasses looking into his eyes over the rim of hers.

'It's a naval toast. It means promotion.'

'Oh, I see.' She smiled and sipped her wine. 'Very refreshing. Only you didn't answer the question.'

'I know. I needed time to think. The truth is I can't leave it. I have to see this whole affair to some sort of conclusion. Though god alone knows what it'll be.'

'Good. I was worried you'd try and stop me running the story.'

Yorke nodded. 'I'd thought about that as well. Here's our starters.'

When she'd finished her mackerel, Catherine passed judgement. 'Delicious.'

The venison was excellent. As the meal concluded each became aware of the tension that had been building between them.

'Would you like anything further? Cheese? A sweet?'

Catherine shook her head. 'I'm fine, thanks. Perhaps a coffee.'

'Right.' Yorke beckoned to the waiter. The coffees appeared, over which they lingered. Finally, as their conversation came to a stuttering halt, they stood up to leave, Catherine giving Yorke an uncertain, almost timid smile. Yorke was aware that they were approaching the Rubicon. *What*, he thought, *will be the consequences of crossing?*

18

CATHERINE AWOKE TO find Yorke on his elbow looking down at her, a smile curling up his lips.

'I hope,' she said languidly, 'you like what you see.'

'Very much. I'd like to show you just how much but we need to get going.'

They had packed up all their notes and had made plans – of a sort. The only way to stop the criminal Hydra, as Catherine described it, was to use the oxygen and firebrand of publicity.

'Very Lernaesque,' said Yorke with a grin.

'Is there such a word?' Catherine smiled in return, running her index finger down his cheek.

'Probably not.' He put his arms around her waist and drew her close. 'But I have to warn you I had something of a classical education in the school I went to.'

'You went to school? I don't believe it. Not a thug like you. What did you learn? Anything useful?'

'The *Kama Sutra*.'

'Now, that *is* useful. However,' she sighed theatrically, 'reading is one thing, practice is another.'

'I need plenty of that. But not now. We need to make a move. Dom's expecting me this evening. I wonder what he'll make of you?'

'Will I meet him?'

'I hope so. He's told me a number of times that it was time I had a girlfriend.' Yorke saw the look on Catherine's face and said, 'Don't worry. Last night wasn't a declaration of undying love. We hardly know each other. You don't strike me as the sort of person to rush into a relationship and I definitely am not.'

Catherine nodded, unable to keep the relief out of her voice. 'Good. My career is very important to me. Last night was,' she hesitated, 'a pleasant interlude. But that's all it was. An interlude.'

'Good. In that case we'd better go.' If he was disappointed, Yorke didn't show it. In the bottom of his holdall Yorke placed the flipchart paper and threw the rest of his stuff on top.

A slightly sour note had entered their conversation and they left with a feeling of awkwardness lying between them. They drove in tandem back to Cumbernauld.

A short while later they were in the air, heading south. 'There's a small airport near Boston,' Yorke said, adjusting the plane's heading by a few degrees, 'we'll land there.'

'Are you going to phone ahead and see if she's there?'

'No. If she died in the attack that's the end of it. But I need to find out for sure. Nothing else makes any sense. Evelyn supposedly left *Phoenix* just before the attack. Jack, Ali and I were there together which was highly unusual in itself. The co-ordination of the attack was either very fortuitous or meticulously planned. I suspect the latter. These people don't leave things to chance. My survival was a matter of luck. If Evelyn Beckworth is alive she may have something useful to tell me.'

He trimmed the Skyhawk, settling her at 8,500 ft. With 80% of power she was cruising at 120 knots but battling a head wind that gave her 109 knots over the ground. The KMD 550 multifunctional display gave a summary of the air traffic and weather. He adjusted the plane's heading another ten degrees to port and engaged the autopilot.

'Good, all I need do is watch the instruments and the world go by. Unless, that is, you'd like to fly her?'

'Me?' Catherine looked at him, startled.

'Why not? It's easy. Let me show you.' He turned off the autopilot and took the column in his hands. 'Place your hands on the controls and follow me through. Gently, now . . . gently. Get a feel for the plane. Now put your feet on the pedals. That's it.' For the next twenty minutes he gave Catherine a flying lesson.

'This is fun!'

'You're doing great. You've been at a level height and on course for the last three minutes or so.'

She glanced at him. 'Only because you've . . .'

He waved his hands at her and lifted his legs slightly. 'Nope. You've had control for the last few minutes.'

Catherine shrieked and the plane's nose began to drop.

Yorke grinned, took the controls and intoned, 'I have the plane.' He quickly brought her back on course and height and reset the autopilot.

'Swine!' Catherine spoke with feeling though with a smile.

Yorke laughed. 'I'll have you flying in a month if you let me.'

She looked pensively at him. 'I might at that. I enjoyed it.'

The remainder of the journey was spent in companionable silence. They landed without mishap just before lunch and took a taxi into Boston town. There, Yorke, using the name of Yarrow, hired a car. The day had turned wet and windy, showers threatening to coalesce into something more sustained. Neither had raincoats and Yorke stopped at an outdoors outfitters to buy a couple of dark anoraks.

'According to the map,' said Catherine, 'Wainfleet All Saints is about three miles ahead.'

Yorke had barely known Kavanagh's secretary only that she lived in the area. Using the internet they had quickly found her address and a map of how to find her house.

'The last time I saw Evelyn she was asking permission to leave early as her mother needed help. If I remember correctly, she has an invalid mother who's a bit of a Tartar. Kavanagh used to allow her to leave whenever she needed to go as she always made the time up. In fact, she did a lot more than that.' He shook his head. 'It's astonishing how little we really know or bother to learn about our fellow . . . what? Compatriots? Not friends. Co-workers certainly. Christ, I know a damn sight more about my enemies that I did my friends and colleagues. What a bloody indictment! We're coming up to the village now. Quaint,' was Yorke's opinion of the old-fashioned houses and well kept gardens.

Catherine said, 'That's the street. Turn left.'

Yorke did as he was bid and they found themselves on the road for Thorpe St Peter. They passed a number of houses and just after the 30mph sign Catherine said, 'We just passed the Wee Inglenook.'

'I saw it. Detached, small front garden with hanging baskets either side of the door.' He paused, 'And a For Sale sign.'

'What now?'

'I'm not one to rush in where angels fear to, so we'll park and stroll past the house. The rain helps. Though we might get a bit wet.'

Yorke pulled into the side of the road and said, 'Wait here a second. I need a few things out of the boot.' He took off his coat, strapped on a holster for the Smith & Wesson, replaced the coat and quickly put on the anorak. The rain was now a steady downpour and he shivered. The Walther PPK he put in his pocket, where access was easier and more immediate. The S&W was for heavy stopping power. The Walther was for immediate defence. *Against what? A defenceless middle-aged lady?* However, he had never been one to be unprepared and today would be no exception.

Catherine joined him in the wet, he locked the car and they strolled back along the lane. Minutes later they passed the house. They did little more than glance at it.

'It looks empty,' said Catherine.

'It does.' They went further into the village. 'She may have died in the attack. I'm only surmising she left before the bombs started to go off. And what about the mother?' It was a rhetorical question and Catherine kept silent. 'There's a post office.'

Yorke stood outside the shop while Catherine went inside and bought a book of stamps. She loitered at the counter and chatted to the elderly postmistress for a few minutes.

Back outside she said, 'The old lady's dead. She died three weeks ago. There's a rumour that Evelyn's selling up to move abroad.'

'So she lied about her mother being ill.'

'She may have used it as an excuse. The attack being a co-incidence.'

Yorke's look told her what he thought of that idea.

Catherine shrugged. 'Just being Devil's advocate.'

'Is she still here?'

'She was yesterday afternoon.'

'Let's go along the footpath that runs past the side of the cottage. Before we do, that shop sells umbrellas. We'll get a couple.'

In a convenience store he also bought two pairs of rubber cleaning gloves. He gave a pair to Catherine.

Her quizzical look prompted him to say, 'We may need them shortly.'

Armed with an umbrella each they walked past the side of the cottage. The day had turned dark and the small windows meant little natural light penetrated the house. There were no lights on and the desolate look of abandonment heightened.

The path continued into a small wood and then skirted a field. They paused under the dripping branches of a tall oak tree.

'What now?' Catherine looked about her, shivering.

'You stay here while I take a look in the house.'

'I'm coming with you. What can be more natural than for a couple to be looking at a house for sale?'

Yorke nodded. 'All right. In that case we'll go round the front and walk up to the door. Put your gloves on.'

Catherine did as she was told. Yorke tried the doorbell and hit the knocker. There was no reply. Either side of the garden was a wooden fence, hiding them from a casual observer. The front of the garden had a low wall and gate. There was nobody walking the pavement on such a miserable afternoon. From an inside pocket he removed a small electronic lock-pick. The door lock was a bog-standard latchkey type. Yorke selected a suitable pick and inserted it into the lock. He pressed the button on the end of the handle and the pick instantly read the tumblers' shape. Tiny pieces of metal filled the space, he twisted the lock open and removed the pick. He pushed against the door and opened it a crack.

'How on earth did . . .'

'Shsh. Can you hear anything?'

'No. It's as quiet as a crypt.'

'Let's go in.' They were speaking in whispers.

'Isn't this called breaking and entering?' Catherine asked nervously following Yorke.

'Of course not. The estate agent gave us a key and told us to feel free about looking the place over.'

'Oh, of course, silly me,' she said dryly. 'I forgot about that conversation.'

Yorke flashed her a grin. They were standing in a small hall with a door off left and right. Stairs on the right led to the bedrooms. Ahead was another door which Yorke opened. It was a modern kitchen and diner, an extension to the house only a few years old.

'If we're going to be open and above board we'd better switch on the lights,' said Yorke.

Catherine looked to the right of the door, saw the switch and flicked it on. Nothing happened and she flicked it a few times. 'Strange. No electricity.'

'Or the bulb's gone.'

'No. The electric timers on the microwave and the cooker are off.'

Yorke had already noticed but merely nodded. 'Let's check the other rooms. Back in the hall the door on the left led to a small sitting room, which from the slight mustiness in the air hadn't been used for a number of weeks. Photographs of Evelyn were on a sideboard, tracing her life from baby to adolescent to womanhood. They appeared to have stopped being taken when she was in her early twenties.

'Not unattractive,' said Catherine, picking up one of the frames. 'Presumably the woman with her is her mother.'

Yorke commented, 'No pictures of a man. A father.'

'Yes. That's what I was thinking.'

'Evelyn never mentioned a father but it's true to say I didn't exactly ask her about her home life. It's not the sort of conversation one has with a secretary. Or anybody else for that matter. Unless someone is being PV'd.

'What's that?'

'Positively vetted. To join *Phoenix* you had your life story trawled over with a fine toothcomb. Whatever skeletons were in her cupboard, if there were any, would have been found by Desmond Kavanagh. And as she got the job, I doubt they were of significance. I think,' he looked slowly around at the armchair and footrest, the small occasional table and the cluttered surfaces, 'that this was the old woman's room. Let's take a look across the passage.'

The other room was similar in size and layout except the furniture was more modern. A TV sat in a corner with a video and DVD player. Remote controls were lying on a small table next to a comfortable looking armchair. Yorke checked the cupboards in the sideboard and found one side stocked with bottles of drink and the other with crystal glasses. The bottles had been opened and varied from port and sherry to gin and blended whiskies.

'She appears to have liked a tipple,' said Yorke.

'Who doesn't? It doesn't mean she was a heavy drinker by any stretch of the imagination.'

'No, that's true. That leaves upstairs.'

'And under the stairs,' said Catherine.

'I'll take a look in the cupboard under the stairs while you have a quick look in the bedrooms.'

Yanking open the door to the cupboard two things happened. Yorke recognised the flashing alarm unit and Catherine screamed.

He took the stairs three at a time. Catherine was standing in the doorway on the left, her hand to her mouth. Yorke touched her arm and she turned in to him, a sob catching in her throat. Over her shoulder he looked into the staring eyes of the body of Evelyn Beckworth.

Easing past Catherine he knelt by the body. It was stone cold and had obviously been there at least twelve hours. Possibly a little longer. The cause of death was evident. She had been shot twice through her left breast. A half packed suit-case stood open on the bed, clothes littering the duvet. He looked around the small bedroom and saw a handbag half hidden under the bed. Grabbing it, he stood up.

'Here, take this. We'd better get out pdq,' said Yorke.

'Hadn't we better send for the police?' Catherine faltered.

'And say what? Anyway, there's a state-of-the-art burglar alarm flashing downstairs and unless I am very much mistaken we tripped it. So they could be along at any time. And I have neither the inclin-ation nor the time to answer questions to Mr Plod.'

They went out the front door and he pulled it shut behind them. There was a break in the rain. Catherine hurried forward and he grabbed her arm. 'Nice and slow. We've just knocked on the door and there's no answer. We'll be back when the owner is home. Take your gloves off.' He stuffed both pairs of rubber gloves in his pocket.

On the pavement they turned right and headed towards the car. There were no flashing lights or two-tone horns signalling the arrival of the police and Yorke was becoming confident that the alarm in the cottage would go unanswered for a while longer. After all, burglary was a common occurrence and the bureaucratically over-stretched police could barely keep up with their workload.

The sound of a racing engine gave Yorke cause to slow down and look back. But he realised it was a trick of acoustics and the car was coming from ahead. No! Two cars. And coming at speed. It started to drizzle.

'Pull your hood up.' He suited the action to his words. 'We'd better hurry.' He was frowning. If the cars were coming in response to the alarm they'd be coming with blues and twos. There was less paperwork if the burglar heard and did a bunk before the police arrived. Two cars swept past and Yorke glanced at them. Each was a nondescript saloon.

'I don't like this one little bit,' he grabbed Catherine's arm and hurried her along. 'Two cars with two coppers in each? For a village burglary? Never in a million years.'

The rain was now coming down in sheets and the wind was bending the edges of their umbrellas. Her head huddled down,

Catherine shivered and looked back. 'They're out of sight. Hell, I think one of the car's coming back.' The sound of a racing engine grew louder and a dark blue Rover appeared around the bend. As it approached the engine note changed and slowed. Brakes were applied hard and tyres screeched.

'Run! Here's the keys. Whoever the hell these people are they aren't police! Get out of here!'

The car stopped alongside them as Catherine broke into a run. Two men piled out of the car, each holding guns. Yorke didn't hesitate. Without removing his hand from his anorak pocket he shot the passenger through the chest, the noise an intrusion in the quiet countryside. Turning to shoot the other man he had nobody to aim at. The driver was already in the ditch on the other side of the lane.

Catherine was at a bend in the road when a chip of stone erupted at her feet. The driver had fired a silenced shot at her the bad light and rain causing him to miss. Yorke dived behind the front wheel of the Rover. The tyre next to his face erupted and the car collapsed onto the rim of the wheel. Catching a glimpse of the man in the ditch, Yorke opened fire and shot three times in quick succession. He missed. Catherine was out of sight when the other car came speeding back around the bend.

19

YORKE DIDN'T WAIT. Diving over a hedge behind him, he landed on his shoulder and rolled onto his back. He scrambled to his feet and found himself in a ploughed field with cereals growing. Rather than risk a twisted ankle over the uneven furrows he ran along the side of the field, grateful that the rain was affecting visibility. Something plucked at his left sleeve and he glanced down to see the bullet torn hole in his coat. The field was coming to an end and ahead he saw an unkempt hedgerow. Ducking and weaving he leapt a ditch before coming to a stop. Woven into the hedge was a barbed wire fence. He looked back and saw the dim outline of one of the gunmen sixty metres back. To the right was a second man, running fast about the same distance away.

Reaching under his anorak, Yorke withdrew his modified Smith and Wesson. He dropped into the ditch and knelt down. With his right hand clasped in his left, his elbows planted firmly on the edge of the ditch, his knees soaking up the rainwater, he calmed his breathing. In spite of his exertions he was gratified to see that the end of the silenced barrel wasn't wavering. Two shots. Less than seconds. *Do it*!

The nearest man was forty metres away and coming in a straight line. Yorke could hear the gunman's laboured breathing. Aiming at the middle of the man's torso, Yorke fired. Immediately he switched aim and fired again. The second man was already diving forward when the bullet hit him in the crown, killing him instantly. The first target stayed down, unmoving. There was no sign of the third. Yorke stayed where he was. The rain eased and suddenly stopped. The wind dropped and the countryside was blanketed in silence. A weak sun shone through, lifting the earlier gloom. The two bodies were hardly discernible amongst the cereal and Yorke ignored them, convinced both men were dead.

The ditch circumvented the field. The road was fifty metres away to his left, another field at least a hundred metres to his right. He could see the rooftops of the houses of the village on the other side, one or two chimneys with smoke rising. Very dimly, from the distance, he heard a car engine. He knew he couldn't stay where he was. Whoever the men were, reinforcements could already be on their way and he knew he'd been damned lucky so far. Time to get away. He thought of phoning Catherine but decided against it. She didn't need the distraction of her mobile ringing just at that moment.

The ditch was well kept and he had no trouble in keeping low and darting along it – away from the road. He had dismissed the idea of reaching the road and trying to get away. He would be too easily spotted. Instead, he decided it was time to yomp out of the area. The mile-eating pace of the SAS and RMs would enable him to cover a lot of ground.

He stopped by the furthest hedge and cautiously looked around, quartering the landscape. Nothing was moving. A few metres away was a beech tree with low slung branches. The bole was his side of the fence while its branches spread over the hedge and barbed wire. Leaping up, he grabbed a branch and swung his legs on to the top strand of wire. He heaved himself over and dropped heavily onto the other side. He lay still and looked back. All quiet. There was no ditch this side of the fence and he felt exposed although the hedgerow was thick enough to hide him from view. He knew better than to walk across an exposed field and followed the hedge, still going away from the road. He walked with long strides, his head turning continuously as he searched for potential attackers. Less than ten minutes later the village was out of sight and he was hidden in a small copse at the corner of a wheat field. He stopped and withdrew his mobile phone.

It rang out and Yorke was beginning to think there would be no answer. 'Catherine? Are you all right?'

'Stephen! Yes! I got in the car and drove like a maniac. I was going to come back and look for you.'

'No! Don't!' There was alarm in Yorke's voice. 'I can manage on my own. It's just after six. I'll meet you somewhere. I know! There's a pub in Stickney. If I remember correctly the village is on the A16. Go there and wait for me. I'm about seven miles away. I should make it in about an hour and a half at the most. You got that?'

'I've got it. What are we doing then?'

'Getting the hell out of here. I'll see you later.' He broke the connection. In the distance he could hear a diesel engine and saw a tractor and trailer move over the brow of a low hill. A wind had picked up and blown the sky clear of cloud and it looked like it was turning into a pleasant English spring evening. Yorke looked about him. 'Where only man is vile,' he said to himself.

He knew the sun didn't set until around 21.00 and so he had no choice other than to walk openly across the countryside. How many reinforcements could the enemy muster? What if the police were called? They'd find him and the guns. He couldn't risk getting rid of them as he might need them again. He didn't underestimate the tight spot he was in. Anger coursed through him. Who had killed Evelyn and why? He still had no idea as to which side she'd been on. The lie about her mother could have been a useful excuse, like Catherine suggested. Or had she betrayed them? Had she been killed as part of the mopping-up operation? The thoughts whirled around his brain, a distraction to the job in hand – survival.

His anger turned to white-hot hatred of the people responsible. He shook his head. He knew such emotion was a distraction and got people killed when they should have been concentrating on the job in hand. He kept close to the hedgerows, his long legs stretching out and eating up the miles. Twice he crossed lanes as he headed west, by-passing a number of small villages and skirting farms and out-buildings. He found

Stickney and the pub without difficulty. The car was in the car park.

Entering the bar, he saw Catherine sitting at a corner table, nursing a drink. He joined her.

'Any problems?' he greeted her.

'None. But the sooner we get away from here the better. What happened?'

Yorke shrugged and said in a quiet voice, 'I shot at least two, maybe three of them. You know, the resources of this lot are astonishing. Truly astonishing. It wouldn't surprise me if they had roadblocks set up under the guise of the police even as we sit here.'

'I hadn't thought of that. What are we to do?'

'If we meet real policemen we bluff it. We'll ditch the anoraks.'

'And if they're bogus?'

'There'll be a few more bodies littering the countryside. I was near here running away from these swine only a few days ago. I can't keep running.'

They left the pub and climbed into the car. Catherine drove. Yorke placed the Walther PPK in the side pocket of the door and the Smith & Wesson under his seat, butt forward.

'Wait a second,' he said as Catherine started the engine. Two high-powered cars swept past, each with four occupants, heading south towards Boston. 'I know this area quite well. Go left and immediately right. The countryside around her is criss-crossed with small lanes. We'll take those.'

They drove through quaint villages with equally quaint names such as New Bolingbroke and Tumby Woodside. Shortly after that Yorke decided it was safe to take a main road and they headed to Coningsby and then Sleaford. They saw no more cars crammed with men and were now mixed in with the hundreds of cars to be found on an English main road. From Sleaford they headed for Boston and the aerodrome. Enroute, Yorke telephoned Dom and reassured the boy that he was all right and that he'd see him later.

It was dusk by the time Yorke finished his pre-flight checks and sent the little plane racing down the runway. As they gathered height they came back into the sunlight, while the world beneath them became cast in deep shadow.

Catherine looked down and said, 'It's awesome. Not like being in a large jet.'

Yorke grinned at her. 'Awesome is the right word. When you fly in a small plane like this you enter a new world.'

Catherine smiled back. 'You can forget all your worries, somehow. They stay back there on the ground.'

'I know precisely what you mean. Unfortunately, as soon as you land they catch up again, often with a vengeance.' He busied himself talking to Air Traffic Control, made height and heading adjustments and allowed the ATC to con him back to Gatwick. They landed on the tail of a 737.

After handing the plane back to the hire people they went across to the main airport buildings and found a taxi to take them to Crawley. The plan had been for Catherine to return to London while he joined Dom. Now, as they stood at the railway station and it came time to part, they were both reluctant to do so.

'When will I see you again?'

Yorke shrugged. 'I'm not sure. But soon. I need to get Dom away. The school's no good. They'll have the place covered. I need to make sure he's *safe*. That above everything. Then we need to expose what's going on. You write the stories while I cover your back.'

Catherine leaned closer looking into his eyes. 'What about my front?'

'I'll cover that too,' he smiled at her.

'So, not just a one night stand?'

He put his arms around her and kissed her lightly. 'What do you think? There's been nobody else since Dom's mother died. I had neither the inclination nor, truth to tell, the time for dalliances.'

Catherine laughed. 'Dalliances. What an old-fashioned word. Then I suppose in some ways you're an old-fashioned sort of man.'

'If you mean one who walks on the outside of pavements, opens doors and pays in restaurants then I guess you're right. Is that a problem?'

'No. I like old-fashioned men. Only I've met so few and had so little experience with them.'

'You've got my numbers and my e-mail. And Dom's mobile.'

'Ditto. I'll call as soon as I get home. All right?'

'Do that. You've got the flipchart papers and all the notes we made?'

'Yes, safe and sound.'

A last kiss and Yorke was gone, striding down the platform for his train. A call to Dom had established that he was still berthed where Yorke had left him at Arundel. The journey seemed to take forever but just before midnight he alighted at Crossbush. It had been a long day. A long few days, and Yorke was tired. Otherwise he might have been more alert. As it was he didn't recognise any trouble until it was too late. But with the recognition came darkness.

Dom was fretting. It was after 02.00 and there was still no sign of his father. He had tried the phone but all he was getting was the message to try again later. It was only then that he decided to try the tracking device. Switching it on his eyes almost popped out of his head as he saw that it showed Yorke moving west. With shaking hands he took the latitude and longitude and plotted the position. Southampton! It didn't make sense. Indecision gnawed at him.

If you can't affect something don't worry it, he remembered his father saying. Always get sleep if you can; you never know when you'll need it. Dom passed a restless and fitful night lying on his bunk. He was suddenly wide awake and much to his surprise found it had just turned 07.00. Memories flooded back and he rushed to the chart room. He checked the tracking signal. It was steady. Quickly he plotted it's position. Chaple Point? Cornwall? Mevagissey? He'd heard the name recently. He clicked his fingers. The radio transmission ordering the boats searching for them to return to Mevagissey. *Why is dad there*? More importantly, why didn't he say anything. Realisation dawned on him. Unless he'd been taken there against his will. Was that it?

Even as the thought took root he was down aft flashing up the diesel. As it warmed through he was letting go the mooring and allowing the current to sweep the yacht into the main-stream. Dom opened the throttle wide and headed towards the sea. He had no plan only an overwhelming desire to be near Yorke. There was gear on the boat that would be useful. Including the tracking device that could be refined the closer he got to Yorke. Within a half-mile radius he'd be able to fix his father's position to within a few metres.

In spite of his anxiety and desire for haste he didn't forget the rules-of-the-road nor the necessity for safe passage. As the *Lucky Duck* reached the open sea he bent on the mainsail and jib, altered course to starboard and settled her on a heading of 250 degrees. Profound relief coursed through him; the wind was a steady 18-20 knots out of the east. Putting on his harness, he hooked on the safety line, hoisted the mainsail and eased the boom out to starboard. He adjusted the mainsheet until he was satisfied that the sail was drawing as much wind as feasible. He then cut the power to the engine. Quiet settled over the yacht apart from the hiss of water under her keel and the sound of the wind through the rigging. He checked her speed; 7 knots.

There were few boats about and he had a clear run to Selsey Bill. He debated with himself whether to set the jib or spin-naker and settled for the latter. If the wind stayed steady he'd get an extra 2 or 3 knots out of her.

From the sail locker he dragged the bag containing the spin-naker up on deck. He clipped the bag to the port rail and attached the halyard, sheet and brace to the sail. Setting the spinnaker pole on the mast, he hauled up the topping lift until the pole was horizontal with the deck. Quickly he began winding the spinnaker out of the bag and back towards the beak of the pole. As he did so the wind caught the sail and began to lift it out of the bag. This was a tricky manoeuvre and one he'd only done with his father there to direct and help.

With the spinnaker pole fixed firmly to the brace, the sail close up to the beak and the topping lift and kicker in place all that was loose was the sheet. At the mast, Dom grabbed the halyard and hauled down quickly, the sail rising and filling as he did. As soon as the spinnaker reached the top of the mast, Dom secured the halyard, pulled on the sheet and tied it off. The bow of the little sloop lifted and she seemed to fly across the water, willed on by Dom's sense of urgency.

Realising he was hungry, he checked the setting of the sails and swept the horizon for other boats before he went below to fry bacon and make a sandwich. A cup of tea in one hand, sweetened with tinned milk and two sugars, and a door-stop of a sandwich in the other. he stood in the bow and looked ahead.

Fear and trepidation mingled with excitement as he pondered his options. Automatically he checked the sea for other craft. Nothing was coming close, and nothing was on a steady bearing indicating the potential for a collision. He had tried Yorke's phone only minutes earlier to receive the same frustrating message – try later.

When he'd finished eating he went below to check on the weather forecast. The pressure was dropping and heavy squalls and rain were expected in the late afternoon. The boat was making good 11 knots, Selsey Bill was abeam to starboard and the distance to go was as near as dammit, 195 miles. 18 hours run at that speed. But that was impossible as wind patterns changed and alterations of course became necessary. Realistically it would take a day to get to Mevagissey. A day possibly his father didn't have. Indecision took hold and he began to swither whether or not to head to shore and find a police station. And say what? His father had been abducted by some men who were trying to kill him? Which men? The ones who'd attacked the house at Gib Point? What did he know about Gib Point and what went on there? The questions went round and round in his head and his answers began to sound ludicrous even to himself. And suppose he got somebody to believe him? If the police went in mob-handed to wherever his father was being held, wasn't there a likelihood his father could be killed? He'd seen how ruthless these men were. That was assuming his father was still alive. Tears welled up at the thought and he angrily wiped them away.

The wind had backed a few degrees and a corner of the main sail was flapping. He adjusted the setting and then busied himself checking the rigging. It was just after midday when two things occurred. He had to tack to starboard to go around the stern of the Portsmouth to Jersey ferry and his mobile phone rang.

'Hullo? Dad?' he asked eagerly.

A woman's voice asked tentatively, 'Hullo? Is that Dom?'

Warily Dom replied. 'It may be. Who are you?'

'This is Catherine. We sort of met on that video link.'

'I remember.'

'Listen, Dom, is Stephen with you? I've been trying his mobile but there's no answer.' Desperation lent urgency to Catherine's voice.

Dom said nothing, his brow furrowed in perplexed indecision.

'Dom? Dom? Are you still there?'

'Yes. How do I know I can trust you? How do I know it's not some sort of trap?'

'What do you mean? Some sort of trap. How? To do what? Look, can I talk to Stephen?'

'No.'

'Why not?'

'He's not here, that's why.'

'But he left me last night to join you on the boat. At Arundel. I was with him when he spoke to you.'

'How do I know you're telling the truth?'

'Dom, for Christ's sake, why should I be lying? Do you have any idea where Stephen is?'

'Maybe.' Dom's uncertainty was mixed with fear and he wondered what he should do.

'Listen, Dom, I know about the tracking device. I was with him when you checked his position in Scotland. Where is he? Have you spoken to him since last night?'

Miserably, Dom answered. 'No. I've heard nothing.'

'I've found some information I think Stephen would like to have. That's why I've been trying to contact him.'

'How did you get this number?'

'Your Dad gave it to me just in case. Dom, what do you think has happened?'

'I don't know. All I do know is that Dad didn't arrive and I can't contact him. I've checked the tracking signal and he's in Cornwall.'

'Near Mevagissey,' Catherine said.

'Yes! How do you know?'

'It was the information I wanted to give your father. I've tracked a number of businesses to a place just outside Mevagissey. It's too complex to explain but I think it's useful information for him to have.'

'Well he appears to have gone there. That's where I'm headed.'

'Maybe he found something out and went of his own accord.'

'He wouldn't go without telling me. Never. And he'd have answered his phone when I rang him. And he'd have come here last night.'

'What are you going to do?'

'I don't know yet. But I'm going to look for him.'

Catherine sighed. 'When will you get there?'

'Tomorrow morning.'

'Okay. Wait for me. I'm leaving right away. I'll phone you in the morning. I think that under the circumstances two heads are better than one.

20

YORKE AWOKE TO a sea of pain. It felt as though he had at least two cracked ribs. He moved tentatively. Maybe not. Just bruised. His head felt twice its size and one eye was half closed. It hadn't been a scientific interrogation. It had been a brutal attack of revenge by the brother of someone he'd killed in the past few days. He spat blood from his mouth and ran a dry tongue over dry lips. Opening his eyes he saw he was in the same small room where he'd lost consciousness. He knew he was lying on a concrete floor, that there was a table with three chairs, two one side, one the other and that a guard stood at the door watching him. He opened his eyes and blinked. Only there was no guard.

A stanza of poetry by Dylan Thomas entered his head.

And you, my father, there on the sad height,
Curse, bless me, now with your fierce tears, I pray,
Do not go gentle into that good night.
Rage, rage against the dying of the light.

Groggily he sat up and leaned against the stone wall. *I'll go kicking and screaming and I'll take a few of the bastards with me.* He stayed still and quietly surveyed the room he'd spent the last eight hours or so in. Maybe longer, he thought, as he had no watch and no way of telling the time. The room was about fifteen feet square, had a solid door and no window. He didn't know whether it was day or night. Somehow though, he didn't think he'd been out for that long. If so, it was the middle of the day, perhaps early afternoon. His immediate thoughts were of Dom. What was he doing? More importantly, was he all right? He hadn't mentioned the boy and neither had his captors.

Since he'd been taken he'd learnt only one thing. They wanted to know what Yorke knew and whether or not he'd told anyone and if so, who? So far the questioning had been crude and the results had been precisely what any professional would have expected – nothing. A big, fat zero. But that was because they weren't set up for modern interrogation techniques but that, apparently, was about to change. Or so he'd been promised. Just as soon as ex-Colonel "Mack" Roberts arrived. He was bringing the right equipment to handle a difficult interrogation. Yorke could well believe it.

As he came to he noticed something else had changed. There was a jug with a glass beside it on the table. He climbed stiffly to his feet and staggered the two paces to reach them. The glass and jug were plastic. He poured water from the jug into the glass, took a mouthful, swilled it around his mouth and carefully spat it down the drain situated under the table. The likelihood of the water being doctored with some sort of drug was far too high. Usually an hallucinogenic. Yorke grinned mirthlessly. He knew as much as Roberts about interrogation.

He poured the rest of the water over his head and felt refreshed though still damnably thirsty. He had already had a good look around the room and was as certain as he could be there was no camera or listening device. The room was lit by a naked bulb hanging from the ceiling. He could easily smash it and plunge the place into darkness. That fact alone convinced him that wherever he was, wasn't designed to hold prisoners.

His coat had been taken, as had his socks, shoes and belt. His shirt was torn but still had its buttons. He felt the collar. The edges were still stiff. The enemy had been careless. There was a noise at the door and he threw himself back onto the ground and closed his eyes.

'He's still out for the count,' said a rough voice.

'Good. He's drunk the water. He'll not come round for the next twenty-four hours.'

'Saves us having to force the stuff into him. Mack ain't here until midnight tomorrow. He said no food or drink. I reckon when Yorke comes to he'll have a raging thirst and an even worse hangover.'

'Good. Serves the bastard right.'

Yorke heard footsteps approach and readied himself. He felt the presence of the man above him. Though he was ready for it, the kick in his thigh made him grunt but otherwise he stayed still.

'He's out cold. Leave him be. I got on okay with him in the mob. Pity really. Mind you, he was always a strait-laced son of a bitch.'

The voice had been nagging Yorke. Now he got it. Tom Littlejohn – a damned good corporal and a better sergeant. Tempted though he was, he didn't dare look. He knew that he was dealing with one, probably two, extremely professional men. The sort you didn't give an inch to as they'd take the whole nine yards.

'Let's go and have a pint. I could murder one. Then I'll give you a game of pool,' said Littlejohn.

'It was damned lucky he was spotted on the train. Trust Ingrid.'

'That blonde bitch. I can't stand her.'

'Me neither, but I wouldn't mind giving her one.'

The door closed but Yorke lay still. Ingrid? Blonde? Vaguely he remembered a slim woman with very fair hair and pale skin on the train. But she'd taken absolutely no notice of him and he'd taken no notice of her. *Luck!* Only the bloody enemy appeared to have it all. He lay still, listening intently. Was he alone? Or was one of them in the room watching him? After only a few seconds he knew the room was empty. Nobody could stay that still and quiet for even twenty seconds. He opened his eyes. From what the two men had said he guessed it was middle to late evening. He would need to be patient before he made any sort of move. Patience was really his forte but he'd manage – somehow. For the umpteenth time he wondered what Dom was doing and whether he was all right. The water Yorke had swilled around his mouth was beginning to have its effect. The chemicals in the water were absorbed through his mouth and gums. He didn't mean to but he couldn't prevent himself from falling asleep.

The wind had picked up as the sun went down. Dom had hauled down the spinnaker and put up the big jib. The wind was gusting over 25 knots and the *Lucky Duck* was flying along, touching 13 knots. She'd never gone so fast. He checked the combined lantern at the masthead, both green and red lights burned brightly and he checked the white overtaking light. Ditto. The radar showed nothing on a collision course – the nearest contact passing two miles to port.

Now it was dark he felt safe. The yacht was just three incidental lights in the night. No form, no substance. Anonymous. He opened the secret compartments in the hull and began removing certain items. Whatever he did, whatever happened, he would be prepared.

Midnight. He checked the sails, took in a reef on the mainsail and changed the jib for the smallest of the three they carried. The wind was now on the port beam and the sails hard up, the hull heeled over. Speed of advance, distance travelled over the ground, was 9 knots. Highly respectable under the circumstances, and now looking like an 05.15 landfall at Mevagissey. He had been thinking about Catherine all afternoon, the biggest question in his mind was whether or not he could trust her. He had decided he couldn't. There was too much as stake.

The rain came in squalls and he hunkered down inside his foul-weather gear. He'd identified Gribbin Head on the radar and had pored over the chart of Mevagissey Bay and Chaple Point. He still wasn't close enough to his father's signal to refine his position which would help him to decide. A last examination of the sails and the ships' lights he could see scattered around him, a final check on the warning buzzer on the radar should a contact come within 5 miles and he settled down to sleep, sure it would be impossible to achieve. A loud crack woke him to a grey dawn as he struggled groggily awake.

The wind had shifted in the night and the boat was virtually in irons, moving at only a knot or two. The crack that had awoken

him was caused by the mainsail flapping. Groaning, Dom climbed
to his feet, checked his position and heading and set the yacht
on a starboard tack. Amazingly the *Lucky Duck* was 3 miles port
of his planned track and only 4 miles from Chaple Point.

He went below, washed his face and brushed his teeth.
Immediately he felt fresher, more alive, his tiredness sloughing
off him like a second skin. He made a Marmite sandwich and
a cup of tea, NATO standard with condensed milk, and returned
up top. It was 04.20. Sunrise at Plymouth was at 05.14. The
rain had stopped and he was looking at a clear sky, pleased
with himself to be able to identify Capella and Vega, and what
was evidently Venus.

Now a mile off-shore, he began refining the position indi-
cator of Yorke's tracking device. It only took a few seconds
but finally he had his father's position pin-pointed to less than
twenty metres. The chart showed a house on the top of the
cliffs, behind Chaple Point.

Satisfied, he dropped the mainsail, trampling it underfoot,
then stuffing it down the forward hatch. Now only the jib gave
the yacht any momentum and her speed dropped off to half-
a-knot. He was only two cables from the cliffs, the boat silent
in her approach, unnoticeable in the pre-dawn grey.

Dom took the *Lucky Duck* in as close to Chaple Point as he
dared. The echo sounder was showing three metres when he
dropped the jib and lowered the anchor. She settled only fifteen
yards off the rocks. He sat in the silence for a few minutes but
nothing disturbed the peace. There were no yells and, more
importantly, nobody took a shot at him. *So far, so good.* In his
cabin he changed out of his bright yellow foul-weather gear
and put on an old can't-see-me-suit of Yorke's. One that Dom
sometimes used when doing a dirty job around the boat. He
ignored the paint splodges on the trousers. It was a bit big
around the waist but his belt took care of it. Under the jacket
he strapped a holster and a modified Smith & Wesson, the
sister of the one his father had taken. In his pockets he placed
two small PE devices.

Back on deck he threw the inflatable into the water and

climbed down into it. He used a paddle to propel him the short distance to the shore. There he clambered onto the rocks and pulled the boat up after him. The rocks behind were about fifty feet high, not sheer, but a stiff climb.

'Wish me well, dad,' Dom spoke in a whisper, addressing his real father. 'You know how much I love Stephen.'

He could barely see his hands in front of his face now he was off the water and in the shadows and so he moved slowly but steadily up the scree and to the cliff proper. As part of his preparations to become a Royal Marine officer, Dom had joined a club and had been climbing on artificial cliff-faces for the past 12 months. He had learnt the rudimentaries of rock climbing, the first being not to trust your weight to a foot or hand hold without trying it first. He began climbing – slowly, carefully, aware that a great deal rested on him getting to the top. He could hear Yorke telling him – 'Dom, there's no point screwing it up before you get started. Slow and steady and get to your destination. There's room for cock-ups when the action starts. Then control passes out of your hands as others are involved.'

He was two-thirds of the way up when a chunk of rock broke off and clattered down the cliff while he hung on with his left hand and right foot. He stayed still, mustering his strength, ignoring the pounding of his heart. After a few seconds he continued his upwards passage. Finally, after what had seemed an age but was only minutes, he reached the top. Grabbing a handful of grass he pulled himself over the edge and lay still, getting his breath back.

He could see nothing and more significantly hear nothing. The house was about a hundred yards away, a dark looming edifice in the early morning. It was three stories high, at least a hundred yards long and God alone knew how deep. From his pocket Dom extracted his mobile phone. It was patched through to the yacht and the readout on the tracking device. He sent instructions down the phone and the position of the tracker was further refined. A picture was transmitted back to the phone. Yorke was somewhere in the left hand corner of the building.

Staying low, Dom ran across the sparsely grassed and stony

ground. There were no lights on and no sign of anybody. The building took on form and he could see a huge archway over the front door. His feet hit gravel and he realised he was walking on a driveway that appeared circumjacent to the house.

He made one last connection to the tracker. Now he was so close to the source of the signal he was able to refine its position to less than half a metre. There! At the corner. The nearest door only yards from it. Treading carefully, Dom made his way to the door and tried the handle. It was locked. He removed one of the PE charges from his pocket and stuck it to the door. How long should he set the timer? While he pondered the problem the door handle turned and the door moved slowly inwards.

Yorke awoke with a start. *Christ, how long had he been sleeping?* It wasn't like him. He knew . . . the bloody water. It was skin absorbent, not just ingested. He just hoped he hadn't slept for too long. But how long? Was it still the evening or the middle of the night? There was only one way to find out.

Getting to his feet, he stretched, eased aching muscles and prepared to go down fighting. Tearing two buttons off the bottom of his shirt, he felt under his shirt collar for one of the collar bones used to keep the fabric stiff. He slid it free. Each button had a slot in its side and he fixed each end of the collar bone to a button. The result was a flat dumbbell about 2 inches long.

He peeled off the backing paper on each button and then bent the collar bone in half before straightening it again. Pressing the buttons onto the deadlock, he stood beside the door and closed his eyes. A few seconds later the device threw out a super white-heat, melting the bolt. Acrid smoke blossomed in the air and quickly dissipated. Smashing the bulb, he plunged the room into pitch darkness while he waited and listened but nobody came.

His thirst had returned with a vengeance, along with his aches and pains but he put them out of his mind. By now the bolt had cooled to red hot and Yorke gripped the edge of the door to ease it open. Drops of the bolt were already solidifying and he had to tug hard to pull the door ajar. The corridor outside was pitch dark. He looked left and right but could see nothing. Which way to turn?

Licking the back of his hand he held it out in front of him, palm sideways. After a few seconds he turned his hand around. There was a definite coolness on the back of his hand coming from the right. He did it again. No doubt about it. There was a slight draft coming from that direction.

With his hands extended in front of him he walked slowly and cautiously along the corridor. It seemed to stretch forever, the darkness Stygnian in its intensity. It was minutes later that he sensed a lifting of the gloom. It was infinitesimal but he looked back over his shoulder to check it. Yes, it was a few degrees lighter ahead. A dozen more paces and he saw a grey dash across the floor in front of him and he came to a halt against a door. He felt its edges carefully. The lock was on the right. A key was in the lock and he turned it slowly. He felt it meet resistance and then the well-oiled tumblers moved. Silently he turned the handle and when it was fully around he pulled the door towards him.

The blackness gave way to the grey and chilly morning. Yorke opened the door far enough to step through and froze as he got outside. He'd heard the unmistakable sound of a safety catch being thumbed.

A whispered voice said, 'Don't move or I'll shoot.'

Yorke's heart soared and he chuckled, 'I do believe you mean it, son.'

'Dad!' Dom spoke in a loud and excited whisper. 'Dad! I don't believe it.'

'Shush, son. Keep it down. What are . . . Never mind. Explanations can wait.' Yorke placed his arms on the boy's shoulders and gave him a hug. 'I think I'd better take that.' He eased the S&W out of the youngster's hand. 'How did you get here?'

'*Lucky Duck*. She's just over there.' Dom nodded towards the sea, a big grin plastered on his face.

Two things happened. Dom's mobile phone began ringing and a man stepped around the corner of the house and stopped less than three paces away.

21

YORKE REACTED INSTINCTIVELY. Because of the awkwardness of their relative positions, he took two paces and hit the man a stunning blow across the neck with his left hand, followed by a blow to the nose with the palm of his right. The man gurgled and dropped, still conscious, reaching for his radio. Yorke stamped his bare foot onto the man's hand, breaking the guard's metacarpals, anger and fear lending weight to his movements. Dom was at risk! The bastards were going to pay like never before. The heel of his other foot shattered the man's throat and the man gurgled his last gasp in agony. Yorke shook his head. It was time to make a run for it. He turned to Dom who had his phone to his ear.

'Hullo?' Dom whispered. 'Catherine? I can't talk now . . .'

Shock froze Yorke for a second. Catherine? What the hell was going down?

'Dom! Dom!' Yorke whispered urgently.

Dom looked up at his father and said, 'It's that woman. Catherine somebody. She phoned yesterday. She says she's at the gates.'

'What gates?'

'Here. This house.'

'Let me talk to her.' He took the phone and said, 'Catherine? Where are you?'

'Stephen? Thank god! I thought you were a prisoner or something.' There was bewilderment in her voice.

'I was. I broke out. Dom's with me. Where are you?'

'At the gates to the house near Mevagissey.'

'Mevagissey? In Cornwall? What are you doing there?'

'*You're* in Mevagissey!'

'Dom where are we?'

'Those lights over there is Mevagissey. Didn't you know?'

'No. I . . . Catherine what is it?'

'Two men are coming. They've got guns.'

'Listen, stall them. Don't break the connection. I'll listen in. Dom, which way did you come?'

'Those trees are the cliff. You can see the sea now.'

In the thickening light Yorke looked the way his son was pointing and saw the grey undulating ocean.

'Where's the yacht?' As he was speaking, Yorke was searching the dead man. He found what he wanted – an automatic. 'Listen, son. Take the Smith & Wesson and hide in the trees. If I don't come for you in fifteen minutes get the hell out of here. I'll meet you in the town harbour tonight. Midnight. Okay?'

Dom nodded nervously. Now he'd found his father he didn't want to be parted from him again.

Yorke understood the youngster's reaction, patted his shoulder and then gave the boy a quick and fierce hug. 'I'm counting on you son. Now go.'

Dom ran across the ground towards the trees. While Yorke covered the boy's progress he knelt beside the body's feet and removed its shoes. They were a size too big but better than being bare-footed. Dom reached the trees and hid behind one of the boles. Yorke waved and hurried away to the corner of the house.

There had been no sign of any other guards. He figured if two men had pounced on Catherine and he'd taken out one other then three had been on watch. A substantial number for a premises of that size. He wondered how many more were in the house. Pressing the phone to his ear he heard Catherine's voice.

' . . . off. I'm a journalist. This is public land. Christ, this is the road. I have a right to be here.'

'Shut your mouth! You're coming with us. We don't like snoopers and until we're told otherwise you're staying here.'

'I'm not! And you can't make me!'

There was silence for maybe two seconds and then the unmistakable sound of a slap and Catherine's scream of pain and rage.

'You bastard!'

A man's voice yelled. 'Ow! Stop the cow, Phil.'

Catherine screamed again and there was silence.

'She still alive?'

'Yes. I didn't hit her that hard. Come on, darling, wake up. I'm not carrying you. You're going to bleeding well walk.' There were a few more seconds of silence. 'Radio in. Wake Erik. It's time he earned his keep. Ask him what we should do with her.'

A voice mumbled in the background while the guard continued, 'Up you get, darling. You're coming with us.'

Yorke guessed that Catherine had dropped her telephone as the voices faded. He placed Dom's own phone in his pocket and stopped at the corner of the house. Sunrise wasn't far away and the daylight was coming fast. He could see the two men, Catherine between them, walking up the drive. One was speaking on a radio whilst the other held Catherine's arm. Yorke turned and sprinted back to the dead guard. Quickly he removed the body's coat and put it on, along with the baseball cap the dead man had been wearing. He ran back to the house in time to see the three stop at the front door.

The man on the radio turned to the other man and said, 'Erik says to put her in the room next to Yorke. This way.' He pushed Catherine towards the corner of the house.

Yorke took four or five paces back and waited, listening to the footfalls of the three. As they came round the corner, his head down, Yorke walked towards them.

'Jim. Give us a hand . . .'

He got no further as Yorke, holding the automatic by his side, swung it hard against the head of the man on the right. He fell, pole-axed.

'What the fu . . .'

Yorke pointed the weapon at the other guard. 'Don't even think about it. I won't hesitate.'

The man raised his hands, nervously licking his lips.

'Move away, Catherine.'

She stepped clear.

'Turn around.'

The man reluctantly turned, raising his shoulders and ducking his head as though to ward off the expected blow. Yorke hit him hard. Very hard. He had been one of the men who had given Yorke a kicking. In repayment Yorke gave him a hairline fracture and rendered him unconscious for a good while.

'Come on, we'd better go. Wait! Where's your telephone?'

'My telephone? Why?'

'Did you tell these clowns your name?'

'No. Only that I was a journalist.'

'They didn't check your bag?' Yorke nodded at the bag slung over her shoulder.

'No. They were bringing me in here first, I guess. What about my phone?'

'If they find it they'll know pretty bloody quickly who you are. It'll be a lot safer if you stay anonymous for a lot longer yet.'

'I dropped the phone on the road. I don't think they noticed. I didn't see either of them pick it up.'

'I'll go and look for it. See the trees? Dom's over there. Now hurry. Whoever was on the other end of the radio may be wondering what's happening. Or become curious enough to come and see who you are.'

Catherine hurried towards the trees while Yorke ran down the drive to the gates. Although shut, they weren't locked and he went through easily enough. The black mobile telephone lay in the middle of the road. He swept it up, dropped it into his pocket, turned on his heels and sprinted back towards the side of the house.

As he neared the trees he waved at the other two to get going. At the cliff edge he found Dom already a third of the way down while Catherine was standing back in horror.

'I can't go down there!'

'You have to. Come on, it's easy. If a fifteen year old boy can do it, so can you.'

'I can't! I hate heights!'

'We've no choice! It's too dangerous to go back to the gates and out that way.' Even as he spoke he was looking back towards the house. Lights began to appear in some of the windows. 'Shit! The whole place is coming alive like an angry beehive. Catherine, we've got to get out of here.'

'All right,' she said in a small voice.

'Good girl. I'll go first and guide you. Give me your bag to carry.' With the bag over his shoulder, he tucked the revolver in the small of his back before scrambling over the edge and feeling his way down until his feet found a firm hold. 'Now come on. Put your left foot here and your right foot here. Keep putting each foot and hand lower than the other.'

They began to slowly climb down the cliff face. Halfway down they went from being in a grey gloom to brilliant sunshine. It bathed their backs and lit the cliff. It was at that moment Catherine slipped and lost her hold.

Yorke had both feet firmly planted, and his right hand curled around an outcrop. His left hand was holding Catherine's right ankle as he guided her foot into a deep crevice. In her fear and agitation Catherine leaned backwards and began to fall. Yorke let go her ankle and slammed the palm of his hand against her behind and pushed, his muscles straining as he tried to prevent her falling. She hovered for a couple of seconds and then Yorke won the battle with gravity and she hit the cliff face with a lung expelling gasp, striking her chin on the rock as she did.

'Grab hold. Find something to hold on to,' Yorke ordered.

After a few seconds Catherine said, 'I'm . . . I'm okay. Got a hold. Oh, god! Oh, god! I knew I couldn't do this.'

'Shut up, Catherine. We haven't far to go. Even if you fall the worse will be a couple of broken legs.'

'What if a land on my head?' She asked with a flash of her usual spirit.

'Then you won't be hurt at all,' came the callous reply.

Catherine, in spite of herself, chuckled. 'I asked for that. Okay, you're right. We'd better keep going. I can't hold on much longer.'

'Move your left foot. There's an outcrop about twelve inches down. That's it. Now your right hand. Okay. Good.'

As they continued slowly down the cliff Dom reached the bottom and put the dinghy in the water. He sat in the boat watching with anxious eyes as the two grownups made their cautious descent. Six feet from the bottom, as the cliff shelved outwards, Catherine slipped again and this time Yorke wasn't ready for it. They both slid to the bottom, barking shins, scraping hands and faces.

'You all right?' Yorke asked, helping Catherine to her feet.

'I'll live. Look at the state of me!' Her trousers and blouse were torn, her hands filthy and her nails were broken.

'You said it. You'll live. The rest is fixable. Come on, into the boat.' He handed her in and jumped after her, pushing the boat away from the rocks. The thrust put them within a few feet of the *Lucky Duck's* hull and a few swift paddles with his and Dom's hands and they were alongside.

'Dom, no engine! Pull up the anchor. Catherine, stand by the wheel and turn her when I say. I'll take the jib.'

The wind was off the land and coming down across St Austell Bay. As Dom announced the anchor had broken free, Yorke hauled up the Jib and said, 'Spin the wheel to port.' The wind caught the sail and the yacht's bow came round to an easterly heading. Slowly she headed away from the land. 'Dom, let's hoist the main.'

Yorke looked back at the cliffs but saw nobody. He prayed their luck would hold just a little longer. Ten minutes was all he asked for.

'Hold her steady on that course,' he said to Catherine as he and Dom worked on the mainsail. As the sails began to fill and draw steadily, the yacht picked up speed and headed straight into the sun. With the running rigging set and the standing rigging adjusted, the *Duck* accelerated like the thoroughbred she was.

*   *   *

Yorke sat in the cockpit, exhaustion etched in his face. The autopilot was set and he was having difficulty staying awake. It was mid-morning and Cornwall was out of sight astern as they headed south-south-east. In spite of his tiredness he couldn't help smiling at the thought of Dom charging in to rescue him, and Catherine coming all the way from London. She'd even walked to the house from the railway station rather than hire a taxi in case she was remembered. When he'd asked her why, she'd shrugged sheepishly and replied, 'I thought it was the right thing to do.'

His reply of, 'You've been watching too many spy films,' hadn't gone down well.

Now they were both asleep. He wanted to do the same but wasn't prepared to risk being taken unawares. If he set the radar alarm at 5 miles he'd not get any sleep anyway and any less wouldn't give him time to prepare if the enemy did come after them. So he was forced to stay awake. He scanned the horizon, decided the three ships and half a dozen yachts he could see would pass clear and went below to make a cup of coffee. With a steaming mug of freshly ground coffee, he returned to the cockpit. In spite of himself, a short while later his head was nodding and he was jerking himself awake. He knew he was falling into that state of micro-sleeps which was the cause of so many motorway accidents and decided the sensible thing to do was sleep properly for ten minutes. He checked the radar, set the radar alarm, set his watch alarm, and lay down on the cockpit cushions. In seconds he was fast asleep. Ten minutes later he was jerked back to wakefulness by the buzzing on his wrist.

A wash and teeth brush left him feeling refreshed and fully awake. He knew he would now be all right for another couple of hours. There'd be no more micro-sleeps. That afternoon he was able to give a great deal of time to his thoughts and he didn't like them one little bit. He knew he was afraid. For probably the first time in his life he knew real fear. But it wasn't for him. It was for Dom. And, he admitted to himself, for Catherine. Christ in a bucket, it wasn't his job to save the sodding world. Let someone else do it. Like the Prime Minister. The sanctimonious, cowardly *bastard*.

Or maybe the PM had his priorities right. If the rest of the world could sit back and watch organised crime and terrorists get the upper hand why should he bother? But Yorke knew the answer, paraphrasing the quote – for evil to flourish all it needed was for good men to do nothing.

Standing up, Yorke altered the yacht's heading 10 degrees to port, adjusted the jib's sheets and tightened the main's in-haul. Satisfied, he sat back down to his ruminations and a mug of tea, no milk and no sugar.

Movement below disturbed his bleak thoughts and Catherine popped her head up through the companionway. 'Get you anything?'

'No thanks. I'm okay. How are you feeling?'

She smiled. 'Better. I've cut my nails and put antiseptic on my grazes. What about you?'

'Healing nicely.' Yorke yawned. 'I could use some shut-eye.'

'I'll be right up. I can keep watch while you sleep.' She reappeared a few minutes later with a cheese sandwich and a mug of coffee.

Yorke gave her a few basic instructions about waking him, settled below on the main saloon settee and promptly fell asleep.

22

MR FROBISHER'S VOICE was softer than usual. Even gentle. A sure sign that his anger was boiling over and if his men weren't careful there was a possibility of heads rolling.

'You had Yorke here and he escaped? What did he do? Just walk away?'

'We're sorry, Mr Frobisher, but as far as we can tell he somehow burnt the lock off the door.'

'Burnt it off? How did he manage that?'

The two men exchanged glances and shrugged. One of them had a bandage wrapped around his head, a splitting headache pounded between his ears and he felt like vomiting.

'Sir,' said the less injured of the two men, 'we stripped him of all his gear and searched him very carefully. How he did it we've no idea. Where he went, likewise. We figured the woman had a car somewhere and they did a bunk in it. We're looking for him now.'

'Where's Colonel Roberts?'

'On his way. His helicopter had a slight problem. He's been delayed an hour. Two at the most.'

Frobisher sighed and waved the men away. He still had to report to Mr Kennedy after telling him the good news that Yorke had been taken. Now they were back to square one. Well, not quite. They knew where the boy and the yacht was. A team had been despatched already. His phone rang. That hope was immediately dashed and he vented his spleen by throwing the mobile against the wall, shattering it.

He took another mobile from the desk drawer and dialled. 'Sir? I have bad news.' He explained the position to Kennedy who, surprisingly, took the news far more benignly than he'd expected.

'Never mind about him. Is everything ready for tomorrow night?'

'Yes, sir. Colonel Roberts is coming to personally take charge of security. All the rooms have been made ready. The caterers have been hired and the menus agreed.'

'Good. I'll be there at 16.00 before the guests begin to arrive. Have the girls been organised?'

'Yes, sir.' If he was at all upset at having his preparations questioned he didn't show it. 'Colour, nationalities and sizes have all been attended to.'

'All the cameras working?'

'Yes, sir. We've checked everything.' Somehow he managed to keep his voice neutral. He did as he was told and did it well. Kennedy knew he could leave everything to Frobisher, his questioning of the arrangements an indication of how important the meeting was.

A helicopter sounded in the distance. 'That's Colonel Roberts arriving now, sir.'

'Bring him up to date and tell him to forget about Yorke. After tomorrow he won't matter an iota.'

'Yes, sir.' But as usual he was speaking to a disconnected phone.

Ex-Colonel "Mack" Roberts marched into the room looking fresh in spite of his long flight. Frobisher thought the man always walked as though on the parade ground, or as one colleague put it, 'As if he's got a broomhandle rammed up his arse.'

Roberts' erect posture added to his stature of 5ft 5ins. He was slim, elegant, had a well-shaped head, a good-looking face and a pencil-line moustache. He also had the reputation of being a womaniser though there had been no sign of it since he'd joined the organisation. There was talk of a wife at one time but if so she was long gone. Roberts had been with them for six months and done an exceptional job as a unit commander. His work in Columbia had been exemplary. With the death of the previous Head of Security when the bomb had exploded on the yacht, "Mack" had been the obvious man to take over. Unknown to Frobisher, Roberts' one regret was that he'd known nothing about the attack on *Phoenix* until it was over. *If only* – the two saddest words in the English language.

Frobisher passed on Kennedy's message about Yorke.

'Thank you, Mr Frobisher. I'd come to that conclusion myself. Can we go over the arrangements together? That way we'll miss none.'

'Of course. In the meantime let me get us a drink. Tea?'

'Please. I think the Darjeeling appropriate at this time of day, don't you?'

Frobisher merely smiled. He couldn't stand the muck. He'd have a coffee instead. A double expresso.

When Yorke awoke it was from a troubled and dream-filled sleep. Groggily he got to his feet and stepped onto the companionway ladder and looked into the cockpit. Dom and Catherine were sitting at opposite sides of the cockpit.

'Everything all right, you two?'

Catherine nodded while Dom said, 'Yes, dad. No problems. Nothing within two miles. We're half a mile to starboard of track. France is painting at thirty-five miles.'

'Thanks, son. I'm going for a shower.' After shaving and showering Yorke began to feel human once more. They'd be in France for dinner. Good. They should be safe enough there. He knew a secure anchorage on the Côte de Granit Rose with a fine restaurant only a short boat ride away.

Returning to the cockpit with a mug of tea in his hand he sat down between the other two. If he noticed any frostiness between them he chose to ignore it.

'We need to decide what we're doing,' he began. The others looked at him, saying nothing. 'Any ideas?'

'Sail away and not come back,' said Catherine, 'gets my vote every time.'

Yorke nodded. 'You, Dom?'

Dom shrugged, looked sheepish and then said, 'I don't know, dad. What about the marines? School? Everything!'

Yorke shook his head. 'I know son. It's a hell of a problem. And it's not fair on you. They don't know about Catherine and there's no reason why they should. We've got new identities which we can slip into. The *Duck* will take us anywhere. Money isn't a problem. But,' he paused, 'nothing will be as we planned and thought.'

Dom nodded miserably. 'That's what I thought. Unless we stop these people somehow.'

'That's about it. And apart from telling the world about them I can't see what else we can do.'

'I don't want to give up everything,' said Catherine. 'I like being on the boat but not forever. Be a nomad? Sail the seven seas? It's not my idea of a life.'

'Nor mine,' said Yorke. 'So we go on? Is that what you're saying.'

Dom shrugged while Catherine looked out to the horizon.

'Okay, we need to think about it. We don't go rushing in. We need a lot more information. And Catherine, you need time to write this stuff up. Also we need to talk about Cornwall.' On that enigmatic note he stood up. 'I'm going below to put a fix on the chart.'

A satnav fix showed they were on a straight run in to the bay at Carantec. He calculated speed and distance to go. Just under three hours. About 20.00 local time they'd anchor – he'd already changed the boat's clocks to French time. He used the forward hatch to go back on deck and stood in the bow, looking forward. Numerous sails were scattered across the gently undulating water and if it hadn't been for the trouble they were in Yorke could have felt contented with his lot. Anger coursed through him and he felt a vein throbbing in the side of his head. Here he was, running again. It seemed that was all he'd been doing since the attack on *Phoenix*. Running from the swine. He shook his head. The reality was he'd been bloody lucky. So had Dom. So had Catherine. The pair of them bungling in like that – this wasn't some sort of game. It wasn't

"happy ever after" stuff. It was real, with death all too close
for comfort.

Still, he was being churlish and he knew it. Part of
the reason was the real fear he was feeling for them both
and the thought of what might have happened. He was proud
of Dom. It had been a very brave thing to do. Of Catherine
too. Thinking of them he looked back. The pair of them were
in the cockpit, side by side, talking quietly, not looking at
him. He made his way aft. They seemed to be getting on
better.

'What are you pair cooking up?'

'Nothing,' said Dom. 'Catherine was asking me things, that's
all.'

'What things?' Yorke cast suspicious glances at both of them.

'Nothing. Just things,' Dom replied vaguely.

Yorke dropped the subject. 'How did you happen to go to
Cornwall?' Yorke asked Catherine.

'I found out a lot of interesting stuff from the computer
information,' she said pensively, excitement underlying her
words. 'When Dom told me where you were I knew the address
from one of the files.'

'Why? What was in it?'

'There's a meeting taking place tomorrow night. It starts
late and is going on until the early hours. The people attending
are the Who's Who of European politics and industry. Which
doesn't make sense.'

'What do you mean?'

'Well, I'd have thought the attendees would be criminals.'

'Maybe they are.'

Catherine gasped. 'You've got to be kidding.'

Yorke shrugged. 'Unfortunately, I'm not. Did you bring the
memory stick with you?'

'Yes. I also left copies hidden in my flat in Woolwich.'

'Let's flash up the laptop and see who's on the list. You got
the weight, Dom?'

'Sure, dad. No problem.'

Below, Yorke powered up the computer and plugged in the

USB stick. He copied the files onto the hard drive. While he did so he asked, 'What were you two talking about?'

Catherine hid a smile. 'You.'

'That's what I thought.'

'He has a deep love and respect for you, you know that don't you?'

Yorke looked slightly uncomfortable. 'I have the same for him. He's a great lad. He'll make a fine Royal Marine officer one day.'

'Is that what he wants or is it what you want for him?'

'Me?' There was surprise, even shock, in Yorke's tone. 'No, it's all he's ever wanted to do. Why? Has he said anything to you?'

'No.' Catherine shook her head. 'I was just wondering. Hero worship can cloud a young person's judgement.'

'Dom's too sensible. He's done everything he can to get into the Royals. And I've helped him as well, of course. But it's still all down to him. If he changes his mind that's all right with me. What else was he saying?'

'Nothing. We were just chatting.' Catherine had the grace to look sheepish. 'I *did* ask about girlfriends.'

Yorke laughed. 'And?'

'And nothing. He says there hasn't been any. Then he said, until now.'

'What did you say to that?'

'I didn't. Well, not much. I asked if he'd mind. About me.'

'What did he say?'

'He said no. He said he did at first but then realised that he was being childish. He's got a sensible head on his shoulders.' Catherine ended the discussion with, 'Let me get the file.'

Yorke hid a grin and slid along the seat while her fingers flew across the keypad. 'Here we are.'

They worked their way through the file. It was amazingly detailed.

'You see what I mean about the names?'

'I do. But there are a dozen I recognise whose names won't appear apart from in the lexicon of international crime.'

'You're sure?' Catherine turned an incredulous face towards him.

'Positive. It's my job to know. The detail in the file is amazing. Either *Phoenix* had somebody on the inside or we were bribing or coercing somebody to feed us with this stuff. Either way, it's dynamite.'

'What do we do with it?'

'In truth, I'm not sure. Yet. Let's go up top and enjoy something of the evening.'

Yorke said little as the small yacht sailed peacefully onwards. He was deep in thought. It lasted as they approached land to anchor between the village of Carantec and the small island two cables to the north. They dropped the port anchor, backed away, dropped the starboard anchor and equalled the lengths of the cable. The Bahamian moor kept the yacht's swinging circle to a minimum, no matter from which direction the wind and tide came.

Satisfied, they sat in the cockpit, a glass of red wine in their hands, Dom's with water added.

'There's a small bistro on the waterfront that serves excellent moules in a local sauce,' said Yorke. 'Fancy it?'

The other two nodded. It was Dom who broke the peace by saying, 'I've been thinking. I should go back to school. I can't just stay away. I think it'll be safe enough.'

'No chance, Dom.' Yorke kept the alarm he was feeling from showing in his voice. 'It's too dangerous. They know who you are. They might try to get at me through you. In fact, they probably *will* do that.'

'I'll be safe at school,' Dom scoffed.

'No you won't, son.' Yorke put his hand on the boy's shoulder and squeezed gently, 'This is a very serious matter, Dom. A lot of people have died. On our side as well as theirs. They may just kill you to get their revenge on me. You can't be kept safe at school, only with me. Here. And right now all I can think of is running away.'

'I thought we'd decided that wasn't a good idea,' said Catherine.

Yorke sighed. 'I know. But I hadn't expected them to find me or the yacht but they did. And look what happened. They took me as easily as kidnapping a baby in a pram.' Yorke drained his glass. 'Which is rather a dispiriting thought. They won't make the same mistake again. If they come after me, us, it'll be a bullet and that will be the end of it. Shall we go ashore?'

In gloomy silence they climbed down into the dinghy. Dom started the outboard and they went slowly towards the little harbour. At a set of stone steps they climbed out, lifted the inflatable out of the water and placed it on the top of the sea wall. The harbour was filled with small fishing boats, mainly engaged in harvesting shellfish. Some yachts were allowed in under sufferance, but they were few. And if the fleet had an early morning start and you were in the way – tough. The fishermen were an uncompromising lot.

The bar they entered was busy, the atmosphere thick with the smell of cooking, alcohol and smoke. In the corner two mongrel dogs lay snoozing. The political correctness of the European directives from Brussels had yet to penetrate that corner of France.

Yorke spoke to the owner, whom he'd met on numerous other occasions, exchanged a fistful of Euros and secured the promise of a table in an hour. In the meantime they settled for a corner of the bar, two large Pernods for him and Catherine and a lemonade for Dom.

There were a number of yachtsmen with their families, eating and drinking, having a relaxing and enjoyable evening. Yorke envied them. They had no idea of the consequences that could affect all their lives if the men who could control a prime minister weren't stopped. He threw his liquorice tasting drink down and was surprised to find the glass empty, merely rattling ice cubes. He ordered a bottle of water.

In a corner three men appeared, one with an accordion, a second with a guitar and the third with a fiddle. They took only seconds to check that their instruments were attuned to the heat and fug before they launched into a French folk song. Much to his surprise, Yorke forgot the problems they were facing and settled in to a night of excellent food and bonhomie. It was midnight when they made their way back to the yacht. They put the inflatable in the water and puttered out to the *Lucky Duck*. On the way Yorke checked the surveillance equipment and found the boat had lain quietly throughout the evening.

Onboard, Dom excused himself and went to his bunk. Catherine and Yorke poured themselves some spring water and sat in the cockpit. The night was star filled, still and pleasant. They were looking up at the heavens, Catherine's head on his chest, when she said, 'What are we going to do about the predicament we're in? I've enough ammunition to write a hundred articles as well as a book but where will it get us?'

Yorke shook his head. 'God knows. I've thought of nothing else all afternoon.'

'I noticed how quiet you were. Why don't we put the whole lot, everything we have, into the hands of the police?'

'And tell them what? Oh, Mr Plod, you know those bodies you found? Well, I did it. But don't worry, I'm one of the good guys. They were the bad!' Yorke couldn't keep the anger and bitterness out of his voice. Nor the sarcasm. 'It's ludicrous. They'd arrest me as good as look at me. Should I ever get out of jail I'll be a very old man. It's what deniable operations are all about. Sounds good until you need political support. Then you know how much you're on your own.'

'You sound angry.' There was surprise in Catherine's voice.

'I am, and there again, I'm not. I'm on my own . . .'

'Thank you . . .'

'Shush,' he placed a finger on her lips. 'Not in the meaning of the word. Only in terms of an operation. I've worked alone many, many times, but I always knew I had a safe haven to run to once it was all over. And that's important. Psychologically it makes all the difference. I'm not sure I'm making much sense . . .'

'Of course you are. Curiously, I do understand. We can vanish.'

'We?'

Catherine shrugged. 'Well, the fact is I told those men I was a journalist. Okay, they didn't get my name. But how long do you think it will take them to find out who I am? A few phone calls at most. I'm not,' she said with a tinge of pride in her voice, 'exactly unknown.'

Yorke nodded. 'You're right. I can imagine the call. She's beautiful, black hair, rounded . . .'

'Enough!' She punched him playfully on the arm.

'Rounded eyes, I was going to say.' He leaned closer.

'Liar.' She stopped speaking as his lips met hers.

After a few seconds he lifted his head and said, 'There's another problem. It all depends on how badly these people want us.'

Catherine sighed. 'The swine intrude at the worst possible moment. What do you mean?'

'We know about Mevagissey. How much more do we know? How much of a threat do we present to these people and their organisation?'

'A considerable one, I'd say.'

'Yes, *we'd* say so because we know. *They* don't know. Do they take a gamble and leave us alone? Or do they ensure our silence? You see the quandary they're in. What would you do?'

'It's easy. I'd have us killed. Just in case.' She spoke with a leaden voice.

'So would I. So the reality is we can't run for it. We're too easily recognisable. A man and a woman, plus a teenager.'

'You mean I am,' said Catherine unable to keep a tinge of bitterness out of her voice. 'With my height and colour and with a white man and boy I stick out a mile.' Yorke looked at her in utter astonishment. 'Don't talk so bloody ridiculous. You're a very attractive woman. I'd even go so far as to say beautiful.'

'Thank you. But it would be better if we ran for it separately. We wouldn't be so obvious.'

'And how far do you think you'd get? Do you have a false passport? No? Then how would you get one? What would you do for money? If you use your bank account they'd track you down in minutes. These people have resources as extensive as a government agency's. So you're going nowhere without us. All right?'

Catherine managed a sheepish grin, relieved at his response but having been determined to make the offer.

'So what do we do?'

'There's only one thing we can do. We must make it clear to these people that we have the information. That we'd expose them if any harm comes to any of us.'

'That's not what you said earlier. Then it was they needed stopping. Why the flip-flopping back and forth?'

Yorke shook his head. 'Because the reality is I am only one man, with you and a child. I have no right to risk your lives for my what? Crusade? The tilting at windmills? The corruption is too wide and deep. So we use what we've got to bargain for our lives and freedom.'

Catherine was silent for a few seconds. 'Will it work?'

'I don't know but I can't think of anything else. Can you?'

There was a small silence before she replied. 'I guess not. Then it's goodbye to the Pulitzer.'

'I suppose you could write the articles and get them published and have the Pulitzer awarded posthumously,' he said in a thoughtful manner, rubbing his chin with his thumb.

'Idiot!' She playfully thumped his shoulder. He took her hand, kissed it and then pulled her close. Silence cloaked them, broken only by the sound of a light breeze in the rigging.

23

YORKE RAISED THE anchors an hour before dawn. He left Catherine and Dom sleeping. After spending half the night discussing their options a number of things had become clear. Although they had damaging information suitable for newspaper articles it wasn't enough. The people involved could deny much, if not all, of it. Hell, companies could be liquidated and restarted again even more untraceable than they were now. And the amount of money and sheer power wielded by Kennedy – assuming he was the top dog – and his cohorts, was vast. Yorke and Catherine had decided that they needed more and the place to get it was the house at Mevagissey that night.

Yorke knew it would be crawling with guards. That had an upside and a downside. On the one hand the adage that there was safety in numbers could be made to apply while on the other there was the danger of him being recognised.

Catherine's admonition rang in his ears. 'It's not much of a plan.'

'I know. Two minutes after I begin it will probably all change. No plan works. It's merely the basis from where to start. After that I'll make it up as I go along. The backdoor where I came out is as good a place to begin as any.'

Clear of the land, he adjusted the sails, set the auto-pilot and went down the forward hatch. He began prepping his diving equipment. Fortunately he owned an oxygen-rebreather set which meant no bubbles appearing on the surface. The gear was kept in good order and it only took a few minutes to check. Sorting out the rest of his equipment took a lot longer. From time to time he'd go on deck and correct the yacht's heading, adjust the sails and search the water for other shipping. This was a ferry route, one to Cork the other to Plymouth, and ferries were notorious for ignoring the right-of-way of small sailing boats.

Making a bacon sandwich, Yorke sat in the cockpit, enjoying the simple meal and the feel of the sun on his back. He had no illusions about what he was going to do but saw no alternative. He knew he couldn't run and hide forever. And any blackmail attempt was, in the cold light of day, ludicrous. He'd been kidding himself. And what Catherine had said was true – together they did stick out like sore thumbs. She was a striking and noticeable woman, and no doubt a photograph of her would be circulating soon enough. And what were they to do? Keep a low profile all their lives? It was a ludicrous notion. Impossible. Catherine was a journalist; she *needed* to write. He had a life to lead as well, though doing what he didn't know. And Dom? He had his whole life in front of him. The thoughts had been going round and round almost all night.

He got up, checked the yacht's position and the speed they were making good over the ground, and tacked to port. They had plenty of time. There was no point in arriving in daylight. He switched on the radio, the dulcet tones of the BBC Radio 4 Today announcer penetrating his reverie.

The fire in Woolwich was started deliberately according to a police spokesman. Two people are known to have died. The blaze began in the flat owned by the journalist, Catherine Colbert. So far there's been no sign of her.

There was more but Yorke wasn't listening. Shit in a basket! They'd already found out who she was and gone in hard. He switched off the radio. Dom came on deck a short while later. After the boy made himself a bacon sandwich and a mug of tea Yorke handed the watch over to him and went below to get some sleep. He looked in on Catherine sleeping in the master bedroom, the only one with a double bed. She didn't even stir. He thought about waking her and telling her about her flat but decided against it. Instead he went forward to the other cabin and dossed down in a sleeping bag. In spite of what lay ahead, he quickly drifted off, his slumber undisturbed until an offer of tea was made in his ear. He came wide awake and looked at Catherine.

'No milk, no sugar. Did I remember it correctly?'

'Quite right. What time is it?'

'Nearly 5pm. We're two cables to port of track and more or less set to hit our ETA. Is that right?'

'I take it Dom told you to tell me that?'

Catherine smiled back. 'Yes.' She leaned closer and kissed him. 'I hadn't realised how restricting a boat of this size was before.'

'Catherine,' he spoke solemnly, 'I've got bad news.'

She looked at him with dread in her eyes. 'What is it?'

'I don't know how to tell you but it's your place. It's been burnt, gutted. Two people have died.'

Catherine gasped. 'How do you know?'

'It was on the news.'

She sat down in shock. 'Oh my god, oh my god. The bastards.' Tears welled up and spilled down her cheeks. 'Did they say who's died?'

Yorke shook his head. 'It was Radio 4. Hardly more than a footnote. If there hadn't been any deaths it probably wouldn't even have been mentioned. I'm really sorry.'

Catherine shook her head. 'It's not your fault.'

'I got you into this.'

'If I remember correctly, you saved my life at Gibraltar Point. I'm convinced of that, even if I wasn't so sure then.' Suddenly she stood up, indignation and anger coursing through her. 'I won't let them beat me, I won't! We must stop them, Stephen, at all costs.'

'We'll do our best. But listen to me, Catherine. You and Dom must do what I tell you. Okay?'

'Of course.'

'Have you ever fired a gun?'

Catherine was startled and shook her head. 'No. My weapon has always been my laptop.'

'In that case it's time you learnt. What are you doing now?'

'I'm making stew. Dom said the forecast is holding true. The glass is dropping and we can expect a 5 or 6 in the next couple of hours.'

The boat was pitching slightly, though not uncomfortably – yet. That was still to come.

'I can feel it. Luckily it's from the south-east, so we'll be okay. Better than battling headwinds. What sort of sailor are you?'

'I don't know. I've never done this before.'

'Get Dom to give you a couple of seasick pills. They'll help.'

'But I don't feel ill.'

'You will. And it's better to get the pills down before you need them. Trust me.'

'I do.' She kissed him again while Yorke struggled out of the sleeping back and onto the deck. He staggered slightly as the yacht hit a wave, the first of many he knew were coming. After brushing his teeth, he went up top with the half empty mug of tea clasped in his hand. Dom was at the helm, setting a new course.

'Hi, dad. I'm just coming 15 degrees to starboard. The wind and tide are pushing us to port so I figured to come round now, rather than later.'

'Good lad. Distance to go?'

'Just about 28 miles. We'll get there earlier than we planned but the storm will bring the dark.' Dom was already dressed in bright yellow, foul-weather gear, the spray beginning to flick across the open cockpit.

'We'll take in a couple of reefs of main and change the jib for the storm jib. Okay?'

'Sure, dad. No problem.'

They went to work. Old hands who'd done this many times together meant the tasks were soon completed. The *Lucky Duck* steadied her movements and settled at 7 knots. Catherine put her head through the companionway hatch.

'You guys want to eat? Stew and toast.'

'Sounds good to me,' said Yorke. 'You dish up while I put on my foul-weather gear.'

Minutes later, with Catherine similarly clad, the three of them were sitting in the cockpit, eating.

'This is good, Catherine,' said Dom waving a mug in one hand and a piece of toast in the other.

'Thank you. It's my speciality. Though it's better with fresh beef than a tin of corned beef. I hope I didn't put in too much cayenne pepper?'

'Never. Not for me, at any rate,' said Dom. 'What about you, dad?'

'It's perfect,' said Yorke. 'Thanks, Catherine.'

When they'd finished, Yorke said, 'Time for some target practice. And it's time I introduced you to some of the yacht's secrets.' He began by opening the ready-use locker under the aft seat. At the back he pressed a knot in the wood and the panelling dropped open. 'This is for fast access and close quarter defence.' He displayed two revolvers and two hand grenades. 'Let's start with the Smith & Wesson. I'll show you the stuff in the engine room later.'

'What would happen,' asked Catherine thoughtfully. 'if the police found this lot?'

'I'd go to prison for a very, very long time. However, let me show you something.' Opening another panel he showed them a handle and button. 'Turn this fully clockwise and press the button and incendiary devices erupt here and down below.'

'Is there a time delay?' asked Catherine, aghast.

'Yes. Five minutes.'

'What happens when it goes off? asked Dom.

'Metal will melt, bullets and dets will explode and the *Lucky Duck* will sink in about a minute and a half.'

'Bloody hell,' said Dom in awe.

Catherine's language was altogether more colourful and Dom looked at her with new respect.

Yorke spent an hour showing them and teaching them what he could. Dom needed little in the way of lessons. Catherine kept shutting her eyes every time she pulled the trigger but at least she pointed the gun in the right direction first.

'That'll do,' said Yorke with a sigh. 'We wouldn't stand

much of a chance against Roberts and his men but we might buy enough time should we need to escape.'

The yacht's bow lifted high and came down with a heavy crash, sending a judder throughout the hull, rattling the crockery and cutlery.

'I'll go below and check everything's secure,' said Yorke.

'I did it while you were sleeping, dad.'

'Good. Then I needn't bother. We'd better take in another reef.'

'What about a sail change? To number three?'

Yorke had hoped Dom would make the suggestion, instead of him having to order it.

'Good idea. Hold her on the storm jib and let's get to work.'

They hauled down the mainsail and pushed it down the forward hatch. Quickly they brought up No 3, attached the halyards and hoists and raised it into position. The yacht liked the change and she settled down to a slightly smoother ride. Though both of them knew it wouldn't last. Yorke checked the pressure gauge. From a high of 1003mb the pressure had dropped to 992mb and was still going down.

Yorke called up Plymouth Coast Guard and checked the forecast. It was predicting a low of about 988mb. Not much further to go. It was clear that the blow wouldn't amount to much. Good. It was about perfect for what he wanted to do. With the wind came the rain and soon squalls were passing overhead, adding to their discomfort.

The wind increase further and the small yacht began a gut-wrenching twist to add to the pitch. Catherine gamely held out until she felt her stomach heave once too often. She just made it to the side before she was violently sick. More by luck than judgement, she put her head over the lee. After a few minutes when there was nothing left to bring up she wiped her mouth with a wet tissue.

'I feel like death.'

'You'll be all right,' said Yorke. 'I've got some ship's biscuits. Have one.'

'You callous swine, I couldn't eat a thing,' she said feebly.

'These biscuits absorb the juices in your stomach. I promise you'll feel better. Then take a couple more pills. Trust me.'

Catherine nodded feebly, unsure if she was going to live more than a few hours, and wishing with all of her soul for dry land. However, after nibbling away at a couple of the white biscuits and swallowing two seasickness tablets, she began to feel slightly better.

'Go below and lie down for a while in the saloon. There's less pitch there,' Yorke spoke loudly against the noise of the wind whistling through the rigging and the up-haul strumming against the mast.

She did as she was bid and went down the companionway, thankful to fling herself onto the couch and wedge herself behind the table. Surprisingly she quickly fell asleep. When she awoke it was to find the yacht moving far more sedately, with the engine running and the noise of the storm abating.

Sitting up she ran her tongue over her mouth. It tasted disgusting. She used the heads to refresh herself before appearing on deck. There, Dom and Yorke were standing next to the helm with mugs in their hands.

'It's hot chocolate,' said Dom, seeing Catherine, 'want some?'

'No thanks. Not just yet. Where are we?' She was looking over the starboard bow at the distant lights.

'That's Fowey,' replied Yorke. 'We were a bit early. The sun's only just set. With the wind backed round to the north we'll head south-south-west for Chaple Point. Let's finish these drinks and get the sails up, Dom. It's about right now.'

Colonel "Mack" Roberts made his rounds. The guests had been greeted, escorted to their rooms and refreshments provided. Dinner would be served at 23.30 and finished an hour later. One hour was scheduled for the meeting and the rest of the night was theirs to do with as they wished. He checked the clipboard with the names of each guest and each escort. Only one had asked for his companion to be a young boy. Surprisingly it hadn't been the Arab; it had been the Frenchman.

The guests had travelled incognito, trusting to anonymity to keep them safe. Even Gordon Whitley – the Home Secretary, had come without his bodyguards. Roberts wondered briefly how he'd managed it but then gave a mental shrug. The master had called them and so they came. Money was a powerful aphrodisiac. Raw power even more so. And Kennedy had both in awesome amounts.

Roberts' men provided the guards that night. In accordance with Kennedy's instructions, the men patrolling the grounds wore camouflage fatigues, while those within the house wore dinner jackets. He wanted his guests to be kept safe in as pleasant an atmosphere as possible. It was, as Kennedy was fond of saying, more conducive to good business.

And in that, he's probably right, thought Roberts. Leaving the house, he made his way around the grounds. They covered 7 acres of mainly lawns but with eight copses of trees scattered over the area. A high wall surrounded the land. There were two gates, the main and a postern. Alarms had been rigged around the perimeter and anything larger than a poodle would set them off. Cameras had been installed at strategic points and fed into a monitoring room in the basement. Thinking of the basement brought to mind Yorke and his escape. And the girl. A reporter. How the hell did she come to be sniffing around? Was it a coincidence? Or were Yorke and the girl somehow connected? He shook his head. Was it the same girl who had been at Gib Point? Idle speculation was a waste of time. Besides which, as each day passed, Kennedy's position became more secure – stronger. Soon, nobody and nothing would be able to touch him. He'd own a country and control governments. And not a backwater like Georgia. Croatia was about to fall to him. Big rewards required big risks and that was something Kennedy was prepared to take. But when would his avarice be satisfied? Or was that impossible? Was there *never* enough for a man like Kennedy? And some of the people who worked for him?

'Is the sledge ready?' Yorke asked Dom.

'Yes, dad. I've double checked the batteries. It should be good for five miles at least.'

'Thanks, son. Now remember, keep a steady speed and don't slow down whatever you do. Then head offshore and stay below the horizon. I'll signal when I'm ready. At the latest I'll leave at dawn come hell or high-water. Understood?'

'Understood. You can count on me.'

'I know I can. You've already proven that. I couldn't be more proud of you if . . .' he didn't finish, but added, 'Your parents would have been equally proud.'

Catherine watched them with a lump in her throat. Nobody mentioned the thought – what if Yorke didn't make it? It was, she was aware, unthinkable. His plan was sketchy, his intentions ludicrous and how the hell he expected to get away with it was beyond her. On the other hand it was audacious and stupid enough to work.

At least he looked nothing like his normal self. His hair had been lightened considerably and parted differently. Rubber cheek implants changed the contours of his face enough to make him an entirely different person. She was looking at a total stranger.

'Where did you learn to alter your appearance like that?'

'We were taught by a make-up artist who works in the film industry. It helped a lot on some operations. Let's hope the info you got from the files is accurate. Can't-see-me suits in the grounds, dinner jackets in the house. With so many security personnel I'm hoping nobody will know everybody. Hell, the files showed fifteen were recruited in the last 3 days alone.' He shook his head. 'The scale of it all is truly frightening.'

Yorke and Dom placed the sledge in the inflatable. The UC(P) – underwater chariot (personal) – was a metre and a half long and thirty centimetres in diameter. A third of the container consisted of three batteries in series while the single speed motor was clamped underneath, causing the water flow to pass under the diver. The variable speed propeller could drag a diver at between 3 and 4 knots, in virtual silence. The sledge had a capacity of approximately 30kgs, depending on the gear being carried. She was negatively buoyant and required forward motion coupled with two small fins either side, used to control depth, not to sink.

The waterproof hold was lightly packed as Yorke didn't want his dinner jacket to get too creased. Now he was dressed in a dry suit. Underneath he wore his black DJ trousers, black socks, white shirt and had a bow tie in his pocket. In the sledge was a Glock 19 and a Russian built VAL Silent Sniper, a rifle the west only learnt about in 1994. It was a silent semi-automatic rifle firing a heavy 9mm bullet at subsonic velocity. It was claimed that it could penetrate all body armour out to a range of 400 metres, a claim that Yorke had proven to be true. With the stock folded it was only 615mm long and weighed a mere 2.5kg. Each magazine held 20 rounds and he carried 3 of them. Other gear consisted of plastic explosive packages fitted with timers and a pair of night vision goggles which had an infra-red detection capacity as well. He had no idea who had sent the file about the meeting but it had been extremely detailed. Providing one caveat – that it was all true – he knew what to expect. But that was the big question, was it true? If it was, who on earth was the mole? Whoever it was, he was an extremely brave man.

'Coming to the drop-off point, dad.'

'Okay, Dom, steady as she goes. What speed are we showing?'

'Seven knots.'

'Ideal. I'll see you both later.' Yorke rolled the sledge over the side and went with it. He had his oxygen-rebreather strapped to his back and a pair of fins on his feet in case he had to abandon the UC(P). He pressed the start button and the motor kicked silently into life. The craft was steered left and right by a pair of handles like a motorbike, while depth was controlled by the right grip, twist forward and she went down, backwards and she surfaced. The left grip controlled her speed. At 8m and a heading of 330 degrees he set the autopilot. All he had to do was watch the echo-sounder, monitor the depth and course and hang on. Sensors in the chariot detected any currents, and compensated for the course over the ground he needed to maintain, working to keep him on track at all times.

In the darkness there was hardly any feeling of motion apart from the press of water on his body. It was far from unpleasant and held the danger of being soporific. To stay awake he twisted his head, kicked his feet and watched the dials. After thirty minutes he knocked off the auto-pilot and slowly twisted the right handle upwards. The fins angled and he felt the sledge rise slowly towards the surface. Manoeuvring the UC(P) was easy, doing so in such a way as to remain undetected took a good deal of practice. At half a metre, Yorke levelled off the angle and slowly put his head above the surface. The house was well lit, less than half a mile away, and dead ahead.

Twisting the handle away from him, he sank gently back to the depths, set the auto-pilot and rode in. Now the most important instruments on the sledge was the echo-sounder and depth gauge. Ten minutes later the depth of water beneath him was five metres, and above it was just touching three. The time of maximum danger was the approach and landing. From the chart he knew he was half a cable from the shore. Allowing the chariot to sink to the sandy sea bed, Yorke abandoned it and went slowly to the surface, paying out a guide rope attached to the handles as he did. Near the surface he stopped his ascent by gripping the rope tightly, then paid it out between his fingers. He inched his way to the surface. As his head broke the water he held himself with only his eyes and the top of his head showing. A flick of a switch on his NVGs and they went to infra-red. He remained suspended, slowly examining the length of the shore-line, covering every square metre. Nothing. Nobody. No heat signature.

He waited for a few minutes, never one to rush in. Satisfied, he pulled himself off the surface before flipping over and swimming down to the UC(P). Once more in motion, he was committed. He drove the sledge into the shore, luckily finding a stretch of sand to land on. Once more he used the infra-red goggles. No bodies showed.

He opened the small hold in the sledge and removed the VAL, cocked it and placed it close at hand. Then he took off his dry-suit, gratified to find that only the sleeves of his shirt were wet, water having seeped in when he'd expanded and contracted the tendons in his wrists. From the sledge he took a pair of black shoes, put the Glock in a shoulder holster and put on his dinner jacket. Over this he put on his camouflaged jacket and trousers. There was one last thing to do. He sent an OK text to Dom; almost immediately he got one back.

Hiding the UC(P), diving set and suit in a shallow grave in the sand, he turned his attention to the cliff face. With the VAL slung over his shoulder he slowly made his way up the rock, pausing often to listen and test the air. He knew it wasn't particularly a difficult climb, after all he'd come down the cliff only 40 hours earlier, but the requirement to keep silent made it a great deal more demanding. He tested each hand and foothold before committing himself, careful not to dislodge any small stones or earth. Inexorably he drew nearer to the top. Just below the lip he paused, straining his ears and sniffing the air like a bloodhound. To anyone seeing him he knew he looked ludicrous, like a twitchy rabbit putting its nose out of its burrow prior to its evening graze. But he also knew the first indication that anyone in the vicinity was the smell of cigarette smoke, deodorant or even body odour. He couldn't smell or hear anything or anybody. Even the wind was easing as the front went through.

24

ONCE HE WAS committed to the cliff top he would have to brazen it out. He paused with his head just below ground level and placed the VAL Silent Sniper in an opportune crevice. He looked across the ground and saw the heat signatures of two people, one about thirty metres to his left, the other the same to his right. He rolled onto the flat and swiftly stood up, looking out to sea. The NVGs he slipped from his head and placed in his pocket. If anyone challenged him he'd say he'd been sent to check the cliff.

Nothing happened. No shouted challenge. Nobody approached. He threw a thin nylon rope down the cliff face and secured it to an outcrop of rock.

Nonchalantly, though feeling far from sanguine, he began to walk towards the corner of the house, only about 200 metres away, feeling very exposed and vulnerable. The night had turned cloudless and as he approached the house, the moon rose above the horizon, casting it's eerie light across the landscape. He heard feet scuffling on stone to his right and he paused. A sentry appeared.

'Got a light?' The man asked in a heavy accent.

'I wouldn't if I were you,' said Yorke in a loud whisper. 'Mack would have your guts for garters if he caught you smoking.'

'Ach, I'm not afraid of Roberts.' The accent was guttural, harsh; Germanic.

'Well, I'm sorry. I don't have one.'

Without another word the man turned on his heels and walked away. Yorke looked around. There was nobody near.

He stopped at the door through which he'd escaped earlier and tried it. To his surprise, it opened. He stepped into the pitch black corridor, paused and took his NVGs out of his pocket. Placing them on his head he switched them on. The darkness immediately vanished to be replaced by a soft blue light. He walked along the corridor and passed the room he'd been held in. At the furthest reaches of the corridor he came to a door, held closed by a Yale lock. His electronic pick made short work of opening it.

Opening the door a crack, he removed his goggles, before putting an eye to the shaft of light. A lit corridor with nobody there. Quickly he stripped off his camouflage jacket and trousers, put the ready made bow tie around his neck and adjusted the Glock 19 under his armpit. He stepped boldly out into the corridor and had only taken a few paces when a voice called him from behind.

'Here, you, what do you think you're doing?'

Yorke ignored the challenge and walked on. The voice was suddenly right behind him.

'I'm talking to you.'

Yorke stopped and turned. He found himself looking into the hard, ancient acne pitted face of a man in green livery. He was about forty, with grey, curly hair and a pencil-thin moustache.

'You are?' Yorke asked politely.

'Maxwell. I'm Mr Kennedy's chauffeur.'

Yorke looked at the telltale bulge under the man's coat. 'Something more, if that's anything to go by.' He nodded at the man's side.

'I asked you a question.'

'I couldn't give a rat's arse what you asked. You're a chauffeur, I'm a guard. I do the asking. However, I'll be courteous this once.' He held out his hands. They were scratched and filthy. 'I was searching along the cliff and fell. I'm here to clean up and take up my duties in the gallery.' Once more Yorke sent out a silent prayer of thanks to whoever had supplied the file of information he and Catherine had pored over. The detail had been amazing and thankfully, it would seem, accurate.

'Okay. It's just we can't be too careful.'

Yorke allowed himself a small smile of acknowledgement. 'I guess you're right. I understand there's a toilet along here.'

'On the right, a few doors down.'

Nodding his thanks, he found the room and went inside. A wash and brush up left him looking more presentable. The corridor was empty and he made his way to the backstairs. He took them two at a time. He heard the gaiety before he saw anybody. Rounding a right-angled bend he found himself on the long balcony that surrounded the room. The room had been converted into a dining room. Trestle tables were covered with heavy white linen and had silver service placements in front of each chair. Waiters moved back and forth, serving expertly and quickly. The noise level was what one would expect in a crowd of diners 44 strong. The gallery he was on went all the way round, to a grand staircase at the furthest end, opposite the main door. The layout was precisely as he'd seen in the file. Along the wall opposite stood 10 men in dinner jackets, guns under their jackets, about 3 metres apart. There were also 4 guards lining the walls to his left and right. He knew there were another 10 similarly armed men under the balcony where he was standing. Around the gallery were a further half a dozen guards who were patrolling the balcony in a clockwise direction, never still, eyes everywhere, missing nothing. Yorke realised they each had one thing in common – they had earphones with thin wire going down the back of their collars.

Yorke began walking around, unhurriedly, at the same pace as the others, glancing at the people below. It looked like a dinner for the senior management of a successful corporation, apart from the jarring note of the armed men. Two of the diners were women. One he vaguely recognised and as she looked up at a waiter who was offering her some wine he placed her. Cordelia Hewitt, European Commissioner for Foreign Aid. Something niggled at the back of his mind at the sight of her and then he got it. There had been an accounting irregularity in her vast department of over 100 million euros. The auditor who had found the discrepancy had died in a car crash. There had been nothing suspicious reported about the death and the whole matter had faded away, as was so often the case when it came to the EU's bureaucracy. Standing there and seeing the woman, knowing a great deal about many of the room's occupants, Yorke wondered about the crash.

Unlike the other guards, Yorke paused often to look down, resting his hands on the waist-height and ornate wooden rail surrounding the balcony. As he did, he did two things. He aimed the flexible camera lens attached to the underside of his wrist at the diners and he stuck shirt-button sized directional microphones underneath the railing. He was about two-thirds of the way round when he saw Colonel Mack Roberts step onto the gallery. Yorke went directly towards him.

'Colonel, can you spare me a moment?'

'Certainly. What do you want?'

'I've no radio, sir. Mine was duff.' Seeing Roberts, Yorke had felt it prudent to approach him and point out the deficiency, rather than be noticed and called to account.

'I've got a spare here.' The colonel reached into a pocket and handed the small radio over.

'As bad as bloody Clansman,' said Yorke with feeling, referring to the highly inadequate radio system the military had suffered with for over a decade.

'You've used Clansman? Where? Iraq?'

'No. Bosnia.'

With a nod Roberts strutted away. A bantam of a man who knew he ruled the roost. Yorke watched him go with a smile. He'd established something. His *bona fides* with the boss, in front of the other guards.

Immediately, he opened the nearest door and looked inside. It was an empty sitting room with its lights on. He stepped back onto the balcony as a guard walked past. 'Check the bloody rooms he says.'

He got a nod of commiseration. He began a second circumnavigation of the gallery, this time opening each door he came to and going in. The rooms were virtually all the same.

Bedrooms with a double bed, a comfortable looking settee and a sideboard laden with drinks. Curiouser and curiouser, he thought. When he quit each room he turned off the lights, giving himself a black background, making less of a target. In each room he hid tiny transmitters similar to those he'd placed around the balcony. Each one could transmit for up to 8 hours but only came on when noise activated at a certain level. The transmitters he'd placed around the balcony rail, aimed at the occupants of the banqueting hall, were narrow path listening devices that at 10 metres covered an area of 1 metre diameter. They sent their messages via satellite to *The Lucky Duck*. There a multi-track, automatic recorder, capable of listening to over 1,000 transmitters simultaneously took down every word. Built-in software took out background noise and sounds not in the same range as the human voice. It made for clean recordings.

In one room, Yorke used the speed-dial on his mobile. 'Dom?' He didn't whisper. He spoke normally. Bluff was safer than any clandestine action. 'The recorder working?'

'Yes, dad. No problems. You okay?'

'Fine. What about you two?'

'Okay. Catherine is sleeping. She'll take over the watch in two hours.'

'Good. Well done, Dom. Bye.'

Yorke walked onto the balcony. The clatter of knives and forks, tinkling glasses and waiters serving had given way to almost complete silence. A glance around told him how much things had changed. The waiters had left and there was an air of expectancy in the room. All the guards had also vanished. Yorke stepped back into the shallow alcove of the room he'd just left.

Movement on the other side of the gallery caught his eye and he stepped further back into the darkness. It was Colonel Roberts. He stood silently in another doorway, looking down at the speaker.

A knife tapped unnecessarily against the side of a glass, demanding a silence that was already there. 'Gentlemen and,' after a slight hesitation and a nod in the direction Yorke knew the two women were sitting, 'ladies, thank you for coming here to-night.' The contempt he felt for the people in the room he kept well hidden. He thought of them, whenever be bothered to allow any of them to impinge on his thoughts, with a feeling close to hatred. They were his playthings. His to command. Controlled by him because of their greed. For Kennedy, it was all about power. The money was a means to an end. Many of the people in the room wielded their own power, some of them a great deal of it, though nothing in comparison to him. Then they didn't have the added benefit of complete ruthlessness, a private army trained and willing to kill, a talent for blackmail which had proved very useful over the years and no form of conscience whatsoever. He could kill a child with as much feeling as squashing a bug.

'I promised you a night to remember and I hope I live up to that promise or my name isn't John Kennedy.' Nobody called out "It isn't", though many there knew he'd started life with a different name, even if they didn't know what it was.

Behind Kennedy a screen smoothly dropped from the ceiling. Yorke noticed Kennedy pressing buttons.

'This is a statement of account.' They weren't to know it wasn't a full statement. Kennedy only told them what he thought they needed to know. Kennedy began a power point presentation. 'It is a summary of what we've achieved in the last twelve months. I have had the figures broken down to show areas of main interest, narcotics, people smuggling, prostitution, money laundering and so on. I would like to draw your attention to two items. The one headed fraud. Much of that is from the European Union. Two areas in particular contributed the most, the overseas development fund and the new agricultural fund, enhanced to cater for the additional fifteen countries in the Union. Such a joyous occasion when the countries of the former Soviet Union joined, don't you think?'

Laughter broke out. One handed, the guests slapped the table while raising a glass in salutation. Kennedy allowed the applause to run for about 20 seconds before tapping the glass again. A few of the guests waved their glasses at Cordelia Hewitt who waved merrily back.

'However, there is still much to do. We have now siphoned

over twenty million, that's pounds sterling, by the way, not zlotys,' more laughter, 'to each of the five ruling political parties in Britain, Germany, Spain, France and Italy. Indications of appreciation have been received and certain contracts are guaranteed, including building the new European Parliament building in Strasbourg to cater for the extra people. After all, if the Scots can be robbed of half a billion I am sure we can do a lot better.' More appreciate clapping and yells of hear, hear sounded for a minute. This time Kennedy let them go on a bit longer. He was enjoying himself.

One voice called out, 'What about a building in Brussels as well?'

'That will be next year,' replied Kennedy, straightfaced. More hoots of derision followed. 'Legitimate business accounted for over ten billion euros of profits last year while our illegal operations accounted for nearly ten times as much.' The truth was closer to twenty times, but that snippet of information he was keeping to himself. 'Those profits represent an increase of twenty-two percent on the previous year. You can see in summary that we are predicting an increase this year of as much as thirty percent, but that's because certain one-off expenses won't occur again. Let me just spend a few minutes talking about the legitimate end of our operations. We now hold large minority stakes in seventeen of Europe's largest banks. Any more and under existing stock exchange rules we'd have to make a bid for the whole company. We aren't ready to do that just yet. However, we will be starting later this year with Britain's National Westminster. We plan to take over at least four banks in the next twelve months. These are spread across Europe for obvious reasons. Technically, with our other investment trust holdings, we have voting control in six banks, but that's not good enough. Not for us!'

Cheers and laughter, more clapping and raised glasses followed his announcement. Yorke, standing back and watching, was reminded of a pack of hyenas attacking a herd of helpless cows, baying in delight, covered in blood, deliriously happy at the carnage they were creating. Anger and intense hatred coursed through him and it took will power not to drop the thin slabs of Semtex onto their greedy, over-fed heads. The Glock would take out a few more and then what? He'd be dead a minute or two later, reality whispered in his ear.

'Let us finish on a high note,' Kennedy said, 'before the party really begins.' He held up a hand to still the fresh laughter. 'Please reach under your seats and take the envelopes you'll find sellotaped there. Please open them.'

Chairs scraped on the stone floor as some people stood whilst others stayed seated and reached underneath them. Hungry and greedy fingers tore open the heavy vellum envelopes. There were collective gasps from around the table.

'Yes, my friends. This year's bonus. Five million euros! Tax free! Spend it wisely. I know a good bank you can cash it in.'

The laughter and cheering erupted. Yorke stood motionless in the doorway, numbed by the spectacle and what he'd heard. How much was enough? Many of the people in the room were more than comfortable. They had position, power, respect. Yet they'd risk it all, for what? More money? More power? No! They'd never have that! Kennedy *owned* them. What drove them? What did they want? Didn't they recognise their betrayal of the people of the world? Not just Europe. But the whole goddamn, sodding world!

Movement on the other side of the gallery caught his eye and he froze. He couldn't be sure but it seemed to him that Colonel "Mack" Roberts was staring his way. If so, why didn't he just walk around the balcony and investigate? Why stand in the shadow of the doorway. Unless . . . Unless he shouldn't be there either! That was a thought. No other guards were around. Obviously what Kennedy had to say was for the ears of the VIPs only. Not the hired help. And whatever Roberts was, he was only the hired help.

There was more scraping of chairs and Yorke's attention was dragged back to events below. The guests stood, cheering Kennedy, clapping and yelling, joyful beyond comprehension. Doors opened and more guests streamed in, on the whole, attractive looking women of different shapes and heights.

Yorke watched as they approached the guests. Then some of the men, now with companions, headed for the stairs. Yorke stood still as the couples entered the bedrooms around the gallery. Cordelia Hewitt was approaching him, her companion dressed in a dinner jacket. Something wasn't quite right. *What the hell was it?* Then he got it. Hewitt's companion was a transvestite. Close to she was very pretty, perhaps her mouth a little sullen, though her eyes were as hard as agates.

Yorke flipped on the light switch and retreated quickly across the room. Grabbing a bottle of Dom Pérignon Champagne he busied himself taking off the foil. Hearing a noise he looked over his shoulder and smiled. 'In you come,' said Yorke gallantly.

Cordelia Hewitt stalked into the room. The wide smile she had on her face turned to a scowl when she saw Yorke. 'What are you doing here?'

'Orders, ma'am. Last minute checking. There was no Champagne in the room.'

'Get out! We can deal with it.' The EU Commissioner for Foreign Aid glared at him.

Yorke shrugged apologetically and placed the bottle in the ice bucket. 'Certainly, ma'am. I apologise.' He figured a little obsequiousness wouldn't go amiss right then, but he needn't have bothered. Hewitt's attention was already focused on the other woman. When Yorke closed the door behind him she was stroking the woman's cheek with a crimson red fingernail.

The guests had thinned out considerably, although a four-piece band had appeared and were playing a complex stylisation of "Yesterday" by Lennon and McCartney. Some of the men were slowly shuffling around a space at one end, their arms clutched tightly around their attractive escorts. Others were sitting at their tables, the women next to them, drinking, hands wandering. It wasn't exactly an orgy, but things were hotting up. Yorke continued filming, pointing his wrists, until he became aware of someone standing on the other side of the gallery looking at him.

It was "Mack" Roberts.

25

YORKE KNEW HE was pushing his luck. He'd stayed long enough. Time for a rapid exit. He ignored Roberts and walked towards the backstairs he'd used earlier. As he did, he checked the time. It was already after 03.00.

He resisted the temptation to look back at Roberts, his imagination feeling the man's eyes on his retreating back. Around the bend in the stairs and he began to hurry, taking the steps three at a time. In the corridor, still in darkness, he put on his NVGs. He found where he'd left his camouflage trousers and jacket and quickly dragged them on over his DJ. The Glock he placed in his right hand pocket after first attaching a silencer. Pausing at the door to the outside he took the handle by his left hand and clasped the butt of the pistol in his right.

He pulled the door open and stepped through straight into the path of one of the guards who was walking around the building as part of his patrol route. The man was startled but it was Yorke who recovered first.

'Morning. I'll be glad when this night is over.'

The man grunted. Whether he agreed or not Yorke couldn't tell and wasn't bothered. He began to walk across the open ground towards the cliff. Tiredness and running on his nerves for so long were taking their toll.

There came another challenge. 'Oi, you!'

'Me?' As he replied and looked back he saw it was Tom Littlejohn, the man who'd been in Yorke's cell just two days earlier.

'Yes, you. Don't I know you from somewhere? I've heard

that voice before.' Littlejohn was peering closely at him. 'But I don't know the face.'

Should he bluff it out or act? There was never a simple answer. Only right and wrong ones. He didn't hesitate. *Right or wrong*? He'd never know. Yorke shot Littlejohn without removing his hand from his pocket. The silenced bullet went through the heart. About to move the body into the corridor he heard numerous footsteps coming his way. He didn't wait. Turning, he moved quickly towards the cliff.

As he reached the edge and kneeled down next to the rope he grabbed the VAL and pressed the lower portion of the safety catch in. He was watching the house as two guards found the body. Whistles blew and arc lights came on, illuminating the whole area in white. The radio in his ear erupted into life and orders were given. He ripped the receiver out and left it dangling. It was a distraction he didn't need right then. A search light began to trace the edge of the cliff and just as it reached him, Yorke fired two rounds from the silenced automatic rifle and extinguished it. Chips of stone and earth erupted near him and he saw the two guards running towards him, firing silenced pistols.

He shot both of them.

No more shots came his way and he reached into a pocket and withdrew a thin pair of cotton gloves. Pulling them on, he took one last look around, took hold of the rope and slid down. There was no time to rappel or fit the rope correctly around his back and legs – there was only time to hold tight and slide. The cotton reduced most of the rope-burn from unendurable to painful.

He hit the bottom with a thump, flexing his legs, staying upright. He hurried to the spot where he'd buried the chariot and diving gear. There was no time to put on the dry suit as bullets suddenly hit the rocks behind him, one ricocheting past his ear. He thought he was being deliberately shot at until he realised that a fusillade of shooting had erupted all along the cliff face. He heard something metallic clatter on the rocks and threw himself down between two large boulders. The grenade erupted about 10 metres away, sending deadly shards of steel in all directions. Scrabbling in the sand he dragged out the chariot and weight belt. He heard more grenades landing amongst the rocks and after only a few paces he threw himself flat. One grenade landed nearby and the nearness of the explosion left his ears ringing but otherwise he was unhurt. Rolling over he took aim at the cliff top. Men were silhouetted against the lights in the background. He put the safety catch to fully automatic and sprayed the top of the cliff. Lying on his back shooting upwards was tricky, but he had the satisfaction of seeing some of the guards fall back with cries of pain when suddenly all of them vanished.

He knew what to expect. He got to his feet, grabbed the UC(P) and weight belt and ran the last few yards to the water's edge. The clatter behind his back told him that hand grenades were raining down. Fear lent him strength. Carrying the chariot cradled in his arms and with the weight belt over his shoulder he waded into the sea, pressed the start button and launched himself flat. The propeller dug into the water and pulled him serenely from danger. He kept his legs together and his feet out flat, not causing a splash, letting the machine do the work. The exploding grenades, reaching a crescendo of noise, began to fade behind him.

About three cables from the shore he looked back. Lights had been trundled to the cliff edge and were being aimed down. He could see guards climbing down the cliff face, the shower of grenades having stopped. He guessed there would be boats somewhere and hoped they were kept safely at Mevagissey, which would take time to be manned and brought round. Attached to the end of the chariot was a short hose with a mouthpiece. It was for use in an emergency in the event of the diver's main bottles either becoming empty or malfunctioning, a very rare occurrence. His diving goggles he'd left looped over the handlebars and he used one hand to put them on, not slowing, knowing distance was vital. The UC(P) moved faster on the surface, as there was approximately a third less drag, an advantage he could improve on if he got rid of his clothes.

Awkwardly he kicked off his shoes and began the laborious task of shedding his camouflage trousers. With them off he reluctantly wrapped the VAL Silent Sniper in them in a tight ball and let go. The cloth rode the water for a second or two before sinking. He shivered. The water was bloody freezing.

Next he kicked off his DJ trousers and managed to peel off his can't-see-me jacket. He transferred a number of items from the jacket into the pockets of his DJ, wrapped the weight belt in the camouflage jacket and let it sink. A glance at the speedometer showed him at 4.6 knots. An increase of 0.8 – not much, but it could make all the difference.

He pressed the transmit button on the right-hand side of the chariot. After a few seconds a light flashed three times in front of his face. Dom knew he was in the water and moving fast.

A glance at his wristwatch gave him a surprise. It was only 03.25. Yet it felt like hours since he was in the house. Thirty minutes had passed and now his teeth were chattering. His legs felt numb and he kicked them up and down in an ineffectual attempt to get them warm or at least keep the blood circulating. Luckily, this far from land, the sea was undulating with no breaking waves. The lights on the cliff were beginning to fade and could be seen only when he was at the top of a swell. Whatever pandemonium he'd created back there meant he wasn't out of trouble. They'd be wanting blood. His.

Looking ahead, he raised his face clear of the sea and caught a flash of red and green, the combined lantern at the mast head of a sailing vessel. Was it the *Duck*? Seeing it gave him renewed strength and hope. He placed his head flat between his outstretched arms and concentrated on being as streamlined as possible. With his face in the water he was breathing off the emergency oxygen, but again, speed was of the essence. The only weapons he was left with were three flat Semtex packs and a throwing knife strapped to his right calf. He hoped he wouldn't need them.

Numbness began to creep in as the cold sapped his strength. Slowly he kicked his legs again, trying to get his circulation moving. He lifted his face. The combined lantern was closer.

He looked back. Now the lights at the house were a hazy glow. His watch told him he'd been in the water for . . . his brain was becoming sluggish. Forty-eight . . . no, fifty-three minutes. If this had been September, when the sea would have had the summer to warm up, even just a few degrees, he knew he'd be in better shape. But now, after a cold winter, those few degrees could make all the difference. They weren't only strength sapping, they were deadly. Using what was almost the last of his energy he reached for the safety clip on the back of the UC(P). The spring hook was attached to a 3m, thin nylon line kept rolled up on a tension-roller. It was to aid recovery by attaching the hook to suitable lifting gear. He got the line around his waist and snapped the hook onto it.

If the chariot slipped from his hands at least it wouldn't go too far without him. His eyes closing, he began a series of micro-sleeps, nodding off for nano-seconds before jerking awake. He knew he was in the first stages of hypothermia. His right hand slipped from the handlebars and this time he jerked awake with a pounding heart. *Come on, you bloody fool, not now. Not when you're so close*!

The masthead light was much clearer. Probably less than a mile. Even as little as 7 or 8 cables. Not long now. The jib and mainsail were obvious. Good lad. She was flying along. But why did he have the engine running? That made no sense! The idiot. Hadn't he learnt . . . the noise wasn't coming from the *Duck*. It was off to his left. He lifted his face and strained his eyes over his shoulder. There! Coming like a bat out of hell was a fast cruiser. He could see the green of her starboard light. It was heading straight for the yacht.

No! It was turning. Coming straight towards him. What the hell? This close he could be painting on their radar. He twisted the handlebars and angled the fins down. The chariot dived, taking him with it. The auto-pilot kept him on course, the depth-limiter safety feature evened the chariot out at 8m, before reaching the depth when pure oxygen became narcotic and dangerous – below 10m.

The spurt of adrenaline had brought him wide awake, his

lethargy diminishing but he knew it wouldn't last. He concentrated on listening to the sounds of the boat's screws. They thrashed overhead and faded, came back and faded again. He could hear them distinctly heading away from him in the direction of the yacht.

He took the UC(P) up to 3m and began kicking with all his might. He was using up needed energy but desperation leant him strength. A faint buzz on the panel on the chariot warned him he was at the rendezvous position. He looked up. The day was dawning and a grey light diffused down the first few feet of water. Enough for him to see the deep keel of the yacht and the sleek hull of the motor boat. Slowly he inched his way up, towards the stern of the yacht.

The motor boat was alongside the *Duck*, their hulls thudding together in the gentle swell.

Dom's voice came clearly to Yorke. 'I'm telling you to get off my boat. You've no right.'

A harsh voice said, 'Shut up, you little bastard. We're going to search this boat and there's nothing you can do about it.'

'Yes I will. I'll call the coastguard and . . .' A loud smack followed by a body crumpling onto the deck followed. 'You shit,' said Dom. 'You wouldn't dare do that if my father was here.'

'What have we here?' said the same voice.

'Let me go, you pig,' said Catherine.

Yorke could hear the sound of a struggle. What was said next he didn't hear as he used the UC(P) to go under the cruiser's hull near the waterline and come alongside on the opposite side to the *Duck*. With numbed, feverish fingers, he took out a Semtex pack, peeled off the adhesive backing and pressed it firmly against the hull of the cruiser. He placed the other two at 2 metre intervals. Quickly he went along each one and set the first to 2 minutes, the second to 1 minute 50 seconds and the third to 1 minute forty seconds. He returned to the stern of the *Duck*, slipped the spring hook from around his waist and attached it to the stern ladder.

The last of Yorke's considerable strength was waning fast.

The debilitating nature of cold water was not to be underestimated and it was with great difficulty he pulled himself on to the platform. He could hear that things on the yacht had gone from bad to worse.

'I know this woman. She was at the house. She's that journalist. That bastard Yorke gave me a bloody headache because of her. Jesus! This little bastard must be Yorke's son. We'd better take them with us.'

'What shall we do with the yacht? Sink it?'

'Yes. No.'

'Make up your bleeding mind.'

'Get back over and radio in and ask for instructions. Erik!'

'What?' A voice on the cruiser replied.

'Sam's going to radio for instructions. Either we take them back with us or we leave them on the yacht.'

'Don't be stupid. We can't just leave them.'

'The yacht won't be floating no more.'

Yorke looked at his watch, the numerals fuzzy. He shook his head to clear it. How long did he have? Fifteen? Twenty seconds?

He was kneeling, the throwing knife in his hand, mustering his strength for one massive effort. How long . . .?

The three eruptions were seconds apart as the bottom was ripped out of the cruiser. The explosion killed the man on the radio outright. The man on the helm had his back broken by the shock wave and collapsed with a loud scream.

The third man spun round to look at the cruiser just as Yorke stood up on the ladder and threw the knife at the man's torso. Instead of hitting the heart or some other vital organ, the knife went right through the man's upper left arm, severing muscle and arteries. The man staggered, yelling in fear and anger. However, he had the strength and presence of mind to reach for the gun in his shoulder holster, drawing it, snarling his hatred.

Yorke had no strength left other than to stand there swaying. His befuddled mind told him to jump into the sea, but his body wouldn't do what he told it.

As the gun came up Catherine reacted. She lurched to her feet, grabbed the 2 metre boathook, and swung it over her head, bringing it smashing down onto the gunman's right arm. Bones crunched, the man screamed and the gun fired, the bullet hitting the transom, inches from Yorke.

Before the gunman could move Dom barged into him with his shoulder and caught the man in the chest, sending him flying backwards and over the railings. He fell into the sinking hull of the cruiser, now floating half a metre away from the yacht. The boats hadn't been attached and continued to drift apart. Suddenly there was an eruption of flame. A small fire that had started in the engine room had reached the main tanks. The resulting fireball scorched the side of the *Duck* as Dom jumped across the cockpit and pressed the starter button. The engine burst into life and he rammed the gear lever into reverse. The propeller bit and the yacht moved away from the already dying embers of the fire as the boat sank. There was no sign of any of the men who'd been aboard.

Yorke stumbled over the transom and collapsed onto the stern seat. He was shivering uncontrollably, his teeth chattering. He managed to say, 'Out to sea, son. As fast as you can.'

'Dad, are you all right?'

'C . . . cold. I need to get out of these clothes. Hot sh . . . shower. The chariot's on the stern. Put the *Duck* on auto and you two get it on board.'

Catherine, in something of a daze, gave Dom a hand. Yorke staggered below and dragged off the remainder of his wet clothes. He knew he needed to get his core temperature up. The thought was fixed in his mind. Grabbing a bar of chocolate, he stuffed it into his mouth as he climbed into the shower. He turned it on, as hot as he could stand it, leaning against the side, his legs rubbery.

'Can I help?' Catherine asked, putting her head around the door.

'Yes. Hot drink. Drinking chocolate with sugar.' He switched off the water, took a towel and roughly dried himself. He found his dressing gown and put it on. His teeth were still chattering and he barely had the strength to return to the galley. Collapsing onto a sofa he said, 'Light the gas rings on the cooker and get me a duvet, please.'

Catherine did as he bid and as she tucked the feather filled quilt around his shoulders said, 'You look awful. White as a sheet.'

He summoned up a smile. 'Thanks. It's the onset of hypothermia. I need to get warm inside and out. Need a fug in here so I suck warm air into my lungs and drink hot, sweet fluids. It's the quickest way.' The kettle began to boil and she went to make the drink.

'Should I put some brandy or something in it?'

'Definitely not. Old wives' tales. Alcohol is bad for you. Opens the pores. Let's heat escape. Glucose is best.' He took the proffered mug in both his hands, trying not to spill the drink. He managed to get it to his lips and sip it, scalding his tongue, forcing it down.

'Is there anything else I can do?' She was frowning at him, her concern obvious.

'No, thanks. I guess I'll live. Need an hour or two to recuperate. Go up-top and help Dom. We're still on the engine. Get the sails up and run before the wind.'

Catherine nodded and left. Yorke drained the mug, placed it in the holder next to him, closed his eyes and promptly fell asleep. He awoke to a muggy headache and the sun streaming through the portholes on the port side.

Groggily he climbed to his feet, crossed the deck and switched off the two gas rings. The cabin felt like the inside of a particularly unpleasant sauna. He found the medical chest and helped himself to three headache pills. He went aft to his cabin and got dressed in jeans and tee-shirt before going forward and opening the hatch. He popped his head up, waved to Dom back in the cockpit before working his way along the hull opening all the port holes. Already the fug was dissipating, the temperature falling, his headache clearing. Each passing moment left him feeling stronger and more alert.

Finally he put his head through the companionway hatch. 'Okay, Dom?'

Dom yawned and nodded. 'I'm okay. What about you, dad?'

'Fine. Where's Catherine?'

'Dom nodded behind him. 'On the transom seat.'

Yorke looked past Dom's legs to the sleeping figure of Catherine, dead to the world, lying along the seat.

'She's only just gone off. She was working on the computer until half an hour ago. Hey,' he smiled at his father, 'she's all right. The way she smacked the boathook across that guy's arm.'

'I guess she is. But it's also thanks to you son, knocking him over like that. Well done.'

Dom shrugged in sheepish pleasure.

'What time is it?'

'Just after eleven. That's the Lizard over there,' Dom pointed to the starboard bow. 'South-south-west means we're running before the wind.'

'Good lad.' Yorke came up beside the boy and put his arm around his shoulders. 'You sure you're okay?'

Dom shrugged. 'I guess so. Only . . .'

'I know, son. Only you've never killed anyone before. It's a terrible, terrible feeling. But you know they'd have killed us without a second thought. There was no way we were going back to that house and coming out alive. And you heard them. If they hadn't wanted us back there they'd have killed us and sunk the *Duck*.'

'I know. Catherine said the same thing. Only . . . It's just not that easy to do or . . . or live with, I guess.'

'Believe me, I do know. If you pair hadn't done what you did I'd be dead now. So thank you.'

'Gosh, don't *thank* me, dad.' There was utter surprise in his voice.

'Well, you did save my life and that deserves thanks. Twice now you've come to the rescue.'

'Heck, dad, I know you'd do the same for me.'

'You'd better believe it, son. You'd better believe it. Now, how about tea and bacon butties, while I take the boat?'

'You got it, dad. Course, 210 degrees, speed,' he glanced at the dial, '6.5 knots. Wind from the north-east, jib and main set. Nothing coming within 3 miles.'

'I have the boat,' said Yorke formally.

A slight sea mist was hovering close to land while out where they were it was clear. He could see two large hulled vessels miles away to port and three sailing boats to starboard. Otherwise the Channel was clear. He hoped it stayed that way.

26

THEY HELD A council of war that evening. They had tacked round Lizard Point and finally got into Mullion Cove there they anchored for the night, using Mullion Island to create a lee. The *Duck* swayed slightly, the undulating sea passing soporifically beneath her hull. Every third or fourth wavelet broke gently against her, causing the softest of shudders.

'We have a number of major issues to face,' began York. 'First of all, we were damned lucky to get away.' He shook his head, the fear he felt not showing on his face. It wasn't for himself, however, that he was afraid, it was for them. Not one to dwell on regrets and ponder the "what ifs", he did so now. Mentally, he shook himself out of it and got back to the matter in hand. 'They know who each of us are. They know we represent a threat of some description to them, albeit one that is unquantified as far as they're concerned.'

'That doesn't seem to bother them much.' Catherine swirled the ice cubes around the glass of her tonic water. She wished she'd added gin to it but recognised Yorke's maxim to keep a clear head.

'They definitely feel safe and powerful enough to shoot first and ask questions afterwards,' said Yorke. He in turn raised his glass of soda water and took a mouthful.

'What are we going to do?' Dom asked, ignoring the glass of coke on the table in front of him.

'We now have the actual evidence we needed,' said Yorke. 'The recordings we have are incredible. I know a lot was lost in the background clutter but there's a lot of good stuff there. And we've only listened to less than thirty percent.'

'None of it will be of any use if we don't stay alive.'

Yorke looked at Catherine and nodded. 'That's so. Hence we need to make some decisions as to what we're going to do. I've been wracking my brains to think of someone we can contact who's in a high enough position to do something and I've come up with one name.'

'Who?' Catherine stood up and went over to the drinks cabinet. She began to refreshen her glass with tonic water.

'The Prime Minister,' was the startling reply.

'What?' She looked at him dumbfounded. 'Are you nuts? After what happened?'

'I don't think the man's a coward. I think he's rightly fearful for his family. We know one of the policewomen guarding his wife and kids is in the pay of the enemy. Maybe more than one. So we have to somehow spirit the family away. Get them to a safe place. Then he can blow the whistle. The only place that can be done is in Parliament.'

'I just don't see it,' said Catherine taking a mouthful of her drink.

'Any better ideas?'

'Offhand, no. But I wouldn't trust him. Look what happened when you did. How will you get in contact with him? You won't get within a mile.'

'I have his family e-mail address. I'll use that.' Yorke shrugged, drained his glass. Dom nodded at it but Yorke shook his head. 'No thanks, son. Any more and I'll go rusty. I'll also try Phil again.'

Catherine asked, 'Can you trust him?'

Yorke nodded. 'Beyond a shadow of a doubt.'

She nodded, the doubt she was feeling evident in her eyes.

'You may be right about the PM. Let's sleep on it. I'm knackered. Are you sure you're okay for the first watch, Dom?'

'Sure, dad. I slept half the afternoon.'

'All right. It's 22.20 now. Shake me at 01.00. Catherine, I'll call you at 05.00. Okay you two?'

Yorke went up-top to check the anchorage and the weather. The forecast had been good and so it was proving. Light breezes from the north, dry, outlook fair. Dom sat in the cockpit, huddled in a thick jacket.

'Okay, son?'

'Yes, dad.'

'Good. Don't forget to call me. Good night.'

Yorke went below and looked in on Catherine. 'You okay?'

'Sure. What could possibly be wrong? My flat is burnt out, ruthless people are trying to kill me and I'm stuck on this small boat with a teenager and a killer.'

'Is that what you think of me?' Yorke tried to keep his voice even.

Tears welled up in her eyes. 'I don't know, Stephen. I'm scared. I'm scared for my life, my future, for everything. You know, I think I'm most scared of what's in store for the world if these people aren't stopped. I've been listening to some of the recordings, matching the faces and voices. Do you know who some of those people are? It's mind numbing. It's the only word for it. Since I've realised the scale of the corruption the horror of what it means has been growing in my head.'

'I know. I feel the same.' Yorke sighed, indecision heavy in his eyes. 'I don't have the answers. I'm blundering around. I've never been in a position like this before. Always, there was back up. First with the Royal Marines and then at *Phoenix*. Operating alone was one thing, but having a safe refuge was,' he paused, searching for the right word, 'comforting. It was there at the back of your mind. If things went pear shaped and you had to do a runner you had somewhere to run to. It's amazing how sustaining that thought is. It goes to the basics of something as mundane as carrying a gun. *Phoenix* had all the right permits. A phone call from Desmond Kavanagh could solve vast sways of problems. If a constable lifted me with a gun on me, Christ, a throwing knife with a blade more than 3 inches long and it's a long prison sentence. Those thoughts are debilitating. They prevent you from thinking straight.' He tailed off, shaking his head.

Catherine placed her hand on his arm. 'Unless you're a criminal. Then you don't care.'

Yorke smiled wanly. 'Or you're as powerful as John Kennedy.'

Catherine nodded. 'I'm at a loss as to what we do. I'm not so sure that talking to Beaton will be of any help. He's frightened for his family. He's hamstrung. He's told you he's getting out. You said he wanted the Chancellor to take over, but in view of what we now know I suspect it will be Whitley that gets the job. The British Prime Minister controlled by a crime cartel! Think of it! The implications are too terrible to contemplate.'

'You're right. Where would that lead us? Democracy as we know it could be destroyed. From the UK they could take control of other countries within the European Union. With eighty percent of all law coming from Brussels and unelected officials just think what Kennedy and his lot could do if they had control. It truly doesn't bear thinking about. That's why we have to fight them.'

Catherine leaned back on her pillows wearily. 'How, in God's name, do we do that?'

'Together! We need to pull the information we've gathered in a coherent and focused way. We need to get it out to the press world-wide. We get a copy to the Prime Minister via e-mail first. I'll tell him what I discovered in Crieff. How his daughter went missing.'

'Then what?'

'We need backup. Serious backup, which is why I mentioned Phil. He's not only a close friend but also a major at Stirling Lines, Hereford.'

'The SAS?'

Yorke nodded. 'He's Regimental Adjutant.'

'Are you sure you can trust him?'

'As sure as I can be. We grew up together. I was best man at his wedding and vice-versa. We joined the RMs together but he jumped ship and went to Hereford. We've been on joint ops and exercises. I can't think who else to speak to.'

Catherine sat up, suddenly excited. 'I can! The Assistant Chief Constable for Devon.'

'Who's he? I mean how do you know him?'

'It's a she. Mary Murray. I wrote an article on her a few years ago when she was a superintendent. We became friends. We see each other maybe four or five times a year, exchange Christmas and birthday cards, that sort of thing. But I'd bet with everything I have she can be trusted.'

'What about with your life?' Yorke asked dryly.

Catherine leaned back, closing her eyes, a tiny headache beginning to take hold in her left temple. 'At some point in time, even with that. If Mary's gone over to the dark side then there really is no hope for us.'

'The dark side about sums it up. Look, let me make a suggestion. I can get you away. False passport and other ID. Money not a problem. You lay low while I try and stop them. If I succeed somehow, then you can resume your old life. If I fail, well . . .' he shrugged, leaving the word hanging in the air.

'No, I can't do that,' she said wearily. 'Somebody has to stand up and be counted and it looks like we're elected. What's next? We can't float around the Channel forever.'

'We lay low. Tomorrow we cross Mount's Bay and go to a small boatyard I know. We'll have the yacht repainted. I've already phoned and made the arrangements.'

'Can you trust the people at the yard?'

'I hope so. He's my uncle. Although I haven't seen him in a couple of years. While we're there I want you to compile the information we have. Edit the recordings we took last night until we have the most damaging. Do what you do best.'

'What's that?'

'Be a journalist. Think Pulitzer.'

'Bugger the Pulitzer. It's a bauble. I want to survive. Are you coming in here with me?' She snuggled down, moving her hips enticingly.

Yorke looked at her with longing and thought about Dom. 'Sorry.' He patted the tops of her legs and in reply got a tongue poked out at him.

The night passed without a hitch. They changed watches, had a leisurely breakfast and then hoisted sail.

As they got underway Dom announced, 'Seventeen and a half miles to go, dad. With this wind from the south, probably four hours.'

Yorke and Dom gave themselves up to the sheer joy of sailing while Catherine continued working at her computer.

Mid-morning Yorke made a phone call. 'Phil? At last! It's Steve. Can you talk?'

'Sure, no problem. I got your message but I've just returned from Bosnia. Had a defaulters' table to take first and then I was going to call you. I gave them ten days pay and confined to barracks for drunk and disorderly and bringing the service into disrepute.'

'How did they do that?'

'Eight yobs attacked three of my men. When it was over only five of the yobs went to hospital and three walked away. Actually, crawled would be a better description. That's bringing disrepute to the service. The lot should have gone into hospital. Actually, in all seriousness, we keep telling the lads to walk away. To ignore the provocation. But what the hell, we pump them full of testosterone, make them the toughest sons-of-bitches alive and expect them to take a load of crap from a bunch of no-hopers. Anyway, to what do I owe the honour of this call and why the urgency?'

'I need your help, badly.'

'How badly? What's happened? Is Dom all right?'

'So far. Phil this is serious. Do you still have the same encrypted e-mail?'

'Sure. What do you have for me?'

'You'll see. We'll send the file at 14.00. I'll phone back at 16.00. And Phil, listen. Tell no one. Show no one. Okay?'

'Sure, Steve, no problem. Where will you be?'

'Uncle William's.' Yorke broke the connection. Phillip Carstairs knew the boatyard. They'd spent enough of their school holidays there. Learning to sail amongst other things. Catherine joined him in the cockpit and sat on the transom seat.

'How's it going?'

She pursed her lips and thought about her answer. 'On one

level, it's fine. On another it isn't. The problem is we now have so much. Between the computer files from *Phoenix* and the tapes from the house there's so much to transcribe.' She shook her head. 'The more I read the more frightened I'm becoming. They're across Europe. I've identified senior politicians, bankers, industrialists, journalists, writers. God above, everybody who's anybody seem to be involved.'

'Everybody?' Yorke chided her.

'Well, not quite. But some real powerful people, nonetheless.'

'I don't doubt it. But we must keep this in perspective. The vast majority of people are *not* involved and in fact would fight these people tooth and nail if they knew.'

'I suppose that's true. But there's a snag.'

'I know. Knowing who the good guys are.'

'That, but I was thinking more from the point of view of rallying the forces of good before its too late.'

York nodded. 'You put it very succinctly. Although I do believe it can never be *too* late, only harder to deal with as time goes by. The more entrenched the enemy becomes the harder it is to dislodge them. A military fact of life.'

Catherine nodded. 'I take it you were talking to your friend?'

'Yes. We'll send him an e-mail at 14.00. The address it's going to ensures it's automatically encrypted. It should be safe.'

'Good. I'll phone Mary. I have her mobile. Okay?'

'Sure, go ahead. The sooner the better. However, we need a backup plan.'

Catherine looked at him in surprise. 'We do? How?'

'I'll tell you in a moment. Dom, get ready to jibe. Jibe-o.' Sails shifted, the yacht's course altered and they settled on the final leg to their destination.

'Dom, how about a coffee?'

'Sure, dad. Catherine?'

'Please. Any chocolate biscuits?'

Dom smiled. 'How many?'

Catherine raised two fingers, paused and added a third. Dom nodded and went below.

'We send copies to our solicitors. To be opened in the event of our deaths. My solicitor already has such an instruction. It's my will in reality. We send discs, in sealed envelopes, with our instructions. If we post them today, guaranteed overnight delivery they'll get there tomorrow.'

'And what do we tell the solicitors to do?'

'To copy the discs and send them to every newspaper and media outlet in the country.'

'Actually, I can do better than that,' said Catherine. She broke off to accept a cup of coffee from Dom. 'Thanks.' With a mouthful of biscuit she spoke around the crumbs. 'I have a data base of all the really serious media players, including agencies. They're formatted on disc. I use it to send simultaneous articles from Australia to Iceland. It's all e-mail. All the solicitors would have to do is load the discs and give the correct instructions. They probably know what to do but I can write a note telling them, just in case.'

'Good. Send them the lot. Use the edited versions for Phil and what's her name? Mary Murray? Distance to go, Dom?'

'Two and a half miles. There's the yard's crane.' Dom was standing in the bow with binoculars to his eyes. 'Romeo's flying. Uncle William's ready for us.' Dom could clearly make out the red flag with the yellow plus sign.

'Fancy going in under sail or shall we motor?'

The entrance was narrow but opened out once past the mole. Sailing her in was the tricky option, or as Uncle William always said, 'The show-off option.'

Dom smiled at Yorke, 'Why not?'

'All right. Nothing too smart. We'll drop the main at half a cable and go in on the jib. With this wind it'll be a doddle. Out fenders.'

Dom put fenders over both sides of the hull. Standing in the bow, he kept one on a line ready to hand, while Yorke had the same in the cockpit.

With a hundred yards to go they dropped the mainsail. The *Duck* immediately lost way but with a steady breeze of about eight knots from the south kept her heading for the entrance.

A lonely figure stood on the wall on the starboard side and watched them critically.

'Hi, Uncle William,' Dom yelled as they passed.

The figure waved back. 'Go to the cradle,' he yelled.

'Okay!' Yorke acknowledged.

The *Duck* tacked to starboard and with twenty metres to go Yorke said, 'Let go the jib.'

Dom dropped the jib, Yorke spun the wheel hard to starboard and the yacht slid round to come to a halt, port side to, a metre from the jetty, the lifting cradle directly astern. Yorke and Dom grinned at each other in silent satisfaction.

Grabbing the boat hook, Dom stood amidships and pulled them towards the side. Uncle William appeared and clapped his hands. Dom threw him the bow line which William caught and dropped the bight over a bollard. He marched quickly aft and dealt with the stern line equally adroitly. He noticed the name change on the hull but said nothing. He knew explanations would be forthcoming.

Yorke leapt the few feet up to the jetty and held out his hand. 'Hi, Uncle William. How are you?'

His uncle grinned broadly. 'All the better for seeing you, laddie. What are the scorch marks on the hull?'

'We'll tell you over a cup of something. This is Catherine.'

William looked at her closely and evidently liked what he saw. He held out his hand and helped her onto the jetty. 'I am very pleased to meet you, my dear.' He tucked her hand under his arm and led her away. 'What's a nice girl doing with a pair of reprobates like these two?'

She looked back helplessly and rolled her eyes. Yorke was laughing silently while Dom had a wide grin on his face.

The yard could hold 6 to 8 medium sized yachts at any one time. William had three craftsmen and five general dogsbodies working there. Due to the high standards and quality of their work the yard was always busy. In a desperate attempt to reduce the work load William increased the prices. To no avail. It seemed the more he charged the more yachtsmen wanted his services. The people on his payroll were amongst the highest paid in the industry, loyal, hard working and always prepared to go the extra mile if needed. Like if a deadline had to be met or a regular customer had an urgent job needing doing. Fitting in the *Duck* had taken sleight-of-hand sophistry but William had managed it.

The yard was immaculate. All equipment was in pristine order and stowed in its proper place. In contrast, the office was a tip, with work surfaces covered with paperwork. Yorke and Dom followed the other two. William swept some papers off a chair and offered it to Catherine.

'Where's Ellen?' Yorke asked after William's super-efficient secretary.

'Gone to have a baby, would you believe?'

'I thought she already had three kids,' Yorke said.

'She does. The daft bugger. And no man either. Still, she'll drop the sprog next week and be back the week after. She'll soon get this place sorted. I'll make coffee.' William busied himself with a state-of-the-art coffee machine. He was in his late fifties, the younger brother of Yorke's dead father. There was a family resemblance between the older and younger Yorke, the same deep set eyes and shape of the head. William was thin and tall, his thick head of hair completely grey.

'How's Aunt Rebecca?' Dom asked.

'Fine. Gone to Derby to her sister's for a few days.' Noticing Yorke's raised eyebrows he added, 'It's all right. Honestly. There are no problems.' Seeing Catherine's quizzical look, he explained. 'I'm a recovering alcoholic. Believe me, my wife's put up with a hell of a lot in her time . . .'

'That's why we call her Saint Becca,' interrupted Dom.

'Cheeky monkey,' said William, ruffling the boy's hair in good humour. 'Anyway, I no longer drink but it does mean I make the finest coffee in Christendom.'

'It's an Arabic drink,' said Catherine with a smile.

'And infinitely better than anything an Arab could make.'

'It's true,' said Yorke. 'He's got about fifty varieties of coffee beans, his own mixture and more flavourings than you can shake a shaggy stick at.'

'This is my own mixture.' He offered a steaming mug to Catherine. Finally they were sitting around the conference table, papers piled on one side, Catherine's laptop booted up and spewed forth information. While this was happening, Yorke told his uncle everything, with contributions to the story from the other two. William asked shrewd questions and though shocked to the core, he didn't show it.

Halfway through the narrative Yorke said, 'It's coming up to 14.00. Let's get the e-mail ready for Phil.'

'Carstairs?' William enquired, raising an eyebrow. 'Good choice. We can trust him.' It was typical of William to identify himself with the problem.

However, Catherine asked, 'We?'

'Certainly, we. From all you've told me these people are a threat to our very civilisation. Possibly even our existence. They have to be fought like we did the Nazis in the Second World War and Saddam in Iraq.'

'Iraq,' Catherine bristled.

Yorke interrupted. 'Don't go there, either of you. Keep it until after this battle is won.'

'Never mind the battle,' said William, 'the war.'

'Ready to send the e-mail?' Yorke asked and received a nod from Catherine. 'Send now. 14.00.'

'Why so precise?' she asked reasonably.

'It's to do with the encryption. Codes are sent into the server, the info is scrambled and then vomited out to its destination. It's not one hundred percent foolproof but pretty close.'

'Shouldn't we have encrypted it this end first?'

'No. Any information is stolen at the server's end. The encryption software meets the e-mail as it arrives and encodes it before it goes into the system. All terribly clever and way beyond my pay grade or understanding. What about Mary?'

'I've tried her mobile. It's going to answering machine. I'll try later,' she said looking at the brass 24 hour clock on the wall over the door.

They continued their narrative until well into the afternoon, their mugs of coffee being replenished often. While they did so, the *Duck* was put on the hoist, lifted from the water and placed on a stand. Two of William's staff began sanding and preparing the hull for painting. The colour was to be a deep blue, like the old Royal Yacht Britannia.

After numerous attempts Catherine finally made contact with Mary Murray. The ACC was alone, driving her new Porsche around an old airfield near Falmouth. 'I'm on the hands free, so talk all you like.'

'Mary, I need to speak to you as a matter of urgency and a mobile isn't to be trusted.'

'Why ever not?'

'It's too complicated to explain. But if you're in Falmouth can you come here?'

'London? Are you nuts?'

'Of course not! I'm near Newlyn.'

'That's different. All right. I was getting bored going round and round in circles. Where will I find you?'

'At a boatyard, called?' She looked at Yorke.

'Yorke's. Two miles south of Mousehole.'

She repeated the information to the ACC.

'What on earth are you doing there?'

'It's a long story. But I promise you not a boring one.'

'Has this anything to do with your flat burning down?'

'So you know about that?'

'Literally only what I heard in the news. I've tried ringing you but your mobile is unobtainable.'

'I lost it. God knows where.'

'All right, sit tight and I'll be with you as soon as I can.'

'Mary, tell no one. Do you understand? No one.'

'Okay. No one. Don't worry. My lips are sealed.'

'Are you sure we can trust her?' Yorke asked. It was the question uppermost in their minds all the time. *Who* could they trust?

Catherine shrugged. 'Like I said, if we can't, then there's no hope for mankind. Believe me, I think Mary is as straight as they come.'

The story was finally told. William's rhetorical question as to what they could do hung in the air, bringing a pall of gloom with it. The workforce came and clocked off amidst a chorus of "goodnights". As the foreman was leaving Yorke handed over two padded envelopes and a £20 note and asked that they be sent registered post. Catherine had prepared them earlier, with short notes to their respective solicitors.

Silence settled over the yard only to be interrupted by the unmistakable thwacking sound of a helicopter. Yorke was out of the office before he'd even thought about it. A dash to the cradle and he climbed the ladder up the side of the *Duck*. A flick of the switch and he had an Italian Beretta AR 70/90 automatic rifle with silencer in his hands. Yorke recognised the new, highly improved Westland Scout Mk.XXV. It landed on the open space between the mole and the hard standing. Yorke kept low, waiting to see who came out. The door opened and a man in uniform jumped to the ground. Yorke was utterly astonished to see him.

27

HE WAITED WHILE Major Phillip Carstairs stood uncertainly looking around him. Nobody else got out of the helicopter. The rotors slowed to a stop.

'Phil!' Yorke yelled.

Carstairs looked up at the yacht, about 100 metres separated them. He could just see Yorke's head. 'I'm unarmed. There's only me and the pilot,' Carstairs called back.

'Tell him to get out and stand where I can see him.'

Carstairs spoke over his shoulder and moments later a second man joined him. Warily Yorke climbed down, the gun held nonchalantly in his hands. His friend wasn't fooled for a second.

The two men were complete professionals. Carstairs knew he had to establish whose side he was on before there was any joyous reunion. And he had to be quick about it.

'As soon as I got your e-mail I knew what was up. We've been tracking personnel out of Special Services from all across Europe. We knew they were joining private companies some of which we didn't like the look of. We also knew, because of who they were, that they were potential problems. Trained by us, used against us. Not a pretty scenario. As soon as I saw the file I knew. Which was why I had to come personally.' He grinned and held out his hand.

Relief washed through Yorke as he took the proffered hand and shook it warmly. 'Am I glad to see you. We're in deep shit.'

'We?' Carstairs raised a laconic eyebrow. He was 6ft 3ins tall, had black curly hair, blue eyes and a dimple in his chin.

He was film star good looking, single and had a way with women that Yorke had always been envious of. Luckily, the only time they'd been in competition with each other was as teenagers.

'I'll explain. You are?' he turned to the pilot, offering him his hand.

'Lt Brown, sir. Alex Brown. Joined 22 SAS six months ago.'

'Welcome. Does he know any of this?'

'Some. We've been working on it together along with Intel. Your names match ours. Except there were a few surprises in your file.'

The office door opened and William came stalking out, followed by Dom and Catherine.

'My word,' said Carstairs, 'she's a cracker.'

'Don't even think about it, Phil. She's spoken for.'

'You? Why, you crafty old dog. Well done, old man.' He shook Yorke's hand again.

Introductions followed as they went back towards the office. As they reached the door they heard a horn sound and watched as a sleek Porsche drove up to where they were grouped together. Yorke, realising who it was, went into the office and hid the rifle under a pile of papers.

They all trooped in, Catherine and Mary Murray bringing up the rear. Yorke did a double take when he saw her. She was beautiful. About 5ft 5ins tall, nice figure, short blonde hair, wide blue eyes and a merry smile. He learnt later that she had always thought her looks a hindrance to her career; so she tried that much harder.

With introductions finally out of the way, coffees at hand, they sat around the conference table. Catherine explained to Mary why she had wanted to see her so urgently. The ACC's response was totally unexpected.

'I've known about some of this for some time. Corruption in high places across Europe is rife. Court cases fail when the defendant is obviously guilty. Fraud has never been so bad or blatant.' She paused and looked down at her neat, ringless hands. 'We have been unable to find enough evidence to do anything other than watch the guilty walk free. I say walk free. More often than not they don't even get to trial. I know you may not think so but we aren't that stupid in the police. We've also been hamstrung by some of our senior officers and political masters.'

The discussion continued until Mary asked, 'Can you tell me more about *Phoenix*?'

'What's to tell? An intelligence gathering operation that passed what it learnt to Stirling Lines at Hereford, MI5, MI6 and other agencies around the world.'

Mary nodded, tapped her strong fingers on the table and then said, 'The first part is true. The second isn't. *Phoenix* had its own oper-atives. Is that what you did, Mr Yorke?'

'Please, call me Stephen. Or Steve. And no, it's not what I did. I was an analyst. I collected and collated information. That was why I was able to bring the right files with me when I escaped.'

Mary's noncommittal nod was a picture in disbelief.

Catherine used her computer, via a projector, to display the contents of the files and to begin going through what they'd learnt. By 21.00 it was Dom who said plaintively, 'I'm starving.' The adults had been so engrossed with what they were seeing that the thought of food hadn't entered their heads.

'Leave it to me,' said William. 'Believe it or not we've a superb Chinese restaurant in Newlyn. It does take-away and delivery. All right?' He acknowledged the nods and added, 'Any preferences or shall I choose for us all?' They left it to him and he went into another room to place the order to allow the meeting to continue uninterrupted. He was hanging up the phone when he heard a cry of surprise. Rushing back through he said, 'What is it?'

It was Mary who answered, her voice shaking with shock. 'That man on the left, he's a Commander with the Metropolitan Police and the man on his right is the Chief Constable of Essex. My God!' She gasped. 'The Home Secretary!'

Yorke sat in silence. Seeing the effect the information was having on somebody as senior as an ACC was, on one level, shocking, on another, satisfying. He looked closely at the woman and realised she was older that he'd first thought. There were fine wrinkles around her eyes and the corners of her mouth. He reassessed her age as probably nearer forty than thirty which made more sense in view of her position. Too old for Phil? He exchanged glances with his friend and had to contain a smile. In spite of the situation they were in, Phil was definitely smitten. Again.

The food came, was eaten, and the meeting continued until finally Carstairs, Brown and Mary Murray were as cognisant of the facts as Yorke and Catherine. Dom had gone to bed after the meal, escaping to the *Duck*, becoming bored with it all.

'Are you prepared to tell us what you know?' Yorke asked Mary.

'I don't understand. What do you mean?'

'I've been watching you. Some information has been a surprise, even, as we saw, a shock. But some of it, a good deal of it, hasn't been. You've nodded or pursed your lips at some of the crimes we've identified. So are you going to tell us?'

'It comes under the Official Secrets Act,' she began only to stop when Yorke laughed out loud.

'Please, Mary, don't feed me that crap. Speaking for Lt Brown, Phil and myself we've seen more secrets than you ever will.'

'That may be so,' said the ACC with dignity, 'but Catherine hasn't. And she's a journalist.'

Catherine was about to protest when Yorke held up his hand and said, 'Hang on, I'll answer that. First of all, the Act is totally irrelevant. If we work secretly then we'll accomplish nothing. Catherine and I have been over this time and again. We must expose these people to the full glare of publicity. It's our only weapon. Think about it. Stop being a policewoman for a minute and think outside the law.'

'Outside the law? You mean something illegal? I can't do that!'

'No!' Yorke said with more vehemence than he'd intended. 'That's not what I mean at all. What we've shown you is all there is. Some more recordings of the same but this is the best. Could you get prosecutions out of this?'

'Well . . .' Mary drew the word out, paused and with great reluctance shook her head. 'Not with what we've got. No.'

'Exactly. But there's enough for you to work with. Get investigations moving,' Catherine said urgently.

'I never thought I'd live to see the day when I said this, but I'm just a lowly ACC. I need far higher approval to investigate the Chief Constable of Essex and a Commander with the Met.' Mary shook her head. 'I can hear the arguments now. Their barrister will say it was all a joke. A comedy played out for the benefit of a charity. I'll give you a cheque for five million euros, you frame it and hang it on your wall and pay £100. Oh, and we were told not to try cashing it as a stop had been placed on all the cheques. The rest was all part of the fun and games of the evening. And so on and so on. Christ they probably wouldn't even lose their jobs. Instead, I would.'

A gloom settled over the room. Yorke said, 'Uncle, you got any scotch in the house?'

'Aye, Steve. I may not drink it myself but I don't begrudge my guests. It's in the larder in the kitchen.'

'I'll get it. I need to clear my head,' said Yorke. 'Ladies? What will you have?'

'Nothing for me,' said Mary. 'I'm driving.'

'No, you're not,' answered Catherine. 'You said you've a few days leave. You can stay on the yacht.'

'Or in the house,' said William. 'We've plenty of room. More comfortable than the *Duck* and we've got hot and cold running water, showers and a loo. Saves climbing up and down ladders.'

'Okay. Then I'll stay. In that case, any gin?'

'I'll give you a hand,' said Carstairs.

The two men took the orders and went out the door and round the back of the offices. It was a short walk to the large, 5 bedroomed and comfortable house where his uncle and aunt lived. They had brought up three children there, a boy who now lived in America, another in Australia and a girl in

Scotland. In spite of their distance apart they were a close family in regular contact.

They walked in silence as far as the kitchen and then Carstairs said, 'You don't take people like Mack Roberts to court.'

'I know. I was thinking that when Mary was talking about the law. You put a bullet in his head.'

'Not just Roberts. The men we've identified so far will fight like cornered rats, no matter what the cost in peripheral damage or deaths. We know the type of men they are.'

'You can't explain that to somebody like the ACC. It's beyond their comprehension. They live and breath the law. We've both operated well outside it, albeit with official sanction and blessing.'

As they talked the two men loaded bottles and cans into plastic bags. The last item they took was a tray of ice. They started back towards the office.

'Nice looking woman, Mary, don't you think?' Carstairs said nonchalantly.

'I hadn't noticed.'

'Lying swine. She's not married.'

'She doesn't wear any rings, that's different,' said Yorke, smiling in spite of himself.

'No, she's not. I can tell.'

'I know, your expertise in that matter precedes you,' Yorke said straight faced but they both knew what he was referring to.

'How was I to know? She was using me to get at her husband.' Carstairs shuddered. 'Christ, that had been close. I was almost named in the divorce.'

'And that doesn't look good on your record, does it?'

'That, as you well know, is an understatement. Even so, I'm going to ask Mary for her phone number. Faint heart and all that. What's with you and Catherine?'

'Ah, now you have me. Just met. Had a good time together one way and a bloody awful time the other. I like her and fancy her. But what does she feel about me, other than a need to be saved? Big question, no answer.'

Back in the office, drinks were poured. A coke for William, beer for the pilot, G & Ts for the ACC and Catherine, whisky and ice for the other two. However, it wasn't a joyous party. It was sombre, fearful and oppressive as the scale of what they were facing and what they had to do took shape and size.

'Look, one thing I can assure you. You can count on the Regiment. The Colonel knows I'm here and why.' Seeing the look of alarm pass across Catherine's face he added, 'He's the only one. Nobody else. Even the flight plan was fixed. Like Mary, we've been working on the problem for nearly two years. At first it was the rate at which men were quitting the service that was alarming and then where they were turning up. Their connections. A lot of it was hearsay but there's no doubt the majority of them were involved with illegal activities. We had neither the resources nor the training to find out what the hell was going down.' Carstairs shrugged. 'I can tell you, it's a Europe wide problem.'

'I'm in a quandary,' said Mary, with a sigh. 'Normally I'd be looking for all sorts of permission before I said too much, but this seems to be the exception that proves the rule.' She ran a finger along the condensation on the side of her glass, considering her options. All her training told her to keep silent but her instincts said she'd better trust these people if they were to make any progress. She seemed to make up her mind for she suddenly sat up straight. 'This is ludicrous.' She looked at Yorke. 'I agree with you, Steve. The Official Secrets Act is bunkum in this situation. We've been aware of some of what you've shown me but it's been useless. There's never been enough to make arrests and get convictions. And where we've carried out the former we've almost *never* got the latter.' There was vehemence in her voice. 'One thing we learnt about eighteen months ago was that the Crown Prosecution Service wasn't following through on some cases we were absolutely certain about. We made our usual protests until finally we were told only months ago that the Director of Public Prosecutions was being hamstrung by the Home Office. Now that's serious crap.' Mary paused and took a mouthful of gin and tonic.

'I didn't like what I was hearing and so I contacted a colleague of mine in Sunderland. He was an ACC, a few years older than me and would, no doubt, have stepped into the top job once one became vacant.'

'Would? What happened to him?' William asked.

'He died in a car crash.'

'That was unfortunate,' said Brown, a can of beer halfway to his mouth.

'It was. Especially as it was on the notorious mountain road near Monte Carlo. He was alone, his car went off the road, burst into flame, and he died. One of those unfortunate affairs. The trouble is, I never believed it, though I couldn't prove anything.'

'Why didn't you believe it?' Catherine asked.

'Knowing the man. It was during the afternoon on a dry, spring day. He was . . .' she paused, marshalling her thoughts, 'more than merely a careful driver. He was obsessed with road safety. He'd passed his advanced driving test. He'd even taken the French driving exam.'

'Why on earth had he done that?' Carstairs asked.

'He'd bought a villa just outside Nice. Years ago. From money he'd inherited when an old aunt died. He was going to retire there. I guess in about five years, if he'd lived. No, the accident didn't make sense. Except, I got a letter from him two days after his death. He'd been investigating a number of cases on his own patch and didn't like what he was finding.'

'What was that?' Yorke asked.

Mary shook her head. 'There I can't help you. He didn't say. Only that he'd be in touch as soon as he had more proof. Of what, against whom,' she shrugged, 'I've no idea. Knowing what I now know, I'm sure he was killed.'

'It's why the law isn't working,' said Yorke harshly. 'You can't fight these people wearing kid gloves. They have tame lawyers and barristers who twist the law to their perverted ends even when they know the defendant is guilty.'

'And with the Home Secretary covering their backs the power they have is truly terrible,' said William. 'It's enough to drive a man to drink.' Seeing the look of alarm on his nephew's face he quickly added, 'But it won't. One thing I've learnt in my lifetime, there's no point in going off half-cocked. We need a plan of action. A few days lost is irrelevant. I can't help with the planning, that's down to you lot. What I can do is offer the facilities in this place. We've computers, space and privacy.'

'That's very kind of you, Uncle William. We'll see. Mary, any ideas?'

She looked at Yorke and nodded. 'Yes. We need a task force. A team we can trust.'

'How do we do that?' Catherine asked. 'We've all seen some of the faces on the video. One has been niggling at me and I've just placed him. The editor of The Sunday Tribune. He's also on the board of a company that owns radio and TV stations in Europe. I'll bet everything I have if we trace ownership of the companies they'll lead back to John Kennedy.'

'You'll get no argument from me,' said Mary. 'I was thinking in terms of a few people to start putting this information together to go to court with. Digging where we can to build up substantial cases. We then pick these people off, one by one.'

Yorke shook his head wearily. Glancing at the wall clock he was surprised to see it was after 02.00. 'That's no good. It'll take forever. We need direct action as well.'

'I can't sanction anything like that,' said Mary in alarm.

'You can't. The Prime Minister can.'

'The PM? How?' Catherine asked.

'Maybe Mary's the answer to one of our problems. Instead of sending him an e-mail,' Yorke looked at the ACC, 'could you get in to see him?'

'Not a cat's chance in hell. Except,' she paused, leaning forward, a smile breaking out. 'I'm going to a garden party in three days time. He'll be there along with Mrs Beaton.'

'What's the occasion?'

'World-wide famine relief. The usual suspects of the good and the great will be attending.'

'Okay. It's a start if you're going to be at the same place.

Speaking of his wife, there's something you need to know.'
Yorke went on to explain about Mrs Beaton's protection detail.

Mary sat back thoughtfully. 'It makes frightening sense. It also makes you think if other details are also working for the enemy. The odds are, they are. Jesus, what a mess. Does the PM know about this?'

'I'm sure he doesn't. Although, to be honest, what he does and doesn't know I've no idea. He's an intelligent man. What he doesn't know he can surmise. Deduce.'

Catherine yawned which set the rest of them off. They agreed to disperse for the night. The three men would sleep on the yacht. The two women in the house. Breakfast would be at 09.00 in the kitchen.

The day dawned to find Yorke keeping watch sitting in the sail loft, his Beretta AR 70/90 at hand. The three men had drawn lots and he'd lost. He'd had the middle from 05.00 to 07.00. He'd barely got to sleep when Phil had woken him. A cup of tea hadn't helped much and he'd walked about, staying awake. They all agreed they were being over cautious, but they were facing a very powerful and deadly enemy. It wasn't beyond reason that Kennedy's organisation had discovered where the yacht had gone and dispatched men to deal with them. Both Yorke and Carstairs had survived tough situations in the past by not taking *anything* for granted.

The more he thought about it the more convinced he became that the only option was the enlistment of the Prime Minister. Parliament was the place to expose what was going on. Coupled with the media. *And military action.* There was no choice other than to use force. Certain people had to be eliminated. Would the PM agree? Realistically, probably not. It was why *Phoenix* had been a deniable organisation. A thought struck him. If the Home Secretary was in Kennedy's pocket, and he'd known all there was to know about *Phoenix*, what had the PM been black-mailed to do? Or tell? Wearily he shook his head. He was going round and round in circles.

The minute hand crawled slowly to the hour and he went up the ladder to the yacht and woke up Brown. Yorke was asleep as his head hit the pillow and didn't wake up until he was called for breakfast.

In the kitchen Catherine and Mary had prepared a full English breakfast and strong coffee. Dom ate with the enthusiasm of youth, the men with the hunger of having been up half the night on watch.

'I've made a list,' said Mary, placing a rack of toast on the table, 'of people I'm sure I can trust. Unfortunately, it's not very long.'

'How many names?' Yorke asked. 'Delicious scrambled eggs by the way.'

'Thanks,' said Catherine. 'They're another of my specialities.'

'The baked beans are mine,' said Mary with a smile. 'Cooking is not my forte. In answer to your question, I've six names. Four men and two women. Of the men, two are ACCs and two are Chief Superintendents. The women, I'm afraid, are relatively lowly Inspectors.'

'That's a respectable rank in anyone's book,' said Carstairs. 'I made a similar list during my watch.'

'You were on watch?' Mary asked in surprise.

Yorke answered. 'We shared the night. We daren't take anything for granted against this lot. Mary, I urge you, take no chances. If they discover you're working against them they won't be prosecuting you. They'll kill you.'

Mary nodded. 'I suppose. Now in the daylight it all seems so ludicrous. Like something out of a novel.'

'Don't forget your friend in France,' said Carstairs.

Mary nodded. 'You're right. This list of yours?'

'I've ten names. All in the Regiment. All officers or NCOs. Including the CO. I think we can network from there.'

'What about non-military, non-police types,' said William.

'What can they achieve?' asked Brown in surprise.

'One hell of a lot, my lad. Especially amongst the elderly.'

'The elderly?' Yorke was flabbergasted.

'Of course. You don't think that men and women who were born during World War Two, raised families and have grandchildren are going to stand by and watch a bunch of crooks inherit the earth?'

The idea came as a surprise to the remainder of them around the table.

'No, I guess not,' said Yorke. 'But how do we use them?'

William raised his fork in the air and said, 'Call them to arms. Marches, demonstrations, letters to their MPs. Questions at shareholder meetings of companies owned by the cartel. Using the internet I identified twenty shareholder meetings taking place in the next three weeks alone. The shareholders' names are still spewing out of my computer as we speak.'

'What do we do then?' Mary asked.

'That's where you come in. Use the police computer or whatever it is you do to identify some of the names. We work out a profile. Background. Age. Maybe social group, though I'm not certain that's so important. Any criminal record could be important. I'm not sure we want anyone who's been convicted of fraud or theft. Some names will be obvious.'

'Such as?' Catherine asked.

'Actors, retired civil servants and professional people. Retired military, especially if they had a senior rank. How about the Duke of Westminster? He's General Commanding Army Reserves, or some such title. I would have thought him unbribable and incorruptible.'

'Hell, yes,' said Carstairs with enthusiasm. 'I've met him on numerous occasions. He's a damn good chap.'

'I take it,' said Catherine acidly, 'a damn good chap is the highest accolade you can give?'

Carstairs laughed. 'Something like that. We said last night that though the corruption is deep and wide it still really only scratches the surface. We can mobilise a lot of people if we play it right.'

'We also need a military option,' said Yorke.

'I'm not so sure,' said Mary. 'The courts are the place to fight criminals.'

The military men left the statement hanging. There would never be a meeting of minds on the subject.

28

MARY MURRAY MANAGED to get her escort's name added to the invitation – Major Phillip Carstairs. For the next three days their tiny team was busy. Carstairs returned to Hereford and together with Lt Brown had a meeting with Colonel Harry Hughes, the Officer Commanding the SAS. He was a tough Welshman, who'd come out of the coal valleys of Wales and who had come up the hard way, having joined the Welsh Guards as a boy.

The Colonel's reaction had been all that Carstairs could have hoped for, as he told Yorke, using a highly encrypted phone service that was foolproof should anyone try to listen in.

'Good. I've also thought of somebody we can trust – I think. He's with Five. I've worked with him on three occasions. I'll try and get hold of him. Phil, by the way,' Yorke paused.

'It's all right, old boy, you don't have to say anything.'

'Thanks, Phil. It's a bloody marvellous feeling not to be alone.'

'I understand that. Now, that's enough maudlin crap. We've work to do.'

Yorke tracked down his MI5 contact to his home. He was in bed with a bad bout of flu. He sounded dreadful and Yorke merely wished him well and suggested they meet when he was up and about.

William joined him. Yorke explained the position. His uncle clapped him on the shoulder. 'Don't worry about it. We've got enough happening, believe me. The British people are slow to rile but, by god, when they are, then watch out. Mary's contacted the people on her list. She's meeting with them tomorrow. In the meantime, Catherine's refining the information you've gathered to be as succinct and hard hitting as only a journalist can make it. I saw some of the stuff about the meeting. How did *Phoenix* get hold of it?'

Yorke shook his head. 'I've no idea. But Kennedy has a traitor in his camp.'

His uncle smiled. 'Precisely. So it's not all gloom and doom. We've a lot going for us. Mary's also identified dozens of potential names for us to phone. Shareholders of the companies Kennedy has large stakes in. Another refinement in choosing people must be that they have e-mail.'

'How do we find out?'

'We phone and ask. Not exactly difficult. Some people will think it's a hoax, others will accept things at face value, especially if we time it to coincide with our press releases. As was said last night, the whole thing will take timing. This is like planning a large, complex operation. When the witching hour strikes everything must be in place.'

'It has to be unstoppable. To do that we must also cut off the head,' said Yorke. 'Take away the brains if only for a short while, before anyone else can take control.'

'That,' said William, 'is your part of ship. Come on, let's inspect the *Duck*. The second coat is going on and I hope we'll have her back in the water tomorrow.'

With that the two men went outside. It was a glorious day, with a force 3 from the south, bringing warm weather from Africa and Spain. It was the sort of day that pulled at the very being of any sailor. Dom was on the deck, greasing shackles, he looked up and waved to them both.

'He's a nice lad. You've done well by him.'

Yorke nodded. 'Thanks, he is that. But the bonds that tie are loosening as he gets older.'

'That's the way of the world, thank goodness.'

'Sure it is. But it means that next year or the year after he won't want to go sailing with me. He'll want his own chums. Girlfriends as well. Which is fine, but it means it's time I began to look to my future. Assuming,' he added wryly, 'I have one.'

'Plan for the worst, hope for the best. It's a good motto. Does Catherine figure in your plans?'

Yorke shrugged. 'I hardly know her, but, truth to tell, I hope so. We'll have to see what the next few weeks bring. Hell, the next few days. What happens when this is all over? *Phoenix* is gone. I'm unemployed.'

William grinned. 'Good! It's about bloody time you came here and took over.'

'The yard?' Yorke said in surprise.

'Yes. I'll be 61 in September. I've got a 40ft ketch ready to go. Your aunt and I want to head south, cruise the Med and then cross to the Caribbean before we're too old and decrepit. You've a talent for what we do here. It's yours if you want it, lock stock and barrel.'

Yorke looked at his uncle in something close to shock. It was never an option he'd ever considered. 'What about Jamie, Frances and Colin?'

'They're well taken care of. You can buy the place over a period of years, pay me rent or buy it outright. I'll give you a very good price.'

Yorke had no doubt his uncle would. His initial reaction was to refuse outright, but as they strolled about the place and the sights, sounds and smells got to him, he wasn't so sure. 'Can I think about it?'

William chuckled. 'Good lad. When you're ready I'll show you the books.'

Mary Murray and Phillip Carstairs showed their invitation at the gate. That was the start of a long and laborious process to enter the grounds of Buckingham Palace for the garden party. Luckily, the fine weather had held though the forecast was for rain later in the day. They passed through two metal detectors, had their bodies patted down and Mary had her handbag searched. That was in spite of the fact that she was known and greeted by those who were on duty. She accepted it with good grace, as did Carstairs. He could easily have enjoyed himself as Mary was proving to be such good company. Instead, the dire situation they were in left him unable to relax and appreciate his first ever royal garden party.

They'd just passed the last of the security points when Mary said, 'There's Dick Winchester. He's one of the ACCs I phoned. Dick!' Mary waved and smiled gaily.

Introductions were made. 'You made it sound urgent on the phone,' he said, kissing her on both cheeks.

'It is. Remember a few months ago we were talking about corruption and organised crime?'

'Of course. It's getting worse by the day and the blasted government is taking no notice. It's astonishing.'

'Take this.' Mary handed him a memory stick. 'When you've seen that lot you'll understand. It's *vital* you tell nobody what's on there until you've spoken to me.'

'This isn't like you, Mary. All this cloak and dagger stuff.'

'Trust me. There's a lot happening and we need to be at the forefront. There's a meeting in London tomorrow. Can you make it?'

'No. I've a meeting with community leaders about racism and Islamophobia. I can't get out of it.'

Mary shook her had. 'Trust me. When you see what's on the stick you will. Please call me on my mobile as soon as you can. Dick,' she placed her hand in his arm, 'we joined Hendon together. We've known each other more years than I care to remember. I helped you after Sarah died. No strings. I was just there for you.'

'You helped me keep sane. For that I'll be eternally grateful.'

'Then trust me when I say you must be at the London meeting. Call off sick. Anything. Look, we have to go. I must find the Prime Minister.'

'Beaton? He's by the marquee.'

'Thanks, Dick. I'll speak to you later.'

Carstairs exchanged a handshake with Winchester and followed Mary as she crossed the lawn. As was the protocol for such events, people didn't approach royalty or senior politicians without an invitation. Minions controlled access with polite firmness.

Beaton was standing with his wife, a few feet apart. He was talking to a fat man with heavy jowls, that were wobbling in agitation. Mrs Beaton had a glazed look on her face as an equally fat woman talked at her. The PM stroked his cheek with his forefinger and a dapper looking man standing nearby stepped forward.

'Prime Minister, I'm sorry to interrupt, but I have an urgent call. The Cabinet Office. Your PPS. It's America. The President.'

'Thank you. You must excuse me. I must speak to the President of the United States of America.' Two other men approached and efficiently led the man and woman away, the man talking over his shoulder at the Prime Minister while Beaton turned his back. There was no sign of any bodyguards. This being Buckingham Palace, a protection detail was deemed superfluous.

Mary understood what was going on and went straight to Beaton. 'Prime Minister, may I speak to you?'

Beaton turned irritably towards her but seeing such a pretty woman approaching he curbed his reply.

'My name is Mary Murray and I'm the Assistant Chief Constable for Devon.'

Beaton nodded and smiled. 'Yes. I recognise you now.'

'Sir, I need to talk to you as a matter of urgency.'

The PM frowned. His wife stepped closer and looked with interest at Mary and Carstairs. 'Can't you go through the proper channels? This is most irregular.'

'No. Please believe me when I tell you this is of the utmost importance.'

Beaton was becoming irritated. 'This is a social event. To raise awareness for world-wide famine relief. We have important announcements to make after the event. Make an appointment and come and see me at No 10.'

'Sir, please just listen to me for a minute.'

'Oh, very well,' he said with bad grace. 'But make it quick.'

'We have proof of corruption at the heart of your government. We know . . .'

She got no further.

'That's enough! I won't have my administration maligned by you or anyone else. This interview is terminated.'

Carstairs interrupted. 'Sir, I'm Major Phillip Carstairs and I'm the Regimental Adjutant at Stirling Lines. Please listen to Mary.'

'The SAS? Go through your chain of command.'

'Sir,' there was desperation in Carstairs' voice, 'we know what happened with your daughter. When she went missing. We know who did it and why. You must listen to Mary.'

Mrs Beaton had gone pale and placed her hand on Mary's arm as though for support. 'How do you know?' she asked.

'Mrs Beaton, Prime Minister, I have a memory stick to give you. It contains a good deal of information. Do not, I beg you, show it to anyone else. Will you look at it as soon as possible and contact me?'

'This is highly irregular.' Beaton frowned, indecision in his stance.

'This was the only way I could get to speak to you privately. Or as private as possible. But I'll not hand over the stick as I will undoubtedly be seen and awkward questions will be asked.' Mary looked at the PM's wife. 'Will you accompany me to the loo, Mrs Beaton? I can give it to you in private. I know this is all melodramatic but when you see the files you'll understand.'

'Sir,' said Carstairs urgently as he noticed the aid approaching, 'it also concerns *Phoenix*.'

Beaton would have made a lousy poker player as he couldn't keep the surprise off his face. However, he recovered quickly and said, 'My dear, you go with Mary, while I go in the tea tent.'

The two women walked away, side by side, towards the tent clearly marked Ladies. Carstairs stood uncertainly and then walked towards a group of strangers. Small talk was the last thing he wanted to indulge in but felt it his duty.

Inside the tent Mary quickly established that there was

nobody else there. 'Please take this. Mrs Beaton, tell nobody about our conversation. Especially your protection detail.'

The older woman looked at Mary in some bewilderment. 'Why especially them?'

Mary hesitated and then said, 'They can't be trusted.'

'What! I don't believe you! It's not possible . . .'

'Mrs Beaton, please! Wait until you've seen the files. But I urge you, I beg you, don't let either of your detail know something is wrong. If you value your life and that of your children . . .'

'Don't threaten my children.' Susan Beaton's voice was becoming shrill.

'I'm not! For Christ's sake get a grip. I didn't come here to frighten you or threaten you.'

'You're doing a damned good job, that's all I can say,' Mrs Beaton spoke bitterly.

Look,' Mary ran her hand through her hair, realised what she had done and opened her bag to take out a small brush. As she repaired the damage she said, 'I know this seems ludicrous but believe me, it isn't. You must get your husband to look at that info tonight. Here's my card. Please get him to phone me. It doesn't matter how late.'

Susan Beaton stood there uncertainly. 'Why did you say that about my protection detail?'

Mary hesitated. How reliable was the woman? Would she fall apart and blow it before they were ready? 'One of them can't be trusted. We're checking the other one now.'

'Which one don't you trust?'

About to tell her, Mary changed her mind and shook her head. 'Just treat them as you always do. Equally. That way you won't arouse any suspicions. Can you do that?'

Susan Beaton squared her shoulders and looked coldly at Mary. 'I have spent my life in politics. Supporting Alex. Smiling at enemies, shaking their hands. Politics is a very dirty game and to become Prime Minister you have to know how to play it. And play it well. I'll do my part.'

'Thank you. You'll understand the need for all the secrecy

when you see the files held on that stick. Tomorrow, the information this contains will be released to practically every news agency in the world. We will do so in a co-ordinated manner if we get Mr Beaton's co-operation.'

'If? And if not? Are you threatening my husband? If you are . . .' there was steel in her voice.

Mary quickly interrupted. 'Of course not. Please believe me. This is of vital importance to the country. To our very democracy.'

'That sounds melodramatic in the extreme.'

'I know it does.' Mary shook her head wearily. 'Just trust me. You will, I assure you, understand later. Incidentally, watch the stick in the residence. Privately. Have no one else with you. Is that possible?'

Susan Beaton nodded. 'Tonight it is. We're having a family dinner and an early night. At least that's what we'd planned.'

Mary nodded. 'Good.' She didn't add that she doubted the early night. 'Come on, I'll walk with you back to the tea tent.'

After she'd done so, Mary found Carstairs and, taking his arm, pulled him away from the group he was with.

'We can't do any more. It's up to the PM now.'

Carstairs smiled down at her. 'How did you get on?'

Her shrewd eyes darkened for a moment. 'I thought I'd blown it at first. But she seems to have grasped the seriousness of the situation. I just hope I've convinced her to get her husband to look at the blasted thing. If not, it's all been for nothing.'

'There's no going back now. We move with or without the Prime Minister. I agree with Stephen on that point. Time will tell.' He suddenly changed the subject. 'This is my first time at a royal garden party. Are they always so boring? What's the protocol?'

'What do you mean?'

'Can we leave? Before the Queen?'

Mary shrugged and then smiled. 'No. That's strictly taboo. On the other hand, as an ACC a crisis has arisen that calls for my immediate attention.'

So it proved. A smile, an apology and a flash of her ID card got them past scowling officials and out of the grounds. It was just before 17.00.

'What are we going to do?' Mary asked, naturally tucking her hand under Carstairs' arm.

'I've no idea. I'm from the sticks. I know London not at all.'

'Me neither. When you suggested we leave I thought you had some master plan.'

'Apart from wishing to get you alone, then I hate to disappoint you.'

Mary looked at him thoughtfully. She liked what she saw. But she was aware that she was a few years older – maybe five or six years. Did that matter, she wondered? There was only one way to find out.

'I'm a lot older than you.'

'And you out rank me,' said Carstairs, 'albeit we're in different services.' He patted her hand. 'I wanted you from the moment I clapped eyes on you. I'm not going to rush you into bed. Even if I could,' he added hastily. 'But I will wine and dine you and get to know you while you get to know me. Fair enough?'

'Fair enough. I think I like you already. A lot. And I don't say that very often. The problem is, when men find out I'm an Assistant Chief Constable they run a mile. And believe me it's worse now than when I was a Chief Superintendent and that was bad enough. It was like being a nun.'

On that note they found a small restaurant and spent the remainder of the evening talking about themselves and their experiences. For a while they even managed to forget the horrors that had brought them together. It was barely 21.00 when Carstairs saw Mary into a taxi to take her to the hotel she was staying in while he walked to the underground to go to Paddington Station. He had to get back to Hereford. They had an operation to plan. He was just settled in his compartment when his mobile rang.

'Phillip? It's Mary. I've just had the Prime Minister on the phone. I think he's in shock. But he's also angry like no man I've ever heard. He wants to see us at No 10. Where are you?'

'Getting off the train, as it's about to depart.'

29

THE *LUCKY DUCK* had been re-named *The Walrus*. This had been the name of an old yacht that William had recently scrapped. He still had the paperwork for the *Walrus* and with a few simple adjustments to its contents the *Lucky Duck* was reborn. Her gleaming blue hull, red stripe 10cms beneath the deck line and freshly painted superstructure left her looking like a new vessel. Once again she was bobbing on the water, sleek and elegant, raring to shed her shackles and race into her natural element. Dom was itching to cast off and hoist her sails. But that day all hell was breaking loose and the yacht would be going nowhere.

Catherine timed her e-mail transmissions with precision. They were sent east first, then to Europe and Africa and finally to the Americas. They went to news agencies, TV and radio stations, newspapers and magazines. Over the years she had amassed a formidable and comprehensive list of names and addresses and with her name as the sender it was guaranteed to reach the addressee. It wasn't long before those who knew her mobile phone number were calling and her e-mail was jammed solid. Though that only lasted for a short while. Suddenly her web-server was no longer working. Precisely as they'd been expecting.

She didn't answer her mobile until she and Yorke had hired a plane from Land's End airport and were half-way across the Bristol Channel. It was far too easy to track the whereabouts of a mobile telephone and the last thing they wanted was Kennedy's men turning up at the boatyard.

She made and answered call after call. Many of it was similar in nature. Was it attributable? Could they name her as the "special correspondent" who'd got the information? Were the film and voice recordings at the meeting real? Five million euros? Was that true? Was it a hoax? Was it a scam? Was it something to do with charity? She fielded them all as best as she could.

Finally, 'Catherine Colbert.'

'Miss Colbert, I have Mr Kennedy for you.'

Suddenly her mouth was dry and her palms moist. She put her finger over the mouthpiece and said to Yorke, 'It's him. Kennedy.'

'What an unpleasant surprise,' said Yorke. 'Don't let him get to you.'

She nodded but before she could say anything he was on the phone. There was no greeting. 'If you do not rescind these lies with immediate effect and apologise in writing you will regret it.'

'I can't do that. As it's all true.'

'You have no idea what you have started.'

'I started nothing, Mr Kennedy. I merely reported it. Are you denying it? I have proof. I've shown the connections that exist between crime cartels across Europe and yourself. I have shown how your criminal activities are intertwined with your legitimate businesses. I can prove your connections with politicians, business people and crooks. It's all there and I mean to expose you.'

'You won't live long enough.'

'I take it that's a threat. Thank you. I've recorded it and will send it to the police and my media contacts. Goodbye, Mr Kennedy.' Catherine broke the connection and sat back with a sigh. She was totally drained. 'He's threatened to kill me.'

Yorke nodded. 'He was going to do that anyway. So nothing's changed.'

'Except being told it makes it all the more real somehow. Oh god, I'm scared.'

Yorke placed his hand on her knee and Catherine placed

her hand on top of his. After speaking to Air Traffic Control he turned the plane eastwards somewhere north of Swansea. 'Nothing's changed. Except Kennedy hasn't time to come after us, he needs to protect himself. This is only the start. All hell is going to break loose around him. The political fallout will begin at lunchtime with the exposure of the Home Secretary in the House of Commons. According to Mary the EU Commissioner, Cordelia Hewitt, will also be arrested. William has pledges from over thirty people already about asking questions at shareholder meetings. Things are going to escalate beyond all reasonable control. The genie is well and truly out of the bottle and there's no putting it back.'

'Is it,' asked Catherine, looking steadily at him, 'a genie for good or evil?'

Yorke looked at her pensively. 'Only time will tell.'

The Prime Minister stood at the despatch box. His demeanour was thoughtful and serious, reflected in the face of the opposition leader sitting across from him. As was the convention, when something of national importance was to be announced the leaders of the main political parties had already been briefed.

'Today,' the PM began, looking around the chamber, 'begins the fight back against organised crime and corruption in this country and Europe. It is in fact a war, which we are determined to win. Evidence has come to light which shows the unimaginable depths to which some people in this country have sunk, into a morass of greed and personal desire the likes of which I would have never thought possible. The cancer has spread its tentacles across Europe's political parties and reached the highest offices. It is with shame and regret that I have to announce, in view of the evidence, the resignation of Gordon Whitley, the Home Secretary. Already the Crown Prosecution Service is looking into the case and I will be meeting with the Director of Public Prosecutions as well as the Attorney General to discuss what action we'll be taking against Whitley.' No "Right Honourable", not even "Honourable", as when referring to members of opposition parties. 'His local labour party committee has also been informed and are meeting shortly to discuss deselecting him with immediate effect.'

The House was in uproar, with the Speaker calling for order and threatening to name members. If he did, the next step would be to have the recalcitrant MP removed from the chamber.

The speech was a long one. It touched on all the issues that were so vital if the war on crime was to be won. His language was flowery, hyperbolic and hard-hitting. He was a master at grand-standing.

'I wish, before giving way to the honourable member opposite,' he nodded at the Conservative Leader, 'to share with you my personal experience.' The House was suddenly silent, not even order papers rustling. 'I was threatened with blackmail when my youngest daughter went missing recently for a heart-stopping half an hour.' The other MPs were electrified. Nothing like this had ever been said by a British Prime Minister in the House of Commons before. 'Thanks to the work of one man I have learnt that the person responsible for kidnapping my daughter was a member of my wife's protection detail. That person was arrested early this morning and is currently at Paddington Green Police Station being questioned. I have a special thanks to make, here in the House, to Assistant Chief Constable Mary Murray who has done so much in the past few days to bring this and other actions to bear on the evil criminals that reside in our midst.' Lifting his notes, to which he hadn't referred once, he sat down.

The Speaker intoned. 'Mr Michael . . .' the leader of the opposition's name was drowned out in the calls and jeers typical of the Palace of Westminster.

Prime Minister's question time was extended. Instead of the usual cut and thrust of political debate, innuendo and outright lies made in the guise of questions, the House sang, as the Liberal Democratic Leader said later, from the same hymn sheet. The importance of what they faced was brought home to every member that day. Exercising parliamentary privilege, when asked to name names the Prime Minister did so, clearly pointing his finger at John Kennedy, born János Kadras in Budapest. He added that a full investigation into the man's background was already underway by Europe's intelligence services.

Yorke landed the plane back at Land's End. Catherine's mobile was now switched off and he'd emphasised to her not to use it again.

'What about my e-mail? Can I use that?'

'Yes, if your server has re-connected you. Mary's already working on the problem. We'll find out when we get back to the boatyard. Listen.' He held up an admonishing finger. The car radio was broadcasting live from the House of Commons. It was electrifying stuff and they sat enthralled as Yorke drove his uncle's Ford along the A30.

The Leader of the Opposition asked a question and the Prime Minister rose to answer it. 'I can confirm that arrest warrants have been issued for some 150 people and are being served even as we speak. Co-ordinated raids took place across the country, indeed, across Europe, at 11.00 BST, as other police forces acted on the information we have been able to supply them with. The operation against organised crime has been going on for some time and this is the culmination of months of effort.'

Catherine and Yorke exchanged surprise looks. 'No doubt,' she said, 'political spin is already at work. Inevitable, I suppose.' She sighed. 'Why can't our politicians just do what's right? Why can't they . . .' she caught Yorke's smile and was forced to chuckle herself. 'They wouldn't be politicians other-wise, right?'

'Right.' He indicated to the right and turned off the main road and headed towards the coast, Mount's Bay in the distance. 'It's time to lay low. Until most of the flak has gone. There's little we can do now apart from let the authorities deal with matters. Do you fancy a cruise? We can take the *Duck*, or should I say the *Walrus*, south to warmer climes, or north to the Scottish lochs.'

'Brrr,' Catherine shivered theatrically, 'I like the sun.' There was a moment's silence and then she asked, 'What about Dom? Will he be coming too?'

Yorke sighed. 'I don't know. I'm loathe to leave him. He's in danger. Kennedy will be wanting his revenge and he still has the power and influence to do it.'

Yorke's mobile phone rang. It had been given to him by Carstairs before he'd left for Hereford and only he and William had the number.

'Yorke.'

'Stephen, it's me, Phil. I've good news and bad. The good news is Mary called to say that some of the men they've arrested are singing like canaries. The Home Secretary, the man who wanted to be tough on crime and the causes of crime, cracked like an egg shell. He's given her invaluable information. The Chief Constable of Essex, by the way, was found in his garage with a hosepipe from his exhaust into his car. No note; no nothing. Dead as a dodo. So far Mary's been able to identify many of the people who were at the meeting in Mevagissey and is working on the rest. Those who are foreign nationals have been reported to the authorities in their own countries. All points bulletins have gone out across Europe and arrests are being made.'

'What's the bad news?'

'The Met went to Kennedy's offices to pick him up but they were too late. A helicopter landed on the roof and took him away, literally from under our lads' noses.'

'Where did he go? He must have had a flight plan.'

'It was false. They were under positive control until Chatham. There they were routed towards Sheerness but they dropped off the radar. Our best guess is they landed on the Isle of Sheppey or they went down in the Swale.'

'Do we know what sort of helo?'

'Luckily we do. One of the cops is ex-RAF. He says it was Soviet, probably a Kamov Helix-C.'

'They didn't land on Sheppey or go down in the Swale,' said Yorke. 'They landed on a ship. Find out if the SS Invergowrie is anywhere in the area.'

'Why that particular ship?'

Yorke explained about following the helicopter from Gibraltar Point out to the ship. 'It's the logical destination. If he's running then a plane or helicopter are no use. He needs a ship with a long range. With the way things are going I suspect Europe will be too hot for him.'

'What about Croatia? It was just about in his pocket.'

'Just about, but not quite. Neither Croatia or Georgia will be of any use as we moved too soon for Kennedy. Thank God.'

'While we've been talking I've had somebody try and find out about the ship. Nothing of that name has asked to pass through the Straits of Dover in the last twenty-four hours.'

'The ship could have gone north about. No! This is all rubbish! Kennedy didn't know about his arrest. He got away by the skin of his teeth.'

'Is it likely that he had an escape route planned? Just in case?'

'Phil, we're fishing, but I doubt it. He was absolutely sure of himself. He wasn't looking to run.'

'Suppose he had some warning?'

'That makes sense. Of course he had a warning. Probably from the time of Catherine's first e-mail. That's when he'd have made plans. So he had what? Twelve hours notice?'

'Something like that. Enough anyway for a man with his resources.'

'The Invergowrie is 20,000 tonnes. A dry cargo carrier. See if anything else is moving through the Channel. A ship that size will have to keep to the separation lanes and report her movements to the coastguard as well as be tracked. No, this is crap. The ship will have gone north. No lanes, no radar control. Much more sea room. The Channel would be a trap and Kennedy would know it.'

'How are we to find the ship?'

'Get a picture from Lloyds. If they don't have one get a description of shape and size. Build it into a computer and use the satellites. Get an identi-fit. It shouldn't be difficult. GCHQ ought to be able to help.'

'Good idea. I'll get on to it right away. If I get anything I'll phone you.'

Catherine and Yorke arrived back at the yard. William was having a great deal of success in contacting shareholders because of the publicity and what had happened in Parliament.

'Middle England's anger is well and truly up,' said William, making fresh coffee. 'The shareholders are going to ask awkward questions of the boards of directors of the companies involved. One will be, how was it possible for a crime cartel to buy shares? It's rhetorical but it will bring home the point. And a lot of questions about blind trusts and off-shore companies holding large chunks of British businesses. They are also lobbying parliament to demand a change in the law to stop this sort of thing ever happening again.'

Catherine accepted a mug of Kenyan high roast and said, 'Did you hear the Labour MP demanding that shares held by a criminal organisation be cancelled? The Conservatives have jumped on that bandwagon along with the Lib Dems. Various government departments have agreed to look at the prospect of introducing a law to achieve that. Along the same idea of stopping criminals from profiteering from their crimes. This is all working out better than I expected.'

Yorke hated the idea of pouring cold water on her enthusiasm but he knew that as long as Kennedy was at large they wouldn't be safe. Even if Kennedy ended up in prison he'd do his damnedest to get revenge and the obvious targets were Catherine, Dom and him. Any collateral deaths like William and Mary Murray would be a bonus as far as Kennedy was concerned. No, there was only one solution and it needed doing sooner rather than later.

His mobile rang and he answered. 'Yes, Phil?'

'There are eight ships of roughly the right size and shape. We're checking each one using long range Nimrods. We should have an answer within the hour.'

'Good.' Yorke stood up and wandered away from the other two. Outside he said, 'Phil, if you find him I want in.'

'I figured you might. I'll have to ask the OC.'

'Remind him he owes me a few favours.'

'To be honest, I'd like you there, so count on me.'

Yorke wandered down to the *Walrus* and joined Dom who'd been pottering around the yacht, carrying out regular maintenance on the running and standing rigging. A smudge of wood stain streaked his forehead.

'Hi, dad. I saw you arrive but I was busy. What about me returning to school?'

'Not yet. There are one or two things we still need to sort out. Maybe in a few days time.'

Glumly the boy nodded. 'Okay. I can't wait to get back and tell them what's been happening. But it'll be so *boring* after all this.' His emphasis on the word made Yorke smile. 'Then again,' Dom added as an afterthought and shook his head, 'it won't do any good. Nobody will believe me. They'll think I'm bragging after reading stuff in the papers or seeing the telly.'

'I suppose that's true. To be honest, this sort of stuff is best kept quiet. You'll see after you get into the marines. You'll go on an op and come back and when I ask you about it you'll quote the Official Secrets Act at me or some such nonsense.'

'I wouldn't do that, dad!' Dom was affronted. 'I'd tell you. Of course I would.'

'We'll see. Look, I wanted to ask you something. What do you think of Catherine?'

'She's cool. I like her.'

'So it's all right if we go away for a cruise while you're at school?'

'I guess,' he spoke hesitatingly. Then his voice hardened, 'Of course it'll be okay. Only, can I borrow the *Duck*, I mean the *Walrus*, in the summer hols and take a few of the guys away for a week?'

Yorke laughed at Dom's manoeuvring and said, 'Sure. We'll work to some sort of plan.'

'I can't get used to the name change. Do we really need to change it?'

'Yes, son. Just in case. It's not over yet. You never know we might need her with the new name.'

Yorke didn't need to explain further. Dom understood. His phone rang. 'Yes, Phil.'

'Nothing. An absolute bust. Each ship is accounted for.'

'Are you sure?'

'We've done just that. Armed teams have been put on each ship, just to double check.'

'Damn and blast. Where the hell could he have run to?'

'We've computed in the Helix's range and speed. Suppose he flew out into the North Sea and went like a bat out of hell northwards? Supposing the Invergowrie was at sea, heading towards him, operating at maximum distances and speeds? She picks up the helo and heads north again. It would take Kennedy well past the Scottish border. I'm talking north of Aberdeen by now. Like the Cromarty Firth or Dornoch Firth.'

Yorke interrupted him. 'Jesus H. Christ. You've got it! I know where he is!'

30

KENNEDY'S ANGER KNEW no bounds. The helicopter had
landed on the deck of the Invergowrie and the ship had turned
north again, ploughing a deep furrow towards the Cromarty
Firth. He was in the captain's cabin, pacing the width of the
ship, the deep pile carpet masking the heaviness of his tread.

'How did this happen? How did a bunch of shits manage
to do this to me? Tell me that!' He screamed at Leo Agnew.

His assistant of 20 years could only shrug his shoulders.
'John, take it easy. We can fight this. We've friends in high
places. The highest. This is a set back, nothing more. We come
out fighting. Already our lawyers are preparing legal, not
defence, but offence. We'll go on the attack like we always do
when faced with a problem.'

'That bastard Beaton. Did you hear him in the Houses of
Parliament?'

Agnew didn't say that as they'd listened to the broadcast
together then of course he'd heard it. Instead he nodded.

'I want Beaton's bastard children taken. I'll teach him!
Nobody thwarts me. Nobody!'

'I'll see what can be done,' said Agnew soothingly knowing
full well there was nothing he *could* do right then. If ever.
Beaton's family were being protected in the safest place in
Britain. They'd been flown to 22 SAS at Hereford. Agnew had
learnt they wouldn't be staying there but that a SAS team plus
members of the Met Protection Squad would be escorting the
family to the Prime Minister's country retreat of Chequers.
Already the men and women who had been on Kennedy's
payroll were being rounded up. What neither man could

possibly know was that Joyce Summers, of Mrs Beaton's detail, was telling everything she knew in the hope that she would get her sentence reduced. Kidnapping a child, even for a short period, carried serious penalties. What Summers did know were the names of many of the others involved. As always in these cases, names led to more names as the dominos fell.

Mr Frobisher entered the room. From the look on his face it was obvious that he didn't have any good news. In fact, quite the reverse.

'Well what is it?'

'I'm sorry, Mr Kennedy, but the assets of the Moscombank have been frozen. The Russian government are talking of sequestrating all the bank's assets. Certainly we cannot access any of the accounts we hold there.'

Kennedy picked up a ship's decanter full of malt whisky and smashed it against the nearest bulkhead. It shattered into tiny pieces, the pungent smell of whisky permeating the cabin. It took a number of minutes before Kennedy was able to get himself under sufficient control to speak coherently. Like many geniuses, and there was little doubt that Kennedy could be so described, he was borderline psychotic. Losing his temper uncontrollably was a manifestation of that psychosis.

Breathing heavily he finally asked, 'Any more bad news?'

'Not yet. But I'm expecting some,' said Mr Frobisher softly.

'What do you mean?' Agnew sat down at the huge desk that dominated the cabin and fiddled with a letter opener.

'We have to be realistic. Our people are being rounded up across Europe. Colonel Roberts and many of his men only just got away before the police started knocking on their doors. He's flying north right now with a contingent to meet us at the castle. Luckily, they all have false ID so its not a problem. For now. But I don't think we can linger in Scotland. Just in case the authorities know about this ship we'll fly ashore. The ship can refuel at Thurso. Let her get customs clearance and depart. We'll follow in the Helix once the Invergowrie's at maximum range. That way, we can move fast.'

'Whose idea is this?' Kennedy asked, then added before he

received an answer. 'Get a steward to clean up this mess and get me a cup of tea.'

Agnew picked up the phone to pass the order while Mr Frobisher replied.

'It was Colonel Roberts, sir, who suggested it. If we stay onboard we could be trapped. At least at the castle there are options if we have to make a run for it.'

Kennedy nodded. 'Make it so. Good. One thing. An absolute priority. I want the man Yorke, the woman Colbert and Yorke's bastard dead. Send Ingrid to deal with them after we get ashore.'

A helicopter picked Yorke up and took him to Hereford. When he arrived at the briefing room large scale Ordnance Survey maps were being projected onto one wall.

'You were right, Steve,' Carstairs greeted him. 'We put out an all-points bulletin in the Highlands and a plod at a small village called Kildonan reported seeing a low flying helo, just here.' He used a laser pointer and illuminated the place. 'The castle is here, fifteen miles north-west. It's in the middle of nowhere. One road access and surrounded by hills, burns, heather and seriously inhospitable country.'

'I had Catherine do some more digging and she found that the whole of the area, some 250,000 acres, is owned by Kennedy via off-shore trusts and cut-off companies,' Yorke said.

'We'd never have found him if you hadn't done your homework,' said a man entering the room. The red tabs on his lapels indicated he was a colonel.

'Sir, let me introduce Stephen Yorke.'

As they shook hands the Colonel said, 'We met nine years ago. A little op into Bosnia to pick up Sakavitch.'

Yorke smiled broadly. 'Yes, I remember. In and out was a piece of cake. Pity the bastard had already flown the coop.'

'It was ever thus in the Balkans. Let's hope it won't be the case here. Are we sure Kennedy's there?'

'As sure as we can be. All indications are that's where he'll be. We also received an anonymous text message a short while ago saying that he would be arriving shortly.'

'No confirmation that he's actually there yet?'

'Not yet, sir.

'Still no idea who the informant is?'

'No, sir,' replied Carstairs. 'Not even a hint.'

'Is this an arrest or a take out?' Yorke asked. 'Because I don't think knocking on the door and asking Kennedy to come quietly will work. And even if it did the fallout will be disastrous. He'll be out on bail within minutes and away before we can blink.'

'The Prime Minister has already given the executive order. He also added and I quote, "I don't want Kennedy to stand trial".'

'Good. We aren't much use at arresting people,' said Carstairs.

'That's what I told the PM,' said the colonel.

'What about secrecy?' Yorke asked, frowning.

'As tight as a duck's proverbial,' replied Carstairs. 'Nobody has yet been told that we know where Kennedy is. Not even the Prime Minister. As far as he's concerned we've blanket authority to take action wherever and whenever we find Kennedy. Even the helicopter sighting we put down to a UFO investigation. As though it was all nonsense and we didn't care that a helo was flying across the Knockfin Heights. However, it won't hold for long. Security at times like this never does. So we need to move fast.'

The phone rang and Carstairs answered. 'Hullo, Sergeant.' He listened for a few minutes. 'All right. Very good. Thank you.' Hanging up the receiver he turned to the other two men. 'We've just received a text message telling us that Kennedy has arrived at Castle Drumbeg.'

'Anything else?' Yorke asked.

'Yes. A number of things. Bring laughing gas.'

The three men exchanged surprised looks. Known as Laughing Gas by special services, the nitrous oxide based gas was a powerful knock-out gas that had been developed in recent years for use in hostage circumstances.

'Still no clue as to who's sending us these messages?' Yorke asked.

'Comms put out a trace. It definitely came from somewhere in northern Scotland. Presumably from the castle itself. It means that whoever the mole is, he has specialist knowledge. Not everyone knows about laughing gas. The message also says there are thirty heavily armed men plus fifteen staff. The staff are Eastern European and loyal to Kennedy and will fight.'

'The odds are more or less what we expected,' said the OC of 22 SAS Regiment. There was a knock on the door. 'Enter.' The door opened. 'Ah, Sergeant Miller. Is everything ready?'

'Yes, sir,' replied Miller. 'Equipment has been issued. The C130 is ready.' He cast a quizzical eye at Yorke in civilian clothes.

To ease matters, Carstairs said, 'Major Yorke is coming with us. Get him kitted out please. Weapon?' He turned to Yorke.

Yorke smiled. 'Do you happen to have a Russian VAL?'

The sergeant's scowl at having a non-SAS man dumped on him turned to a grin – albeit a nasty one. 'You know the VAL?'

Yorke nodded. 'My favourite.'

'Mine too. Come along, sir, we've one left in the armoury.'

When Yorke returned he was wearing full battle fatigues – a grey mottled can't-see-me-suit – and had a VAL Silent Sniper over his shoulder.

'Everything okay?' Carstairs greeted him.

Yorke grinned. 'It is now. Miller asked a few adroit questions which I appeared to have answered to his satisfaction. I don't think he sees me as such a liability any longer.'

'Good. After we drop we have a five mile yomp,' said Carstairs. 'These plans just arrived. We got them from the local planning authority but as you can see they're fifty years old. God alone knows what, if anything, has been changed inside. We found estate agents' particulars that are five years old which was when Kennedy bought the place. We've had our Intel lot make enlarged copies of the photographs. You can see the library, dining room and one of four lounges. This is the master bedroom.' The glossies were 12ins by 12ins and showed large rooms needing a great deal of work done to them.

'It looks a decrepit hole,' Yorke said.

'We understand that a vast sum of money has been spent doing up the inside of the building but how it's changed, if at all, we've no way of knowing.'

'I don't suppose there's been any structural alterations,' said Yorke.

'That's our feeling too,' said the Colonel. 'Right. A full brief in ten. Off on schedule?'

'Yes, sir,' said Carstairs.

Roberts knew they were coming. It wasn't even a question of when; it would be that night. This was the one window of opportunity the British had to get Kennedy. After years in the military and special operations he knew only too well how the establishment thought and acted. Beneath the veneer of civilisation, political correctness and demand for human rights beat a heart as tough as steel and as ruthless as the devil. The world always had, and still did, underestimated the determination of the British to look after the interests of the UK. Roberts grinned wryly. Their mixture of caring for the underdog, generous spirit, courage and, that word again, utter ruthlessness, had made them the proud bringers of civilisation across the world. But it had always been on their terms. Which was why . . . His thoughts were interrupted.

'I've deployed the guards, sir.'

'Good. It should be a quiet night so let the men catch up on their sleep. Nobody knows we're here and I'd like to keep it that way.'

The other man shivered. 'This is a bloody bleak place.'

They were standing on the castellated south facing wall. The house wasn't a castle in the English sense of battlements and moat. It was a large house with thick, fortified walls and roof space from where fighting men could defend the place. There was no moat and no inner or outer courtyards. The main door faced west. A drive meandered to the main road nearly five miles away. The nearest village was Kinbrace, nearly 8 miles as the crow flies. The nearest inhabited house belonged to the gillie who looked after the estate's wild life, and that was two miles distant.

The wind was cold and damp, from the west, and was bringing the threat of rain. Moonrise was still four hours away, in the early hours. An owl hooted close by and was answered by a nerve-jangling screech.

'What the bloody hell was that?'

'Relax,' said Roberts. 'That was the attack call of a bird of prey, though don't ask me which one.'

'It frightened the life out of me.'

'It will have done worse to the poor stoat or whatever it was it had spotted. The animal freezes, the bird swoops and,' he snapped his fingers. 'It's a vicious and nasty world out there, even amongst the heather and hills of Scotland.'

The man left Roberts to his thoughts. Which way would they come? Parachute in using the new helium wings? No. Helos hard and fast? They couldn't be certain of the defences he had to muster. No, there was only one way. A route march. A yomp. From where? The east. Distance? Five to Eight miles. That's what he'd do. Well, he'd better get ready.

'Ten minutes,' the pilot announced.

His charges began a final check, preparing to shuffle aft when the drop doors opened. The pilot ordered them to stand-by and they got into line. Carstairs was leading. The Colonel would be staying onboard the plane to monitor progress and to take overall control.

'Green. Go, go, go.'

The men jumped left and right, their parachutes opening automatically. It was a lo-lo drop – low level jump, low level parachute open. As soon as he left the plane York felt his shoulders jerk up and his feet drop. He had the jumpers surge of relief that the damn thing had worked and then concentrated on his movements. The panel in front of him showed him his heading, rate of descent and his height above ground on a Doppler display. A quick glance around and he could see the others, dark shadows against the starlit night. Less than a minute after leaving the plane a warning buzz told him to prepare for landing. He looked down, saw nothing but darkness and looked back at his display unit. The parachute was really a wing, controlled by inflating its leading edge using helium which gave it extra lift. He pressed the inject button at 1 metre above the ground, felt his shoulders being raised and touched down as gently as gossamer landing on a feather quilt. The wing enabled troops to land in rough terrain with a vastly reduced chance of a twisted ankle or worse.

Using their portable radios all thirty men reported a safe landing. They split into four teams and moved out at two minute intervals. Yorke tagged on to the last team, led by Carstairs.

31

EX-COLONEL "MACK" Roberts put the high-powered night vision goggles to his eyes and swept the countryside yet again. Nothing. He looked at his watch. 02.00. A text-book attack meant *now, damnit*.

Wearily he started the process again. Left, in close, work out. Back in, move right. Back out . . . Yes! Movement. A red deer? There were enough of them, even though many were starving, as over-population eroded their habitat. He focused closely and smiled in satisfaction. Here they came. Right on schedule and as predictable as the tide, provided you knew how to read the tide tables. *Time to save lives*.

He was on the south facing part of the roof. A guard loitered nearby though he didn't have Roberts' type of binoculars. Instead he was counting on his natural vision and hearing skills to warn of impending trouble. However, 22 SAS were moving like ghosts, in spite of the gear they carried.

A physical attack was always a hit or miss affair. You didn't hit a man over the head just hard enough to knock him out and leave no long term or serious damage. If the man fell unconscious then the likelihood was his skull had been cracked or other brain damage sustained. And killing him wasn't an option as far as Roberts was concerned. Instead, he took a syringe out of his breast pocket and held it in his left hand.

'Take a look at red three zero through these.' He handed over the binoculars.

The guard raised them and looked for a few seconds. The oath that sprung to his lips died there as the hypodermic was thrust into his right biceps and its contents injected into his body. He would have collapsed in a heap if Roberts hadn't caught him and lowered him to the stone battlement. Quickly he walked towards the west wing. One down, three to go.

The same tactic worked on the second guard and Roberts nodded in satisfaction. He was approaching the third man, who was covering the northern approach, when he clearly heard the sound of metal on stone. The guard heard it too as he stiffened and looked over the wall.

'What is it?' Roberts asked in a loud whisper, as he approached.

'Christ, you frightened the life out of me, sir. I'm not sure, but I heard something. There's somebody there, I'm sure.'

'Use these and take a look.' Roberts handed over the glasses and the guard began to raise them to his eyes. Time was running out as the fourth team was bound to be nearing the walls and so he didn't wait. He rammed the syringe into the man's left arm and pressed the plunger. The guard turned in shock, looked at the ex-Colonel and collapsed with a clatter.

Roberts broke into a run towards the fourth and final guard. If he raised the alarm all would be lost and many men could die that night. What was the man's name? St Juste. Oliver St Juste. Ex-French legionnaire.

'St Juste! St Juste!' he called in a loud whisper.

'Oui?' The guard turned towards Roberts and took a step forward.

The little ex-Colonel barrelled into St Juste's chest. The Frenchman was one of the few guards smaller than Roberts and he went down heavily, knocking the back of his head on the flagstone. In spite of his size he was as tough as they come and dazedly he reached for his gun. Roberts dropped onto the man's arm and thrust the hypodermic into his neck. The ex-legionnaire sighed and stopped struggling.

Looking over the wall, he was in time to see the last of the north attack team climb through a window. He sprinted for the roof door, reaching for a gas mask as he did.

*   *   *

Ingress was synchronised and completely silent. Alarms were found to be switched off, windows and doors unlocked. Perplexed whispers between team leaders solved nothing. Was it a trap? Were they going into a fire-fight from which they wouldn't escape?

They knew from the plans where the mains switchboard was and the two soldiers tasked with switching off the electricity did so. Through his NVGs, Yorke could see that the place had been renovated to a high degree.

Carstairs said, 'Move in. Every room. Use the gas.'

The men of the SAS put on gasmasks connected to their own oxygen, supplied under a slight positive pressure. It was the only sure way to ensure they didn't get a whiff of the knock-out gas. They moved silently through the house, placing hose pipes under each door and giving each room a heavy dose. They finished the downstairs rooms in under three minutes. In six of the rooms they found sleeping men with guns next to them. They would sleep for at least another eight hours.

There were three sets of stairs, two at the back of the house, one at the front. Yorke was leading the way up the main stairway when a gun opened fire and the peace of the night was torn asunder. The noise came from above and he took the steps two at a time.

Somebody yelled a warning and he threw himself flat in time to feel the bullets from an unsilenced automatic cut the air around him. He spun around to shoot but held his fire. Mack Roberts was pointing a silenced pistol above Yorke's head and down the corridor. The pistol fired twice and a body fell from the doorway at the end.

'Move it, Yorke,' said Roberts, 'before Kennedy gets away.'

What the hell was going on? Roberts was the mole?

The man behind Yorke leap-frogged him and headed for the doorway, Yorke on his heels. A door directly to Yorke's right opened and instinctively he threw himself against it, barging it open.

The person on the other side fired an automatic pistol blindly, unable to see in the gloom of the house. Yorke fired two shots, killing Leo Agnew.

The other SAS members were hitting the rooms hard. Flash/bangs were thrown into the rooms, the grenades' noise and blinding light debilitating in the extreme. They were followed by the soldiers. Now that the gas was no longer in use it was no holds barred. Their instructions were unambiguous. Give no quarter and expect none. For the SAS that was SOP – Standard Operational Procedure.

'You all right, Yorke?' Roberts asked crouching in the doorway.

'Yes. I take it you've been the one feeding us the information.'

'Affirmative. I'll explain later. Kennedy is in a bedroom above this room and the only way up to it is via a small staircase behind you.'

Yorke frowned. 'I don't remember that being in the plans.'

'It's not. He had the room installed. But that's not the worse of it. There's a fully serviced and fuelled Lynx sitting up there.'

'What about a pilot?'

'Kennedy can fly.'

'Bugger it! We'd better move.'

'That's the door,' said Roberts. 'It's steel lined and locked.'

Yorke took out two flat packs of Semtex, stripped off their backing paper and pressed them securely over the hinges. He set the timer for 5 seconds. Both men stood to one side and hid their faces. The explosion ripped the door off.

While Roberts knelt at the door Yorke stood behind him. Instinctively they fell into the roll of high and low.

'Nothing.'

'Nothing,' repeated Yorke.

They moved slowly and carefully up the narrow stairs. It was plushly carpeted and their feet made no sound as they ascended. At the top was a second door. Yorke pressed himself against the right hand side while Roberts reached up and tried the handle. It turned. He pushed. The door stayed closed.

'Any more plastic?'

'Last two.' Yorke quickly pressed the Semtex in place, set 10 seconds and both men ran halfway down the stairs.

They placed their hands over their ears as the explosion erupted. They ran back up, Yorke crashed the door, fell into the room, rolled and came to his knees in the middle of the floor. Roberts stopped in the doorway and surveyed the room, giving vital backup. There was movement on the right and a figure stepped out, aiming a gun at Yorke's back. Roberts fired three shots and the gunman fell. Neither man moved as they surveyed the place.

'Clear,' said Yorke.

'Agreed,' replied the ex-Colonel.

The dead man was the chauffeur, Maxwell.

Just then the unmistakable whine of rotors starting penetrated the room and both men ran for the door on the opposite wall. It was slightly ajar. Yorke was about to charge it when Roberts grabbed his arm and stopped him.

Cautiously he pushed the door open. A hail of bullets shredded the door, expending their energy on the wall opposite.

'Yellow one, this is red leader, do you copy?'

The radio in Yorke's ear burst into life. 'Copy, red leader. I'm on the roof with Mack Roberts. He's our mole. There's a helo flashing up and about to take off. We're certain Kennedy's onboard.'

'Copy that. I'm heading for the roof.'

'Roger out.' He turned to Roberts. 'Carstairs is heading for the roof. He's got a Stinger or two.'

'Okay. Let's distract them. Throw a flash/bang.'

Yorke threw his last grenade. As it erupted he went high and Roberts went low. They found one gunman with his eyes screwed shut and his hands over his ears in pain. A double tap from each of them put the man out of his agony.

The downdraft hit them first and then the sound of the helicopter lifting into the air. Instead of going straight up it jumped over the edge of the roof and headed in a gentle curve downwards and away. Yorke and Roberts reached the edge and opened fire with both weapons on fully automatic. They couldn't tell if either had scored any hits as the helicopter opened the distance before gaining height.

Carstairs appeared alongside. The trooper with him was unslinging the Stinger from his shoulder even as Carstairs said, 'Where's the copter?'

Yorke pointed at the helicopter now about a mile away. 'You need to hurry.'

'No problem. We've improved the design. The range has almost doubled to 10 miles. Ready?'

'Yes, sir.' The trooper had the 5 feet long missile, packaged in its disposable launch tube, on his shoulder, following the helicopter. At that moment the pilot made an error. He began turning to starboard, heading towards the coast. As a result, instead of increasing the distance between them as quickly as possible, he was significantly slowing it down.

The missile was designed to provide protection against low-altitude targets – fixed-wing aircraft, helicopters and cruise missiles. The system was fire-and-forget, using an infrared seek and lock system. When the trooper pulled the trigger the rocket fired at supersonic speed.

The men stood silently and watched the missile's trajectory as it headed unerringly towards the helicopter. It erupted against the engine block and blew up the aviation fuel. The helicopter fell to earth in a blaze of death and destruction. It would take a forensic team to prove that the bodies were those of John Kennedy and Mr Frobisher, using their dental records. Their deaths wouldn't be announced for another two days.

'I guess it's all over,' said Yorke.

'I'm afraid it's not,' said Roberts. 'I found out about two hours ago that Kennedy has sent Ingrid Kahn to kill you and your boy. And the reporter, Catherine Colbert.'

Although the words caused Yorke's stomach to contract in fear he said in a steady voice, 'He had no idea where to find us.'

'Your uncle's boatyard in Cornwall,' was the shattering reply. 'She left here nine hours ago.'

*   *   *

Ingrid drove like a maniac for no other reason than that she loved driving fast. The Aston Martin stuck to the roads like glue while speed limits meant nothing to her. She was in Inverness when she made her first stop to refuel.

There was no chance of her taking a plane. She would have to drive the whole way if she wanted to reach Cornwall with her guns. According to the car's computer she had 719 miles to travel and she relished every one of them.

The car had been fitted with the very latest anti-photographic number plates and she sped down the notoriously dangerous A9 setting off the speed cameras with impunity. She passed other cars as though they were stationary as the Aston reached speeds of over 120mph. Her intention was to reach her destination at about 03.00, which meant she needed to average 86mph. In spite of the high speed at which she was driving she wasn't reckless. She didn't overtake on blind bends or drive on the wrong side of double white lines. She merely drove the car at what she felt was the safe limit of her ability.

She was held up at roadworks near Pitlochry and again around Perth, but she'd reached Stirling by 20.00. Still with 600 miles to go, she was on time at her planned speed.

The traffic had thinned out and she flew past Cumbernauld, hit the M74 and began to gain time, reducing the overall speed required. The road reduced from a three lane motorway to two lanes but as the only traffic was lorries trundling south at 56mph, in convoy, she was able to hold the car at over 90mph.

She reached the services at Southwaite. The computer told her that she needed to maintain 79mph to get to the Yorke boat-yard at 03.00. Throughout the journey she had been listening to Abba disks, singing along with abandon in a voice that was almost, but not quite, in tune.

Her next stop was at Keele Services at 22.30. She needed petrol, a pee and a snort of cocaine. Back on the road, her nerves as jumpy as the car was powerful, she put her foot down. Astonishingly she reached the outskirts of Exeter just over 2 hours later. There the M5 ended and at junction 31 she turned onto the infamous A30.

It was 00.50. The road proved worse than she'd expected. In preparation for the summer when the road would be packed with cars towing caravans, when the wear and tear would be at its maximum, road works were everywhere. Where she could, she ignored the red lights of the temporary traffic lights and drove on anyway. Only on one occasion did somebody flash car lights at her.

It was 02.48 when she arrived at Penzance. That was the precise moment when Kennedy's helicopter was shot down in flames and he died.

Fifteen minutes later she was outside the boatyard listening to a diesel engine starting up. Gun in hand she ran towards the water's edge.

32

YORKE PHONED WILLIAM. No answer. *Come on, come on*!
He'd try Dom. The trouble was he slept like the dead. He
looked at his watch. 03.03.

The phone rang and rang and he was about to give up.
'Hullo?' A groggy Dom answered.

Thank you, god, thank you. 'Dom! Wake up. Shake it, Dom.'
Fear lent harshness to his voice.

'Dad? What is it? What's the time?'

'Never mind the time. Are you paying attention?'

'Sure, dad. I'm awake.'

'Good. There's a woman on her way to kill you. You got
that? To kill you and Catherine.'

'Bloody hell.'

'Bloody hell is right. I don't know when she'll get there but
it could be soon. So take the *Duck* and get away, right now.
Just start up and move her. Go to sea. Head for the Scillies. Is
Catherine onboard or in the house?'

'She's here.'

'Good. Wake her up and bloody well shift, Dom. And listen,
son, no questions, no arguments, you got it? And don't take
any crap from Catherine.'

'Where are you, dad?'

'Northern Scotland, so I'm not much help. I'm relying on
you.'

'What about Uncle William?'

'He's sleeping. Leave him be. Now shift.'

Dom scrambled out of his sleeping bag, thought about
waking Catherine and realised he'd be away quicker if he didn't

have to explain. Up on deck, barefooted, he let go all the lines
and allowed the yacht to drift away from the wall even as he
pressed the diesel's starter button. The engine was cold and
turned over harshly before coughing into life with an eruption
of smoke.

With the boat gathering way, he spun the wheel and turned
her sharply to port, towards the sea. A gun fired behind him
and a bullet nicked the mast, making an odd pinging sound.
Dom ducked, his back hunched, expecting a bullet between his
shoulder blades at any moment.

The yacht's bow began to lift and fall as she nosed her way
into the swell. As the stern passed the wall Catherine put her
head through the companionway hatch.

'What on earth's happening, Dom?'

'Dad phoned. He said to get away because some woman
was coming to kill us. She's just shot at us. There's a bullet
hole in the mast.'

'What!' Catherine's voice was a shriek.

'I'm not kidding. Somebody fired a gun at us. It must be
the woman dad phoned about.'

'What about William? Is he all right?'

'I don't know. Dad said to get away. To head for the Isles
of Scilly. I don't know what he's planning but knowing him
he'll have something up his sleeve. Take the wheel and hold
her steady, Catherine, while I get the main.'

Ingrid stood watching the yacht vanish in the moonlight. Now
what? She needed a boat.

A voice called behind her. 'What's going on? Who the hell
are you?'

She spun round and saw an old man wearing a tee-shirt and
jeans. Outlined against the light of a door, he was holding a
large adjustable spanner in one hand, gently hitting his left
palm with its head.

Ingrid walked towards him, holding the gun to her side, got
to within 3 metres, stopped and fired. The bullet hit William
in the back of his right hand and smashed into the steel of the

spanner. The bullet ricocheted into the ground. If it hadn't been for the spanner the bullet would have killed him. As it was he was thrown off his feet and he hit his head, falling unconscious for a few seconds.

Ingrid approached carefully. Blood was pouring from William's hand and he was groaning. She was disgusted with her shooting. She'd been aiming at his stomach but had timed the shot badly.

Looking around, she saw an outdoor tap with a bucket underneath. Filling the bucket, she threw the water over William's face. The cold water brought him round. With consciousness came a searing pain in his hand and abdomen along with a throbbing headache.

He felt a hand grip his throat and a young woman's voice say, 'Listen, you old goat, I want a boat to go after the yacht. Where will I find one?'

William groaned, partly from pain, partly to give himself time to think. He said nothing until Ingrid rammed the barrel of her gun into his left knee and said, 'Tell me or I'll blow your knee off. You'll bleed to death in serious pain.'

William gasped. He was a brave man but not a foolhardy one. If she carried out her threat she'd find the work boat and follow Dom. If he could manoeuvre it so that she took him with her then he might be able to turn the tables on her.

'There's a run-about,' he gasped. 'A work boat. Down by the steps.'

'Good.' She lifted the gun and pointed it at William's head, her intention unmistakable.

'Wait! For god's sake, wait. If you shoot me you'll never follow the yacht.'

'Why not?'

'The boat's an old cow. As temperamental as hell. She's diesel and her tanks are contaminated with water so she keeps cutting out unless you change filters and clean them. Can you do all that? Or are you going to get a couple of miles out to sea and breakdown? There's no AA out there and there's a storm coming. Look.'

Catherine glanced over her shoulder and out to sea. Sure enough, a bank of cloud was beginning to blot out the stars and drift across the face of the moon. Maybe the old bastard was telling the truth.

'All right. Get up and no tricks. You can drive the boat.'

William tried to sit up but he didn't have the strength. Groaning, he collapsed onto his back.

'You're no use,' said Ingrid, pointing the gun again.

'Wait! Wait for Christ's sake. I can get up.' With a super-human effort William got to his knees and staggered to his feet, using the wall to steady himself.

'Come on, get a move on.'

'Let me bandage my hand first.'

'I said, move it.'

William was getting a little of his strength back and with it his courage. He shook his head. 'The yacht's not going to get away. If I lose any more blood I could easily pass out and be no bloody use at all. I'll fix a bandage and take a painkiller.' Expecting a bullet in the back at any moment he turned and went into the kitchen.

Ingrid stood still for a moment, tempted to shoot the old man. Instead, she followed him. William placed his hand under the cold water tap, and washed the blood away. His hand was a mess but looked worse than it really was. The bullet had drilled a neat hole just behind his middle knuckle and though it was extremely sore his fingers still worked. He took four Paracetamol tablets, drank a glass of water and began wrapping his hand with a bandage.

'That'll do. Get going.'

William led the way down to the jetty, staggering, holding his hand and midriff, making more of his injuries than was the reality. The workboat lay alongside, fully fuelled and ready to go, as she was left every night. She was a tough, old Royal Navy glass-reinforced plastic whaler MkII. The single screw, 11.2 bhp engine, could push her along at 7 knots and she carried enough diesel to last 13.5 hours. Backup propulsion was a bank of oars. Opening the engine cover, he flicked the cut-off switch

to off and back to on, primed the engine and turned the ignition key. The engine turned over without firing.

After a few minutes of impatience Ingrid said, 'If you don't
get this piece of crap moving now I'll . . .'

'I know,' said William wearily, 'you'll shoot me. Give me
a moment.' He fiddled with the primer again but still the engine
refused to start. 'I need to change the filter.'

Curses and threats from Ingrid didn't make him go any
faster. She had the sense to know her limitations but promised
herself the satisfaction of killing the old man after she'd dealt
with the kid and the reporter. With the filter changed, William
knew he couldn't risk any more delaying tactics. He flicked
the cut-off switch to off, primed the engine and turned the key.
She burst into life in a cloud of fumes.

William sat down at the stern next to the tiller and gasped
in pain.

'Get this boat moving or . . .'

'Shut up! Or nothing. I'm not sitting here just for the benefit
of my health. You see the instrumentation just there. That's the
oil-pressure and engine temperature gauges. We wait until
the left needle stops flickering and the right needle goes into the
green. Otherwise the engine will cut out and we'll have to wait
at least 15 minutes before trying to restart her.' He was lying
but Ingrid didn't know that. He was trying desperately to give
the yacht more time to get away.

After a couple of minutes, impatient at the best of times,
Ingrid threw off the lines and said, 'Get going! Now!'

The engine and gearbox control was a single lever on the
port side. William pushed it into ahead and the boat moved
slowly away from the side.

'Faster.'

William increased the revs and the boat slowly picked up
speed. The boat was double-ended, 8.46m long and 2.26m wide.
She had superb sea-keeping qualities and was capable of
carrying 22 persons or 1,500kg of stores. In-built polyurethane-
foam blocks made her virtually unsinkable even if she filled
with water.

The light was thickening and already, though they were a cable from the land, they could see the outline of the yard fading behind them. Ingrid sat up for'ard, trying not to shiver, wishing she'd brought a warm coat with her.

Down aft, William reached under the housing, extracted a yellow foul-weather jacket and put it on. Ingrid didn't notice as he slid another three jackets over the stern. Let the bitch freeze.

Holding onto the combined lantern stanchion in the bow, Ingrid balanced herself, her other hand holding the gun by her side. She hated the sea but she'd do as Kennedy ordered. Was Yorke onboard the yacht? Or just the kid and the woman?

'You!' She looked over her shoulder at William sitting hunched in the stern, a small, inoffensive man, fear and pain diminishing him. 'Is Yorke on the yacht?'

About to answer in the negative, he said, 'Yes. Yes he is.'

There was something in his voice that Ingrid caught and she said, 'Liar. Good. It makes my job easier. I can catch up with him later.'

Please do, you bitch. You'll die for sure.

The *Duck* had a head start of nearly 50 minutes. The wind was from the south-west which meant if they were sailing they'd be tacking back and forth, and the whaler would be closing inexorably on them. Looking to the south, William was pleased to see that the clouds were well and truly beginning to form, cirrus and cirrostratus the forerunners of an approaching warm front.

'Can't this bucket go any faster?' Ingrid interrupted his thoughts.

'No! This is as fast as she'll go.'

Ingrid stomped aft, stood in front of William, placed the gun to his forehead, reached down, took the engine control and shifted it a few more degrees forward. Immediately the revs picked up and the boat began to increase speed.

'I'm not an idiot. Lie to me again and I will kill you.'

'If you do,' said William with an equanimity he wasn't feeling, 'you'll never find the yacht.'

'I may decide to take that risk. Now shut up!' She went back into the bow and stood looking ahead. After a few minutes her vigilance was rewarded. A sail, just to the left. She saw the yacht alter course to starboard and begin to go right. 'Turn this boat to the right. Go on, do as I say!'

With a sigh, William pushed the tiller hard over, making Ingrid totter.

'Not that far, you fool. Don't turn the sodding thing! Turn back. There! Hold that course.'

Ingrid didn't realise it but by following the *Duck's* course, aiming at her, the whaler wasn't gaining as quickly as if they stayed on a steady mean course that the yacht was forced to tack around because of the wind. William, having spied the sail, wasn't going to enlighten her.

Ingrid sent the whaler left and right, aiming at the yacht each time she altered course. Even so, they closed inexorably on the *Duck*. With sunrise the sail gave way to glimpses of the hull. The wind was backing towards the south and increasing, and the temperature was rising slowly. The sky was becoming more overcast and the visibility was beginning to deteriorate. A squall ruffled the water and caused the boat to rock slightly. William was satisfied to see Ingrid shiver violently.

Due to the fact that the weather forecast was lousy, there were no other small boats at sea only the whaler and the yacht. Ingrid didn't notice that they were now out of sight of land, or that the sea was beginning to undulate more strongly or that the visibility was worsening.

Catherine walked up the companionway with two mugs of tea. As she handed one to Dom she looked astern.

'There's a boat chasing us. Or following us. Look.'

Dom looked over his shoulder and immediately recognised the whaler. 'That's Uncle William's workboat.' The whaler was perhaps 5 cables away and closing. Grabbing the binoculars hanging around his neck he lifted them to his eyes. 'Uncle William is at the tiller and there's a woman in the bow. She's pointing this way.'

The gunshot came clearly across the water and the bullet thudded into the transom next to Catherine. She screamed and dropped her mug, Dom swore and knelt down to start the engine. A second bullet went through the mainsail causing a small hole.

With the engine kicked in, the yacht began to pick up a little speed, though with the wind from the current direction Dom knew they couldn't outrun the workboat. Their only hope was to go about and run before the wind. Kneeling next to the hidden ready-use locker, Dom opened the cover and took out a Smith & Wesson. Using his left hand he pushed down the safety catch at the rear of the slide and took aim. His first shot hit the side of the bow of the whaler next to Ingrid.

Before Dom could fire again Ingrid darted aft and stood alongside William. 'Stop or I'll blow his insides out! I mean it!' she yelled.

Dom heard her and wondered if it was a bluff. Before he could say or do anything Ingrid opened fire and William yelled in pain as the bullet went through the fleshy part of his thigh, missing an artery and bone by millimetres.

'All right! All right! Don't shoot anymore! We're stopping!' He knocked the gears into neutral and leapt to lower the mainsail. As it dropped, way came off the hull and the *Duck* went into irons.

The whaler closed rapidly, Ingrid standing next to William, her gun firmly against the side of his head.

'Put the gun down,' she yelled at Dom.

In surprise, Dom looked down at the pistol in his hand and dropped it as though it had suddenly become red hot. The whaler came alongside and Ingrid gestured with her pistol.

'Both of you stand in the front where I can see you. You, old man, get into the yacht.'

William, his teeth gritted in pain, began to climb into the yacht.

'Nice and easy. No sudden moves because believe me I will use this. Good. Now sit by the wheel.'

While William did so, Ingrid climbed onboard after him,

picking up the gun Dom had dropped. 'This is nice and cosy. You're Yorke's bastard,' she said looking at Dom, 'and you're the journalist.'

'He's my step-father,' said Dom with dignity, 'and this is Catherine Colbert.'

'Good!' Ingrid raised the gun and aimed it at Dom.

'Wait!' said William in a husky and pain laden voice. 'If you shoot Dom you'll be stuck out here.'

The yacht rolled as a heavy wave appeared from nowhere and a gust of wind rocked her hull.

'The weather's deteriorating. There's no land in sight. If you kill Dom I won't help and neither will Catherine. You're going to shoot us anyway.'

Ingrid looked from William to the sea. For the first time she seemed aware of the fact that there was a storm brewing. 'I'll shoot her. The boy can get us closer to land. He'll live that bit longer that way.'

'If you shoot Catherine, I won't help you,' said Dom defiantly.

'How about I blow her knee off? Which one should it be?'

Catherine dropped to the deck, landing on her knees, fear leaving her mouth dry and anger making her hands shake. She wanted to kill the bitch.

'Wait! I have an idea,' said Dom. 'Let my uncle and Catherine go below. I'll sail the *Duck* for you.'

At that moment, like divine intervention, the unmistakable sound of a mobile phone ringing came from below.

'Like hell! You devious little bastard. You knew the phone was there.'

Dom didn't say, as well as a radio and a distress beacon. Instead he said, 'No, honest, I wasn't thinking of that. Then let my uncle and Catherine sit in the whaler. We can tow them. They won't be able to hurt you.'

Another gust of wind brought a rain squall. Ingrid was suddenly aware that the other three all wore warm jackets while she was freezing her arse off in a fancy blouse and cotton coat.

'Give me a yellow jacket,' she ordered Dom.

'They're down below, in a locker.'

She didn't risk Dom out of her sight and said, 'You, bitch. Throw me your coat.'

Catherine did as she was told and Ingrid quickly put it on.

'Now come back here and help the old man into the other boat.' The whaler and yacht had drifted about half-a-cable apart. William sat with his hands clenched around his leg, unsuccessfully trying to stop the blood seeping from his wound.

'You!' Ingrid pointed at Dom, 'Come and drive this boat over to the other one.'

Dom clambered into the cockpit, started the engine and neatly took the yacht alongside the whaler.

Ingrid said nothing, merely gestured. Catherine moved aft and helped William into the other boat. 'Tie the rope to the back.'

With the whaler sitting about 4 metres away Ingrid added. 'Now sit still in the back of the boat. And don't move. You, Dom or whatever your stupid name is, get us moving towards land.'

'I need to take a fix. To find out where we are and work out a course.'

'No you don't! I'm not an imbecile. Head north. England is that way. And I know the needle thing points north so line up the compass.'

Dom spun the wheel and lined up the yacht's heading on north. The weather continued to worsen and the yacht began an uncomfortable pitching. Ingrid was no seaman and she sat in the stern beginning to feel green around the gills. She needed to get this over with fast. As soon as land was sighted she'd shoot all three of them and steer for the coast.

'What are you going to do with us?' Dom asked. If he was afraid he wasn't going to show it to her.

Ingrid said nothing, merely looked at him, swallowing bile nausea building in her throat.

'You're going to kill us, aren't you?'

She still said nothing. Merely looked at him.

33

YORKE HAD DRIVEN like a madman to Inverness. There a Search and Rescue helicopter had been placed at his disposal and flew him to Glasgow. Now that the operation was over that was where the C130 had landed to re-fuel. A dash from helo to plane and he was in the air and droning south by 04.00. Take-off had been by special permission because of the time of day and the noise disruption to the people living near the airport.

He learned from Dom that the woman had arrived at the yard and that they'd only just got away in time. He contacted Carstairs who in turn phoned ACC Mary Murray. She had an armed response unit on its way to the yard in minutes. Yorke was flying over Carlisle when he got the news that the yard was empty and that there was no sign of William or the woman but that an Aston Martin was parked there.

In minutes he ascertained that the workboat was missing.

'Phil? Tell Mary that Catherine and Dom are heading towards the Isles of Scilly. Are there any search units we can send out?'

'Yes. I'll get the SAR boys onto it. What about the coast-guard?'

'The nearest will be Newlyn. But they can't go without backup. Can Mary get an ARU to them?'

'No problem. Leave that to us. Have you seen the weather for the area?'

'Yes, the pilot just handed me a report. A warm front is passing through. Visibility will be shit by the time we're there and the sea rough. We'll have to play it by ear.'

08.00 found the C130 flying a box search pattern 500ft above the surface of the sea, the centre fifteen miles south west of Merthen Point. If the weather hadn't been so bad they'd have seen the yacht much sooner and Yorke was beginning to despair of ever spotting the *Duck*. Another search pattern was being followed closer inshore by the lifeboat, carrying three armed policemen. The plane's and the boat's radar was picking up intermittent signals and each one had to be investigated, more often than not proving to be sea-clutter caused by breaking waves or bits of rubbish. A whaler and a small yacht made lousy returns on a screen.

'I've got something firming up,' said the navigator. 'This looks more like it. Two contacts in the north-west quadrant. Course to steer,' he said to the pilot, 'three one three.'

The pilot banked the C130 onto the new heading and, without prompting from Yorke, went lower. She levelled off at 100 ft.

'There's the *Duck*!' Yorke pointed through the windscreen.

Even as they spotted her there was an explosion and fire erupted out of her from bow to stern. Immediately, she began to sink. Yorke looked on with horror.

'You're going to kill us, aren't you?' Dom repeated. 'As soon as we see land.'

Ingrid knew that if she spoke she'd be sick and so stayed silent, concentrating on not throwing up her guts.

Dom put the yacht on auto-pilot and left the wheel to sit on the starboard side. 'Why do you hate us?'

'I don't. Now shut up. Why aren't you on the wheel?'

'I've put on the automatic steering.' Recognising the symptoms of seasickness, Dom knew he had one chance. He moved until his right side was next to the hidden firearms ready-use locker. Looking over the stern at the whaler he said, 'They don't look too good.'

Human nature meant that Ingrid looked back at the other boat. Catherine and William looked the picture of misery, huddled in the stern of the boat, William losing blood, Catherine soaked to the skin and freezing.

Dom reached inside the locker, turned the handle one full turn and pressed the button. The *Duck* had five minutes to live. He kept looking at his watch, willing the time to pass, knowing that if he moved too soon it would be all over for him. The same if he left it too late. At four minutes he couldn't stand it any longer and he suddenly stood up. The incendiary devices were right next to him and if they went off he'd be killed. Sweat suddenly broke out on his brow.

'Stay still!'

'I can hear something. It could be rocks. We don't want to run aground.'

In her misery Ingrid didn't question the stupidity of Dom's statement. Instead she watched as he went forward and into the bow. The yacht suddenly pitched high and came down with a crash that proved too much for Ingrid as she vomited all down her front.

Dom didn't hesitate. With fifteen seconds left on his watch he dived over the side and swam under water along the length of the yacht's keel before coming up for breath almost alongside the whaler.

Grabbing the side of the GRP hull he hung on as Ingrid, in a fit of rage, raised her gun and fired at the boat. The pitching whaler spoiled her aim and she flicked the safety to fully-automatic. As she did so the incendiary devices throughout the yacht went off. Bullets exploded in all directions and plastic explosive added to the flames, burning with an intense blue light.

Ingrid was hit twice by bullets; once in the thigh, shattering her femur and secondly in the elbow, leaving her ulna and radius hanging by only the skin. Her scream of pain and terror as the boat sank beneath her could have been heard a mile away.

Catherine helped Dom over the side. As he sat up he said, 'Quick, cut the rope before we're dragged down.'

He handed her his Swiss army knife and she jumped forward and sawed at the bow rope. The rope parted and the bow of the whaler sprung free and upwards. All around them debris from the yacht was floating, cushions and lifebelts a sad reminder of a beautiful boat.

Air trapped inside Ingrid's yellow jacket kept her afloat for a few seconds. She was face down but feebly she mustered her remaining strength and turned over to look up into Dom's eyes.

He looked down at her and found he had pity in his heart. Her eyes went blank and her weight took her down as the air finally escaped.

The sound of the circling C130 made them look up. They waved. The plane banked and a figure parachuted out of the rear doors.

'It's dad! I bet it is!'

Yorke landed in the water only metres away. He hit the release button and the parachute floated clear before collapsing. His automatic life vest inflated as he swam the few strokes to the boat. Dom helped him into the whaler. 'I knew it was you, dad!'

'Hi, son. You okay?'

'I'm okay. Only Uncle William isn't so good.'

Yorke knelt by the side of the older man. As he did the lifeboat appeared out of the gloom and came alongside, having been conned there by the Hercules. William was taken off and given first aid as he was ferried at full speed back to shore. Knowing where they were, Yorke, Dom and Catherine set a course for the boatyard. As they motored towards land Dom told him what had happened.

'I'm sorry about the *Duck*, dad. But I didn't know what else to do.'

'You did exactly the right thing,' said Yorke, putting his arm across the boy's shoulders and hugging him. '*Exactly*. You don't for one minute think that the yacht, or anything else for that matter, means as much to me as you? Or Catherine,' he added as an afterthought. 'I couldn't care less about the *Duck*. Things we can replace, people we can't, don't ever forget it, Dom.' Yorke had a wide smile on his face, reflected by Dom's.

They arrived at the boat yard to a welcoming committee of the police and the news that William would be all right.

'Thank God for that,' said Yorke with feeling. 'We'll visit him later. Come on you two. Into the house. Hot baths and warm clothes are the order of the day. After that, young man, we need to see about getting you back to school.'

Dom was about to protest but he hesitated for a moment. After what had happened the thought of school was suddenly very appealing. He couldn't wait to get back to the peace and tranquillity of an inter-school cricket match. He nodded to his father and led the way indoors.

Carstairs met with Yorke two days later. With him was Colonel "Mack the Knife" Roberts. Mary was due at any minute and the three men sat in the sunshine, a bottle of cold white wine on the table in front of them. Catherine joined them, bringing a tray of glasses with her.

'Dom get away okay?' Carstairs asked.

'No problem. He couldn't wait,' Yorke replied. 'Thanks, Catherine.' He turned his attention back to Roberts.

'It had been Desmond Kavanagh's idea,' said Roberts. 'He and I went back a long way. Joined Sandhurst together in 1968. He'd been on to Kennedy for quite some time but didn't have enough to justify any sort of action. The fact was, he wasn't certain it was Kennedy. Suppose the real brains behind the crime cartel had been Frobisher? Kennedy's death wouldn't have achieved anything. But not only that, Desmond had known that the death of one man, even at the top, wouldn't destroy the whole organisation. He needed information and a lot of it. I started feeding it to him as soon as I arrived but to be frank, it was low-level stuff.' Roberts took a mouthful of wine and placed the glass back on the table before resuming.

'I was doing a job in Columbia for a few weeks in the run-up to the attack at Gib Point. Kennedy operated a tight ship of need-to-know.'

The military men nodded. It was to be expected of any large and successful organisation. Especially one run with a quasi-military background.

'With the death of my predecessor, Kennedy recalled me to

the UK. I was actually in the air when the attack at Gib Point took place. I'd known nothing about it. I found out afterwards that they'd been planning it for months. Even if I had been in the job I doubt I *could* have stopped it. But I could have warned Desmond to get everybody out, with all the information. After all, Gib Point was only a building. The men and women working there were irreplaceable.'

'What happened to your predecessor?'

Roberts glanced around the table and shrugged. Very dryly he said, 'He was meeting a man named Salondi in the South of France.'

'Jack's last op?' Yorke queried in surprise.

'The same. Desmond didn't know it at the time. He was there to assess Salondi for absorption into Kennedy's organisation. He was collateral damage and very fortuitous. That's when I got the call to return from South America and was catapulted into the top job. It saved me the trouble of having to create the vacancy,' he added dryly.

Yorke nodded. 'When did you know about Evelyn Beckworth?'

'Again, after the attack.' Roberts looked at the three faces in front of him and said, bleakly, 'I ordered her death, under the guise of mopping up. Kennedy was all for letting her go away and enjoy her ill-gotten gains. I couldn't do that. I'm Desmond's daughter's god-father.'

'Did you know it was me back at Mevagissey?' Yorke asked.

'Of course. I saw through your disguise. You could have knocked me down with a feather when I saw you. I managed to delay them when you were scrambling down the cliff. Even so, I couldn't prevent what happened afterwards. Sorry about that.'

'It's all right. Any op where you achieve your objective *and* walk away from is a successful op, as Desmond always said, and I concur. One thing puzzles me. How did they get on to me so quickly after the attack on Gib Point?'

'The men had been deployed around the area, covering all the escape routes. When you used your credit card they knew you were on the loose.'

Yorke nodded. It was just as he'd thought. They heard the sound of a high performance car arriving and seconds later Mary Murray was with them.

'Who's is the Aston?' she greeted them.

Yorke replied. 'We haven't got round to that yet. Can you run a check on the number plate and find out who it's registered to? Because I think Phil is about to become the proud owner.'

'Me?' The startled SAS officer said.

'Why not? If we mop up properly we can clean up as well,' said Yorke. 'That was SOP at *Phoenix*.'

'It may have been at *Phoenix* but it isn't with the police. You aren't serious?' Mary asked, pausing with her glass of wine halfway to her mouth.

'Of course I am. You don't have to keep any of it. If it bothers you, give the proceeds to charity. But I know the vast amounts of money swilling around the whole rotten edifice. The lawyers and bankers will be on it like a shoal of piranha, believe me. Then some of the lesser, but still very senior men in the organisation will step in and start picking up the pieces. The whole cartel is fracturing into tiny bits, scattering like corn. The problem is, some of that corn will take root and grow, rising from the ashes. The more we can strip it clean the better.'

'The proceeds of crime act only allows us to go so far,' said Mary. 'And it's not nearly far enough for these circumstances.'

'By the way, Mary,' Yorke said, changing the subject deliberately, 'what's to happen to the men we captured at Drumbeg?'

Mary shook her head. 'Another inadequacy in our laws. We can't get them on anything other than possession of unlicensed firearms.'

There were disbelieving shakes of their heads.

'That's ludicrous,' said Catherine in outrage.

'I have spent hours with the DPP and his staff trying to find something. As you can imagine, the prisoners aren't doing much talking. They're too well trained to fall for any of our legal tricks. And torture is out of the question – as is injecting them with drugs. Still, we matched fingerprints on guns so we can have them sent down for anything from five to eight years. In fact, we're talking to a judge right now who'll probably be trying the cases. Suggesting he gives the maximum term.'

'I thought the judiciary was independent,' said Yorke.

'Oh, it is. Only some parts of it are more independent than others. But I'll tell you, a hell of a lot of people are going to get away with it. The only winners in this lot are going to be the lawyers, as usual.'

'You know,' said Yorke, 'this is why we need an organisation like *Phoenix*. It's the only way.'

Mary shook her head. 'I'm not so sure. What happens if such an organisation came into being again and was corrupted? What then? What about the balances and controls we have in society to *stop* such power falling into a few wrong hands?'

That started a debate that continued late into the night. The discussion was heated, passionate, informed – and very enjoyable. Yorke lit a barbecue and cooked steaks he'd soaked in his own mustard and honey sauce, while Catherine and Mary prepared green and bean salads. The wine flowed freely.

The following morning William returned to the house, brought there by his wife, Rebecca. Yorke was saddened to see his uncle looking so old and frail, but after what had happened he wasn't surprised. A younger man would have found it equally tough to get over, and being the wrong side of sixty didn't help.

In the evening, Carstairs, Mary and Roberts left while Yorke stayed on. The fact of the matter was he had nowhere to go. His flat in London no longer held any appeal and Catherine's would not be habitable for many weeks if not months.

His aunt trapped him and Catherine in the kitchen after William went early to bed.

'Stephen, your uncle's had enough. All he's talked about these last few days is selling up and going to visit the kids. We can split our time between Scotland, America and Australia. I have to tell you I'm all for it. So is he. Only . . .'

'Only he doesn't want the yard to pass out of the family.'

'Something like that. Oh, I know he started it. He'd hoped

one of the boys would have wanted to take it on but it wasn't to be. What about you?'

Yorke shrugged. 'I don't know. Uncle William mentioned it to me and I've been giving it some thought. Only, I've a few things I want to do. And I'd feel tied down here. How long have you been here?'

'Twenty-eight years. A lifetime.'

'It proves my point. Instead of selling it find a good manager, set in proper supervisory controls and then go. Postpone the decision.'

His aunt nodded her blonde head, now streaked with grey. She was a handsome woman who'd had to work hard all her life as well as bring up three kids and look after an alcoholic, though loving, husband. It hadn't been easy. It had been thanks to her they hadn't lost everything 15 years earlier. Now she wanted to enjoy the fruits of her labours, before, as she told William, it was too late.

'Aunt Rebecca, give me a while to think about it. Not long. Say a few days?'

'A week, Stephen. If you haven't decided by then I'll either sell the place or do as you suggest.'

'Of course,' said Catherine, 'you could do both. Sell it to Stephen and let him find a manager.'

Rebecca smiled. 'I knew I liked you enormously. I think you'll be very good for my nephew. Anyway, good night. If anyone phones, we're not in.' On that note she left them sitting in the kitchen.

'I've had enough wine. I need something stronger,' said Yorke. 'Especially with you women ganging up on me.'

'We're not! It's just they're such lovely people. It makes sense and it makes them happy.'

'I'm not sure I can afford this place. It's got about 10 acres of land attached to it. It's valuable beyond belief especially as I suspect planning permission for houses is possible.'

'That gives me an idea,' said Catherine. 'Following on from last night's discussion.'

'Which one? Before or after we went to bed?'

'I don't remember much talking after,' she said archly.

In the process of pouring a large whisky, he paused and then said, 'I can't remember a thing. Perhaps we'd better try again tonight just to remind me.'

'Why you . . . you . . . chauvinist pig!'

'Is that the best you can manage in insults?' he grinned. 'So what's this idea?'

They discussed it late into the night. When they finally went to bed Yorke was reminded why there'd been so little talk the night before.

In the morning they established an off-shore company and began to acquire assets by the simple expedient of transferring ownership. Three properties in central London were held by off-shore trusts. The cut-off arrangements meant that whoever had the deeds owned the properties. Getting the deeds proved simplicity itself. Yorke telephoned a lawyer in Kingston, Jamaica. He gave him a password he'd found as one of two items owned by a company registered in Liechtenstein; the second item was shares held in an off-shore trust which in turn owned the deeds. It was all walls within walls. It was all very complex and would take many years to unravel, if it ever happened. An hour after his phone call to Jamaica, he received an e-mail telling him the deeds had been despatched.

'This is frightening,' said Catherine. 'I don't want anymore. I don't need the money. I'll earn my own.'

'Give it away,' Yorke said with enthusiasm. 'You said that third-world debt was close to your heart. Pay it off. Who's to stop you?'

Catherine stood up and paced the office. William had given it over to them, as he was taking it easy in the house.

'I don't know, Stephen. With money comes huge responsibility. I'm not sure I can handle it.'

Yorke sat back in his chair wearily. 'You're right. It's not my thing either. Okay, let's make an agreement. It's now 12.30. We spend today finding as much money and assets as we can. We stop at 17.00. We liquidate the assets and give the whole lot to charity. Will that suit you?'

Christine pursed her lips. 'I wouldn't go that far . . .'

When they finished they had no concept of how much they'd acquired but knew it was a vast sum.

'We give it away anonymously, yes?' Yorke said.

'Definitely. What was that smirk for just now?'

Yorke couldn't keep the grin off his face. 'I found a rather large yacht berthed in Spain. I've now taken ownership of all sixty-four shares which makes up any vessel. I consider it recompense for the *Duck*. Fancy a trip to Algerciras?'

The next few days saw them consolidating their ill-gotten gains, aquiring as much of Kennedy's assets as possible. The three London properties were valued at over £150 million. They looked at the total of over £300 million with trepidation.

'We have to get rid of it. All of it,' said Catherine.

'Okay. But we won't panic. We'll get rid of most of it. I'm going to use a chunk to buy the yard from uncle William.'

'How much?'

'I don't know. I'll get it valued. That and the yacht is more than enough. I also want to give uncle William something for the pain and stress he's suffered. We'll see. What about you?'

Catherine shrugged. 'I don't know. Say a couple of million to pay for the horrors I've been through? How does that sound?'

'Sounds fair. Look, don't get hung up about the money. It's going to vanish into a black hole. I know. I've seen it happen before. Lawyers and banks are going to walk away with most of it. What we've done will help a hell of a lot of charities.'

'I know, but I still feel unclean, somehow. But,' Catherine sighed, 'you're right.' She shook her head. 'Yet I feel guilty.'

'We'll learn to live with it. Already I suspect the vultures are gathering.'

The telephone interrupted their discussion. 'Yorke.'

'Stephen, this is Mack Roberts. Can you come to London to a meeting?'

'What for?'

'The Prime Minister wants to see us. Tomorrow at midday. Does that suit you?'

'Em ... Yes. Of course. I'll be there.' Hanging up the receiver he told Catherine.

'He probably wants to thank you personally. You know, we're rich, yet I don't feel comfortable with it.'

'Me neither. I don't want vast wealth. I just want enough to enjoy the good things in life without worrying about it.'

The following morning they went together to London, catching an early flight from Plymouth. Catherine went to see an editor at the Sunday Times while Yorke went to Downing St. After a good deal of showing ID and being searched he finally found himself in the Cabinet Office Briefing Room A, known as COBRA. There he found Beaton, Roberts, and Brian Calthorpe.

'As you know, Yorke, the Chancellor is the new Home Secretary. And contrary to what the press says, he asked for the job. Correct, Brian?'

'Correct. With Britain's finances on such a sound footing I decided I wanted to sort out the Home Office. Or at least,' he added with Liverpudlian wit, 'try to.'

Whatever he'd been expecting, it wasn't what was said. The meeting lasted an hour at the end of which hands were shaken and he and Roberts left.

One issue Yorke had brought up with the P.M. The setting off of the alarm at Beaton's house. Blind panic had been the reply. Regretted as soon as he'd done it. He'd apologised whole-heartedly.

'I don't know Mack,' said Yorke. 'I'd more or less decided I'd had enough.'

'It's a lot to take in. But listen, already the vultures are circling.'

'That was more or less what I told Catherine this morning.'

'When the criminals realised there was no central power they took over. Exactly as we expected. The only way to fight them is with an organisation such as *Phoenix*. We didn't tell you the best bit,' he chuckled. 'We're going to take over Castle Drumbeg. It has everything from satellite broadband to a computer network. You heard the PM. I'll take Desmond's place, though he'll be a tough act to follow. You'll be my number two. We're not asking you to be in the field, but directing. I can give it two, maybe three years, and then you can take over.'

'It's a lot to think about.'

'There's no hurry. Phone me Monday. You've got my card. Look, even if you decide it's not for you, how about giving me three months to pick the staff? To get the organisation established.'

Yorke knew he was being suckered in but the suggestion was a reasonable one and he nodded. Has the organisation got a name?'

'Oh, yes. But not very original. *Phoenix II.*'

'Jesus. A real *Phoenix* rising from the ashes.'

Yorke gave the organisation three months and quit. One of the last people he persuaded to join *Phoenix*, the *II* already having been dropped as too cumbersome, was Phillip Carstairs. He took over from Yorke and became Roberts' second-in-command. The Aston proved useful for commuting south for his visits to Mary. However, like all long distance relationships something had to give. Both were committed to their jobs. Mary was already tipped as the next Chief Constable of Essex and, with much regret, their affair petered out until finally even the phone calls stopped.

William and Rebecca retired. They accepted a valuation of £3 million for the yard and a further £3 million for William's pain and suffering. Yorke insisted on it and William was tickled pink to take the money when he learnt where it had come from. The wound in his leg healed completely but his hand was becoming arthritic. He was, Rebecca said one day in confidence to Yorke, old before his time. They spent their days visiting their children and grandchildren. Rebecca insisted they travelled first class. William didn't argue.

Yorke took to the job of running the boatyard without a single regret. The staff already had the place running smoothly, his input merely, as he put it, a gentle nudge on the rudder from time to time. Plans were laid to open a marina. However, it still gave him plenty of time to indulge his passion for sailing. He and Catherine finally got away to Spain and their newly acquired yacht, the *Salamander*, which proved to be a 60ft, modern, twin-masted vessel. She was luxuriously fitted-out and had the latest navigation and communications equipment. Their journey back to England was slow, easy and idyllic. It was during the journey that Catherine made her decision to give up journalism and turn to writing fiction instead. When Yorke asked her about the *Pulitzer* she snorted in derision. There were, she told him, more important things in life. He suggested she write political thrillers but she told him no way. She'd always hankered after writing *chic lit*.

Dom's future in the Royal Marines appeared assured – subject to him passing certain exams. When Yorke brought up the idea of marrying Catherine, Dom was all for it. Yorke was proud of the fact that his stepson agreed to be his best man. At the time of the wedding Catherine was 3 months pregnant.

The End

Havoc

by Paul Henke

Europe is a seething cauldron of hatred. Islamophobia and xenophobia sweep the continent as incessant terrorist atrocities terrify the population. Legal and illegal immigrants are blamed for attacking the white, Christian establishment. Whipped up by the press, non-whites and non-Christians are being hounded and persecuted in retaliation for the deaths caused by the terrorists. A backlash begins.

But all is not as it seems. The immigrants are as much victims as the whites. Who is masterminding the race war? Is this an Islamic plot against the west? Or something even more sinister?

Once again this master storyteller has highlighted the fears and prejudices of a world on the edge. As always, Henke's meticulous research creates a background that is rock-solid and thought provoking. The conclusions drawn by his imagination are disturbing in the extreme.

As hero Nick Hunter battles against this latest threat to democracy, Henke fearlessly brings forbidden issues to the fore in an action packed story that enthrals the reader from beginning to end.

ISBN 1–902483–06–5

Débâcle

TIFAT File I

A Nick Hunter Adventure

Following a summit meeting in Paris an alliance of interested countries form an elite fighting force to combat terrorism throughout the world. Based in Britain and under the command of a British General, the team is made up of Western, Russian and other non-aligned countries' special forces.

Without warning the terrorists strike. A group of bankers, politicians and industrialists are taken prisoner off the coast of Scotland and the new, untried force is sent to search for them.

The Scene of Action Commander is Nick Hunter, Lieutenant Commander, Royal Navy, an underwater mine and bomb clearance expert with experience in clandestine operations.

The enemy is one of the world's most ruthless and wanted terrorists – Aziz Habib! Hunter leads the team against Habib, backed up by two computer experts: Sarah from GCHQ and Isobel, hired by the General to run the IT for the new force.

While stock markets take a pounding and exchange rates go mad, the state sponsoring the terrorism is making a fortune. It has to stop. At all costs.

This is non-stop adventure from beginning to end. A riveting story told by a master story teller. You are guaranteed not to want to put it down!

Débâcle mixes fact with fiction which will cause you to wonder, how true is this story? Did it really happen?

ISBN 1-902483-01-4

Chaos

TIFAT File III

A Nick Hunter Adventure

Ambitious Alleysia Raduyev has inherited the family business – the largest crime cartel in Georgia. Operating on the classic theory of supply and demand, she caters for her customers every desire – narcotics, arms, prostitution, forced labour. Her payroll has extended to include lawmakers and law enforcers. No one is safe from her tyranny and oppression.

Power base secured, Alleysia moves on to her next objective – the formation of a super crime cartel, whose actions will result in global chaos. As a deterrent to those who would oppose her, she chooses the ultimate weapon – three nuclear warheads.

Desperate to prevent a new, anarchic world order, the West declares World war III against the cartels and their terror organisations. As violence escalates, the now battle-hardened troops of TIFAT are pitched against their toughest adversary yet.

Spearheading the battle is Lt. Cdr. Nick Hunter, the fearless explosives and diving specialist seconded to The International Force Against Terrorism.

The latest TIFAT novel is a clarion call to the Western world as it comes to grips with the realities of modern terrorism.

ISBN 1-902483-04-9

The Tears of War and Peace

by Paul Henke

It is 1911 and David Griffiths is in Wales, bored and lonely. He travels to London at the behest of their family friend, John Buchanan, to start a new business in banking. There he gets caught up in the suffragette movement and falls in love with Emily. Against the backdrop of women's fight for votes and the looming First World War, the Griffiths build a vast, sprawling company encompassing banking, aircraft manufacturing, farming and whisky distilling.

The enmity of a German family follows them tragically throughout this period, leading to murder and revenge. At the end of the war, thanks to a change in the Constitution, Evan is invited to run for President of the United States. The family rally round for the most important battle of Evan's life.

With the Brown-shirts running rampage across Germany, David and Sion are soon involved in a battle for survival.

Sir David Griffiths is a colossus of a figure, striding across the world and through the century, a man of integrity and bravery, passion and dedication. Determined to win, nothing comes before the family.

The story is as compelling as ever. Historical fact woven into the fictional characters makes a breathtaking tale of adventure you will not want to put down.

ISBN 1-902483-03-0